Secret Matilda

Jon Gray Lang

SECRET MATILDA

Cover Image by Tithi Luadthong

ISBN: 978-1-7323305-3-5

Library of Congress Control Number: 2021920528

Jon Gray Lang

To Lyndsie, thanks for the long discussions about writing, worlds and characters.

Oh, and keeping me on track.

Jon Gray Lang

THE MATILDA SERIES
The Matilda
Twistin' Matilda
Black Matilda
Secret Matilda
Waltzing Matilda

Also, by Jon Gray Lang
Nun with a Gun: Town with No Name

one

Crazy Horses

An effluvium of burnt copper and spoiled vegetation permeated the Matilda as the jump engine forced a hole through the skin of the universe. The small freighter was dragged into the 'other space' that existed within the cracks and folds of regular space. Enormous creatures that called this place home trumpeted their arrival as the rift closed behind the ship.

"By God's bones! We're right in the middle of them!" Anton cried.

"Push the engines hard, Anton!" Ordered Captain Delahaye.

Anton pushed the sublights to max, "Do they seem pissed to you?"

"More than normal?" quipped Derain, then shouting, "That one's coming after us! Brace for impact!"

Jon Gray Lang

The Captain glanced at the cyborg holding herself up near the hatch, "We've got this, Lu. Get back to the sickbay."

Luli wearily nodded and stepped off the bridge as a colossus brushed against the freighter. The hull rang with the clangor of bells as the ship leaned to her starboard side.

"It's only a short jump," she murmured as she stumbled into the lift.

Luli hastened to the sickbay as an angry squall reverberated through the cargo bay. She looked in on Galena's sleeping form before heading to her med tube. As the lid closed, she stretched out safe in the knowledge that the torture ship lay in fragments behind her. Even as the freighter rolled hard, sleep enveloped her quickly. She barely noticed the Matilda falling back into normal space.

Suddenly, a rumble vibrated through the hull and the Matilda lurched. Emergency medical protocols kicked on, automatically injecting stimulants into the occupied med tubes.

"Huh... what?" Luli jerked awake and slammed upright into the lid of her med tube.

Alarms blared as warning lights bathed the sickbay with a garnet glow. The main overhead lighting fixtures hung precariously from the ceiling. Her med tube leaned drunkenly in its cradle and Luli was pressed against the side of it.

Woozily, she slapped at the med tube controls, "What in all of Tom is going on?"

She cursed in frustration as her fingers kept

missing the controls. Her arms felt heavier than usual and it took her a moment to figure out why. The whine from the Matilda's stabilizers fought against the screams of the alarms as the gravity in the med lab swung from port to starboard and back.

As the entire ship rocked from another impact, Luli's tube was thrown clear out of its cradle. It came crashing down and cracked against the decking.

Sparks shot wildly from Doc's track assembly. The automaton's bleats echoed crazily as it slid along the track and slammed into the plas-glass that covered one side of the med lab. The panels shattered, sending shards flying in all directions.

Luli struggled to get out of the damaged med tube while it lay on its side. A crack ran across the viewing window, but she wasn't able to break through. Abruptly, the entire tube was dragged out of the debris, then righted. The clips popped and the lid was pulled free of its hinges. Luli looked up into the haggard face of Lieutenant Chadov.

"Luli!" Galena cried. "Are you alright?"

"Yes. Any idea what's going on?" Luli asked as she struggled to free herself.

Galena grabbed one of Luli's arms and helped pull her out of the broken container, "No idea. Last I remember was blacking out on some old wreck out in the middle of nowhere."

The entire ship shuddered and one of the ceiling plates crashed against the operating table. Doc screeched loudly as it slid along its track and smashed into the back wall. Luli slipped and fell backward into the med tube. Galena lost her footing and fell across the pilot.

The sirens stopped screaming and the emergency lights went dark. Galena pushed herself off of Luli and rolled onto her side. Only the lights from Doc's chassis illuminated the room.

"What just happened?" Galena sputtered out.

"Shh!" Luli stared into the darkness, straining to listen for any sounds. "Life support isn't running. The engines are down too. I... I think the Matilda is dead."

Doc chimed in, "Ee che dae le..."

"Yes, well I am running, too," grumbled Luli. "Do you have anything constructive to add?"

"Li do tong sa," sang out the automaton before its guttural squeaks quieted. "Te cho da..."

Galena murmured, "He's not getting a response from the Matilda either."

***

The rift in space had barely begun to close before the Matilda suffered under the barrage of weapons fire. The ship bucked like a bronco when the sublight engines were blasted to pieces. The concussion sent the freighter into a slow spin that gradually picked up speed as smaller rockets hammered the hull of the old boat.

"Can you see what the hell is pounding the ever-living crap out of us?" shouted Captain

Delahaye, as the Matilda rocked from another coil gun slug.

"Not a damn thing, Jacq," cursed Anton. "Whoever they are, they've taken out our sensors and comms."

"Matilda's weapons are down, too," added Derain. "Coil guns aren't responding and the missile bays are flashing disabled."

Another volley rocked the ship and Luli's starman figurine slid off the dashboard. The bridge lights sputtered out and all the electrical systems went dark.

"Gods be damned! Who the hell is out there?" cried Jacquie.

The statue slowly floated past Jacquie's head and bounced off the bulkhead behind her. The Matilda continued spinning and the view out the bow port began changing. Tiny pricks of light from the stars segued into a lazy spiral. There was nothing more to see until a long dark shape appeared in the bow port.

"Did you see that?" asked Anton.

"Not enough to figure out who it is..." answered Derain.

The crew held their breath and kept their eyes glued to the bow port as the Matilda continued its inexorable roll. The enemy cruiser swung into view. The attitude jets on the big ship began to burn on the port side.

Derain groused, "Is that another one of those black-ops Consortium cruisers? How many of

Jon Gray Lang

those damn things are there?"

"And what do they want with us?" added Jacquie.

"Those marauders are trying to match our spin," cursed Anton.

***

The latest impact to the Matilda flung Barney against the jump engine's cradle. He rebounded and caught himself against his workbench before the next strike sent him flying through the open hatch. The electrical systems cut off as he floated down the main shaft.

"Really? Now?" Barney grumbled as he tumbled down the main shaft. The lights sparked and went dark as he bounced against the wall. Barney tried his best to scrabble for a handhold but couldn't stop his uncontrolled way down the shaft. "Bloody fine time to remember I didn't install those ruddy handrails."

He reached into one of the pouches that hung from his belt and retrieved a small tube. With the press of a button, a small grappling hook launched and latched onto the handle of the port container hatch. The cable retracted until he was able to get a solid handhold. Shock hit him as the Matilda shifted when another impact grazed the outer hull. He listened intently as the sound of something scraping along the hull quickly came to an abrupt end. Then a loud crash resonated through the ship. He lined up his feet before he let go and his magnetic boots clicked on the deck of the main shaft.

"Where in all the nine hells is my 'case of trouble' when I need it?" he growled as he proceeded to the engine room.

***

Captain Kaplean waited until the spin between his vessel, the M33, and his prize, the Matilda, matched up. He felt good. They had led him on a grueling chase, but he finally had them at his mercy. The navigation lights flickered along the hull of the trawler before the entire ship went dark.

Scanner Technician Cordelan relayed, "Target has lost power. I repeat, target has lost power."

"Officer Shimada?" asked the Captain, "Any communications coming from her?"

"No sir. Her comm array was destroyed," she replied.

"Alvarez, fire the boarding harpoons and drag that thing into tunnel range once the spins match up," ordered Captain Kaplean.

"On it, sir," replied the Gunnery. "Harpoons away."

The Captain looked on as four harpoons launched and punctured holes into the skin of the freighter. He clicked on the comm, "Chief Bull? There are two airlocks on the target. Prepare boarding teams for both. Oh, and expect trouble."

Chief Bull's voice came back, "Understood. Authorization on lethal force?"

Dr. Wyeth rubbed her hands together and shook her head in the negative, "I won't allow it. I want my test subject unharmed, do you hear me?"

The Captain brooded for a moment before he answered, "Denied for now. Capture them alive, but don't take any unnecessary risks."

"Understood, Captain."

***

Chief Bull shouted to his men, "You heard the Captain! Prepare to board a hostile vessel. Lethal force is not authorized. Load the rubber rounds and stunners."

"Stun shots?" moaned a couple of the marines. "We might as well just throw rocks. This'll be a right mess."

"Stow it, Johnson," barked Chief Bull. "We don't know how many will be on the other end of the tunnel. Go in expecting the worst."

The clap of magazines into rifles echoed in the locker room.

"Higgins and Gavriel, get your squads on a lander," ordered Chief Bull. "You'll be breaching the upper decks."

"On it, Chief!"

Chief Bull grinned through the grumbles of his people as they loaded rubber crowd suppression rounds and stun cartridges into their weapons.

"Johnson, grab shock sticks for your team."

"Understood, Chief," replied Corporal Johnson. "Any particular reason why?"

"Because I want you and your squad taking point, greenie. You'll be leading this charge, Johnson."

***

"Keep the guns trained on her," ordered the Captain. "She might have a few surprises left."

"Understood, sir," replied Gunnery Alvarez. "She's not getting away from me again."

Captain Kaplean leaned back in his command chair and studied Dr. Wyeth, who paced back and forth in front of the viewport, eyeing the dead freighter.

"So close and yet so far," she caviled. "How long is this going to take?"

Lieutenant Hayley caught the almost imperceptible nod from the Captain. She stepped away from her station and approached the woman, "Clearing a ship can take time, Dr. Wyeth."

"Time is the one commodity I don't have, Lieutenant. Set up a tight beam to the Ankara jump gate immediately with the highest directive. I'll take it in my cabin." She turned on her heel and strutted off the bridge. Over her shoulder, she called out, "I expect updates as they happen. Do not disappoint me again, Captain."

***

Galena stumbled out into the cargo bay and stopped when the hull shook from a series of small impacts. "Sounds like boarding harpoons."

Luli asked, "Do we have anything down here to fight them off with?"

Galena rested her hands on her hips and looked around, "We have a couple of pistols... Wait! That mark looks familiar. Check that crate. Mr. Leon must've left it here at some point."

"I thought they were only chock full of mazuma." Luli ran to the crate and kicked it over. A handful of rifles fell out followed by a large ammo box.

"Are those Hail-Storms?" Galena positively glowed as she strode toward them.

"Hail-Storms?"

A satisfied grin lit up the Lieutenant's face, "They sure are. Inaccurate as all hell, but they'll throw up a wall of slugs fast and hard."

Luli bent down and read the label on the top of one of the other boxes, "This one says it's full of grenades."

"That's a good start," Galena pondered. "I wonder if those refraction camo suits we got from the Cyclops are still in here?"

two

Gun Fever (Blam Blam Fever)

Jacquie pressed herself against the bow port as two small landers flew past and disappeared around the port side of the ship. Derain quietly pulled out his pistol and made sure it was loaded before he slid it back home in its holster.

Jacquie pounded the plas-glass, "They've got a tunnel to the cargo bay. Looks like they got a couple landers going for the upper airlock, too."

Anton slipped out from under the nav station and floated over to the bridge hatch, "Should we lock this?"

"Leave it for now," she answered. "I don't want my boat more damaged than she already is."

"The Matilda's already a wreck," said Derain. "Where's the good in saving a door?"

She spun on Derain and the strain on her face was clear to see, "You take that back!"

Jon Gray Lang

Derain threw up his hands in surrender. The ship clanged as four more harpoons slammed into the hull. With their conversation forgotten, the three of them glanced out the hatchway.

***

Chief Bull and his team stood in the access way while they waited for the tunnel to extend out to their target. Unlike commercial vessels, the M33's tunnel had been designed for boarding actions. Reinforced plasteel ran the length of the shaft to prevent high-end rifle rounds from punching holes through it into space. It had shunts built along the sides in case of concussive blasts. The tunnel was constructed for clawing its way to a foothold onto other ships and creating a safe haven for Consortium Marines to keep pushing forward.

The metal teeth bit firmly into the skin of the Matilda's hull. Johnson's team launched themselves down the tunnel. The pounding of their magnetic boots reverberated the entire length until they came to a stop at the hatch.

Corporal Johnson directed, "Eldin, cut this sucker open. Let's get inside the damn tin can."

Eldin and his mate popped the sparker on the cutter and set the flame to the locking mechanism. After a few minutes, the lock popped, flinging ribbons of hot metal against the outer layer of the airlock.

The flame was minimized and the two-person

team backed out of the way. An incredibly large man moved up front and wedged a hydraulic bar into the seam. His muscles bulged against the skin of his suit as he worked the end of the bar farther into the crack. Once the tip of the bar cranked open a gap that was big enough, he jammed the bar halfway in and hit the switch. The bar split open into a pressurized jack. The hatch continued to open until three other people ran up and pushed it all the way into its housing.

"Eldin? One more time, please."

"Got it, Johnson," Eldin replied as he began cutting through the inner lock mechanism.

When this one popped, the molten metal spilled onto the decking on the other side of the hatch. Once again, the big man stepped up with the hydraulic wedge and set to work. As soon as the gap in the hatch was wide enough for the other three to dive in, the big man stumbled back and dropped the wedge. The sound of a gunshot rang down the tunnel. Blood spattered down the arm of the big man's armored suit. Two riflemen took up position within the open portion of the hatch.

"You see where that came from, Ramirez?" asked Johnson as he waved the medic over to Private Singh.

"Not a thing, man. This hallway is as empty as your dating card," replied Ramirez. "Oh, shi...!"

The hallway rattled with gunfire, as slugs burst against the hatch, the decking, and the back wall of the airlock before exploding outward into tiny fragments. The two marines fired back until the return fire petered out. Two other soldiers pushed the hatch into its housing and a two-layer firing wall formed up just past the opening.

"Keep an eye out, people," Johnson cautioned into the quiet. "Ramirez, you first."

"On it, sir."

Ramirez slinked forward into the open. The rest of the squad slowly spread out through the dark cargo bay on the Matilda. After all the noise, everything was eerily quiet. The marine's boots ground fragments of plas-glass into the decking. It glinted in the light from their handheld flashes. Johnson's beam hovered over a couple of smashed crates that lay in a pile. Only the sound of gears whirring and pneumatic pumps popping drifted from the med lab that was highlighted by small pinpricks of colored lights.

"Malik and Roma? Check that out," commanded Johnson. "Ramirez and Eldin, lock down that lift."

Johnson's team split off in twos. One pair headed into the sickbay as another moved to the lift doors. The bay remained quiet until their voices called out, "Clear."

Johnson activated his comm, "Chief?" Looks clear on this deck."

A flood of soldiers entered the cargo bay and took up positions along the airlock wall.

"Did you check out the crawler?" asked Chief Bull.

The faint sharp tinks of thin metal pins proceeded a hail of grenades that clattered across the decking amongst the marines.

"Incoming!" screamed Ramirez.

Smoke canisters burst overhead. As some of the soldiers looked up, the grenades exploded and tore through their body armor. Heavy suppression fire erupted from above the crawler and between the water and fuel tanks on the far wall. The marines fired back. Sparks popped from the armor plating on the crawler and shots ricocheted off the heavy liquid tanks.

"Pull back!" shouted Chief Bull. "God damn it, pull back!"

Two more smoke canisters burst in the air of the cargo bay. The heavy gunfire from the crawler dwindled down to nothing. Then a taped bundle of grenades landed in the airlock. Johnson threw himself on the bundle, but it wasn't enough. Pieces of his body exploded throughout the airlock and down the M33's boarding tunnel. Screams echoed down the shaft as soldiers dragged themselves away from the Matilda. The unmistakable whirr of a Hail-Storm gun whined above the screaming soldiers.

"Get down now!" shouted Chief Bull.

***

The rear hatch on the troop lander opened up and Higgins' team maneuvered out into open space.

The hatch on the other lander slid open and Gavriel's team floated free of their lander. Higgins waved at them and then directed them to the Matilda's airlock. Tiny attitude jets sparked out into the night sky. Magnetic boots clamped to the hull of the freighter as soldiers scattered into position around the airlock. Two of Gavriel's team hunkered forward and engaged their cutter on the locking mechanism.

Hot metal fragments spit into space as the hatch was shoved hard back into its housing. The two-man team floated forward and began cutting through the inner lock mechanism.

Once the lock was sheared open, the cutter team moved out of the way. The airlock was filled almost to capacity and the outer hatch was pulled closed. A plasteel patch was thrown over the burnt lock, then the inner hatch was pushed open. A small amount of atmosphere bled out into space before the patch expanded and held.

Three teams broke into the main hall of the upper deck of the ship. Defensive positions were set up quickly as the last team popped the doors on the inner airlock. "Airlock is secured."

A pair of two-person teams pushed out into the hangar. Aside from the two vessels anchored to the decking, nothing more was found. One of the teams unlocked the hatch to the upper Engine room.

***

Jon Gray Lang

Barney slid back as muffled explosions and gunfire sounded from the deck below. With the ship's power cut, the comms were down as well as the anti-grav. Strangely, the jump engine exuded its own gravitational force even with the power off.

Wiping his brow, Barney hunkered down behind his long rifle. He jammed his boots against the raised cradle for the engine that dominated the center of the main engine room. The long rifle was clamped to the decking and pointed down the main shaft of the ship.

As the concussive reports petered out from the cargo bay, an alarm chirped on his wrist pad. Muttering to himself, Barney pulled back his sleeve and silenced the alert.

"Upper Engine room's been breached, eh? I was hoping I'd never have to use these." He grimaced while he swiped his finger against the screen, "Dismal end for whoever you are."

***

A sonic burst flung the invading marines out of the Upper Engine room. One of them shot up toward the rafters while another smacked against the sides of the parked Waratah and Cyclops. Their screams and pained moans filled the personal comm channels. The other two found themselves scattered throughout the hangar. Corporal Gavriel watched as one of his people crawled toward another. The soldier barely moved forward, trailing a leg that was bent in the wrong direction.

Gavriel snarled, "Who in the cursed heavens are these people?"

***

Jacquie glanced over at Derain, "You got this?"

Derain shrugged on his refraction coat and zipped it closed. He withdrew both of his pistols and silently counted to three before he turned and threw her a slight nod, but she wasn't there to see it. "Yes," he whispered.

As she ran for the hatch, Jacquie shouted, "Anton? You're with me."

Anton hovered next to the hatch on the bridge and kept an ear to the corridor. He looked back and threw a quick grin to the hazy blur that was Derain, then he noiselessly followed after the Captain.

Derain looked down at his pistols a final time as he grimaced, "This plan isn't going to work."

***

Private Zere had sighted down his rifle with the rest of his squadmates when he suddenly caught sight of a man and a woman making a break for it. "Movement!" he shouted before his rifle bucked repeatedly into his shoulder. A satisfied smile spread across his face as the man's leg buckled and he

Jon Gray Lang

bounced off the decking. Then the smile disappeared as his target continued to pull himself down the hall.

"Damned lack of gravity!" he growled as he sighted down his rifle again and fired off another barrage of rubber rounds. "Stupid, pointless safety ammo..."

Higgins' voice bellowed through the comm, "Teams Two and Four! Move up and seize those two! Go, go, go!"

Two marines stepped out into the hallway in staggered positions, followed closely by their companions. The first pair moved to the front of the open hatch of the bridge and scanned for signs of life. They nodded to the next pair and moved off toward the lounge.

***

Derain kept watch from the left panel while the next three marines moved on past the open hatch. His eyes slit as he brought his pistols up and pulled the triggers. The one closest to him went down before the next marine even had a chance to react. She turned just in time to catch a shot through her faceplate.

The one closest to the lounge backpedaled as he was riddled with slugs from Anton's and Jacquie's pistols. His boots disconnected from the decking and he bounced against the wall. Rubber rounds from the other end of the hall ricocheted off the walls near the lounge. The back of Anton's hand was struck and his big pistol Henon slipped from his grasp. Derain lost sight of Anton as he backpedaled into the lounge.

Derain shot the last of the forward team in the back as more soldiers from the airlock slipped forward and slid against the far wall. Multiple rounds slapped into the frame of the hatch, so Derain stepped back into the confines of the bridge.

***

"Hold your fire!" shouted Gavriel.

The only people left in the hallway were the two forward teams and they floated silently where they had died.

Gavriel's hands clenched into fists. "Screw this. I want stun grenades in every single room!"

Higgins replied, "We're supposed to bring them in alive."

"They aren't suffering under the same compunction. If one of them dies, you can lay it on me." Corporal Gavriel lifted a grenade off the man in front of him and affixed it to his rifle, "Fellas? Make them regret breathing today."

The hallway rang with the deep-throated thump of grenades launching off the ends of their rifles. Shockwaves rolled down the hallway and blackened the bulkheads. Once those grenades had detonated, Gavriel ran forward and lobbed a stun grenade into the bridge. There was a loud bang followed by a scream. A hand clutching a pistol fell through the hatchway, but the arm remained hidden.

"The prigs have optical camo," Gavriel grunted into the comm. "Be aware." He flagged down a female marine, "Lloyd, help me truss this one up."

As she walked over, the clump of magnetic boots hitting the deck hard shot past her. The heavy thump of grenades being fired at point-blank range into the lounge followed. She bent down to the hand lying on the decking and ripped the pistol free. The Corporal pulled at the edge of the refraction coat until he was able to peel it off of the tall man. Private Lloyd spotted a gun in the other hand and wrestled it free. She tied his wrists together while Gavriel tied his ankles together.

The Corporal commanded, "Lloyd, drag this one over to the lift. And keep him covered."

"You think it's necessary?"

"If it was up to me, I'd space the lot of 'em. But it's not, so they get to keep taking in canned air. We don't know what other tricks these civvies have up their sleeves and we've lost enough already."

***

Anton stumbled into the lounge and fell to his knees while rounds pelted the wall near the hatch. He grabbed at his right leg and rolled onto his back. Jacquie grabbed his free arm and dragged him further into the lounge.

"You okay?" she asked.

"I'll live," he replied. "I think we got them."

The patter of bullets against the bulkhead trickled to a stop and silence reigned. Jacquie ran to the long table and kicked it with enough force to snap it at the base. The tabletop twisted to its side with a wobble and she tugged it into a position where it could be used as a shield.

Anton watched in mild confusion before he understood, "Aah, good thinking."

Suddenly, dull thumps echoed down the hallway and three stun grenades slammed into the ceiling of the lounge. Jacquie dove for the protection of the table.

"No way this ends well," Anton cursed.

The grenades detonated one after the other. Anton's boots disconnected and his body lifted off the decking. He slammed with a sickening crunch against the ceiling. Jacquie was thrown against the viewport when the tabletop bashed into her. It skittered into the galley and crashed amongst the pots and pans. Soldiers burst into the room while Anton's body spun lazily in the lack of gravity.

"Get that man down," ordered Higgins.

One of the soldiers reached for Anton's leg, but it twisted unnaturally in her grip. She pulled him down until his boots clumped back to the decking, then proceeded to tie his wrists and ankles together. Two more soldiers ran over to Jacquie's unconscious form and tied her ankles and wrists. They dragged her body next to Anton's and clicked her boots to the decking.

Higgins growled, "They have optical camo, folks. Check every single nook and cranny and do not leave anything to chance. Got it?"

Gavriel entered the lounge and detailed two people to cart the two prisoners back with the other one. The marines didn't find anyone else, so the team tromped back to the lift. One soldier was left to guard the prisoners while two others pried open the lift doors. The top was opened and a handheld winch was connected to the cabling of the lift.

The last of the marines piled in. The doors were left propped open and the winch slowly forced the lift down to the third deck.

Gavriel keyed the comm, "Chief? Top deck is cleared, three prisoners are sequestered. We're heading down now."

***

Luli slithered away and took up position near the water tanks. She caught the slight blur that was Galena shifting her way beneath the Rabbit's Folly. Both of them were running on pure adrenaline and Luli knew they wouldn't be able to hold out much longer.

The last rush by the marines had been brutal, but they hadn't gained a foothold in the cargo bay. She knew their luck couldn't last. The pilot strained her ears and caught some shouting coming from the tunnel of the attacker's ship. The voice was too muffled for her to make out exactly what was said.

***

Chief Bull nodded while he listened intently to Corporal Higgins as he explained what they had found on the top deck. They had suffered heavy casualties for the number of prisoners they had captured. Thankfully, the next deck down had been completely empty.

"They have optical camo, eh? I'll relay that, Higgins. Chief out." Chief Bull let his gaze rest on the men under his command as they awaited his orders, "Lock and load stun grenades. I want pulped eardrums in there, you hear me? I want every single one of them knocked out 'til next week."

"Got it, Chief," rang out and the click of rifle-loaded grenades clunked in the reinforced tunnel. He let his hand drop and the first barrage of stun grenades was launched into the cargo bay of this bastard of a boat. As soon as the last had detonated, he had them reload and launch a second barrage in there. Gavriel was right, they had lost too many already.

***

Barney felt the ship tremor from a series of explosions out in the cargo bay. He shook his head slowly as he blew out a pent-up breath and placed his eye against the scope of his rifle. He knew that they would have him eventually, but after everyone else had fought so hard to keep them out, there was no point in surrender. He could already hear the tromping of boots in the wake of the detonations.

***

The Chief waited for the "All clear" calls before he made his way back into the death trap of a ship. The place was crawling with his troops who were ransacking every corner of the open space. Blackened soot covered the decking and the walls and the few crates that hadn't been ruptured in the blasts had been tossed willy-nilly. Slivers of plas-glass intermixed with chunks of faux-wood and plastics littered the deck. Rubber bullet rounds were everywhere.

His eyes turned toward what he could only assume were the remains of a med lab. The place was a disaster. A med tube had been flung against the operating table that had skittered into the cabinetry on the far wall.

Private Kovit's data pad was locked into the medical robot that hung precariously from its track. Three other Marines were in the process of opening each med tube in the search for prisoners.

"Sir! I found one!" said a voice over the group comm.

Surveying the room for the source of the voice, Chief Bull spotted a trooper with her arm up. He strode toward her, making sure each of his boot steps made full contact with the decking. From the corner of his eye, he saw the lift come down to the deck above with what was left of Higgins' and Gavriel's teams. He acknowledged their arrival and waved them toward the open hatch just past the railing.

"What did you find, Banerjee?" the Chief asked as he hunkered down near the water tanks.

The trooper pulled on a heavily bandaged arm that lay within the space between the two tanks. He bent down to give her a hand and, with the two of them working at it, they finally got the body to budge.

"This one is pretty stiff, Chief," Banerjee muttered. "Might not have made it."

All of a sudden, the body shifted and shot out of the gap, throwing the Private on her backside. The Chief was able to hold onto one arm while Banerjee righted herself. The body collapsed to the decking and didn't move again. Banerjee pulled at the face mask of the optical camo suit until she was able to make out what was behind it. What she saw was the work of savagery. Tattered skin hung loosely over the gleaming metal skull where thick stitches had been torn free. Wisps of black hair floated out from the edges of the hood of the suit. Something was familiar about her, though.

"Somebody did a number on her. These bandages go up past the elbows and her whole head is a mess. Whoever did this must've really hated cyborgs," Banerjee added offhandedly.

Jon Gray Lang

"I swear I've seen her before. Wait... this is Luli Qing!" shouted the Chief in surprise. "I saw her on stage on... where was it... Right! It was on Qunis 4. What, by the ghost of Tom, is she doing on this boat?"

Three loud bangs followed by a muffled scream broke over the comm before a call for retreat was shouted. Everyone in the cargo bay looked up toward the second deck as the squads up there backpedaled out of the hatch. Two troopers dropped to their knees and pressed against the door frame. They fired into the room while two more stood behind them and fired over their shoulders.

"Status report, Corporals?" Chief Bull grunted into the comm.

Higgins replied, "Tuco and Layeni got hit by some large caliber round. Damn things tore a hole in the armor and ripped their way through. Baris got hit in the back. I don't think he's going to make it."

"How many down there, you think?"

"Small room at the back," answered Gavriel. "Can't be more than one or two."

"Grenades," interrupted the Chief. "Leave nothing moving in there. Got me, Corporals?"

"Understood," replied Higgins.

***

Barney slid another round into the breech of his rifle. He had hit at least three of them before they had backed out into the gym. They would be coming back and they would be coming for blood. Barney rubbed his chin, evaluating the attack on the Matilda. The ship was dead in the water. Her engines were gone. There was no power. The heat was already dissipating. The rest of the crew had either been captured or killed. That left just him.

He jumped when a canister smacked into the back of the room. It was followed by another, then another. He caught some movement toward the very edge of the main shaft and squeezed the trigger. The rifle bucked in his hands as all hell broke loose.

A blast shattered his work console before the pressure wave picked him up and slammed him into the bulkhead. Another blast went off and his headphones were ripped free in the process. The cradle that held the jump engine cracked and the sphere rolled loose. A third and fourth blast threw him into the ceiling and wall before he blacked out.

***

Minutes later, the decking rang with the clang of magnetic boots. Two marines grabbed Barney's small frame and bound his wrists and ankles. He looked so tiny next to the long rifle that lay nearby.

"Soften him up, folks," ordered Corporal Gavriel. "For Tuco and Layeni."

Their fierce grins shined through their faceplates. The squad formed a circle around

Barney and kicked him with their armored boots. Their laughter sounded ugly and grim in the private comm.

"That's enough. Get his ass to the Chief."

Gavriel waited until his team carted the Titan out past the gym. He gave the room a final once over before he switched the comm channel to wide, "Only one down here, Chief, and it was a Titan at that."

The Chief's voice came back, "No genorgs then?"

"Not a one."

"Captain's not going to be happy to hear that," muttered Chief Bull. "Not one bit."

three

Always on the Run

With a sudden gasp, Galena regained consciousness. When she tried to sit up, her forehead slammed against a large slab of metal. She slumped back to the floor and rubbed her head. Her eyes opened slowly, "Where am I? Last thing I remember is a bunch of flash-bangs."

She studied her surroundings and from what she could tell, she was trapped under the Rabbit's Folly. The runner had snapped its tie-downs and now it was smacked up against the cargo bay doors.

"What in the nine hells did they hit us with?" she muttered into the thin air. "Lu? Lu, you there? Are you okay?"

She listened intently but there was no response. "How am I going to get out from under this behemoth?"

Debris lay strewn about and her boots

Jon Gray Lang

couldn't find purchase. She got her hand inside one of the wheel housings and pulled herself free.

Her body scraped against the decking which made her pause, "We got the gravity reinstated?"

She came to her feet and rubbed her hands together to shake some of the dust off, "Well, hooray for progress."

The Matilda took a sickening lean. She tried to catch herself when she stumbled away from the crawler. Her entire world came crashing down as the hull of the ship slammed hard against something. She was thrown clear of her feet and crashed into the closest fuel tank. Knocked unconscious again, she slid down and slumped into a pile of refuse.

***

Lieutenant Hayley's voice came through the comm, "... I'm sorry, Doctor. We cannot re-angle the ship for your direct comm until the freighter Matilda has been secured."

"Delays! So many delays!" Dr. Wyeth slammed her fists against the built-in desk in her cabin. She keyed the comm, "If you do not redirect this ship soon Lieutenant, I will get your commission pulled and leave you destitute on an airless rock. Do you understand me?"

As she cut the comm feed, the Doctor drummed her fingers against the desktop, "I'll see this whole ship's crew spaced." She glanced over her shoulder at the single mercenary guard she allowed in her cabin.

"Is your team ready, Zhao?"

The mercenary dropped into a quick bow, "We are at the beck and call of the House of Khanda. What are your orders?"

A dark smile graced her lips, "Prep for Protocol 8472."

***

Chief Bull activated his comm, "Sir? We have the Matilda secured in the hangar. Any further orders?"

"Get a team of engineers on board," Captain Kaplean ordered. "Their priority is to figure out the freighter's jump capability."

"Understood, sir."

"Where is the crew right now?"

"The prisoners are en route to our sickbay," answered the Chief. "Should I prep them for interrogation, instead?"

"Let the medical team examine them first," replied Captain Kaplean. "They won't do us much good if they die without telling us a damn thing."

Chief Bull grunted, "Should I inform Dr. Wyeth that her drone was not found on board?"

"For right now, let's just keep her out of the loop."

"Keep the Doctor out of it. Got it, sir. Chief out." He turned back to the hangar, "Anotol, get your team in there and figure out how this demon ship eluded us for so long. Sinix, the Captain wants those prisoners prepped for interrogation as soon as possible."

"I don't think they can handle it, yet," Dr. Sinix said as he looked over the preliminary scans.

"Doesn't matter, Captain's orders," replied the Chief. "Have them checked out but get them prepped as soon as possible. We need to know where they left the genorg butcher."

"Understood, Chief. Nurse Valdez, wake the woman and get her moved to sickbay, stat."

In a parting thought, Chief Bull added, "Oh, Sinix? As a personal favor, can you take extra care with the cyborg? Her hands are worth their weight in gold."

The Doctor looked down at the woman's hands and frowned, "I'll see what I can do."

***

Only long-serving crew members would even notice as the destroyer swung slowly to the port side. The stars through the viewport barely moved before the ship settled.

"Lieutenant? The M33 has been repositioned for tight beam communications per your instructions," stated the pilot.

"Thank you." Lieutenant Hayley sighed as she keyed the comm to Dr. Wyeth's cabin, "Doctor? Thank you for your patience. The freighter has been secured in the hold and the ship re-angled for your comm request."

There was no reply as the comm cut off from the receiving end. A large file was transferred to the laser comm. Lieutenant Hayley delayed the message as she made a copy of it and shunted it over to her decryption software. As soon as the copy transferred over, she had the tight beam laser comm complete the send.

She muttered under her breath, "Please crack it this time, damn it."

***

The sound of boot steps clanging their way through the cargo bay brought Galena back. She could make out two technicians and their levitating equipment box as they headed to the lift.

Tech Anotol stepped gingerly over the shattered plas-glass, "The Chief sure did a number on this boat, didn't he?"

"Serves them right," replied Tech Danislav. "Who do they think they are to take us on? We're the Gods-be-damned Consortium."

Anotol grinned wolfishly, "Yes, it does serve them right, doesn't it?"

Once the two of them stepped into the lift, Anotol perused his data pad, "Let's see. Gavriel said there was an Engine Room off the hangar bay..."

Danislav interrupted, "Higgins said there was one on the second deck, too."

"Second deck, then?" asked Private Anotol.

"Yeah," grunted Danislav. "We'll make our way up. Have to check out the bridge for controls, anyway."

"Good point," replied Anotol as he slapped Danislav on the back. "I knew we kept you around for some reason."

"Har-de-har..." Danislav grumbled as he hit the lift controls.

The lift doors closed and Galena watched them reopen on the second deck. The two technicians stepped out dragging their equipment case behind them. Once they disappeared into the gym, she took a peek at the airlock.

"Looks like the Matilda has power again, but I've got so many more questions. As Rabbit would say, The best place for answers is the source that is right in front of me. Hope that's true."

***

Dr. Sinix examined the Titan on his table. It was a rare chance to get to see one up close. He found the diminutive man fascinating.

"I know I'm a beauty, but are you done with me yet?" grumbled Barney. "Your yeoman wants your attention something fierce. And I could use less of you ogling my crotch!"

"What?" exclaimed the Doctor accompanied by the laughter of his team. "I was doing no such thing!"

Barney leered through his bruises at the poor

man, "That's what they all say."

Dr. Sinix backed into the Yeoman breathing down his neck. He glanced over his shoulder at the hulking man, "Yes, what can I do for you?"

"These prisoners pass muster, Doc?" asked Yeoman Fitzpatrick. "The Captain wants them ready for a lengthy interrogation."

The Doctor sniffed contritely, "Besides some bumps and cuts, they're ready enough. All except the cyborg." He stared into Fitzpatrick's eyes, "Special orders, you know."

The Yeoman stepped back, "Special orders? What about the genorg? She in here somewhere?"

"I'm not aware of a drone," replied the Doctor. "But why would anyone bother with one? They're a dime a dozen."

"Right," agreed Fitzpatrick. "I'll take this lot to the brig, then."

"They're just taking up space in my lab. Have at it. I just need to give the Titan some pain neutralizers."

"Titans can be feisty, Doctor," muttered Yeoman Fitzpatrick. "Might want to add some sedatives to the mix."

"Uh, right you are. Nurse Valdez, can you assist this fine young officer in his duties?"

"Of course, Doctor," she replied. "If you'll follow me."

The nurse and Fitzpatrick quickly reattached the bindings to the captured crew of the Matilda.

Dr. Sinix walked over to the table that the

Jon Gray Lang

cyborg lay on. He pursed his lips at the damage done to her skin. Rot had started to set in at the seams. He rifled through a drawer until he found the vial he needed.

"Miss Qing?" asked Dr. Sinix. "I'm going to inject you with something that will stimulate your skin regrowth. You may feel some irritation as it grows back."

She hesitated before she nodded in acceptance.

He chuckled good-naturedly, "I can understand your lack of trust, but my job is to save lives. And that's what I do."

Yeoman Fitzpatrick barked a short laugh as he signed a release document.

Dr. Sinix stiffened for a moment, but relaxed once Fitzpatrick pushed the crew out into the passageway.

"That Yeoman is trouble, Miss Qing. I would avoid him at all costs."

***

"Looks like you're not needed until the cyborg is released," muttered the Yeoman as he checked his data pad. "Get a move on."

Jacquie and Derain stumbled forward. Anton was shoved from behind when he went to help Barney. It wasn't a long walk before they were unceremoniously thrown into the brig.

Fitzpatrick addressed the guard, "Captain

wants them under wraps. No visitors." He turned to the bounty hunter as he stepped past the cell barrier, "You're a Tiwi, right?"

"Yeah, that's right." Derain cautiously replied.

Jacquie looked over her shoulder as Anton carried Barney into one cell.

"Sorry to hear about your family. I heard they had a rough time of it recently." Fitzpatrick laughed harshly as he slammed the cell door shut. He quickly shoved Jacquie into the neighboring cell.

"What do you mean?" screamed Derain as he pounded at the window. "What do you mean?"

The Yeoman's laughter rang out in response until the brig hatch swung shut with finality.

Jacquie found the retractable bed controls and waited for it to slide out of the wall. She dropped onto the hard surface and rolled back onto her shoulders. The visit to the sickbay had been good. Her eardrums had taken a lot of damage from the stun grenades, but the ringing was down to a tolerable level. Despite the aches and bruises from the fierce fight, it was nice to know that the crew was in better shape now than when they had arrived.

"Even if the interrogation leads to our execution, at least my people are alive to resist," she whispered into the empty cell. "Only one thing left to do. Find where they're holding the Lieutenant."

***

Lieutenant Hayley looked down as her

decryption system chimed softly when it finally broke the Doctor's code. She shunted the details over to her data pad. As the message unfolded, she studied it,

'House of Khanda... Subject 4296-E-2631-H retrieved... Once in custody, will make haste to base of operations. Potential system expansion through 'de trop aspect' can be achieved with subject.'

She read it through a third time. '*While the House of Khanda makes headway through the council, they rob the families of other worlds. And it all has to do with the Doctor's genorg program.*'

She tight beamed the full message to the jump gate with the highest directive for the Council Heads of the Amiran Dynasty. "Now, it's in their hands."

"Is that a private comm, Lieutenant?" asked Captain Kaplean.

As she altered the message, she replied, "Yes, sir. Same destination but the endpoint is still an unknown."

"Meet me in my ready room."

As Captain Kaplean left the bridge, Lieutenant Hayley sent the altered message by tight beam and removed all traces of her recent comm history. She stood up and followed her Captain. Her fingers slid away from the control pad as the door shut behind her.

"You asked for me, sir?"

"At ease, Lieutenant," responded Captain Kaplean. "Is that the message we've been waiting for?"

She nodded in ascent, "We still don't know the final end."

"Send what you have to the Clan Ganbat and wait for further instructions."

Lieutenant Hayley saluted, "It is done. The Doctor's comm has been relayed."

"Now, we just await our orders," murmured Captain Kaplean. "Thank you, Lieutenant, it is good to have friends in dark times."

A vague queasy feeling rose in the Lieutenant's gut, "It is, sir. It's a pleasure to serve with you. I'll return to my station. As soon as I receive a reply..."

"You'll let me know. Yes, thank you."

***

As the two technicians entered the Engine Room, they both noticed how the gravity was heavier as soon as their boots touched the floor. Large caliber casings littered the decking amongst spatterings of blood. Bits of shrapnel lay embedded in the now, non-functioning, work console. But the strange sphere resting against the aft bulkhead of the small room dominated their view.

"By the ghost of Tom, they sure did a number in here, didn't they?" cursed Danislav. "I don't think there's enough left to even guess how much they destroyed."

"A grunt's gonna do what a grunt's gonna do..." grumbled Tech Anotol.

Jon Gray Lang

Danislav brushed the broken hammock off the orb and pulled it from the crevice between the sphere and the cradle. Anotol just stared at it with his hands on his hips.

Tech Danislav rubbed his gloved hand along the surface of the ball, "Well? I think we found it, whatever the hell 'it' is..."

"You ever see anything thing like this?" asked Anotol.

"Hell to the no. I've never seen anything even vaguely resembling anything like this," answered Danislav. "Damn thing gives me the creeps, it does."

"Can't say that I'm a fan of it, myself," muttered Anotol. "But it's not going to figure itself out for us. Let's get to work."

"Yes sir, right away, sir," mocked Danislav.

Just as Danislav turned away, Anotol felt a hand go around his throat and throw him against the wall. As he struggled to get up, a shimmer moved toward Danislav and lifted him off the floor. Danislav's scream was cut short as his body was slammed against the back wall of the room. Anotol tried to get to his feet while Danislav's unconscious form slid its way to the floor.

The shimmer moved back toward Anotol who brought up his arms to block whatever it was. Something with preternatural strength wrenched his arms apart and kicked his legs out from under him. He spun around until he faced the decking and a weight fell onto his back. He collapsed against the decking with the breath knocked out of him. As he struggled to inhale, his arms were restrained behind him.

"You will answer my questions, technician."

The voice, more mechanized than lifelike, came from the shimmering apparition. This alone frightened him more than whatever this was that had trapped him with no way to escape. The grip on his wrists tightened until his skin burned.

"What... what do you want to know?" he burbled.

"What have you done with the crew of this ship?" the voice demanded.

"I, I don't know. Last I heard was that they were to be interrogated."

"Interrogated by whom? Interrogated for what?"

"By the Captain! I don't know what for."

"You don't know?" asked the deadened female voice as Anotol's arm slowly twisted behind him.

He could feel the bones slip as the torque pulled his arm out of its socket, "Rumors say it's about a genorg! That's all I know! I swear!"

"Good enough for me," muttered the shimmer as it slammed Anotol's head into the decking until he stopped moving.

Galena blinked and she was in the engine room. "How did I get here?" Confusion hit her as she regarded the two men. She slipped Anotol's data card out of his pocket and slid it into her own. A disconnected memory floated to the surface of her mind, "They're after me? But why?"

four

Sad But True

Time was running short. Mr. Leon hurried to his cabin on the Copperhead only to find the one person he was growing tired of running into waiting by the hatch.

"Mr. Leon?" asked Hau Hung. "Have you given any thought to my suggestion? About getting me transport to a station or planet?"

"We've had this conversation, Mr. Hau. Besides the debt you owe me, I still find you useful." Mr. Leon ran his hand through his hair, "You are aware our agreement isn't concluded."

"And I'm good for it," replied Hung. "I located that shipyard you were looking for. It wasn't easy, but I found it for you."

Mr. Leon looked the man up and down, "You did well. And you have been a boon to my business, both personal and commercial. But a debt is a debt."

"I'm no soldier, Mr. Leon. I'd be more useful on the ground somewhere... anywhere."

"If it's that important for you to leave, an airlock lies not fifty yards from you," sighed Mr. Leon. "I don't know why, but I still like you, Mr. Hau. I hope you decide to stay on. Now if you'll excuse me, I have much to do."

Hung's eyes dropped as he nodded in grim acceptance. He bowed deeply and headed back to the cargo bay.

Mr. Leon quietly locked the hatch to his berth. With a light exhale, he assumed the lotus position on the center of his bunk and lapsed into a deep meditation state as he closed his eyes. His brothers throughout the systems slowly enfolded with him in the gestalt of the mind. His eyes opened and he could see the cabin aboard the Independence, the office on Mithuna as well as other locations all across Consortium space. A sense of calm washed over him as their brother on the Silk Road station joined them. They exalted at the taste of tea as it slid down the back of his throat.

"Welcome, my brothers," stated the padrone of the brethren. "Progress is made, but still we must push forever forward to achieve that which we must. And time grows short."

Murmurs echoed through the minds of the Leons as each responded in his own way. Even when they were connected, there still existed a sense of separateness. Their fundamental core remained essentially the same, but different life experiences changed their individual views and ideas. And that which set them apart became more prevalent as they were forced to compensate for the response from the Council natural-borns.

"Supplies needed by the Consortium core systems and their military have been interrupted and sent elsewhere. Hefty profits have been made from their sales on the black market," echoed the voice from their office on Jard. "The inner planets are now beginning to feel the sting. Needless to say, but whispers abound through the halls of the Council. They don't see the damage as debilitating as of yet."

Another voice spoke out, "The sisters have effectively destroyed the transport of genorgs. Every last slaver ship has suffered a mutiny of sorts."

"The remnants of that trade are trapped in the orbit of numerous skylines," uttered another voice. "The number of factories and mines that have shut down, due to riots or lack of workers, only grows." The gestalt of minds resonated with mirth.

***

Aboard the Independence, Rex Leon felt the nods of understanding from the members of his family. A quiet sigh escaped him as he shifted slightly to rest his lower back. "Even though our experiments with the sisters failed, they prove as useful in their individuality. Their agreement with our orders has increased their numbers under our command. Can we depend on them for more?"

"Can we?"

From the nondescript berthing of one of the newer M Class Destroyers, came the voice of a young Leon, "I have some insight on the experiment. My ship has captured the Matilda, and I have gained access to the freighter's medical records. It appears that the test subject has been contaminated with the otherness."

Whispers erupted throughout the gestalt mind. Questions floated to the surface and were quickly answered:

"Should we attempt it on another test subject?"

"The change takes too long..."

"... there isn't time."

"Should the Lieutenant be disposed of?"

"She still has uses..."

"... she is proving to be a good figurehead."

"Would she make a good martyr?"

"She is not within reach..."

"... when the time comes, yes."

"Yes..."

As the chorus of agreement accumulated into a cacophony, Rex Leon spoke out against it, "She has proven useful in ways not initially foreseen. Let us not be shortsighted in this. We must wait."

"We must wait..."

"... yes. Yes..."

As the echoes died off, the padrone on the

Silk Road spoke, "We must begin to wrest control of the jump gates. The military craft stationed at each gate has to be disabled or destroyed. As soon as a gate is taken, we'll have to work fast. Dismantling will need to be done quickly before more of their ships arrive. While they waste time tracking down leads on who we are, we have to leave the gates dysfunctional."

Dry chuckles were felt more than heard, "More time for us to spread out and take out their communications. Limit them to their ships with FTL capability only."

"We need attack ships with FTL capability to complete this," grumbled their component from the Independence. "While the crews we have may not be the most trustworthy sort, there is no love lost between them and the Consortium. All we require are vessels."

"We have discovered the coordinates for the M class shipyard. Do we have a deadline on when the new cruisers will be ready?"

"We have freed as many of the genorg sisters as can be done safely. Their teams can make their way to the shipyard, posthaste."

"The attack will need to be quiet. We cannot allow news of it to spread," added another.

"While they try to get their jump gates back online, they will hardly notice a few stolen ships," chuckled another.

"Soon, my brothers. Soon," intoned the padrone. "We will leave our mark and usher in the needed changes for the natural-borns... under our guidance."

Rex slowly broke the communication and rubbed his eyes. He scanned the walls of the cabin until he felt the separation complete. A small grin appeared on his face as he realized that he was beginning to prefer the sense of solitude.

"For that, I blame you, Captain Delahaye."

***

Jacquie felt the bulkhead of her cell press into her back as she slowly leaned forward and opened her eyes. She looked over and Luli was asleep in the bunk next to hers. "Not sure how they got you in without me noticing. I must've been more tired than I thought."

Luli didn't move on the mat that passed for bedding in the tiny room. "She looks so comfortable," murmured Jacquie. She threw the woman a quick nudge, "You ever get that sense, like a feeling that someone is thinking about you?"

"Uh?" muttered Luli as she blinked herself awake. "You mean like someone is walking on your grave?"

"No, not like that at all," grimaced Jacquie. "Like in a good way. You know, positive feelings."

Luli stared at her blankly as she rested her head against the raised cushion, "Not in a long while, Jacq. Besides, it's hard to be positive in a place like this." A grimace of pain shot across her face, "By Tom, my fingers ache."

Jacquie crawled over to her friend and checked the new bandages wrapped tightly around her hands. The splint holding the digits in place felt solid underneath the bandages. Remembering what they had looked like under the original bandages, she hoped the ship's medic had performed some amazing reconstruction work.

"They dosed you pretty high with painkillers, Lu. If it's any comfort... from what I saw, you should be able to play your uke again. Maybe not today or even this month, but sometime."

Luli's red-rimmed eyes stared back at her Captain, "I... I don't know if I want to ever play again, Jacq. After everything that happened out there, I still struggle with what's real. Am I really human or am I just a log entry inside the belly of a machine?"

"You're real to me, Lu," Jacquie said as she embraced her old friend. "You'll always be my Luli Qing and no being, real or imagined, can say otherwise."

Luli collapsed into her arms for a long moment before she pulled abruptly away, "I hate to say this Jacq, but you stink."

Jacquie laughed as she pulled Luli back into her arms, "You don't smell too good either. What I wouldn't give for some time in a fresher, right now."

Luli smiled up into Jacquie's face, the woman she had helped raise, the woman who had rescued her from the clutches of a mad man. She felt safe, if only for the moment. Her laughter joined in with Jacquie's, "Me too, Jacq. Me too."

***

"Damn that sailor," muttered Derain.

Anton glumly looked over at his cellmate, "Which one? This boat is full of them."

The bounty hunter's eyes took in the small form of their engineer, Barney, as he lay comatose on the bunk in their cell. He had barely moved since they'd been tossed in here, but his chest continued to pump oxygen into his lungs.

He rested with his back against the wall and watched Anton fiddle with the heel of his boot, "The one that dropped me in here. The Yeoman that gave his condolences for the loss of my family. That smirk never left his face. The prig knows something and it's eating at me."

Anton stopped fiddling with his boot and set it aside, "With everything that's been happening, that had slipped my mind." He sighed, "I know saying sorry won't help, but I've lost family, too. Even if you didn't always get along, it still cuts deep. If you need someone to talk to..."

"Nothing I can do about it while I'm trapped in here."

Barney's breathing became labored and then he sat up, "Grenades in the engine room?" he blurted. "What kind of idiots are you?" As suddenly as he sat up, he slumped back to the mat.

Anton snickered, "Third time he's said that since we got here. Those tranqs must be strong. Man, is he going to be pissed when he comes to."

***

The marine who stood guard at the M33's hangar glanced both ways down the corridor before he leaned in repose against the wall. The area had been pretty busy of late. After the Chief dragged the freighter crew through to their cells, foot traffic had slowed down. But then it had picked right back up when the technicians boarded that beat-up trawler.

The crew hadn't been much to look at when they passed by. More like a parade of living scars than the gang of criminals who had tweaked the Captain's nerves. The next one in line, more beaten than the last. Especially that cyborg the Chief had gotten worked up about. Scuttlebutt was she was one of those legendary deep spacers.

"But what would someone famous like that be doing with that bunch of miscreants?" He shrugged, "Maybe they're the roadies or something."

He grabbed another view of the vessel they had captured. He didn't know much about freighters, but as far as he was concerned, she was an ugly brute. There were peculiar rents in the hull like some enormous beast had clawed at the little ship. On top of that, there was a weird aura about it, almost unsettling. He felt queasy even thinking about it.

The hatch to the hangar opened of its own volition and a light breeze blew past him. As it clanged shut, he could've sworn he heard the rustle of cloth. But when he searched for the source, there was nothing there.

"Something must be in my eye," he murmured as a vaguely out-of-focus spot moved across his view. "A floater," he decided, as the smudge slipped further down the hallway. He rubbed at his eyes and the blur was no longer there.

"Huh." With a shrug of his shoulders, he straightened up and turned back to standing at attention. He had to be careful these days. He had been caught slacking once already and he didn't relish another day of PT.

five

The Trooper

"There she is," whispered Rosa Keri as she brought the Independence closer to their destination.

The small moon of Sheba spun its forlorn way through space around an even larger, lifeless rock. The Independence settled into a high orbit around the satellite. With bated breath, Rosa and the crew waited to see if their arrival triggered a warning system. So far, the skies remained empty and the comms remained silent.

Rosa looked up from the comm station and shook her head, "Are you sure this is the right place, Mr. Leon? Their space-based defense system is pretty outdated. Even by outer system standards, that thing is old."

Mr. Leon grinned briefly, "Please, check again, but include a run on all frequencies. You might be surprised at what you find."

Commander Keri hummed to herself as she altered the parameters of her scan. While it might seem as if her search took no time at all, running through each of the bands was a time-consuming process. Not only because of the sheer number but also for the care it required to keep the search from alerting anyone monitoring those frequencies.

"Well, I'll be damned," whistled Rosa. "You were right, Mr. Leon. That is some high-end monitoring equipment to be skipping through each band wave so quickly. What in Gehenna are they storing down there?"

"Have they seen us?" asked Delta.

"Looks like we're still in the clear. I'd say the mission is a go."

Rex addressed the genorg, "Captain Delta, I need your people to take control of the facilities on that moon. It is an automated facility, so ground personnel should be nonexistent. We cannot fail here."

"Understood, sir," replied Delta. "Is there anything, in particular, we should make a priority?"

"Control of the communications station is tantamount. Communications from the moon cannot happen. If a message gets out, the revolution would fail before it started and we would all die an unsatisfying fiery death. Got it?"

Delta saluted as she spoke into her personal comm, "Rho-11, have your squads and Daphne's troops assemble to meet me in the cargo bay." Her voice resounded triumphantly as she disappeared through the hatch, "We've got a job to do."

***

The Independence, once a pirate ship named Garuda, had come with a strange assortment of gear and systems. One of the more exciting finds, as far as the genorgs were concerned, were the four cargo crates that contained military-grade drop suits. All told, there were a total of twenty suits. After the two genorg squads suited up, six were left in reserve.

Drop suits were specifically designed for atmospheric entry from a low orbit to planetfall. Airtight and armored, each one was built with a set of attitude jets for controlling their descent and landing. Each suit was also equipped with chaff dispersers to confuse tracking systems.

While older models, the suits were still from the top of the line. Where an old pirate ship had found them was beyond anyone's guess. How often did pirates need to make planetfall undetected? Considering the suits seemed factory fresh, not terribly often.

The genorg's excitement at their discovery had amused Mr. Leon. Rosa found it oddly fortuitous that the suits were on board and that the genorgs were familiar with their use. Military-trained genorgs still surprised her.

The Independence was slowly moved into a lower orbit while Daphne's team was stationed inside the airlock. Once the signal came through the comm, the airlock was lit by a red light as it cycled open to space. Each member of her team counted to three as the sister in front of her disappeared from view. As soon as they were all through, the outer airlock hatch closed. The inner door opened once the chamber was bathed in green light.

Rho-11's team shuffled into the airlock and disappeared from view.

***

The genorgs held their formation as they fell through the thin to almost nonexistent atmosphere. Billows of dust blew up from the surface of the moon as the first of Daphne's team landed.

Daphne's comm chirped with three tones. She chirped back twice before she slapped the attitude jets on the suit. She was coming in too fast and had to brake hard not to miss the landing zone. Dust billowed up in a cloud as she landed heavily, but the suit's servos performed admirably and took the brunt of the landing.

She was already on the move as the dust cloud settled and the rest of her team followed quickly. By the time they were in sight of the facility on the small moon, Rho-11's team had made ground fall on the other side. Daphne sent a single chirp on her comm before it cut to static.

***

"Confounder away, Delta."

Delta nodded as the audio signals all changed to static. "Keep a watch out for any launches, Alice."

"Understood. Priming coil guns," Alice stated as her eyes tracked the weapons board.

"And now, we wait," said Mr. Leon.

***

As the drop-suited genorgs fanned out around the single structure on Sheba, automated guns burst up from the surface. The weapons swiveled to find targets as Daphne's team released their chaff into the sky. Rho-11's team followed suit moments later.

The genorgs jogged past the gun emplacements. Shells sputtered out into the sky as their rounds slammed into the chaff creating bright puffs in the night.

Rho-11 reached the fencing that surrounded the single structure and leapt over it in a single bound. She fired a single flare toward the building. Once it burst, the rest of her team directed laser tracking beams to the gun emplacements.

***

Mr. Leon moved closer to the bow port in an attempt to see what was happening down on the surface. Even though the only sound was the crew's breathing, the bridge was taut with excitement.

"Targets painted," Alice stated in the background. "Rounds away."

***

Coil gun rounds slammed into the gun emplacements and cracked the ground beneath them. The genorg teams moved inexorably toward the building as the skies lost the sparkle from the exploding chaff and grew dark.

Carla made it to the facility door first. By the time Rho-11 came to a stop next to her, Carla had already pulled the hatch plating off and was rewiring it. Other genorgs made it to the door and waited silently for it to open.

Carla slammed her armored fist against the locking mechanism and the hatch slowly slid open into its housing. Rho-11 motioned toward the hallway inside and a two-person team slipped into it. Daphne gave Rho-11 a quick nod as she landed next to her. Rho-11 signaled back and the rest of her team entered the building.

The above-ground structure was empty of life except for the troops making their way to the command center. Rho-11's team met no resistance when they arrived at the main door. Carla dropped to her knees and blasted the lock with the flame of a handheld cutter built into the suit. The metal bubbled until the internal locking mechanism splattered on the floor.

Rho-11 pushed open the door. The room was empty. Lights blinked in patterns across the machine interface that ran the systems for the facility, but no one was there to monitor them.

***

Mr. Leon saw two flares burst in the night sky as Agnes relayed, "Signals received. Disengage the confounder."

Anne added, "Confounder disengaged. Moving to intercept."

"Why waste a perfectly good confounder," smirked Mr. Leon.

***

Within an hour, the Independence landed on the small moon of Sheba just outside of the single structure on the surface. Mr. Leon was joined by a contingent of troops as he stepped into the building. Rho-11 flagged down his group and led them to an enormous pair of doors.

"Like warehouse doors," murmured Rosa Keri. She had decided to join him on the surface. Curiosity as to what lay in this establishment that Mr. Leon thought might be useful drove her decision.

"... this is the only coded lock your teams found?" asked Mr. Leon.

At Daphne's nod, Rosa watched as Mr. Leon pulled a flimsy out of one of the pockets of his commercial-grade spacesuit. He keyed in a code on the recessed number pad.

As he stepped back from the rather long door, Rosa asked, "How did you get the access codes to this place, Mr. Leon? "Why do you even know this place exists?"

"Hmm? Well as a businessman in the shipping industry, one has a tendency to get the odd request or two." He winked at Rosa as the door slowly slid open, "Like this one for example. At one time it had been requested by our illustrious Council that I get a rushed shipment to a Battle Cruiser in some system or other. At the time, it took little work to get the code from an easily duped representative."

The door came to a trundling stop and the lights automatically clicked on.

"And voilà!" cried Mr. Leon. "Much needed weapons for the fight ahead of us."

Surprise followed by a deep sense of trepidation hit Rosa as she looked up from the strange man and out into a warehouse loaded with planet-killer missiles.

six

Cruel Melody

A heavy clang rebounded through the brig before a sharp click emanated from the cell door. Jacquie shot up from the uncomfortable slab. She tried to see down the hall through the small bars that decorated the only window. She couldn't see anything from this angle.

"Lu," she whispered. "Lu? Time to get up."

Luli slowly stirred from the slab, "Uh?"

The slab that Jacquie had been resting on automatically retracted into the wall. The one under Luli followed shortly.

"Wha?" Luli gasped as the slab disappeared under her. "Ow!"

Shouts rang from the hall, "Up! Up! Naptime is over!"

Jacquie bent down to help Luli up when the cell door popped open. By the time she had Luli standing on her own, rough hands had clicked manacles around her wrists. She was pulled roughly away from Luli and pushed through the doorway.

"Hurry up, you bunch of slackers! The Captain's a busy man. He hasn't got all day!" rang out from the end of the hall.

Luli fell against Jacquie as she spotted the rest of her crew being dragged from a neighboring cell, "Derain? Are you guys okay?"

"Just another rough night; we're doing alright," Anton replied.

Derain stared past Jacquie, "Barney's standing, but he's not in the best shape."

"No talking!" yelled one of the sailors. He slammed Derain against the wall and slapped an auto-muzzle over his mouth.

Someone grabbed the back of Jacquie's head and roughly strapped a muzzle over her face. She could feel the tube snake down her throat and choked on it. Her ability to speak would be gone until the thing was pulled free.

Anton slammed the back of his head into the guard behind him. "You aren't putting one of those in me!"

"There's always one," sighed Chief Bull as he jammed a shock stick square into Anton's chest.

Anton's body shook from the electrical current rushing to his nerve endings. Spittle foamed at the corner of his mouth and his eyes rolled up into his head.

"Que cabrón!" grunted Fitzpatrick as blood

from his ruptured nose ran down his face. He kicked Anton savagely in the ribs.

"Fitzpatrick!" yelled the Chief. "Do your job and gag him!"

Fitzpatrick kicked Anton again. Blood splattered Anton's mouth. A sinister glow lit Fitzpatrick's eyes as he said, "Of course, Chief. Caught me by surprise is all."

He bent down and rammed the auto-muzzle into Anton's mouth. Another of the guards helped the Yeoman get Anton to his feet. Fitzpatrick fished in a pocket for a stim-patch and slapped it onto the exposed skin of Anton's neck. Anton's body stiffened and his eyes nearly popped out of his face.

"You up and compliant, prisoner?" Fitzpatrick grunted into Anton's face. At the slight nod from Anton, he said, "Good." A savage grin lit his face as he kneed him in the groin. Fitzpatrick kept him from buckling to the ground and nodded at the Chief.

Jacquie saw Barney step into line and threw a small nod to him. She slipped her hand into Luli's and gave a light squeeze. Luli and Barney waited patiently while the auto-muzzles were affixed to their faces.

"March 'em out boys," commanded Chief Bull. "The Captain isn't a patient man."

***

Captain Kaplean went through the files

Mariko Shimada had put together of the Matilda's crew. Some, like Barnabus de Lagnel's, were barely a paragraph, while others, like Anton Roane's, were impressively thick. He spread them out onto the table's screen and Derain Tiwi's file opened up to his holo. The bounty hunter's image spun in place. It brought to his mind the memory of the man's brother as his body bag was sealed closed.

"Lot of anger in him..." he said offhandedly as he studied the spinning holo.

The door to the interrogation room burst open and in strode the bane of his existence. Dr. Wyeth slammed the door shut and glared daggers at him. The Captain swept over the bounty hunter's holo and it disappeared back into its file.

"Dr. Wyeth! What can I do for you?"

The woman paced angrily in front of him. In some way, he found this rather impressive as the room was tiny. There was barely enough room for the heavy table that dominated the space, never mind the two chairs on either side.

"You've been trying to keep me out of the loop, Daveed..." she said with a touch of acid.

Captain Kaplean chuckled lightly, "First names now, Judith? I don't know if I should be concerned or flattered."

Her palms slapped hard against the tabletop, "Don't play games with me! You're in the wrong league."

"Now Doctor, that isn't the case..."

Her finger wiggled in his face, "I know who

you are. I know all about the backwater rock you came from. I know the only thing you have left to care about is this command. I have friends in high places, Captain. One word from me and I can take all of it away from you. I can leave you as poor and destitute as what's left of your kin."

Her arms crossed as she kept staring at him, "And yet, somehow you keep playing with your future by ignoring my mission."

"We have been tracking your test subject for months..."

"Enough!" she shouted. "Where is my drone?"

Captain Kaplean unknotted his fingers, "We don't have your genorg."

"What do you mean you don't have her? From your own reports, she had to be on one of those vessels trapped in your hangar." She yanked her data pad free from her inside breast pocket, "Let's see, the Matilda, the Waratah, and the Cyclops." Her eyes glared into his, "You have all three in custody, correct?"

"Well, yes..."

"Then by your own account, you should have my subject, 4296-E-2631-H, in lockdown." She waited until he drew in a breath to respond and spoke over him, "But you don't. You never did. And you dare to call yourself a Captain."

A growl rattled in the back of his throat, "There is one other ship that she might be on called the Independence. That is what I'm trying to find out from the prisoners."

"Give them to me, I'll break them."

The Captain shook his head in the negative, "The dead have few words for the living, Judith. I won't have a repeat of the Tiwi family."

Her lip curled in disgust, "You're weak. Do not fail me again, Daveed. If you learn anything from that motley crew, you report it to me immediately. Do you understand me? Immediately!"

"Of course, Doctor..."

Dr. Wyeth sniffed in contempt as she angrily swung the interrogation door open and stomped out into the waiting room.

'*Someone is leaking her information,*' thought Daveed. He knotted his fingers together as he wondered, '*Who is acting against me?*'

seven

Laisse Tomber Les Filles

Jacquie glanced ahead and her eyes followed the thick red line painted down the wall. This section of the ship was painted a somber gray and it smelled dusty as if it wasn't used often. A heavy hatchway at the end was the only thing that didn't blend into the drabness of the area. The chain that held her in line yanked her off balance. She struggled for a moment to recover her steps and fell against the wall.

"No lollygagging!" a guard from behind yelled as she shoved her back into line.

The first through the hatch was Derain, then Anton. As each of them entered the chamber, they were forced into place by the guards. The hatch shut with a finality that shook the breath out of her. Before she knew what was happening, the guard in front of her slammed a stun stick into her gut. She

Jon Gray Lang

folded over and fell back onto the bench that ran the length of the wall. The chain that linked her with her crew tightened as it was locked into place.

Anton's voice mocked, "This a grape hunt or something? I know I don't know a damn thing... oof."

Anton doubled over and Fitzpatrick held him down.

Chief Bull yelled, "Leave it, Yeoman! Captain wants them alert, not out."

"His muzzle came loose, sir," answered Fitzpatrick. He slapped another stim to Anton's neck.

Anton looked a little scrambled, but he was alert.

The door to the interrogation room swung open and a dark-complexioned tall woman with wiry gray hair stomped out. Her eyes scanned over the muzzled crew of the Matilda with disdain. "Worthless," she muttered as she left in a huff.

Jacquie caught the small signal from Yeoman Fitzpatrick as the woman left. She also noticed Derain react as if he knew her.

***

"Come on you! You're up!" Fitzpatrick grinned as he pulled Derain to his feet.

Derain was a tall man. Fitzpatrick was shorter, but he easily outweighed the bounty hunter. He lifted Derain and slammed him against the wall.

He unfastened the buckle that held the muzzle in place and it retracted from the depths of Derain's throat.

Fitzpatrick opened the door. He shackled the bounty hunter to the table as Derain struggled to get his breath back.

"Derain Tiwi as ordered, Captain."

"Thank you, Mr. Fitzpatrick. Please close the door behind you."

Derain heard the door shut behind him. *'That woman was the target Mr. Leon contracted me to kill. She has to be Dr. Wyeth.'* His nostrils flared as he fought to keep his composure.

"Derain Tiwi, licensed bounty hunter for the Consortium. That is who you are, correct?" asked his interrogator.

Derain studied the man. Bereft of insignia and sitting at this dingy table, he still had the bearing of someone used to command. His uniform was clean and simple, but the material wasn't high quality. *'Not a showboat from one of the inner systems, then.'*

"That's right. And who might you be?"

"I am the Captain of this vessel and you may address me as such."

Derain leaned back and cracked his neck. He took a long meandering look around the tiny room and appraised his situation, *'Not much in here to work with.'*

"Of course, Captain. I assume you aren't looking to hire me," he said as he shook the manacles. "What may I do for you?"

"Quite an interesting record, you have here, Mr. Tiwi. Some infractions as a minor, followed by registering as a bounty hunter once you were of age. What made you choose that line of work?"

In the back of his mind, Derain calculated, *'There might be a chance, if I time it just right. When that prig Fitzpatrick unhooks me, I can push the table into this bloke and grab his stylus. One quick stab to the Yeoman's eye and he's down. It should give me enough time to turn the stylus back onto this one.'* He gazed at the Captain, "I was looking for a way off-planet and it fit my skill set."

Captain Kaplean nodded as he perused Mr. Tiwi's file, "You appear to be quite skilled, if your retrieval record is correct. Even I recognize some of these names. Quite skilled indeed."

Derain nodded in assent as his eyes tracked to the two-way mirror. Who else might be watching this? Not the Doctor. With the way she had left, there was no love lost between these two. *'If I time it just right...'*

"What do you know of Lieutenant Galena Chadov?"

"I never tracked her myself," replied Derain. "But from the court proceedings, they made her out to be one hell of a monster. Having met her, I can't see it. But you know what they say, war makes..."

"... monsters of us all," finished Captain Kaplean.

Derain nodded, "So the saying goes. But I haven't been to war, so I wouldn't know. How about you?"

The Captain ignored the question. "When did you last see the Lieutenant?"

"I think it was in the Erebus system. The Captain gave her a pirate ship she helped liberate, but I wasn't with them then."

Captain Kaplean nodded, "You were on Mithuna with the convict Anton Roane."

Derain mused, "Convict, eh? I thought he did his time. I'll keep that in mind for a rainy day."

Captain Kaplean smiled, but it didn't hit his eyes. "How did you end up on the Matilda, if I may ask?"

"It has..." Derain hesitated a moment, "...sentimental value to me. My family used to own it."

Captain Kaplean cleared his throat and toggled a switch on the under-surface of the table. "Aah yes, your family. You have my condolences for their loss."

At the signs of stress in the prisoner's eyes, Daveed Kaplean reached out and gripped Derain's hand. "It was an... unfortunate accident." His eyes slid to Fitzpatrick as the door opened.

"An accident? What the hell do you mean? I saw what you left of them! That was no accident!"

Derain choked when Fitzpatrick pulled the auto-muzzle across his face. He tried to jerk away as the oily tube plunged down his throat. But the Captain steadfastly held onto his hands until the Yeoman lifted Derain out of the chair.

"Thank you, Mr. Fitzpatrick," Captain Kaplean said as he swept over to the next file open on the table. "Bring in the Titan next."

***

Fitzpatrick backed out of the interrogation room with Derain in tow. The fight in the bounty hunter had drained away by the time he locked him into position on the long bench. The Yeoman stood back and admired his handiwork.

"Quit preening, Fitzpatrick," said Chief Bull. "Who's next?"

"The little one."

"The little one? Did someone shit in your breakfast, Yeoman?" Chief Bull shook his head and removed the plasteel strip from the Titan's bindings.

Barney stood up when commanded to. He entered the interrogation room as the Chief instructed him. Once his manacles connected to the tabletop, Chief Bull removed the muzzle and stepped out of the room. The door shut quietly behind him.

Captain Kaplean looked the Titan over. He had a shiner over his left eye and hugged his ribs on that side. "I've never met a Titan before."

Barney chuckled, but didn't say a word in response.

"Your people aren't known for traveling out of your home system. How did you end up way out in the boonies?" At the lack of a response, Captain

Kaplean said, "Questions for another time then. Tell me, what do you know of the dead Titans on Mithuna?"

"See one Titan and think we all know each other? Typical." Barney shifted in the seat and tried to pull his legs up to his chest, "I've had quite enough of your hospitality, thank you. Just put me back with the others."

Captain Kaplean tapped his stylus against the table's screen, "I can send an ident request to your home world."

Barney simply looked away and rested the back of his head on the chair.

"What do you know of Lieutenant Galena Chadov? Did you travel with her? When was the last time you saw her?"

"Look mate, I'm not saying a word." He stared into Kaplean's eyes, "You can beat me to death and I'll still tell you nothing."

The Titan broke eye contact and began humming quietly.

Captain Kaplean toggled the switch under the table, '*I won't be getting anything from this one.*'

Chief Bull swung the door open a minute later and slipped the muzzle over the Titan's face. With a quick yank, he pulled Barney's manacles free of the table.

"Take this one back and bring in the pilot next, Chief."

"Yes, sir."

***

Luli watched as Barney was led back to his spot on the bench. He didn't say a word as the Chief slipped the plasteel strip through his cuffs and locked it into place. The room was silent with all of them muzzled. The Chief walked right by Anton and settled in front of her. As he unlocked the strip holding her wrists in place, the sudden pain made her eyes water.

Chief Bull smiled, "I'm sorry about the need for this, Ms. Qing." His fingers danced on the interface to the device strapped to her face and she felt the tube retract. Fresh air rushed in when the auto-muzzle slipped free of her mouth.

It took her a moment to recover and he stepped back to wait until she was ready. Luli rose unsteadily to her feet and looked back at her friends. Each one was locked in place, fighting the feeling of suffocation from the muzzles. *'Was saving me worth this?'*

"If you'll follow me, Ms. Qing." Chief Bull held the door open to the interrogation room.

As she entered, he gingerly clicked her manacles to the desk. "Sir? Please be gentle with her."

Captain Kaplean smiled in amusement as the rough-n-tumble man acted like a doting mother. "I'll do what I can, Chief."

He went back to his file on the woman across the table as the door clicked closed. "I had no idea he was such a fan of yours, Luli Qing. I'll be quite honest, you have to be the most famous person I have ever interrogated."

Luli looked a little perplexed, "I'm not really famous, Captain. I just happen to be really old."

"And personally responsible for all of these populated worlds."

Luli laughed lightly, though it sounded strained, "Not all by my lonesome, not by a long shot."

Captain Kaplean smiled in an attempt to set her at ease, "Well, I for one, thank you for bringing my three times great grandparents to my home world. If it weren't for you, I wouldn't exist."

"Oh stop, Captain. You flatter me too much."

The Captain's data pad chimed repeatedly until he turned it off. With a wry smile, he set it aside. "Your arrival is making waves, Ms. Qing. My ship's doctor is already requesting your return."

"Oh? Dr. Sinix is a sweet man, but I think he's more interested in checking on his surgery." She smiled back at him, "I'm sure you have questions for me."

Captain Kaplean laughed, "You are correct. Apparently, I'm more star-struck than I expected. I'll keep it short so as not to keep the Doctor waiting. What can you tell me about Lieutenant Chadov?"

"Galena? She is unlike anyone else I've ever met."

"Do you recall the last time you saw her?"

Luli's forehead wrinkled in thought, "It would've been after we made planetfall on Mithuna. A lot happened there and I can't remember all of it."

Captain Kaplean looked down at the file, "You were abducted on Mithuna, is that correct?"

With a pained smile, Luli replied, "Yes, though I don't like to think about it."

"Of course; I am sorry to bring it up." Captain Kaplean toggled the switch and Chief Bull opened the door. "Please take Ms. Qing to Dr. Sinix. He would like to check on her recovery."

Chief Bull pulled out the muzzle and adjusted the clips that would hold it in place.

"No need for that, Chief. Take her to the Doctor as soon as she is able. Oh, and bring in the convict."

"Thank you, sir."

Captain Kaplean leaned back in his chair. He studied the back of the deep spacer as she was led out of the interrogation room. *'That's two for leaving the genorg on Mithuna. With a new ship under her command, the Doctor's creature could be anywhere.'*

***

Chief Bull helped Luli through the doorway. "You two, open the hatch." He ordered over his shoulder, "Fitzpatrick, take the convict in next."

"Which one is that again, Chief?"

Chief Bull glared at him as he stepped through the hatch, "Just do your damn job and get

Jon Gray Lang

him in there!"

Fitzpatrick smiled as he looked down at Anton, "On it, Chief."

Anton leaned away from the Yeoman as he was unbuckled from the bench. He still caught an elbow to the head for his troubles.

Fitzpatrick grabbed the cuffs in one hand and yanked Anton to his feet. Anton could feel Fitzpatrick's hot breath on the back of his neck as he stumbled and was swung against a wall. Fitzpatrick pulled the auto-muzzle off Anton's face, dragged him into the interrogation room, and manhandled him into the chair. His manacles were clicked into the ring on the table.

"I'm gonna look forward to seeing you later," Fitzpatrick whispered in his ear.

Anton froze until he heard the door close behind him. "Man! That sailor is a piece of work. You should see about changing his diet or something."

"He has his uses."

"I bet he does. By chance, is he in the employ of that woman who was in here earlier?"

Captain Kaplean looked up from the file on the table quizzically, "Why do you say that?"

Anton laughed, "What? With all the winks and nods between the pair of them? It's either that or they're sleeping together, though I don't think she's his type."

Captain Kaplean stored that tidbit away. "You are Anton Roane, correct?"

Anton nodded and continued babbling, "He have anything to do with that murder sandwich on Aketi? I wonder if she had him do it. You know, the rumors say it was a brutal affair. Now, I've seen plenty of shit in my day. But if even half the stories are true, that was brutality for no other reason than someone's pleasure."

Captain Kaplean leaned back and watched the one-time freedom fighter. He seemed twitchy and nervous for no obvious reason that he could see. But the man's speculation rang true. "It was an unfortunate accident. Things were taken further than was necessary."

"Definitely something wrong with that guy." Anton gazed frankly at his interrogator, "Do you need him gone? I mean, I know people who can make him disappear. No, that's not your gambit. Were you looking to offload some illicit goods somewhere? I could help with that. You tell me what you need and I can make it happen. Yes, sirree."

"That's good to hear, Mr. Roane. I do need some help with something I haven't been able to figure out."

"Yeah, of course. Rabbit is at your service."

"I've been curious, and it's more of a personal curiosity than anything else. How did your crew end up with the Titan yacht?"

Anton sat there in vague surprise, "Where did we get the Cyclops? Didn't Barney tell you? It was a family heirloom or something. His people delivered it to him on Mithuna, if I remember correctly."

"A gift then? Interesting." Captain Kaplean flipped through the file on the Titans, "Were you aware that two Titan bodies were discovered in orbit around Mithuna?"

"Oh, they're dead? Well, that's a shame. They seemed like kind folks," replied Anton. "Can't say I'm surprised, though. A lot of crazy shit happened on Mithuna. Did you know that's where Luli was kidnapped? Who knew that rock was such a hotbed for criminal activities? I sure didn't. Did you?"

The Captain shook his head, "I had no idea. I was wondering what you could tell me about Lieutenant Chadov?"

"The genorg? Don't see one of them every day. Well, I guess unless you're a miner or factory worker or something, then you probably do." Anton caught the bitter stare, "Oh, you mean Galena? Yeah, we have a history. Last I saw her was when she was on trial."

"I understand both of you were being transported on the prison ship that was attacked."

"Oh, you mean after the Vogelgesang?" Anton hemmed and hawed, "You're right, you're right, she did travel with us for a bit. Must've slipped my mind."

Captain Kaplean tapped his stylus against the tabletop, "She was also sighted with you aboard the CBC Remus."

"Oh yeah, that was her in Ninguiz. I'm glad we made it out of that mess."

"So, I ask you again. What can you tell me about the Lieutenant? When was the last time you saw her?"

"That would be Mithuna, I guess. The Captain gave her a salvaged ship and she flew off into the twilight of space." Anton made a ship with his hand and a wooshing sound. He tried to fly away with it but the manacles clattered loudly when he reached their limit.

"Your Captain gave her a ship on Mithuna." Captain Kaplean scribbled into Galena Chadov's file. *'The man's a terrible liar, but he backs up the other two.'*

He set the stylus aside and watched the man carefully, "You have known Lieutenant Chadov longer than most, Mr. Roane. Is that true?"

Anton gave it some thought. "I've known her since the Battle of Timmony Bay, so I suppose that would be true. Why?"

"Does she strike you as different? More so than the average genorg or human?"

"Different, like weird?" Anton asked. "Well, aren't all genorgs different? It's not like they're treated like people, you know. Can you imagine if the Consortium treated humans like they treat genorgs? That would really mess a person up, wouldn't it?"

eight

Captain of a Shipwreck

Jacquie looked up when Yeoman Fitzpatrick shoved Anton out of the interrogation room and surreptitiously watched the middle-aged man wearing a clean and nondescript uniform who followed behind them. As Fitzpatrick locked Anton in place, the officer looked over the muzzled people strapped to the bench.

He glanced at his data pad, "Which one of you is the Captain? Jacquotte Delahaye?"

Fitzpatrick thumbed in her direction as he stepped back from the bench, "That'd be her, sir."

The man stared at her as if trying to ascertain what kind of a person would command such a motley bunch. "Bring her in." He stared at his Yeoman, "Get those muzzles off them."

Fitzpatrick grinned as he walked over and disconnected the plasteel strip to her manacles. The chain around the cuffs grew tight as he pulled her up, led her in, and shoved her into the chair of the small interrogation room. He guided her wrists to the ring mounted on the table and attached her chain with an audible click. He yanked off the muzzle and Jacquie choked as the tube that ran down her throat was pulled free.

"The prisoner is restrained, sir."

Fitzpatrick threw a hard salute at the man on the other side of the table before he walked out of the room. The man had a thoughtful expression on his face as he stared at the back of the retreating sailor.

"Recording set to on," the gray-haired man officer said as he flicked a finger against a small screen built into the table. "My name is Captain Kaplean of the Consortium destroyer, designation M33. Please state your name for record purposes."

"Uh," Jacquie leaned forward, "I am Captain Jacquotte Delahaye of the merchant ship, Matilda. What can I do for you?"

Captain Kaplean's lip curled in vague amusement. "There is no need to speak overly loud for the microphones to pick up your voice. As to what you can do for me, I will be asking you a series of questions and I need you to answer them as truthfully as possible. We have full spectrum monitoring on you and will know if you decide to be deceitful in any manner." He sucked in a deep breath as he gave her a halfhearted smile, "I would prefer not to resort to chemical inducement. Please, let's keep this as civil as possible."

Jacquie's eyes roved the room before she relaxed into the chair. "Alright, I can do that for you. But would you be willing to answer one question for me before we get started?"

Searching her eyes, Captain Kaplean replied, "Depending on what it is, I may not have an answer. But I will attempt to do so."

Jacquie settled her nerves and stared directly into his eyes, "What have you done with Galena?"

At his shocked silence, she continued, "What have you done with her? Where is Lieutenant Chadov?"

***

Galena hugged the wall outside of the sickbay on the destroyer. It turned out to be another dead end as she saw no sign of the Matilda's crew. She hurried away in the latest of long hallways she had wandered down in her search. She wasn't exactly familiar with this vessel model, but there was a standard to military construction practices. So far, this ship seemed to be built in reverse.

Her optical camo was still holding despite what had begun to feel like days of wandering the halls. Even with the blackouts and gaps in her memory, she had not been discovered. Funnily enough, no one seemed to be looking for her either. This could only mean that the Consortium thought they had captured everyone. Jacquie and the rest were probably locked up, so her priority was finding the brig.

As she moved along the hallway, she followed the red stripe painted on the wall. She had picked it up when she discovered the sickbay. The red stripe had separated from the blue and green lines a couple corridors back. An orange one had joined up with it, briefly. The orange line snaked off to starboard while the red line continued straight toward the aft of the ship.

***

"Please follow me, Ms. Qing."

Luli felt the insistent grip on her bicep from the soldier who led her out of the interrogation waiting room. She looked over her shoulder as she left her friends behind. She turned and smiled softly, "Of course, Chief Bull."

The grizzled man smiled in deference before he led her down the hallway. Her eyes tracked the stripes painted on the floor. There were only two at the moment, a red one and a green one.

The two stripes ran parallel to each other until they came to a branch in the corridor. Chief Bull followed the green stripe and left the red stripe in their wake.

Luli cleared her throat, "This is not the same way we came. Where does the green stripe end?"

"Excuse me, Ms. Qing?"

"Oh please, call me Luli." She smiled

deprecatingly as she pointed over her shoulder, "We followed the red stripe earlier, but it went elsewhere."

Chief Bull came to a stop and released her forearm. "The red stripe leads to the brig, Ms. Qing..."

"Luli, please," she offered again.

He looked thrilled as he dropped into a short bow, "Of course, Ms. Qing... uh, Luli. I'm taking you to Dr. Sinix in our sickbay, which is where the green stripe leads."

"Oh?"

He smiled sheepishly and Luli raised her cuffed hands to her mouth to cover a giggle. "I'm not laughing at you Chief Bull, just at my bewilderment."

"No offense taken... Luli," he replied as he directed her down the corridor. "There are other marking stripes in the M33. Orange leads to the Engine Room, yellow to the Barracks, and blue to the Command Deck. There are other shades too."

"That is very fascinating, Mr. Bull. The old colony ships didn't have colors since only one person was ever awake. With so many people on board, I can see why these stripes are so important." She chuckled in surprise, "Look at me being so informal! Please forgive me, Chief Bull!"

The long-time soldier relaxed as he reached out a hand and took hers. He bowed as he said, "Where are my manners, Ms. Luli? I would be honored if you called me by my first name, Kiran."

She let her hand fall free, "You are a ray of light in this place, Kiran."

"I am a shadow in comparison to you, Luli. My only hope is to see you perform again."

"You've been to one of my shows?"

He laughed in exuberance, "Like so many others, I read about you in the history books. I know all about your childhood on an asteroid in the Sol system. How you left your home and family behind to give humanity a chance." An easy grin appeared on his face, "I grew up a 'roider' too. And that always hit home. As luck would have it, I was stationed on Qunis 4 when you passed through. I couldn't miss seeing you sing for all the worlds."

Luli smiled and the slightest tinge of pink colored her cheeks. "You don't know what that means to me right now, Kiran. From one 'roider' to another, thank you."

The big man grinned again sheepishly as his eyes tracked down to the braces that covered her hands up to her elbows. "I'm hoping Sinix can get you back on the path to recovery."

"Me, too, Kiran. Me too."

***

Captain Kaplean forced himself to keep his elation from showing. He keyed in a quick command for a marine detail to search the target ships again, 'Drone aboard the freighter. She might still be there. Initiate immediate search.'

Jon Gray Lang

Once the command was sent, he studied the woman in front of him. The accounts, scanty as they were, seemed to fit the bill. He murmured, "The individual crew reports would dictate otherwise."

"What was that?" she asked.

The woman looked exhausted and dirty, but not beaten. He wasn't sure what it would take to break this woman. At the same time, her eyes stared into him with an earnestness that he couldn't quite fathom.

"Why would you care what happens to your drone?" he asked genuinely. "Any drone for that matter?"

"Why would I care?" she asked. "You can honestly look at me chained to this desk and ask me that? Well, I have an answer for you."

Jacquie pulled herself closer to the loop that anchored her wrists to the table. "Strangely, it was one of those drones used as fodder by the industries, by the people, and by the so-called Consortium which was built for the people by the people." The rattle of her bindings echoed in the small room. "Let me see if I can remember exactly how Galena Chadov put it. Oh yes." She nodded with dark satisfaction, "Wisdom is born on the bloodied scythes of the downtrodden..."

***

Traffic lessened considerably once Galena

cleared all of the major intersections. Down here, it was only the occasional cart of engineering parts or the random messenger. She had almost run into a handful of guards at a most inopportune time, but had managed to sneak past them.

The red line came to an end at a pair of heavily fortified hatches. Luckily, the outer hatch was propped open and only a single guard was on duty. Galena kept a watch on her for a few minutes. The marine barely moved as she sat at her station and monitored the video feeds from a series of cells. But from what Galena could see, each one appeared to be empty.

Galena snuck up behind the woman and whispered in her ear, "Where are the new prisoners?"

In quick reaction, the guard pushed herself away from the desk. Before Galena could blink, the woman slammed into her and sent her flying. Galena crashed into the wall behind her and slid to the floor. But the optical camo held. She quickly scurried away and looked up. She couldn't believe how big the woman was.

The guard looked around and couldn't find her. She began squinting and her lip curled into a vicious little smile, "Optical camo, huh? Fun. I'll find you, whoever you are... wherever you are..."

Galena fished a screw out of one of her pockets. With a quick flick of the wrist, she threw it on the floor to her right. The guard swung around and Galena leapt onto her back.

The two women crashed into the desk and sent the chair skittering across the room. It bounced against the inner hatch before it rolled to a stop. Galena wrapped an arm around the woman's neck and squeezed, but the guard just pushed herself up and backpedaled into the wall.

Galena wheezed as she was sandwiched between the wall and the back of the guard. She held on to the woman's neck and squeezed tighter.

"I just want to know where they are..." coughed Galena.

The woman jabbed her elbows into Galena's ribs and growled, "I'm not telling you a damn thing."

Galena could feel the change this time, like a switch being slowly flicked. Her choices became simpler, more direct. She stopped struggling for breath as the machine took over.

Galena's dead voice echoed in the small chamber, "If you have no answers, you are no longer needed."

With a sharp retort, the guard's neck snapped and she slumped to the ground. Galena's labored breathing sounded ragged in the suddenly quiet room. Fear at the realization that she had been no more than a passive passenger in her own body pounded in her chest, "I'm not in control..."

Of all the questions swirling in her mind, there were only two she could voice, "Did Jacquie see this? Is that why she fears me?"

***

Jon Gray Lang

Captain Kaplean kept his eyes riveted on the woman across from him, '*A conundrum indeed.*'

She glared back in response.

"A drone told you," he scoffed. "Where would such a thing learn that?"

Jacquie's retort was biting, "She heard it during her time as a courier for the Council on Jard. Before she was sold to your vaunted military for experimental usage. Long after her time in the factories and the mines. It stuck with her. At the time she didn't fully grasp what it meant. But I think she understands now. Don't you?"

Captain Kaplean smiled oddly as he recalled the news feeds that had been coming through of late. His fingers tapped against the tabletop in a nervous staccato. "I would have to agree, Ms. Delahaye. But why is it personal to you?"

Jacquie's reply was quick, honest, and personal, "She's my crew... and my friend. She's been unwell lately and... She may be a danger to herself and others. But mostly, I want to make sure she is alright." Her eyes darted away from his face, "After all we've been through, I have to believe she is."

***

Anton tried to get comfortable, but the bench had obviously been designed with other purposes in mind. He glanced over and noticed Derain straining against his shackles with a haunted look in his eyes.

"Are you okay, man?" asked Anton. "You look like you've seen a ghost..."

Derain turned to stare at him. Thwarted purpose had etched lines into his face.

Anton continued, "... Or your worst enemy."

Barney leaned over, "What's going on?"

"That woman was Dr. Wyeth," hissed Derain.

"Who the hell is Dr. Wyeth?" asked Barney in confusion.

"The woman Mr. Leon contracted me to kill."

***

Captain Kaplean stared at her a moment longer, "I would like to be honest with you, Captain Delahaye. You are not the band of killers and cutthroats I was expecting."

Jacquie shrugged, "Must've caught us on a good day."

"Considering the staggering number of bodies left in your wake, I was prepared for a boatload of murderers. Instead, all I have is you and your ragtag bunch."

"We're good at what we do..."

He sighed in frustration, but continued, "I must consider the chase you led me across Consortium space. While I do applaud you and your crew's penchant for survival, I am afraid it has come to an end. Thankfully, you have given me what I needed."

Jon Gray Lang

"And what was that?"

He toggled the switch under the table, "Now you will be returned to your cells to await trial for your crimes against the Consortium. Tell me, is there anything your people require in the meantime?"

The woman's shoulders stiffened as she rattled the manacles strapped to the table. Her eyes caught his and held them as sardonic laughter escaped her, "Well, I don't know about the rest of them, but I could use some time in a fresher. I think those stun grenades made me piss myself. I can't imagine the rest of them smelling much better." Cheeks ablaze with heat, she leaned forward and murmured, "I can't believe you can stand being in such close proximity to me."

"I was born on Purgos in the Kos system. You might not have heard of it..."

Jacquie barked, "Purgos? Yeah, I've heard of it. That's the place where they eat the dead, right?"

Captain Kaplean continued as if he had not been interrupted, "...but I lived there during the great famine. I was a young boy when the protein factories first fired up and the back of the famine was eventually broken." His eyes grew cold, "I've smelled much worse in my time, Ms. Delahaye. Much, much worse."

***

"... Not what I expected you to say and that

doesn't bode well," muttered Anton.

Barney whispered harshly, "What do you mean by Mr. Leon hired you for a hatchet job?"

"Hey! No talking amongst yourselves! Next one who speaks gets muzzled!" Fitzpatrick yelled from across the room.

Derain stared daggers at the Yeoman who wandered off to speak with the other guards. The only noise in the room was the sound of their hushed voices and occasional laughter.

As the guards bantered and lost interest in the prisoners, Barney whispered, "Hey Rabbit, what did you mean that doesn't bode well?"

Anton leaned forward and the others leaned toward him. "From what I was able to ferret out, Dr. Wyeth is the one responsible for the execution of Derain's kin. Every last one of them. My guess is she used that prig over there to do it."

"Oh, Derain, I had no idea," Barney whispered in shock.

Anton jerked as a shock stick was jammed into the side of his neck. It was held there much longer than was necessary before the Yeoman pulled it free.

"Hey! What did I say?" Fitzpatrick, grabbed Derain by the forehead and smacked the back of his head against the wall. "No talking amongst the prisoners, understand?" He brandished the shock stick in Barney's direction, who shivered in response, "Do I need to demonstrate the rules one more time?" He walked over and joined the other guards against the wall, "I thought not."

Derain watched him as he laughed at some joke, "I won't forget you..."

***

Galena was still a little shaky after she left the brig. If she was lucky, no one would find the marine's body for a couple of hours. Entranced in her own thoughts, she almost didn't hear the voices coming up the hallway. With only seconds to spare, she pressed herself against the wall as two armed marines walked toward her deep in conversation.

"You see those civvies that lit up Johnson's team?" grumbled the one on the right.

The other replied, "Yeah. Looking forward to seeing them hang by the neck. I wouldn't waste a bullet on any of them."

They continued to chat as they passed her. Galena stopped holding her breath and got it under control. The damage done to her was taking its toll. She only wanted to lay down and rest. But her friends needed her now.

Galena had an idea where she would find them, too. "Full muster is required for an execution. Only one place on this boat is big enough for that. The hangar."

***

The sound of a buzzer went off and the

interrogation door swung open. A guard entered and held Jacquie in place while the strap holding her to the table was disconnected. She was led out to join the rest of her team as they were brought to their feet. Her manacles were linked to the others. Fitzpatrick swung the hatch open as he directed the prisoners outside of the waiting room.

Captain Kaplean exited the room and called out, "Yeoman?"

"Sir?"

"See that the prisoners have access to one of the ship's fresher chambers."

"Of course, Captain."

Captain Kaplean turned to gaze at Jacquie and gave a slight bow, "And issue a ship-wide alert. We have a violent genorg loose on our ship. Inform the crew to keep her alive for Dr. Wyeth's sake. But if there is no other way, lethal force is fully authorized."

"Yes, sir." Fitzpatrick saluted and led the crew of the Matilda back to their cells.

nine

Heavy the Beat of the Weary Waves

Gamma felt the ground under her bare feet as she shuffled forward, but she couldn't see a thing. From what she had heard of the Dome of Kuái, there wasn't much to look at.

Earlier this afternoon, she was stripped out of her fatigues and thrown on an auction block with a handful of her sisters whose clothing had been taken as well. The whole zone reeked of controlled fear and rapacious greed. The moon's synthesized breeze, while cold against her skin, did little to blow the stench away.

A nondescript female's voice yelled out from below, "On the block, we have a fifty drone group of mixed ages and skills. Included in the lot are an additional four drones at no cost. Opening bid is twenty thousand mazuma!"

Gamma tried looking into the crowd as bids

were rattled off, but with all the lights focused on the auction block, the glare was too bright.

"Going once, going twice! Sold to Samuel Moraldi!"

Before Gamma knew it, the whole process was over. She and the others were led off and everything went dark when blinders were placed over her eyes. Her wrist fetters were attached to a line that led to who knew where. They marched for over an hour before being brought to a stop. The ground under her feet was hot and sticky. The air held an acrid scent and it felt like tarmac. The blinders were pulled from her eyes and ahead of her was a heavily armored ovoid ship that hunkered on its landing gear.

"Hey Mbuni, can you believe the auction today?" a malnourished male laughed as he clapped a bulky man on the back. "The whole lot for thirty-two thousand mazuma. What luck to find a batch of drones out here in the old moon sector."

"No lie, Jorge," chuckled Mbuni. "They look healthy enough too. Bet we make a killing."

"A killing will be had, my friend." Jorge bowed with a flourish, "Drones, your chariot awaits. Welcome aboard the Scorpio!"

Gamma felt the yank as she and the line of genorgs were propelled through the airlock of the significantly battered ship. They passed through a large hatch into a low ceilinged hold. Mbuni shoved Gamma and she slumped against the bulkhead. Leg irons were clamped across her ankles as the next genorg in line dropped down beside her. This went on until the last of the sisters were locked into place.

The lights dropped to a dim red and the hatch shut with a heavy clang. Her nose curled at the smell of old sweat and poorly cleaned-up body excretions. The bulky man, Mbuni straddled a chair near the hatch and gazed over the incarcerated genorgs. Gamma caught his eye and quickly looked away.

"Are we heading to our work duty?" stuttered the voice of a young genorg. As she looked up at Gamma, fear crawled across the young girl's face and her eyes glistened wetly in the dim light.

"What is your designation?" Gamma asked.

"My designation is Phi-IK97, sister."

"Is this your first work duty assignment?"

The young genorg nodded as her eyes searched for anything familiar in the hold. "Is it always like this?"

Gamma pressed her shoulder against the young genorg for comfort, "This is the life of a genorg, I'm afraid."

The hold rocked as the roar of sublight engines filled the room. Breathing became difficult while gravitational forces pressed the genorgs against the bulkhead. The cold of space seeped into their bones through the walls once the ship broke atmosphere.

Phi-IK97 shivered and tears leaked from her eyes, "So cold..."

Gamma smiled in sympathy. This was her fifth walk on the block, but she still remembered the terror from the first time. She didn't know what was happening, where she was being taken, or what was expected of her. Rumors in her pod whispered of natural-borns wanting to eat the young, untested genorgs as their flesh would be supple and fresh.

"They won't eat you, Phi-IK97. At least I've not met a natural-born who would."

The young genorg started in surprise, "They won't?"

Gamma laughed lightly, "No, they won't." She stared into the young girl's eyes and frowned, "They might let you starve to death alone. They might leave your body broken in a deep hole. They might leave you to die to save some mazuma. Or they'll sing you a song."

"A song? What's that?"

Gamma grinned and red light glimmered on her teeth, "Let me show you something. See this lump on my arm? It's a multi-phase cutter used by jewelers. A natural-born named Rabbit showed me how to hide it under my skin in case I ever needed to escape. Would you like to escape this life for the hope of something better?"

Phi-IK97 nodded dumbfounded.

Gamma brought a fingernail over to the arm with the oblong lump. With a hiss, she stabbed the sharpened nail through the skin and cut along the edge of the eight-millimeter-long object. Phi-IK97's eyes were huge in the dark as blood pooled along the slit on the older genorg's arm. Her two fingers pushed into the flesh and fished out the multi-phase cutter. Once she had a solid grip on the little slim device, Gamma nodded emphatically at another genorg. Tau-SA43 winked in response and set her head against the wall. Gamma sparked the cutter and worked feverishly at the leg irons.

Tau-SA43 started to hum a tune. Some of the genorgs near her added their voices to hers. The sound slowly built up until it resembled the inside of a beehive. Suddenly, Tau-SA43 broke into song,

"You may bury me in the East,

You may bury me in the West,

But I'll hear the trumpet sound in a-tat morning

In-a that morning..."

The bulky guard sneered in her direction, "Hey, cut the singing. You'll have plenty of time for that on whatever backwater moon we sell you off to."

Tau-SA43 ignored him and sang louder. Nu-M12 joined in and the genorgs near her began to hum along. Mbuni grumbled as he stood up and hunkered over to the singing genorg. He popped her in the mouth. The hums died off and Nu-M12 stopped singing.

But not Tau-SA43. She glared at their captor and began singing again. He belted her in the face, and all she did was spit out the blood and sing louder. Mbuni grabbed the shock stick that hung from his waist and jammed it against her chest. The singing cut off like a switch was thrown. The only sound in the hold was the genorg gurgling on her blood. Eventually, that dwindled and the hum from the shock stick turned off.

Mbuni scanned the hold, "Next one who makes a noise, gets the same or worse! Got it?" He looked around and caught sight of a tiny light near Gamma. "Hey! What you got there?"

The cutter bit into Gamma's ankle and she grimaced in pain. Instead of answering she took up the song,

"In that dreadful Judgement day
We'll take wings and fly away.
  But I'll hear the trumpet sound in a-tat morning
  In-a that morning..."

Mbuni grabbed her wrist fetters and surprise was writ large on his face as they came free. A growl bubbled up from the back of Gamma's throat as her legs wrapped around his and dropped him to the decking. Mbuni let go of his shock stick and went for his pistol. Gamma scrabbled for his hands but she wasn't quick enough. A shot rang out deafeningly in the enclosed space, followed by two more. The pained scream of a genorg reverberated over the grunting of Mbuni and Gamma. Mbuni's grunt ended abruptly as the shock stick cracked over his head and snapped in half.

"It broke," murmured Nu-M12 from behind the man's body.

Gamma leaned back and sucked in one ragged breath after another. "Took you long enough. Report."

Nu-M12 glanced back at the others, "Two sisters are dead from the gun. I'm not sure if Tau lives."

Tau-SA43 coughed and hacked up a bloody spitball, "I'm here. By the Lieutenant, that hurts."

Gamma smiled and glanced at the young genorg, silently sitting in awe, "And that, my young sister is a song. It is a powerful thing, no?"

***

Rex Leon leaned against the bulkhead on the bridge as the Independence broke orbit. He closed his eyes and sent out the call. He tuned out Rosa's voice as she flew the Independence to their next rendezvous point. A shipment had been made under the ship's name to cover their tracks for the jump gate personnel. Now they coasted toward their ride out of the system.

He whispered, "Appearances must be kept up as the truths must be hidden. Riding in the hold of another craft through the jump gate should slow any pursuit for the Independence."

Slowly, Rex reconnected with another of his brethren. It was only the two of them, he and the padrone at the Silk Road. He waited until the union fully coalesced.

"How goes the mission?" asked Mr. Leon.

"My brother, the cargo has been retrieved and fills our hold. We only await our connection for the next step in the plan."

"The timetables come together." responded Mr. Leon in agreement. "Soon it will be out of our hands."

"No plan stays unchanged till the end," agreed Rex.

"Let us hope that the other tasks come together as cleanly."

"And our allies answer the call."

Mr. Leon grimaced, "To rest on the laurels of hope is a path filled with chaos."

"But chaos that could be in our favor," added Rex.

"We can only hope..."

Rex felt someone shake his shoulder; and the sensation felt worlds away. "It looks as if we are to make our arrival now. Until the future, my brother."

"Until the future," murmured Mr. Leon before the connection trance dissipated.

Rex opened his eyes. Delta was in front of him with a concerned expression on her face, "Are you alright, Mr. Leon?"

Rex smiled deprecatingly, "Only time taking its toll, Delta. Are we there?"

Delta nodded in affirmation, then rejoined Rosa at the helm. Commander Keri piloted the Independence into the hangar of a ferry. Rex had prepaid the berthing fee, and, if the timing worked correctly, the Consortium wouldn't notice the missing ordnance until after they were long gone and star systems away.

Rex ambled over to the pilot's station. As he

approached, Rosa asked, "Are you sure these guys will drop us in the Acigöl system?"

Rex nodded, "Mazuma has changed hands, Commander Keri."

"Well, alright then," Rosa replied. "We've got the go-ahead to dock. Heading in now."

Rex Leon closed his eyes in a silent prayer, "Tom, bless us on our journey."

***

Captain Moraldi kept a watch out the bow port of the Scorpio. The heavily armored trawler designed to be an asteroid breaker rolled off the surface of the old dwarf planet. It lumbered up through the shallow atmosphere. Once the ship broke past the gravity well, it joined a cluster of moons, planetoids, and satellites that littered the surrounding skies.

"By Tom, I hate the old moon sector. Such a dismal stretch of space," muttered the squat pilot, Iago Suarez. "Never mind that old dome on Kuái. What a shit hole."

"Yeah, but we got a good haul," replied the balding Captain. "Just over fifty genorgs and most of them in their prime." He laughed, "Whoever owned them last took good care of 'em. Each one more fit than the next."

"They look well-fed, too," piped up Jorge, the ship's skinny navigator. "We can probably cut their rations and water intake for the entire ride!"

"Ha, yeah. Save some mazuma!" agreed the Captain. "With them all in top shape, we can sell them for top credit, too. I smell profits!"

Without warning, a bulky being flew past them and smacked against the viewport. The body slid down to the decking as the crew of the Scorpio watched in stunned confusion. The unconscious person was covered in cuts and bruises.

"Mbuni?" the Captain asked. "What are you doing out of the hold?"

A woman's voice shouted defiantly from the rear of the bridge, "Being used as an object lesson."

Captain Moraldi looked over his shoulder and took a step back, "How'd the lot of you get out?"

Gamma strode up and hit the Captain square in the temple with Mbuni's gun. "You would be surprised what we genorgs have learned doing nothing but dirty work for natural-borns. Tau-SA43, take comms. Nu-M12, take navigation. The rest of you, gather up the last of the slavers and lock them in the hold."

"Yes sir," chorused the recently freed and exuberant genorgs. Three of them grabbed Iago, Jorge, and Mbuni's comatose body and headed to the hold. The others formed into teams and dispersed deeper into the ship.

Captain Moraldi shook himself and blinked at the genorg who straddled the pilot's seat. "A drone pilot?"

Gamma looked faintly amused as she stared back at him, "As I said, you'd be surprised." She turned back to the pilot's console and adjusted the Scorpio's course to the jump gate that hovered a few days out.

"What do you want with my ship?" Moraldi bellowed.

Gamma flipped through the delivery manifest, "Let's see, you were going to sell us for a tidy profit in Orsova for menial construction. Does that sound correct?"

Captain Moraldi pushed himself up to his knees and unclipped the shock stick that hung from his waist, "I said, what do you want with my ship?"

With a swift kick, Gamma knocked the shock stick from his hand. "We won't be completing your manifest, and it will be at a loss," she said. "Oh, by the way, your ship has been commandeered in the name of Lieutenant Galena Chadov."

Moraldi quailed, "The Butcher of Timmony Bay?"

"One and the same," quipped Gamma. "And she taught us well." A minacious grin darkened her face.

"What do you want with me?"

Gamma threw a sucker punch to Moraldi's chin. He went down hard and flopped dazed against the decking. "For now I need you to say 'hello' to any Consortium crews that might swing by to see why we're hanging out here. Later we can decide what to do with you on a more permanent basis."

***

Hau Hung stood outside of Mr. Leon's cabin on the Copperhead. He ran his fingers through his hair and smoothed the front of his vest. He closed his eyes silently counting backward from ten. When he reached one, his eyes snapped opened and he rapped out a quick tattoo on the cabin door.

He whispered to himself, "This is your chance, Hau. Don't fuck it up..."

The cabin door swung open and Mr. Leon stood there looking a bit disheveled. He blinked a few times before recognition hit him, "Is that you, Mr. Hau?"

"It is." Hung glanced down the hallway before he tried to step inside, "I need to discuss something with you."

Mr. Leon threw up his hand, "It is three in the morning! Can't this wait until a time more reasonable?"

"It can't. May I please come in?"

The door opened wider, "Very well. Let me get a kettle started."

Hau Hung walked into the cabin and made sure the door clicked securely behind him. He stood indecisively in the room as Mr. Leon wandered off to start the heat cycle on an old pot.

Mr. Leon glanced over his shoulder, "Come in and make yourself comfortable. Someone might as well be."

"Thank you, sir."

Hung sat down in the single chair next to the

only table. He watched intently as the monstrous crime lord waited for the kettle to hit a particular temperature. The man who could kill a person with a snap of his fingers reached into a drawer and withdrew a small satchel. He measured out two scoopfuls of a leafy material and deposited them into a tiny clay pot.

"What is that you're doing, Mr. Leon?"

Mr. Leon smiled, "At this hour? I'm making tea. Would you like to see how it is done?"

"Not right now," answered Hung. "I have too much on my mind to pay attention properly. Maybe another time."

"Another time, then." The most dangerous man in all of the Consortium poured hot water into the pot. He counted quietly to himself before he poured the contents into a couple of rustic cups.

The two cups were placed on the tiny table and Mr. Leon leaned against the wall, "It is rude to have tea alone. Would you care to join me?"

"Of... of course, sir."

Hung dutifully reached out for the cup closest to him and hugged it to his chest. Mr. Leon smiled and raised his cup to him. Hung did the same before he took a sip. The flavor was unexpected and it brought him up short. Grassy and full of life. It reminded him of a hot afternoon sitting with his mother on a grassy hill when he had been a little boy. His reaction surprised him.

The pungent green liquid slowly cooled in his cup as he watched the foam on the surface break apart, "This is... this is quite good. It isn't what I expected."

"It can be surprising," replied Mr. Leon as he took a healthy sip from his own cup. "It has a tendency to lose its je ne sais quoi over time. I wouldn't let it cool much longer."

"Oh." Hau Hung swirled the liquid in his cup before he quaffed the last drops. His eyes closed as he let its magic work through him.

His eyes opened again to see Mr. Leon studying him. The crime lord's cup sat on the table empty of its contents. Hung placed his cup next to it and slowly released the breath he held in his chest.

The intelligence behind Mr. Leon's eyes disconcerted him, but he stood at the precipice of now or never. "I have given a lot of thought to what you last said to me. And I had to question myself. What am I doing out here? Why do I want to run?" he stumbled over the next words, "Am I a coward?"

He expected condemnation, but the man across from him was quiet. Still, that intelligence stared into him and it did not judge him. Hung swallowed the lump in his throat.

"Perhaps I am, but I'm not a fool. I have been given an opportunity and it's staring me in the face. Do I take it and see where it leads me? Or do I run and learn nothing new?"

His hands curled into fists and he squeezed them tightly, "Fear is a strong animal, Mr. Leon. Where I've wanted to run and couldn't, I've been pushed in ways I didn't know I could succeed. I feel like that is what lies ahead for all of us." He quieted and forced his hands to open.

Mr. Leon reached out and shook Hung's open hand, "Welcome to the team, Mr. Hau. We can use all the help we can get."

***

Captain Kaur held fast to the railing of the Peking Empress and looked over her crew. The only people left were long-timers and she had personally vetted each one of them. They'd been with the old luxury liner since she herself had joined as a junior officer. Long-time friends, one and all. She turned to her first officer, "Latiff, we ready?"

"Of course, Captain." At her nod, he addressed the crew, "Captain has a speech. Sit back and give it a listen." He nodded and stepped to the side.

"Morning everyone. We all know this will be the last flight of our beautiful, old vessel. The Peking Empress is being retired."

"But she's still running, Captain! Why are they taking her down?" cried a voice from the crowd.

Harjeet Kaur smiled with bitterness, "She is still space worthy and that's thanks to you and your team, Mr. Dauber. Can we give a round of thanks to our engineers?"

Once the applause petered out, she continued, "Our Empress is being decommissioned and there's not much we can do or say about it. She's an old bird and the Consortium has need of her FTL drive. It's a sad day as there aren't many like her still plying the glorious heavens for the rich and well to do."

"Ain't none out there for the poor and destitute neither!"

Harjeet laughed at that, "Never was before, was there Ovi?"

"Only those that got us here in the first place, Captain," he replied through the guffaws of the others.

"Truth," she agreed. "This'll be her last voyage and it's only to take her to a shipyard and have her stripped. But I don't want this grand old lady to go down without a fight!"

Cries of "Here, here!" billowed up from the crowd.

She quieted the crowd until the air was still. "There's an offer on the table that'll rub right into the noses of those Consortium bastards. It'll be dangerous but we get to keep the old girl flying for another day. Any of you old hands interested?"

"Where do I sign?" shouted Mr. Dauber with great enthusiasm.

Through the cheers, she asked, "It's going to be dangerous. Some of us might not make it out alive."

"I've got no home to go to, Captain," answered Ovi. "I'll stay with the Empress and damn the Consortium!"

"Aye!" others cried out. "Damn the Consortium!"

Harjeet looked at Latiff, "Well, that's that. We're all rebels now."

ten

The Passenger

Galena ghosted through the halls of the Consortium ship as she made her way back to the hangar. Gunmetal walls with colored stripes leading to other places. No one was near her when she came to.

"How did I get to here?"

She shook her head in exasperation. Time had slipped again. Suddenly, a klaxon blared loudly and red lights flashed in warning. Startled, Galena pressed her body against a corridor wall. Her uncontrolled reaction surprised her. Something in her body growled, then inhaled the air as if searching for a scent.

"What is this?" she wondered. Another whiff jogged her memory, and some deep part of her screamed, "You! I know that scent!"

Galena felt an alien intelligence take control

Jon Gray Lang

of her, but it was not the same as before. It seemed more animal-like in nature, while exhibiting a vast intellect.   The entity that controlled her body vibrated in excitement as it dashed down one of the long hallways.

"Where am I being taken?" she cried.

***

Despite the unnerving distraction of the noisy klaxons, the M33's Captain carried out his promise to Jacquie. Chief Bull arrived with Luli an hour after she and the rest of the crew had been locked back in their cells. The Chief's squad led the shackled members of the Matilda deep into the bowels of the destroyer. They were brought down to one of the many crew barracks. The marines immediately set up guard at the hatch to the storage room and also placed a couple guards at the open fresher chamber.

"Come on you lot," the Chief demanded. "Captain said you all could freshen up since none of you reprobates smell like daisies. More like the shit they grow in. So, drop your muftis and get to it."

"Uh..." Barney stammered.

"No need to be shy, it's not like we haven't seen it all before. If you want to stop smelling like freshly turned garbage, then hurry it up!   The freshers are through that hatch." He glared at all of them, "And be quick about it!"

Jacquie unfastened her drawers and pulled her

filthy shirt over her head. She quickly stripped off the rest of her layers and stood in the buff amongst the pile of clothing.

Luli struggled to remove her bio-suit, but was unsuccessful. Her eyes searched the room for Jacquie. "My bandages..." she implored, "I can't..."

Jacquie passed by Derain and Anton, who were busy shedding their own clothes, intent on aiding her friend. "Here Lu, let me help."

Jacquie pulled the seams that ran along the arms of the bio-suit until they split open past the elbows. With a practiced move, she undid the seam at the base of the neck, too. When the garment opened up, she pulled it over Luli's head. The bio-suit slid over the new braces that ran from the base of Luli's elbows to the tips of her fingers. Removing the rest of the suit was short work as it easily slid past Luli's hips down to her ankles.

Barney turned around as his pants finally fell free of his legs and glanced at her. Dark, angry bruises ran the length of Luli's back. But it was the bunched skin at the base of her skull down to the center of her back that held his gaze. "By the nine hells Lu, what did that lunatic do to you?"

Luli remained mute. She tried to look in any direction except toward her friends as they all stared at her in horrified fascination.

Her skin hadn't healed properly. The split left by Jarl's henchmen hadn't closed. Instead, it had darkened and begun to rot. Bacteria had gotten in between the suit and her endoskeleton and bloated outward, but it couldn't escape the bio-suit. Under pressure, her flesh had eventually flattened, cracked, and become leathery. Even the skin that had been cut along her hairline didn't look as bad.

Luli trembled and tears spilled down her cheeks, "Dr. Sinix said I have a good chance of recovery, but I don't know if I believe him..."

Jacquie fiercely pulled her into an embrace and glared at Chief Bull until he looked away, ashamed. Luli leaned into her and broke into sobs. Barney hurried to her side and hugged her with all the compassion he had.

"I won't let anyone do this to you ever again," he murmured through his own tears.

Anton yanked off his remaining sleeve and approached the group. He threw his arms around all of them and pulled them tight. "Luli, you are still the most beautiful woman in all the worlds," he soothed. "Nothing will ever change that."

***

Derain observed this tableau of grief in remorse. Guilt consumed him, '*If only I had been faster... done more... chosen sooner...*'

He felt Jacquie's eyes burn into him. Humbly, he stepped over and wrapped his arms around the only people left who truly mattered. The realization hit him, that after years of searching, he had finally found his home. The smile that graced his lips carried more sadness than hope.

"Jimmy, take their clothes to the laundry... and get them mended... double time," ordered the Chief.

***

Even though Galena remained a passenger in her own body, at times her memories merged with the being inside her. That odd odor was familiar to both of them. Whatever was driving the entity through the ship in search of an aroma was also dragging Galena through its reminiscence. Flashes of overlapping memories struggled for dominance within her.

Galena's actual view of the hallway clouded, vaguely replaced by... a large, dark chamber... circular... almost saucer-like. The chamber encircled a huge sphere that almost reached the ceiling. An inner light emanated from the sphere that shifted through the color spectrum like iridescent oil on water. Shadowy humanoid forms lay prostrate around the center of the space.

Part of Galena cried out in recognition, "Those are my sisters!"

"Less than ants..." replied the being within her.

"You speak?" Galena uttered in surprise.

Even as her body continued to run down a port side passage, she could feel the entity's eyes focus on her. "All things speak. Listening is what most beings cannot... will not... do."

Galena was quiet for a moment before she

Jon Gray Lang

asked, "What is that place? What are my sisters doing?"

The creature just hissed in reply.

Galena was pushed out of this memory and into a new scene. Now she was face to face with a pair of sailors. Her arms rose to slam her elbows into both faces. Blood erupted in a fountain from the right one's nose. The one on the left bounced off the wall and fell stunned to the decking. Her foot slammed down and crushed the sailor's neck. In the process, her optical camo snagged and tore. She couldn't tell how much of her was still hidden before the entity launched her body down another passageway

"I must find it!" the being within her growled.

Galena couldn't stop herself, "Find what?" A humanoid form flashed in her mind, "Find... who?"

But the creature ignored her.

Galena's body came to a sudden halt as it sniffed at the air. "Close..." echoed in her mind.

Her head swiveled harshly to the right and her legs pumped at the decking to pick up speed. In the distance ahead, Galena could make out a single person wearing a lab coat with wiry gray hair. An aching hunger bit into her soul at the sight of the woman.

Galena's own memories spiked to the surface of her mind. There was something about the way the woman moved. The pressure of a hand on her shoulder evoked an urge within her to smile.

A voice from the past echoed in her mind,

"You have done well.   You have exceeded our expectations..."

"Why do I wish to make her proud of me?" asked Galena. "Who is she?"

As she moved ever closer, the woman spun around to face her. Recognition hit Galena hard and a swelling rage bubbled up from the creature inside her.

Galena whispered, "Dr. Wyeth?"

Many strange things happened once that name passed her lips. The Doctor murmured a phrase that Galena could barely register. The being within her screamed in anguish as the mechanized presence came crashing in. She fell to her knees in front of the woman and vomited a thin stream of dark aqueous fluid. Her shoulders shook from holding up the sheer weight of her body.

What could only be her voice, though lacking in all emotion, enunciated, "Dr. Wyeth, what is your command?"

eleven

Anonymous Club

Dr. Wyeth watched as Galena's body slowly came to its feet and stood at attention. She adjusted Galena's torn optical camo until the too recognizable figure once again became a vague, shimmering blur. Judith placed her finger under the genorg's chin, "We have much work to do, you and I. And it must be done away from prying eyes. Attend me."

"As you command," Galena's flat, emotionless voice responded.

The Doctor bent down to take a sample of the black fluid her test subject had vomited up. She slipped it into a small vial that she quickly hid away in an inside pocket. With a snap of her fingers, she headed toward her cabin. The genorg followed docilely behind. Judith uttered a sigh of disappointment. This drone had been her last hope. Unlike all the others, it had survived entry and exit from the 'de trop aspect'. Even so, it was now showing signs of contamination.

The klaxon rang loudly throughout the cruiser. Each deck was bathed in the alarm's red light. Dr. Wyeth opened the door to her cabin, entered the space with a shimmering blur, and shut the door behind them. The klaxon's relentless blaring was muffled by the door and Judith was infinitely grateful for that.

She pulled the latch on the med tube that rested horizontally against the starboard wall. It opened with a hiss of escaping gasses as the lights on its interface flickered to life.

"Enter the med tube and prepare to be scanned," she ordered.

"Yes, Doctor."

The drone stepped into the med tube and began to lie down. "Stop! Remove the optical camouflage first." Dr. Wyeth ordered with haste.

Galena immediately stopped and unfastened the garment. It slid off her shoulders and settled onto the floor next to the tube.

The Doctor's lips curved into a slight smile as the genorg laid down without complaint. She keyed a quick series of commands into the med tube's computer and it began running a diagnostic on her patient.

The klaxon continued to wail in the hallway. In a huff, Judith stomped over to the comm and stabbed the buttons with force.

"This is Officer Shimada, what may I do for

you, Dr. Wyeth?"

"Shut off that incessant racket! How is a person supposed to think with that going on?"

"My apologies, but the alarm must remain on," Mariko replied. "There is a ship-wide search for a violent genorg from the Matilda. The subject is considered dangerous..."

"Stop making excuses and put me through to the Captain immediately."

There was a muted pause before Captain Kaplean's voice came through, "Doctor, the safety of my crew is more important than your hearing at the moment. We have reason to believe that your genorg is loose on my ship."

"An inept search and seizure? I had initially thought better but I see that the crew is just as incompetent as its Captain."

A note of anger crept into the Captain's voice, "The alarm will continue until your creature is captured."

"Oh? Well, I have the drone with me at this moment in full lock-down. Frankly, I am surprised that a vessel full of the Consortium's supposedly finest weren't able to capture a single drone."

Suddenly, the klaxon died and the lighting returned to normal. "Thank you, Captain. I am glad to see that you can, at least, follow orders."

"Three of my crew have been found dead, Doctor. The actions of your creature are not inexcusable. I will need you to bring your subject to me for questioning and justice."

Jon Gray Lang

The med tube pinged when the medical report completed. Dr. Wyeth fed the information to her data pad. She read it over carefully before she returned to the comm.

"My, my," she quipped. "Three dead, you say? Fascinating... Unfortunately, I cannot comply with your wishes. My creature, as you call it, is not for you to interrogate. It is for the future survival of the Consortium."

"I must speak with that... that thing..."

"I have one more order for you, Daveed Kaplean, and hopefully you can complete it without fail. Have my shuttle prepped and the gate notified of my arrival, immediately. I no longer require your services, such as they were."

There was a long pause before the Captain replied, "Your shuttle will be ready for launch within the hour."

"Thank you, Captain. Oh. I have an addendum. Have Yeoman Fitzpatrick attached to my detail. Dr. Wyeth, out."

She glanced at the report again. Perhaps the subject wasn't a complete waste of resources. The battle computer she had illegally installed in the drone's brain was still functioning. The damage it had taken was extensive, but it still kept the alien presence from having complete control.

She studied the impairment and murmured, "The chip is trying to achieve its purpose, albeit in a random manner. Its restoration might prove irreparable to the subject, but it also means I can monitor the chip within a controlled environment. "

A wild light gleamed in the Doctor's eyes as she realized, "There is still a chance to gain a foothold in the 'de trop aspect'. Maybe even a chance to destroy the Masters."

***

Captain Kaplean slammed his fist against the comm console. "Damn that woman!"

"Sir?" asked Officer Shimada.

The Captain rubbed the bridge of his nose as he stared off into space. A frustrated sigh escaped him as he ordered, "Have the Doctor's shuttle readied for immediate launch."

Officer Shimada nodded, "Anything else, sir?"

"Notify the gate that her shuttle will arrive soon with first priority status!"

"Of course, sir."

Officer Shimada keyed the hangar comm and relayed the message concerning the shuttle.

The Captain turned to his inner thoughts, *'I should've seen what that convict Roane saw in minutes. How did I let a damnable mole on my ship? Not only a mole, but a spook for that lunatic of a scientist and whatever council member she works for. Nothing to be done about her now, I suppose...'*

As Officer Shimada completed her conversation with the gate personnel, she asked, "Sir? Is there anything else?"

"Yes, Mariko." The Captain's face was grim as

he leaned toward her, "Trouble is coming. Contact Lieutenant Hayley and only her. Have her dispatch a surveillance team to the Doctor's shuttle and tap its comm and nav system. Tell her to report to me once this is done." He gripped her hand tightly, "Do you understand me?"

She gave him a shaky nod as he released her hand and headed to his ready room. "Two can play your game, Doctor. I am one order away from stopping you in your tracks and robbing you of whatever world you call home. Think you can destroy me so easily? You'll see what you've bitten off..."

***

Lieutenant Hayley woke up abruptly when her cabin comm chimed. She wiped the sleep from her eyes and stabbed at the button, "This is Hayley."

Mariko Shimada's voice came through, "Lieutenant? I have special orders for you from the Captain."

"Oh."

The Lieutenant stumbled out of her bed and slapped a stim patch to her neck. Wakefulness exploded through her body. She shook herself as she reached for her uniform.

"I'm ready, Mariko."

After a brief pause, Mariko continued in a hushed tone, "The Captain says get a surveillance team to the Doctor's shuttle to tap its comm and

Jon Gray Lang

nav system. Once the bugs are active, track the shuttle. Do you have a team?"

Lieutenant Hayley shrugged into her dress shirt, "I have a detail ready. Tell the Captain I'm on my way."

As the comm cut off, Hayley noticed a blinking icon on her data pad. She keyed it and a decrypted message appeared for only a minute before it was erased.

She read it twice, then said it out loud, "Per Amiran Dynasty... Stop... Execute subject 4296-E-2631-H... Execute Khanda representative if needed... Stop... Orders supersede those of vessel Captain... Stop... Orders supersede those of vessel Captain..."

She pinched the bridge of her nose, "The Captain won't like this. I don't like this. But he'll understand, orders are orders."

She keyed the comm, "Corporal Higgins, assemble your squad and meet me at the bay."

As she smoothed the front of her uniform, she repeated, "Kaplean will understand. Orders are orders..."

***

Jacquie stood under the recycled water flow. Ultrasonic waves pummeled the bacteria and dirt off her body. When the fresher's timer ran out, the water stopped and Jacquie stood there dripping. Behind her, she could tell that the others were dressing in the single-use coveralls.

"Here ya go, Jacq," Anton called out.

He tossed her a towel. She caught it and finished drying herself off. Derain threw her the remaining set of coveralls on the bench. She shimmied into the rough cloth outfit, and watched as Barney helped Luli into hers. The sleeves unraveled and he slid them over the metal braces.

"Anton, Help Luli with her shoes." Jacquie called out as Barney moved off to finish dressing.

Anton nodded and bent down to slide them over the pilot's feet. They cinched closed around her ankles. Everyone looked better after their baths.

They had needed them even more than they realized. In those anguished moments before they entered the freshers, they had bared their souls and expressed more to each other than they ever dared to in the past. Those warm showers had washed away more than their physical filth and grime. The waters had washed away doubts and barriers, too. Their spirits felt refreshed and their hope was renewed.

The blaring klaxon finally stopped and the silence seemed loud in its absence.

"Damn, they caught her," Anton murmured.

As they continued to dress in the barracks, they could hear bits of conversation clearly not meant for their ears.

Chief Bull's voice was distant, but quite distinct, "She caught the drone alive, eh? Well... at least we don't have to worry about the trouble her creature could've stirred up."

Although Jacquie couldn't hear the other end of the conversation, she knew they had to be talking about Galena. The Lieutenant might be in dire straights now, but she was alive. Jacquie regarded her companions, her family, as they laughed and bantered at each other's expense. "We might not be free. But we're alive. Every single one of us."

"... I'm taking them back now, sir. Understood, Captain. Chief Bull out." The Chief gazed at the prisoners, "Form up! Cahya, get those binders back on them. Captain wants them under lock and key and I have better things to do than watch a bunch of grungies bathe. No offense, Ms. Qing."

Luli smiled at the man, "None taken, Kiran. I haven't been that dirty since I was a child." She held out her wrists and the marine carefully closed her shackles. "Could you let Dr. Sinix know that I'm feeling better? I think I might get some sleep tonight."

The big man bowed, "I'll do that. I regret the circumstances, but it is an honor to be in your presence." He turned to his men, "Get 'em lined up and out of here. Double time!"

The brisk walk back to the brig seemed too short. Derain, Anton, and Barney were hustled into the first cell and the armored hatch closed with a heavy clang. Jacquie and Luli were led into the next cell and freedom was on the wrong side of the door that closed behind them.

"Galena's alive, Lu."

Luli smiled as she sat on the edge of her slab, "I never thought otherwise, Jacq. Thinking I'd never see you all again would have been too much to bear." Luli struggled to get into a position that was comfortable with limited success.

"Here, let me." Jacquie moved over to the other slab and slid Luli's head to her lap. She brushed the sparse hair on the cyborg's head away from her eyes and did her best to make Luli comfortable. She was struck by the urge to softly sing a lullaby. A tiny smile crossed her lips as an old memory of her mother singing to her came to mind.

Jacquie could almost feel her mother's arms holding her as she sang the song to her friend, to her sister,

"Sleep, baby, or Cuca will come and take you,

Dad is in the fields and mother went to work..."

She sang the verse over and over until both she and Luli drifted into a much-needed sleep.

***

Dr. Judith Wyeth sat at her desk with only the muted hum from the med tube to keep her company. She had begun a process to map out repairs to the chip in the genorg's skull and spinal column. Her comm chimed in a three-tone pattern, stopped, then repeated the sequence.

"You asked for me, Doctor?" said Fitzpatrick

through the comm.

She smiled lightly, "Yes. Please come to my cabin at your earliest convenience."

"Of course, Doctor."

She tapped at her lip and let the comm hiss and pop with light static. "We need to accelerate the timetable, Yeoman. Initiate protocol 8472."

There was a momentary hesitation on the comm line before Fitzpatrick responded, "Understood. At my earliest convenience. Fitzpatrick out."

"Dr. Wyeth out." She killed the comm and glanced behind her. "I'll have to prep you for travel now, won't I?"

Judith peered through the med tube window. Galena made no response. Her expression remained blank.

***

Anton awoke in the darkened cell. The only sound he heard was the breathing of his two cellmates. He checked the timepiece built into the wall above the cell door. Only a few hours had passed since they had been locked in here, but it seemed like forever.

He watched Derain and Barney as they slept on the other slabs, and he did his best to keep quiet as he snuck over to the door. The tips of his fingers felt along the exposed part of the locking mechanism as his eyes traced the seams of the unit.

Eventually, he placed his ear against the box and nodded.

He crawled over to the first slab in the room, "Hey Derain, are you awake?"

Derain responded drowsily, "Huh? What do you want, Rabbit?"

Anton grimaced in the dark of the cell, "Well, I don't want to be in here. I have this thing about prisons, you see. They make me itchy."

"I don't want to be in here either. What's your point?"

"Well, the lock on this cell door is a real piece of crap. I can get us out of here in a couple minutes."

Derain rubbed at his eyes, "You can get us out of here?"

Anton's teeth glimmered in the faint light, "Of course I can. Not too many locks out there I can't get through. But this one? This one's not even a challenge."

"Wait," Derain muttered. "You mean all this time you could've gotten us out of here? Why the hell didn't you say something earlier?"

Barney whispered sharply, "What are you two on about?"

"Anton says he can get us out of here, but he decided to wait for some damnable reason," grumbled Derain.

"The idiot always takes his sweet time," added Barney.

Anton hissed, "Listen, I didn't get a really

good look at it until now. I thought maybe we should get the lay of the land first. With our walkabout for the interrogation and the freshers, we got that. I don't want to go out there half-cocked or anything."

Barney started laughing, "You do everything half-cocked, you lunatic."

Derain started chuckling and eventually, Anton joined in.

"Yeah, I guess I do. So, should we get to the getting?"

"And get out of here?" added Derain.

Barney cracked his knuckles, "Oi. Let's get to the gettin'."

***

The sound of hushed voices on the other side of the cell door woke Jacquie from her light slumber. She placed a hand over Luli's mouth before she squeezed the woman's shoulder. Luli jumped, but recognized the code and quieted immediately. Jacquie placed her finger against Luli's lips and pointed to the cell door. Luli nodded, then hopped to her feet. They hunkered around both sides of the cell door.

It slowly opened and a head poked in, "Jacq, you awake?"

Jacquie reacted quickly. She grabbed the protruding head and pulled in the owner. Luli yanked the cell door all the way open and the other two collapsed into the cell.

"I'm not one of the bad guys," pleaded Anton. "Will you let me go?"

Shock colored Jacquie's voice as she said, "Rabbit? Is that you?"

Luli giggled as she helped the shorter one to his feet, "Looks like we've got the whole gang back together."

"Except for Galena," added Anton.

"Sorry about that." Jacquie released Anton's head, "I thought you might be some of the crew looking to work off some frustration."

"Some of that is probably on the way. I figure they've got to be coming soon," said Derain. "We should shove off in a twinkling."

A scuffle echoed down the hallway of the brig and everyone grew quiet. The thud of a large body hitting the decking ended it.

"Or they could be coming now," added Barney.

twelve

SAIL

Near the destroyer's hangar, Lieutenant Hayley and her squad of marines kept an eye out for Dr. Wyeth. A technician disembarked from the Doctor's shuttle and threw a quick salute to the Lieutenant, then headed off to join the main body of the M33. The distinctive voice of the Doctor came floating down the passageway. Lieutenant Hayley waved her squad up to flank her entrance.

Around the corner came Yeoman Fitzpatrick with an oblong tube. The Doctor quickly stepped aside to give Fitzpatrick more space as he pushed the levitating med tube toward the hangar bay. The Doctor's personal detail of four mercenaries flowed around the two of them and took up defensive positions. Each was armed with a heavy rifle slung over full-body armor.

Lieutenant Hayley was impressed by the

mercenaries' state-of-the-art gear, "They're going to be a tough nut to crack, but orders are orders."

Inside the med tube lay the genorg who had been responsible for the massacre at Timmony Bay. Since running free, the abomination had left a pile of bodies in her wake. A gutted prison ship with all aboard dead. One of their own black-ops ships opened to space. The corpses of a pirate crew left to float where they died. Not to mention the shootouts on a handful of the outer worlds.

Intelligence reports were rife with conspiracies. A common thread was Lieutenant Chadov waging a personal war against the very Consortium that gave her that rank.

Lieutenant Hayley whispered, "Damned thing should be spaced. Break the backs of the drones who call her a hero."

Corporal Higgins glanced at her in concern, "What was that, sir? Thought the Captain only wanted us to find out who the lab coat speaks with and where she makes her home."

Hayley shook her head, "My orders come from the heads of the Amiran Dynasty. They want that creature dead."

"Direct from one of the twenty-three?"

The Lieutenant scratched at her ear and got a slight nod in return from one of the deckhands. "And we exist to do their bidding, Higgins. Understand?"

"Works for me," whooped the Corporal. "Tuco and Johnson need some payback." He grabbed another marine by the shoulder, "Eldin, we have a second crack at the creature who shot up Singh. Take her and anything else that stands in your way, down."

"With extreme prejudice," grinned the Private.

An announcement resonated from the hangar comm, "Clear Landing Bay 17! Repeat, clear Landing Bay 17!"

"That's our cue. Form up!" shouted Lieutenant Hayley.

A second squad of marines led by Corporal Gavriel ran forward and blocked the entrance to the hangar. Dr. Wyeth's party screeched to a halt just outside the entrance.

Hayley swaggered up from behind her little group and stated, "Good evening, Judith Wyeth. By orders of the Amiran Dynasty, you will release the genorg you have sedated into my custody."

Dr. Wyeth laughed heartily, "That won't be happening, lackey."

Flames exploded from the tunnel behind the Doctor. A second detonation erupted in the hangar itself. Fire alarms blared as the deck of the hangar bucked from a third and fourth explosion.

Dr. Wyeth's mercenaries opened fire on the marines as they ran for cover. Fitzpatrick pushed the med tube as fast as it would go toward the shuttle. Dr. Wyeth followed closely behind him.

"Damn it! Get that drone! Kill them all if you have to!" shouted Lieutenant Hayley into the unfolding chaos.

Jon Gray Lang

***

"Do we have a plan?" Jacquie asked as she helped Luli to her feet.

Anton blinked in bewilderment, "Besides, getting out of this place? I hadn't really thought that far ahead."

Luli whispered in the dark, "Head to the hangar and steal a ship. I can fly anything."

"Nice and simple," reckoned Jacquie. "Good enough for me."

Another crash came from the passageway. Barney hunkered low beside the cell door and Derain slipped behind him. Jacquie helped Luli to the back of the chamber. Anton dropped to the other side of the cell door, pushed it slightly open, and peeked through the crack.

The click of heels came closer, then stopped on the other side of the door. Anton tensed as Derain prepped to rush whoever came through. Barney glanced at Anton and nodded with a grim smile.

A familiar voice spoke through the door, "Captain Delahaye? Are you still in here? Or have you already fomented your escape?"

Anton swung the cell door open and Derain grabbed the short man in the Consortium uniform with KOVIT stitched over his left breast. Barney tackled the man's legs. He went down quickly and without a fight. Derain kept hold of his arms as

Anton checked the brig hallway for others.

"All clear," whispered Anton.

Jacquie moved in quickly, but stopped short in shock. "Mr. Leon? What is one of you doing on a black-ops ship? And I didn't think you could look any younger?"

Suddenly, a klaxon began blaring in the distance, but it wasn't coming from the brig.

Mr. Leon smiled mischievously, "At your service, Captain Delahaye. But might I suggest we make haste? Affairs have been put in motion that should ease your escape."

The ship's lights cut off and the crew was enveloped in absolute darkness.

"Like this?" quipped Anton.

***

Fitzpatrick backpedaled as gunfire raked the shuttle's airlock. The shell of the med tube was peppered by stray rounds and its rear anti-grav generator died. He left it where it hovered and searched for cover.

"What are you doing? Get back out there and put it on the shuttle, Fitzpatrick!" cried Dr. Wyeth as more rounds pockmarked the plating on the shuttle.

The Yeoman peeked over the crate he hid behind. It was a pitched battle in the hangar. The Doctor's mercenaries were pinned down just outside the bay. "They won't be much help," he cursed.

One of the mercenaries launched a grenade

deep into the bay. The explosion shook the walls and flipped a lander onto a pocket of marines. In the commotion of the moment, the Doctor made a break for the shuttle. Fitzpatrick bolted from his safe spot and grabbed onto the med tube. Cursing up a storm, he dragged it into the shuttle.

"Get us off the ground, now!" the Doctor screamed as she mashed the airlock button.

"What about the mercs?" asked Fitzpatrick as he hopped into the pilot's seat.

"They've been paid," she replied. "Let them find their own way out. Now to ease our escape," she said with a knowing smile. She hit transmit on her data pad, sending a quick order to the M33.

The engines on the small ship sparked into life. With a roar, they burned the decking and the ship lumbered forward.

***

"Stop that shuttle!" shouted Lieutenant Hayley over the bursts of gunfire.

A flight deck controller ran in front of the shuttle and tried to wave it to a stop. The craft continued to trundle its way forward. Open space lay just past the hangar bay doors. The controller leapt out of the way as the shuttle's afterburners ignited.

Lieutenant Hayley cried out in defeat, "Take it down, damn it!" The marines kept firing at the shuttle, but the munitions loaded into their rifles weren't designed to penetrate the thick plating. At last, the shuttle blasted out into space and disappeared from view.

"Keep thinking you've escaped our grasp," growled Lieutenant Hayley. She glanced down at her data pad in triumph, "I know exactly where you're going." She keyed her comm for the bridge.

***

Captain Kaplean's comm chirped and Hayley's voice came through, "Dr. Wyeth initiated an attack during her departure! We're trying to lock down the shuttle but her mercs are blocking the way! Damn it, they're out of the bay!"

Kaplean's fingers beat out a rapid tattoo on the arm of his chair, "Did you retrieve her destination?"

"She's heading to Jard, sir," replied Hayley.

"Lock down those mercs, Lieutenant. Kaplean out."

Alarms blared loudly throughout the bridge as sensors registered explosions on multiple decks.

"Damn that woman," the Captain cursed. "Gunny, can you get a shot at her shuttle?"

"The shuttle's too small and too far out now, sir."

"We'll get her at the other end. Wind up the FTL and set our course for the Malina system."

"On it, sir. Winding up the wormhole generator."

***

The lights on the M33's navigation console blinked through a patterned code. The same sequence repeated three times before the lights went dark. Officer Grissom sent a silent reply that the message was received.

He covertly eyed the bridge crew. No one was looking in his direction as he keyed different coordinates into the nav system. With another keystroke, he took control away from the pilot and cranked up the FTL drive.

The quarks launched seconds before the pilot realized it, "What in the nine hells? Our course was changed."

"Where did the command come from?" yelled Captain Kaplean. "Who did it?"

Officer Shimada ran a quick system track as a wormhole bloomed in front of the ship. "Command came from Navigation, sir.

The pilot cried out, "Now I've lost control of the ship! The wormhole is pulling us in!"

"Navigation? Grissom, step away from your station. Marines! Arrest that officer! Remove him from my bridge!"

Grissom stood up and pulled out his service weapon. Before anyone could react, he pointed it at the Captain, "My will is to obey. This ship is now under the control of the Family Senai..."

A marine brought up his rifle and shot off a

round. The bullet tore into Grissom's abdomen, leaving a ragged hole in its wake. As Grissom folded from the shot, his finger twitched. His service pistol fired loudly against his faint gasps for life.

The Captain went down as blood spouted out from his chest. "What...?" escaped his lips as he slumped back.

"Sir! We're past the event horizon!" shouted Officer Shimada.

As life drained from the Captain, the Consortium ship M33 slipped inside the wormhole.

***

"Someone has wound up the FTL," muttered Mr. Leon as he sniffed at the air.

Anton yelled over the rumble of their hurried footsteps, "How can you tell?"

Mr. Leon ignored him and kept running in the direction of the hangar bay. Smoke and flames billowed from a few passageways that rang with the screams and shouts of wounded crew members. Fire raged from the starboard engineering hatch as they bolted past.

"You did all this to get us out of here?" Derain wheezed, as they came to a rest at an intersection.

"Me?" asked Mr. Leon. "Certainly not! This is from infighting between the factions of the Consortium. The bloody government is built like a house of cards." He grinned fiercely, "All it takes is a little breeze to blow it all to hell."

Mr. Leon faded through the smoke and the others hurried to keep him in sight. As they got closer to their promised escape, the unmistakable rattles of gunfire joined the screams of the wounded. Mr. Leon jerked and dropped to his knees with a groan.

"Gods be damned, what in all the universe is going on?" cursed Anton.

Jacquie knelt next to Mr. Leon. She watched him pull a bloodied hand away from his torso as a scarlet stain spread across his chest. He grabbed her by the collar, "We're cut off here. The hangar bay is about one hundred meters straight out and to the port side."

Jacquie brushed his hand away, "You're hurt and none of us are armed. You have a plan?"

Mr. Leon blinked in pain. He pulled a brace of grenades out from under his jacket, "I think I can create some confusion for you to get your people to your ship."

Jacquie's eyes grew dark, "This bunch of corsairs gutted my ship. She doesn't run anymore."

"Not true," he whispered. He smiled weakly at her, "My time grows short. You'll figure out a way."

"We'll steal one of the others, Jacq. Then we could tow her out of here," said Anton.

"And what good would that do?" she countered. "Are we going to wish ourselves away or something? The Matilda is trashed! She's a wreck!"

Jon Gray Lang

Mr. Leon continued, "The engineers were trying to piece together your jump engine. Some repairs were completed. There's a chance you might be able to fly away."

"Someone has been messing with my engine?" Barney growled.

"With the way things are going, the sooner we're out of here, the better," muttered Derain.

"What about you, Lu?" asked Jacquie.

Luli grinned halfheartedly, "Can't be any worse than being trapped in the middle of a shootout, right?"

Jacquie scrutinized the faces of her people. Yes, the grime the freshers had removed had been replaced with the soot and filth of warfare, but nothing soiled their hope. "You have your answer, Mr. Leon. What next?"

A fatalistic pallor colored his cheeks, "Head toward the port side and wait. Once you hear the signal, run."

"What's the signal?"

Mr. Leon smiled as a rivulet of blood trickled from his mouth, "Oh, you'll know."

"Alright everyone, you heard the man!" yelled Captain Delahaye. "Once we hear the signal, run with everything you have! Let's go!"

Jacquie disappeared into the smoke with Anton hot on her heels. Barney helped Luli through and they both faded out of view.

As Derain readied himself to follow, Mr. Leon grabbed him by the arm, "Remember your contract,

Mr. Tiwi. Dr. Wyeth is still on board. She ended your family's existence and you still have a chance to pay that balance. Figure out a way to end her and our deal is satisfied. Now go!"

Derain nodded emphatically and rushed away through the haze. Someone began shouting amidst the gunfight, calling for peace. As the voices quieted down, he could distinctly hear Mr. Leon shout, "For the glory of Lieutenant Chadov!"

A huge explosion ripped through the passageway with shock waves that impacted the ship's outer hull. As the hull tore open, Derain saw the skin of a wormhole tunnel spiral past. The internal gravity kicked in harder as bits of flotsam and jetsam spilled through the crack in the hull.

"Did he just blow himself up?" Anton asked dumbfounded. "Why would he do that?"

"Move it!" screamed Jacquie. "We have to get out of here now!"

Derain followed as the crew ran toward what they all hoped was the hangar. Smoke and fire blinded them as the barks of rifles answered each other all around.

When the battered hull of the Matilda appeared through the haze, five figures rushed toward her with a collective sense of awe and homecoming. The old freighter was the worse for wear, but she was still in one piece.

"Everyone, get on board!" screamed Captain Delahaye as she entered the ship.

Luli ran with all her might and dashed

through the airlock. Barney struggled to keep up. Anton rushed up behind him, grabbed Barney by the waist, and carried him aboard. Jacquie waited until Derain was safely inside the Matilda, then cycled the airlock closed.

"Let's hope they left no guards on board."

Barney hurried to the lift and rode up to the second deck. When the doors opened, he ran out across the gym to the engine room. Responding to a call light, the lift returned to the ground floor. When it arrived, the Captain and Derain hopped on board.

"Drop me on the second deck, Jacq. Barney may need my help."

Jacquie cast a dubious look his way, but honored his request. Derain didn't look back as he ran full tilt through the gym. When the lift doors closed, the Captain shook her head and continued up to the bridge.

***

Luli threw herself into the pilot's chair and inserted the jack into the socket built into the back of her skull. Her mind activated a connection with the Matilda. Errors flashed by in a continuous stream.

"Hey Lu, any good news?" Anton asked as he slipped into the seat at the nav station.

"Looks like they got power restored, but not much else." She pulled the visor over her eyes, "Mr.

Leon was right, they were obsessed with the engine. Too bad they didn't get something useful like the sublights running. Attitude jets still function though."

"Not much here either, I'm afraid. Internal and external comms are still down. They made a hash of the nav records, too." He glanced in her direction, "But on a good note, she's still airtight."

Jacquie joined them, "How's it look?"

"Not great..." answered Anton.

Luli continued, "We're getting bombarded by shrapnel from whatever is going on out there. Sublights are toast and it looks like we're in the middle of a wormhole jump." She pulled the visor away from her eyes, "We're heading somewhere fast and wherever it is, it can't be good."

"Think you can pull out of this hangar with the attitudes only?" asked Jacquie.

Luli murmured, "Can't hurt to try," as she slammed the controls to full.

***

Chief Bull burst into the sickbay. Fires raged uncontrolled near the pressurized tanks. Nurse Valdez struggled with the lock on the door.

"Here, let me help," cried Chief Bull as he grabbed the handle and shoved it closed with all his strength.

Nurse Valdez clicked the lock in place just in time. The pure oxygen tanks exploded in a chain reaction, blackening the single window to the storage room.

Dr. Sinix stumbled into the room as the deck shook from another explosion. He spied the Chief with Valdez in front of the storage room. He shouted over the noise, "Is it that bad, Kiran?"

Chief Bull nodded in resignation. "The ship is lost. The witch's mercs are holding the hangar. The only way off ship is by escape pod."

Dr. Sinix nodded in grim acceptance. He had survived the battle in the Tuls system when his ship had burned up on entry into the local planet's atmosphere. "Just like on the Gloire, eh?"

Chief Bull grimaced, "Just like it, Tom. I'm getting too old for this."

Dr. Sinix glanced at Nurse Valdez, "Any hope for our patients, Ellie?"

As she shook her head in the negative, another explosion rippled through the ship. "No sir, and I don't want to join them."

Chief Bull pointed to the door, "The nearest pods are a deck down. Go, go, go!"

***

Derain stumbled into the heavier gravity of the engine room. Barney was tearing through a wiring rig left by Consortium's engineers. Derain steadied himself against the hastily repaired rack that contained the ugly sphere in its center. A low throbbing light emanated from the center of the orb.

"Is this thing on?" Derain squeaked as he jumped away.

Barney grunted over his shoulder, "They've got power to the rig, but it's not responding. Not that it should matter as the thing doesn't even use conventional power. Theoretically, it should be working."

The ship's lights flickered in the engine room and down the main shaft.

Derain grabbed a handhold above his head, "What about the sublight engines?"

"Dead," replied Barney.

"Think you can get a jump out of this thing?"

Barney hemmed and hawed, "Well, it should just work..."

The orb in the cradle glowed with a bright white light and a hum vibrated the air around them.

Barney looked somewhat elated, "Oh! Well, that's a good sign..."

Derain stared into the center of the sphere, "What would happen if we triggered the jump engine in the middle of a wormhole?"

"Probably tear the ship we're inside to pieces. Might tear us to pieces, too. I can't imagine anything good..."

***

Luli pushed the attitude jets past maximum safety and the Matilda shook as it fought against the gravitational pull of the M33.

Jon Gray Lang

Anton held tightly to the console when his comm chirped. With surprise, he engaged it.

"Anton, it's me, Derain."

"Figured that," grimaced Anton. "Now isn't the best time. What do you need?"

"You need to trigger the jump engine and I mean now!" answered Derain.

"What?" exclaimed Anton.

"Can you push it any harder, Lu?" asked Jacquie, as she gripped onto the back of the pilot's seat.

Anton glanced out the bow port and the Matilda had barely moved. The old freighter just strained and trembled in place.

Luli growled in the background, "Not enough power from the jets to pull us free!"

There was an urgency in Derain's voice, "Trigger the jump engine now!"

"It could kill us," hissed Anton.

Derain's voice came through stonily, "We'll probably die anyway and it's my last chance for revenge on those who murdered my family. I'm calling in my favor. So, just do it!"

Anton gulped, "Isn't there anything else that we could try?"

"Flip the damn switch now, or I'll kill you myself!"

thirteen

Rabbit Rabbit

The jump gate in the Ankara system grew
larger as Dr. Wyeth's shuttle continued its journey
toward it. Fitzpatrick wasn't thinking about the gate,
though.   He was recalling the events that had
brought them to it: the horrors of the burning
hangar and the shuttle bursting free only to see the
M33 disappear into a wormhole going who knows
where. *'Did they pull our trajectory? Are we going to get
shot out of the sky?'*   Tiny beads of perspiration
shimmered across Fitzpatrick's forehead, "I did not
sign up for this."

Dr. Wyeth slipped into the co-pilot's seat of
the shuttle, "Check with the gate personnel to
confirm my direct comm was relayed. We need our
cards in play. That bastard of a Captain may have
survived to throw another wrench into my plans,"
she grumbled. "I should have ordered his execution

earlier. No time. Never enough time. Have you checked with them yet?"

Ensign Fitzpatrick grimaced, "Not yet."

"Well, hurry it up!" she shouted as she hopped out of the seat and disappeared behind him.

He clicked on the comm, "Shuttle 501-S calling the Ankara jump gate. Please come in jump gate."

"Shuttle 501-S, this is the jump gate Ankara. Destination please."

Fitzpatrick grimaced, "Please verify retrieval of priority laser-comm to Jard, code 219-33-9."

"Destination, please," repeated the bored technician.

"Check the priority code, soldier. Or do you want to give me your serial number?"

There was a long pause before the shaken voice of the technician came back, "Priority message retrieved and relayed. Is there anything else I can do for you?"

"Malina system and front of the line," answered Fitzpatrick.

"Of course, sir. Relaying destination to the next three jump gates. Have a pleasant journey."

Fitzpatrick looked over his shoulder to see the Doctor staring fixedly at the genorg in the med tube. Her expression was more perturbed than concerned.

"We're next in line to cycle through, Doctor. It took some doing, but you finally caught her."

"That I did. Despite all the bungling of that inept Captain," replied Dr. Wyeth. She swiped something on her data pad, "Send this direct to Consortium HQ. No delays, got it?"

"Of course, Doctor. Sending now."

Tagged with the priority code, the comm was accepted with no delay. "Maybe this is what I signed on for," Fitzpatrick murmured.

He angled the shuttle to the front of the line and settled the vessel into place. "Your drone looks to be in bad shape. Do you think it will survive the trip?"

"Oh, she'll survive, Yeoman. Never you mind that." Judith smiled oddly, "She has survived creatures that would have killed us both."

The comm opened up, "Shuttle 501-S, prepare for entry to the wormhole."

Fitzpatrick swung back to the console, watched as the wormhole spiraled open within the framework and expanded to fill it completely. The shuttle bucked under the sudden gravitational force and was pulled into the wormhole.

"Entering the wormhole now."

***

Anton clicked off the comm as Luli pushed the attitude jets deeper into the red zone. His eyes were riveted on the switch Barney had hard-wired in for the jump engine. Anton's hand hovered over it as he wrestled with his decision.

Jacquie glanced at him and recognized his fatalistic look, "What are you doing?"

Jon Gray Lang

"Might be our only way out," he whispered.

"No! Don't!" she cried.

But it was too late. The Matilda twitched and the air felt electrified. The odor of burnt copper was followed quickly by the stench of overripe and rotting pineapples. Black lightning skittered over the Matilda as a bubble of 'other space' encased it. When the bubble pushed against the hull of the M33, the warship split open. The decking buckled underneath as the ceiling above warped around the ever-growing sphere.

There was nothing that could be done to stop it. People down in the hangar ran as fast as they could to escape. Some were swept into the growing sphere while others were pulled apart by the edge. The hangar bay burst open and the slithering skin of the wormhole slid past. Bodies shot through the rent in the hull and out into the wormhole.

***

As the entire ship convulsed, the M33's comm erupted with the message, "Attention! Attention! Abandon ship! I repeat, abandon ship! Attention..."

As the Doctor and Chief Bull rounded the corner, they ran into Mariko Shimada. Ellie Valdez followed up quickly behind them.

"Your work, Shimada?" cried Chief Bull.

Mariko shouted, "The Captain is dead! Grissom shot him point-blank! You heard the orders, get to the pods!"

The tiny woman blasted past and disappeared down the corridor. Dr. Sinix ran after her followed by the other two. Mariko didn't stop at the lift. She headed for the anti-grav shaft and slid down to the lower deck. The rest of them jumped in with the Chief keeping an eye out in the rear.

"This is when people lose their minds," Kiran muttered.

He pulled his service pistol and verified it was loaded. As he slipped it home, he hopped into the anti-grav shaft and pulled himself down. He swung through the open door onto the lower deck. The only one waiting for him was the nurse. He waved her forward and kept close behind her.

Shots rang out ahead and he pushed Ellie through the door to the pod room. He dropped to a knee and pulled his pistol. One of Dr. Wyeth's mercenaries barreled through and Chief Bull pulled the trigger three times. The mercenary dropped like a sack and his heavy rifle skittered free. Kiran leapt forward and grabbed it before hightailing it into the escape pod chamber.

"What are you doing, Kiran? We've got to go!" screamed Tom Sinix. He waved the old man over and once he was through, slammed the pod hatch shut. "We're all on. Fire it up, Mariko!"

Kiran fell to the floor and took stock of the situation. Besides Ellie, Sinix, Mariko, and himself, Privates Lloyd and Zere were also on board. "We're running two people heavy, Doc. You know that."

"We'll deal with that when the time comes."

The escape pod lights went blue and the small craft shot like a round out of a cannon into the mess outside of the M33. Other escape pods arced their way through the sky as gigantic monsters swam toward them and swallowed them whole.

"What the hell are those?" screamed Private Lloyd. "Nothing is supposed to live in the wormholes!"

"You didn't mention we were in a wormhole, Mariko," grumbled the Doctor.

"We can make it," she grimaced. "We just have to punch through."

Chief Bull pressed his hands together and prayed, "Ancestors, please see our way out of here so that we can live for another day."

The nose of the escape pod smacked into the skin of the wormhole and everything went topsy-turvy. Blackness filled the viewport as the small craft tumbled out of control. Slowly, pinpricks of light began to sparkle like stars.

"Nothing but empty space," grimaced Officer Shimada as she checked the nav system. "No planets, no signals, nothing."

Chief Bull choked for a moment as he slapped his hands together, "So, we live another day. For that, I thank you."

***

Luli stared in horror as the coalescing spill of colors bled through the tear. The hues of the 'other space' pressed against the surface of the wormhole. As the two collided, a ragged tear was forced through into real space. Wonder mixed with fear at the sight of stars shining through the walls of the tunnel.

Luli spoke in awe, "I can see three different dimensions..."

Everything went crazy in the instant of the dimensional intersection. The wormhole tunnel tore under the force and the M33 split open like a rotten tin can. Humans and their garbage spilled out like flotsam past the rift of the cruiser. Smoke and flame emblazoned the skies. Gargantuan creatures swam through the bubble, and the Matilda was surrounded on all sides.

Jacquie grabbed onto the nearest console and shouted, "We have to get out of here!"

The living and the dead were ripped apart by the plunging horde of insectile and fleshy creatures from nightmares. Many of the beasts streaked through the wormhole in both directions and disappeared from view. As the decking of the M33 broke apart, the Matilda listed off its axis and spun free. Everyone on the bridge was thrown hard against the belts of their seats.

The Matilda smashed through the ragged wall of the wormhole. She crashed into normal space inside a fiery ball of lightning. The tumbling wreck of the M33 destroyer spilled out its contents behind her as the FTL engine fell offline.

"What did you do?" Jacquie quelled in horror.

Luli couldn't pull herself away from the viewport. Bodies twirled in space like marionettes on broken strings amongst the remnants of their former prison. In many ways, it was a strangely beautiful and utterly fascinating sight. Too bad no one aboard the M33 had lived to see it.

***

Luli's interface was inundated with new data from the Matilda's functioning sensors. Communications were still down along with the sublight engines. Life support was functioning properly with no atmospheric leaks. She flicked through the alarms until the ringing in her skull stopped. Jacquie shook herself into alertness and Anton stirred moments later.

"Why?" asked Jacquie as she slid over to Anton's chair.

Shards of the ruptured M33 pelted the hull of the Matilda. Intermixed were the bodies of her crew. She glared at Anton who did his best to avoid eye contact.

"Did I give you the order to jump?"

"Well, no. You see... It was um... Well, I had a debt to pay..."

It didn't register with Anton that Jacquie's fist was in mid-swing. The blow connected with blinding alacrity and his head rocked into the headrest. Before he could gather his wits, Jacquie grabbed the front of his jumpsuit and pulled him closer.

She hissed out with barely contained anger, "Did I give the order to jump?"

"We're free, aren't we? Come on, Jacq..." He didn't get to finish his thought before she slapped him hard.

"I don't remember giving the order. I am the Captain, correct?"

Anton spat the blood from his split lip, "Yes, you are the Captain and no, you didn't give the order."

She leaned back and waited patiently.

"Look, it was the heat of the moment. We needed a way out and they weren't going to let us live. And we're alive, right? This has got to be better than whatever hole they were taking us to. You said it yourself, we had to get out of there." He gestured briefly toward the bow port, "It was either them or us. And I chose us. They got what was coming to them."

"Were you sure we'd make it?" Luli asked from behind the Captain.

Anton unbuckled the straps to the chair and brushed Jacquie's hands away, "It was a calculated risk. We were dead either way. Now, if you'll excuse me."

Anton stomped off the bridge. Within seconds, the swoosh of the lift doors revealed his destination. Jacquie gazed through the bow port and shook her head.

"Poor devils," she sighed. "Not all of them

deserved this."

"They paid the costs for their line of work," quipped Luli. And we get to live another day."

"That's pretty harsh coming from you, Lu."

Luli glared, "One thing I've learned recently is that the universe is an uncaring bitch. I might as well emulate her. Though I feel bad for Kiran." She slipped the pilot's visor back over her eyes. "Now if you'll leave me to it, I'm going to see what I can fix on this boat before the ache in my hands gets to be too much."

Concern covered Jacquie's face like a mask as she studied the woman who had been the most caring person she knew. Doubt gnawed at her heart, "Too much, too fast. Are we changing for the worst?"

***

Barney brushed himself off as he got back to his feet, "Damn it, Derain! What in the name of the ancestors were you thinking? We could've been killed!"

"But we weren't, were we?" Derain replied angrily.

Barney glared at the bounty hunter, "Still, this bloody thing isn't a toy!"

Derain's hands curled into fists, "I did what I had to do, damn it. Worst case scenario was either die in a prison or go out in a blaze of glory. Neither happened, so calm yourself."

Sensing the bounty hunter was on the verge of violence, Barney relented. He kicked a bent bracket that lay on the decking. "I need to put this room to rights, Mr. Tiwi. See your own way out."

Barney turned away from Derain. He gathered the loose fragments in the engine room and tossed them in a pile. Derain punched the wall, stomped out of the engine room, and disappeared from view. Barney shook his head in irritation and returned to his work muttering under his breath.

***

Derain silently cursed to himself as he headed to the lift. He pressed the button and crossed his arms. His foot pounded out a rhythm as he surveyed the cargo bay.

Wreckage lay everywhere. Remnants of containers were scattered over most of the decking. The Rabbit's Folly still lay on its side against the cargo bay doors. The water and fuel tanks sported new dents. There wasn't a solid piece of plas-glass left in sickbay.

He placed his hand against the wall, "Do I still want you for myself, Matilda? Do you still need me?"

The lift dinged and the doors parted. Derain spun around and nearly collided with Anton as he stepped out.

Anton glared into Derain's eyes, "I did it. I jumped the Matilda from inside that destroyer. Took a swat from Jacq for it, too."

"Is the M33 still intact?" asked Derain. "Did it follow us through?"

"It followed us alright. It's in pieces all around us, man. No idea if any of them survived and I don't particularly care right now." He crossed his arms, "So, we good? No more debt?"

"Your debt to me is cleared." Part of him deflated with the news that Jacq was angry. "Do we have a clue where we ended up?"

Anton walked past him and stared down into the cargo bay, "No idea. It's a mess out there, what with that vessel busted wide open. Not that we have a whole lot that's working right now, either."

"Yeah," murmured Derain as he joined Rabbit against the railing.

Anton leaned over and peered into the sickbay, "We're going to have to drop the gravity down there to right the crawler."

"How are the ship's comms?" asked Derain.

Anton glanced back at him, "No change since they took the ship. Still down. Why? You got an idea where we can get parts?"

"Should be a ton of parts out there, right?"

Anton laughed as he slapped his hand against the railing, "Ha! You're right, there is plenty to pick through out there. More than enough to salvage what we need."

"Just a short push to get out there, too. Let's grab our suits and get rolling."

Anton grabbed him by the shoulder, "Let's

keep it between us for now. Galena might be out there. If she's alive she may be trapped. No need to get everyone worked up, yet."

"Good point," replied Derain.

***

The lift opened with a ding. Derain and Anton snuck past the bridge and into the dressing chamber near the airlock. They quickly donned their spacesuits and cycled open the chamber. Both of them stepped out into the hangar bay.

"Could've been worse," muttered Anton.

The Cyclops had broken free of one of its mooring straps, but didn't appear to have suffered any damage. The two of them quickly dragged the small ship back into place and slipped a new tie-down through the ring on the decking.

They hopped over to the Waratah. The troop carrier had stayed within its straps, but it also sported a new dent. Derain cycled the rear hatch and boarded the craft. Anton undid the restraining straps holding it to the deck. As the small ship floated free, he ran over to the hangar bay door controls and smacked the door switch. The relay hesitated for a minute, but finally kicked in with a jolt.

As the huge doors slowly rolled open, Anton backpedaled into the hangar and hopped over to the troop carrier. He cycled the hatch closed, threw a quick thumbs up to Derain, and slid into the copilot's seat. Derain nodded as he brought the attitudinal jets online. The Waratah spun around and shot out into the void of space.

***

Luli sighed as she pulled the visor away from her eyes. She rubbed her forehead with her bandaged hands and winced at the sudden pain, "My meds are wearing off."

She glanced over, "Hey Jacq, I should have internal comms up in a few minutes. Nothing I can do for external. We're going to need a new array."

Jacquie looked up from the star charts as the computer cycled through them searching for a match to the system they were in. "Internal? That's something, at least. Hopefully, we can get ahold of Barney and find out what condition we're in."

"Hopefully," agreed Luli.

A bright spark caught Luli's eye through the bow port. She leaned forward to get a better look. "What is that?"

"What was what, Lu?"

"I swear the Waratah is headed toward the wreck."

Jacquie joined Luli. They both stared out the bow port watching to see if an attitudinal jet would flash. Suddenly, there was a bright spot that dissipated as quickly as it appeared.

"Yep, that's the Waratah, alright," answered Luli. "Did you say something to Derain?"

Jon Gray Lang

"Not a gods-be-damned word," grumbled Jacquie.

Luli thought about it a moment, "I guess it's not disobeying orders if you haven't given him any."

fourteen

I Drove All Night

The Peking Empress sailed through the tail end of the wormhole their FTL engine had generated. The energies that sustained its creation collapsed around the luxury liner's hull and dissipated into the darkness. Small planetoids decorated the heavens in a dizzying spectacle of orbits around a larger world.

"Welcome to the bosom of the Acigöl system! View the crown of the old moon sector as it hangs lopsided above the pate of its owner," intoned Latiff Ghilzai.

Thadie Dimba chimed in, "Topped by the beautiful Kuái dome! Aaah, home sweet home. It is good to see you again."

There was laughter amongst the bridge crew. Harjeet joined in the laughter, "We don't have time to stop by your mum's, Thadie. You getting any pings from our clandestine allies?"

"Nothing yet, Captain."

Ovi's eyes reflected in the blinking lights from the nav screen, "We have one, no two bogies coming our way. They're flying in a staggered pattern. Should we hold or should we run, Captain?"

"Keep your fingers nimble, Ovi. If this isn't who we're supposed to meet with, they'll have the jump on us."

Captain Harjeet Kaur wiped at the drop of sweat that slid down her cheek. She was a tall, imposing woman who prided herself on protocol and decorum. "Thadie, tight beam this code to the lead ship," Harjeet said as she placed a slip of paper on her console.

Thadie brought up the comm-laser and keyed in the code. The beam wasn't visible, but it showed as received. Everyone waited for a sign with bated breath. Latiff squinted out the bridge port in an attempt to see the incoming craft. Abruptly, three flashes of light blinked through a pattern, then repeated two more times. Then the pattern flashed again, but this time from the ship that trailed behind the lead one.

Captain Kaur smiled, "That's what we've been looking for. You can relax, Ovi. Latiff, flash the pattern back, would you?"

"On it, Captain."

"Thadie, inform Mr. Dauber to open up the Ro-Ro bays for a two-ship contingent. But keep the internal hatches locked for now."

Jon Gray Lang

***

"There's the signal," said Rosa. "Should we head in?"

At Rex's imperceptible nod, Rosa tapped the sublights to give the Independence a slight push. The FTL capable vessel that Mr. Leon had spoken of, hung in space ahead of them.

As they edged closer, their bow lights hovered over the old ship's curves. Bits of gilt and polish glinted back in the beams. Clean lines ran the length of her as decorative flourishes faded in and out of the light.

"Where did you find her? She's like a ghost from an antiquated past. I've never seen the like," Rosa murmured in wonder. "And she's headed for the scrap pile?"

Enormous panel doors that ran the length of the cigar-shaped craft opened up from the undercarriage. The attitude jets on the Independence fired and the ship slid forward. The docking lights of the Peking Empress glittered between the shutlines until the Roll-on/Roll-off hangar bay hung open invitingly. Everyone on the bridge stared in wonder at the height of workmanship from an era long past. Even the ship's bay cranes were carved with ornamental artifice.

Captain Delta broke the silence, "Rho-11, have Gamma follow us in."

Rho-11 keyed the comm, "Independence to

Scorpio, are you receiving? Please reply."

"Independence, this is the Scorpio. We await guidance."

"Follow our course in, Scorpio. Prepare for docking."

"Course set."

The Independence floated within range of the crane locks. They reached down to embrace the ship into the Empress' bosom. The beaten hull of the Scorpio hovered into view as it ambled its way to another berthing.

Gamma's voice came back over the comm, "My, she's a graceful one."

***

The rumblings from the visiting ships when they locked into place in the Ro-Ro bays vibrated through the deck. Even in the lift, Captain Kaur felt the ship shudder as the large panel doors swung closed. The lift settled and she stepped out into the lower depths of the liner. The long hallway lay before her. Airlock hatches for each berthing stood at attention on either side.

"Follow me, Vadik," she stated as she launched herself down the hallway. As she moved along, she admired the lack of dirt. Her people still kept the old queen spotless, even if there was little point to it. She keyed her comm, "Latiff, unlatch the hatches, but keep the lift under lock-down."

"The hatches are no longer latched, Captain."

Oxygen particulates that burst from the next port side hatch melted in the ambient heat of the corridor. "Keep your firearm close, Mr. Vadik."

The hatch slid open and a short man with a cane entered. He made his way along the carpeted corridor toward the tall figure who was here to greet him.

Captain Kaur put her hands on her hips, "Our benefactor, I presume?"

Rex Leon smiled at Harjeet as he nodded, "You may call me, Mr. Leon. Thank you for coming to pick us up, Captain. It is most appreciated."

She looked down at the short man, "You knew we would come, didn't you? How?"

"I do not choose my compatriots lightly. Especially this far into the game, Captain." He smiled benignly, "Were you able to scare up the rest of our associates?"

"They were waiting where you said they would be. We have them in cold storage in the ballroom of all places." Harjeet smirked, "You have very dangerous friends, Mr. Leon."

The crunch of boots echoed down the hallway. Gamma saluted, "The rest of us have arrived, sir."

"And it is good to see you. How did the liberation of the Scorpio go?"

Gamma frowned for a moment as she thought over her answer, "It required the taking of prisoners. Otherwise, it went smoothly." She looked over to Harjeet, "Permission to come aboard,

Captain?"

"Where did you find a genorg with manners, Mr. Leon?" asked Captain Kaur.

"Oh here and there. You may call her Captain, Harjeet. She has earned the right."

Harjeet's eyebrow arched in surprise at the snap in his tone, but she didn't lose a beat, "Permission granted, Captain Gamma. Welcome aboard the Peking Empress, the last jewel left in the scepter from a bygone era."

"She is a wonder to behold," murmured Gamma.

The hatch behind them opened and Captain Delta stepped through. She reached out to Gamma and clasped her hand before she addressed Harjeet, "Permission to come aboard, Captain?"

Again Harjeet's eyebrows arched in surprise, "Permission granted, Captain...?"

Delta bowed at the waist, "My apologies. Captain Delta of the Independence."

Rex Leon smiled, then winced. His hand rubbed his temple, "Would you give my people a tour of your fine vessel, Captain Kaur? I must step away for a moment. If you would excuse me, ladies."

"Of course. Welcome aboard, Captains. If you would follow me?"

***

Mr. Leon entered his cabin on board the

Copperhead. He let the door close behind him as he sat on the edge of his bunk and bent down to take his shoes off. As they fell to the floor, he wiggled his toes in pleasure.

He smiled at this, "It has become more difficult of late. When did this help me to connect, I wonder? No matter..."

He sighed and curled his legs into a cross-legged sitting position. His eyes closed and his mind reached out for the connection to his brethren. As each brother interlinked, the connection grew until he was able to find the one he sought. The one he needed to speak with.

"Are you there, named one? Can you hear me?"

He felt his brother laugh in amusement, "Named one, eh? I am only of the brethren, nothing more. How goes your journey?"

"The Copperhead makes its way to the Orsova system. We have a priority shipment to deliver to a wayward station. I will have you know it is a most serious business."

Rex laughed, "It is my brother, it is. For our part, the Independence lies within the hold of our carriage. The Scorpio lies as a counterweight to us and our coach flies to its decommissioning."

"The pieces move closer, then," Mr. Leon replied.

"Closer indeed," replied Rex. "Let us hope that we have foreseen all that the future holds."

"All that is left to us is the gates to Chaos."

Rex opened his eyes on the Independence and blew out a breath. He stepped over to the comm, "Anne, please inform Captain Kaur that the timetable has been escalated. Assemble the teams at the earliest convenience. It's time to discuss what the future holds."

***

Captain Harjeet Kaur stood at the long table that Mr. Leon had requested be placed in the ballroom for the meeting. She observed the armed genorgs as they stood guard at the doors and along the walls of the chamber. Each one displayed a confidence she hadn't seen in a drone before.

"They're a little disconcerting, no?" asked a familiar voice.

She looked over and saw a big man with an even bigger grin on his face as he dropped into a slight bow.

"Etsiddy? Is that really you?"

He laughed, "The one, the only." His index finger tapped at his jawline, "Now, when was the last time we saw each other?"

She quirked an eyebrow at him, "If you don't remember, don't expect me to tell you." She grinned at him as she shooed him away, "Go find a seat. The show is about to start."

"Your wish, as always, is my command."

As he wandered off, she watched as the merchant crews and mercenaries she had been told to procure as sleeping cargo filed into the room. There were quite a few faces she recognized from her earlier days.

She waved at Lexi and Oluchi as they found places amongst the crowd. Jong the Giant threw a salute her way as she made a beeline for Zahid in the back.

She almost didn't see Mr. Leon as he slipped through the crowd. He stopped next to her, slapped a data pad into the slot on the table and pressed a series of keys into the interface.

"Quite the bunch of pirates and buccaneers you've had me collect, Mr. Leon."

He grinned up at her, "Only the finest ones in all of Consortium space, Harjeet."

She bit back a laugh as he chuckled. She watched as the people he had summoned finished finding a place to stand or sit. Many of them hung back from the genorgs that now peppered the crowd.

***

Rex Leon rapped at the table with what she first thought was a cane, but the shape said otherwise.

"Thank you, my friends, for answering the summons. And thank you, Captain Kaur for providing the transport."

She bowed slightly as she moved over to the side.

"Hear, hear!" cried Commander Etsiddy. "A finer Captain hasn't sailed a finer ship!"

Over the guffaws in the crowd, Rex Leon smiled. "I'm sure you're all wondering why I brought you all out here."

"Give a hell of a shiner to the Consortium," shouted Ovi.

"Much more than a shiner, much more. "Tell me, what does the Consortium prize more than their jump gates?" At the silence, he said, "I'll tell you. It is their ability to appear anywhere when needed with their FTL ships."

Harjeet nodded along with the crowd.

"And what did I promise you in return for your help?"

Zahid said, "You promised us a return to the space lanes with a vessel under our legs."

Rex paused as he gripped his cane, "I did, didn't I. Luckily, I know where an armada of brand new boats wait for crews to take them." His fingertip swiped the table and the hologram of a shipyard floated above the table. He expanded the image until it was large enough for everyone, even those against the wall in the back. Shock filled the room as the crowd recognized the shipyard.

Latiff whistled, "Those are Consortium destroyers, Mr. Leon. I don't think they'll give them up without a fight."

"Right you are, Mr. Ghilzai. That's why we're bringing our own muscle to clear the way."

Oluchi stood up, "I've seen Etsiddy's team in

action, but are they enough to take that?"

"Not by a long shot," answered Rex. "That is why these Consortium military-trained genorgs will be joining us."

Murmurs erupted in the crowd. Rex stood quietly under the light. This is when it could all fall apart. He had done his best, but old prejudices were hard to quantify.

As the crowd quieted down, one woman walked forward.

"Did you have a question, Molly Quaig?"

"I've only ever seen a drone do things a person couldn't pay me to do. Can we trust them to do this? Can they be trusted not to run?"

Rex's smile looked pained, "Have you ever seen a genorg shirk their duties? Or seen a genorg run from the punishment bequeathed to them? They are more than what you have been told they are. If you don't believe me, you can ask Commander Keri."

Molly glanced over at Rosa Keri who stood next to Delta. Rosa nodded fiercely, "The sisters won't run, Molly. They have more invested in this fight than all of us combined."

Rex continued, "You fought by Rosa's side during the revolution, did you not?"

"I did," replied Molly.

"Would you consider her to be a coward?"

Everyone watched as Molly Quaig tapped her foot in thought. She looked up, "If ole Rosa vouches for them, who am I to say naught? I'll fly with the drones." She glanced back at Delta, "Begging your pardon, I'll fight with you and your, uh, sisters."

Mr. Leon relaxed just the tiniest bit. "Are there any others with a question about the genorgs? No? Excellent."

He manipulated the image of the shipyard, "We'll be heading in from two different docks on the station. I have discussed this with the individual teams. Etsiddy, your squad is to get these crews to their new vessels."

"Depending on the level of surprise, it won't be easy. But we'll get it done," answered Etsiddy.

"Delta, your team is to retrieve the docking keycodes from the station commander."

The genorg stepped forward, "It will be done."

Rex nodded as he moved the image to the part of the station that controlled the communications, "Another team will take care of the internal comms." He smiled briefly, "By the way Delta, Omega says hello."

Rosa nudged Delta in the ribs.

"What about external comms to the station?" asked Etsiddy.

"Oh, there is a contingency in place for that. Captains, I'll need you to keep your crews together and be ready to launch as soon as you are able. The Consortium's response will be swift and hard. Right now, we have the element of surprise on our side. With a fleet of our own FTL ships, we can keep that edge and take the fight to them."

"A right bloody nose for the Consortium this is!" cried Ovi as he whooped loudly. "About bleeding time!"

Harjeet smiled broadly as she looked over at him, "Leave it to Ovi to pump up a crowd."

Rex looked over the crowd and beamed. His chest swelled with a sense of pride. He felt a connection to these people which surprised him. It was different, but almost as powerful as the bond he felt between himself and his brothers.

***

Hours later, Rex clamored down into the hold of the Independence. Racks upon racks of planet-killer missiles recently liberated from Sheba stacked six high filled the storage space. On the outer hull, travel crates hung loaded with more of the same ordnance.

"Will these bolts be enough?" he whispered into the empty bay. "They are all we have, so they must be."

He ran his hand down the length of the fuselage of the nearest one. "It helps that old ore hauler Scorpio is loaded with a hold full of incendiaries. Good on Gamma for that bit of work."

An announcement played over the ship-wide comm, "Arrival to Orsova system imminent. Prepare for entry into normal space."

Rex Leon patted the warhead before he headed to one of the crash chairs bolted to the hull. As he clicked the harness into place, he ticked off the items on his mental list. Consortium contact had been completed with this old FTL-capable luxury liner. She followed through on her summons to the shipyard S-3465 for decommissioning. Each of the disparate pieces slid together as the brothers had designed. Everything was going according to plan.

"Soon we find out if the cost is worth the price." A tight smile spread across his face, "Perhaps this will be the end of the whole venture?"

The Independence shook in its brackets as the Peking Empress slipped into a wormhole toward their objective.

"Wormhole formation completed. Passage to Orsova system is in process."

fifteen

Space Junk

The Waratah nimbly flew toward what was left of the M33. The small pieces of wreckage from the destroyer hung trapped in the gravitational pull of the main hull. Derain ran a scan along the bulk of the craft, but the signs for life were negative. No power readings registered, either.

"Nothing coming through. She's dead," said Derain.

Anton sighed, "I'm not giving up hope for Galena. Let's head to the rear and see what condition the comm array is in before we go inside."

The Waratah fired its attitude jets and floated down the length of the vessel. The port jets flamed for a half-second then darkened. The troop carrier turned in space as the aft section of the M33 came into view. Derain ran the scans for life and power. They turned up negative.

"Pretty impressive what the Matilda did to this thing," remarked Anton. "The outer hull looks undamaged except where the hangar used to be."

"The jump engine almost split her in two," added Derain.

"That's a lot of blood on our hands..." murmured Anton.

After a long pause, Derain frowned, "Too much..."

The comm went silent after that. Derain adjusted the direction of the Waratah and Anton played the spotlight over the hull.

As the Waratah crested the edge of the cylinder, Anton pointed toward a shadowy spindle, "There! The comm array should be..." he studied the scan, "... just over ninety meters from the tear to the aft."

Derain ran his eyes along the hull. The bow lights didn't pick up anything until they flickered across the metal branches of the antenna that sprouted from the hull. He re-angled the troop carrier and searched for a place to lock onto the hull. "Got it."

Derain tapped at the port jets and the Waratah swung out wide. He played over the controls and brought the ship to the base of the antenna array. The boarding harpoons sunk into the hull plating. As he fired the starboard jets, the ship slowed to a drifting standstill. Anton was already up and rummaging through the toolkits.

"That thing is huge. You're certain the

Matilda's array is gone?" asked Derain.

"I sure am," replied Anton. He yanked a laser cutter free from one of the larger cabinets, "Look, Jacq's still going to be pissed. But if we bring something back that we need..."

"She'll go easier on us. Makes sense. Once we're done with that thing, I want to pull the comm records."

"You think Galena might've escaped?"

Derain coughed to cover up his embarrassment, "Uh, yeah..."

***

Luli pushed the visor away and tugged the cord free of her skull, "That's all I can do, Jacquie. The coding looks clean, but some of Matilda's prime systems are still down."

Jacquie's voice came from under the weapon's console, "You've been at this for hours, Lu. Go ahead and take a break. She'll still be here needing repairs... if we ever get her fixed."

"Don't forget to take a break yourself, Captain."

"After I finish with these three fibers..."

Luli left Jacquie to her repairs on the bridge and hopped on the lift. She hit the button for the second deck, "Might as well see how Barney's doing."

The doors opened and she headed to the engine room. She could hear Barney cursing up a storm as she slipped weightlessly down the main shaft. His wrench tapped a staccato beat on the mangled cradle as she dropped to her feet. "How's it going?"

"Not good, lass. Those idiots made a hash of the sublights. It's going to take me all night to even figure out what doesn't work. Aagh!" he shouted as his wrench clanged against the cradle.

Luli patted him on the back, "I'll leave you to it, then."

He barely noticed her leave as he pulled a clump of wires out of a ragged laser-cut hole. "Looks like rats were at this thing..."

Luli sighed as her feet touched down in the gym. She wanted to talk to someone without having their attention divided, but getting the ship functioning needed to happen first. None of them knew if the Consortium cruiser had gotten a distress call out or how they would be treated if 'rescuers' did come to investigate.

She slowly made her way down to the cargo bay and peeked into the sickbay. Doc's chassis still hung off balance on his track and appeared to be powered down. Her bandaged hands settled on her hips, "Looks like you could use some help my friend, and I need someone to talk to. You can listen to me while I get you up and running. After air, water, and food, health is most important. And that's in your wondrous eight hands."

She walked over to where the automaton hung. Hydraulic fluid had spattered onto the decking and the ceiling. His track was blocked by a med tube that stood on its end. When Luli gave a solid shove with her shoulder, the med tube tipped over and crashed to the decking. Doc's chassis lit up like a Christmas tree.

"Et cho?" it chortled.

"I forgot what a one-sided conversationalist you are. I'm working on it," she replied.

"Et cho da kae?"

She looked up at his profusion of tubes. Two of them had popped free of their connectors. She grimaced, "I can see that you're stuck."

"Da kae to cha? De ta? De ta?" it chirped and crackled.

"Of course I'm working on it!" she grumbled. "Do you think I came just to visit? By Tom, what else would I be doing down here?"

She reached for a handhold on Doc's chassis and noticed the bandages wrapped tightly around her hands. For the first time her curiosity outweighed her fear. She closed her eyes and slowly undid the wrapping on her left hand.

The automaton's voice echoed in the sickbay, "Cho lo te?"

Opening her eyes, Luli gasped and stared in wonder at the damage. Scars ran down each fingertip and met in the middle of the back of her hand. She flipped the hand over and examined her palm. Luli pressed her index finger and thumb against each other. The sensation felt weird, almost unwieldy, like something that hadn't been used in a while. Slowly, she unwound the bandage on her right hand. The same scar pattern ran across the back of it as well. She curled and uncurled each finger on each hand in succession.

"Amazing work Dr. Sinix. Color me surprised that they look whole. I wonder if you survived..." Emotionally drained, Luli left the braces that ran from her wrists to her elbows in place. "I'll take a look at those another time."

"Che du tong sa?" the automaton warbled.

"I had to know if I had been repaired first, Doc." A sad smile clouded her face, "Don't worry. You're next."

She leapt up and seized a handhold on Doc's chassis. In one swift move, she grabbed the disconnected lines and popped them into their sockets. The hydraulic line slipped into place and Doc's chassis vibrated as his mobility returned. Luli let go and landed on her feet laughing along with Doc's burbles and chirps of exultation. In the midst of their celebration, something caught Luli's eye. A chain of memory cores, that had fallen from the med tube she'd knocked over, glistened on the decking.

***

Barney swiped his data pad in disgust. The report was ugly. If it hadn't been the Matilda, he could've whistled in appreciation at the marksmanship required to leave a vessel with no avenue of escape, yet prevent it from cracking its shell in its attempts.

The data pad pinged and he read the latest entry, "The sublight cores are gone. There's nothing left to work with." He ran his fingers through his graying hair as the list of damaged components continued to grow, "Guess who will be blamed for not getting them up and running? The engineer! And who's that? Why that would be me!"

He sighed and set the data pad onto his workbench. "And I just got my place back. What are we going to do? What can we do?"

His expression grimaced in determination, "Not lose hope, that's what."

***

Jacquie perched on the weapon's station, waiting anxiously while the Matilda generated a damage report. She hugged herself and shivered slightly, "Great. The heat must be on the fritz in here."

Her data pad blinked as the report finally flashed across the screen. She sighed in disappointment when she perused the list. "Too many damn things are broken."

The ship's defenses were a shamble. The missile tubes all registered as being nonfunctional. The coil gun barrels were twisted beyond repair. She swept the report from view in frustration. Angry tears gathered in the corners of her eyes.

After everything the Matilda had been through and everything that she had by sheer luck escaped, this might be the end for her. She was dead in the water... nothing more than an oxygen bloated husk in the blackness of space.

"My home is a ruin," Jacquie whispered to herself on the empty bridge.

sixteen

Under the Milky Way Tonight

"That's the last one," Anton announced over the comm. "On my way in."

"Got it," replied Derain. "I'll be waiting for you."

The hatch opened and Anton floated over to the copilot's chair. He strapped himself in and smiled through the faceplate, "Shall we?"

It hadn't been easy, but they had successfully secured the comm array to the top of the Waratah. The landing harpoons pulled free as the ship turned back the way it had come. Derain drove along the hull of the M33 until they got closer to what was left of the hangar bay.

The Waratah entered the epicenter of the damage. Derain fired the bow attitude jets to slow the troop carrier. The Waratah continued past the twirling wreckage entangled with the bodies of the destroyer's crew.

Anton motioned toward a jumble of small ships that hung suspended in their moorings, "Looks like some of those fighters might be salvageable. You know, depending on how things go."

"Just be on the lookout for a hatch that'll get us to the bridge," murmured Derain as tiny fragments pelted the bow.

Anton pointed to starboard, "Looks like there might be some options over there."

Derain brought the Waratah in as close as was safe and locked in the harpoons. Once the ship was secured, both of them disembarked and headed toward one of the opened decks. Flames spurted from their jet packs as they floated over the ruptured decking. One floor level had space showing through to the other side so they kept going. Anton pointed through a rip in the hull to evidence of a hallway, "Hey, stop here. I think I see a way in."

Their magnetic boots clicked against the ragged chunk of decking. The rent in the warship's armor was narrow.

Derain stared through the crack, "We'll have to ditch the packs."

Anton opened the buckles and slid his jet pack free. Derain anchored them both to the decking. Exchanging a satisfied nod, they headed deeper into the ship.

***

Jon Gray Lang

Luli bent down and reached for the chain of memory cores that hung from the overturned med tube. As she pulled them free from the wreckage, they clinked against each other. She held them in her hands and arched her left eyebrow as she appraised them. Considering how long they had been hidden, they were oddly warm to the touch. "Like someone had been holding them in their hands and then left them here for me to find," she murmured.

Her eyes played over the individual surfaces. Each one had a series of grooves that traveled down the length of the shaft. Pitting existed along the surface of two of them. She rolled the most pitted of them over in her hand. Stamped into the body along the end was the code L-12 069. She rolled the other pitted one over until she found the code M-11 988. She rolled each of the others between her fingers and realized each code started with a letter followed by a series of numbers. Surely those letters corresponded with the last name of each of the deep spacers.

"My friends," she whispered.

***

"Another dead end," muttered Anton.

The hatch at the end of the corridor was bent inward from an explosion and blocked their way through.

Jon Gray Lang

"No way we're getting that one opened." added Derain as he inspected the area for other openings, "Let's head back and look for another one."

"This is our fourth one, Derain. You think we'll find an intact hatch?"

As Derain pulled himself down the hall, his voice echoed in Anton's helmet, "We'll only know if we look."

Anton sighed as he kicked off the floor and followed. The first hatchway into the ship had been ripped apart. A close proximity blast just past the hatch had collapsed the hallway into itself. The second hatch had been open, but had been blocked with crates and containers where the walls were pockmarked from gunshots. The one before this had just opened out onto space.

Anton clicked his boots to the decking and joined Derain. The flooring had been sheared free and sharp edges glittered in the beams from their flashes.

"One of these damn shafts has to go into what's left of the actual ship, right?" Anton groaned into the comm.

"So logic would dictate," grumbled Derain. "It's your turn to choose, which one?"

Anton peered up a couple of decks to an opening where a corpse floated eerily, "That one. It looks clear past the body."

Derain looked up and saw the figure, "The one with the swaying stiff? Might as well. At this point, it can only be a good omen for the likes of us."

He leapt straight up and caught the edge of the protruding deck in his gloved hands. As he pulled himself over, Anton shot past him, spun, pushed off the ceiling, spun again, and landed on his feet.

"Neat trick..." muttered Derain as he headed down the hallway.

"You have to admit, that was pretty cool!" Anton cried after him.

***

Luli stepped over to Doc and slid her back down his chassis. As her bottom hit the decking, she leaned into the robot.

"Che shi lo?" it asked.

"I am okay, Doc, just thinking..." She dangled the chain of memories and lamented, "This is all that's left of my friends,"

"Da kae da cho?"

"Yes," she chuckled. "I still have my other friends. But this is all that remains of my oldest friends." She singled one memory core out and held it up, "This one here is Vijay."

She could hear the automaton's eyes swivel around to look at the object in her hand.

"I got to watch him die..." Her bitter chuckles became gasps as she held up another core, "This one is Folami. He used to make me cackle like no one

Jon Gray Lang

else."

She felt more than heard the torso of Doc twist around. The small hollow in its chassis enfolded her. She slid into the hollow and smiled up at Doc's visual assembly.

Her fingers shook as she separated another of the cores, "And this one is Yannick. We would play these ancient sea shanties and the rest of them would laugh and sing along... and those... were... the happiest times... of my life!" She shrieked as she threw the chain into the cargo bay. Luli sobbed into the crook of her elbow and her chest heaved with one shuddering breath after another.

One of Doc's eight arms encircled her as another arm pointed at the cluster of cores, "Shae lo da?"

"Huh?" Luli asked as she wiped at her eyes.

"Shae lo da? Es ed to do?"

Her soft reply was tinged with sadness, "Yes, they are all important to me. Even that monster Jarl."

Doc's arms forcefully pointed at the memory cores, "Sho sho! Du ka klo tet! Sho du kla!"

***

Anton was bent over the panel of a hatch they had finally found intact, steadily working on the lock. Derain checked his oxygen levels that registered only sixty-nine percent.

"Will you hurry it up?" Derain barked as he

clicked and unclicked one mag boot in an attempt to tap his foot.

Anton muttered as he slid the plastic strip into the locking mechanism again, "Shush your protein-hole! It'll open soon enough!"

"Now is way better than next week, Rabbit. I only brought so much air."

"You're breaking my concentration!" Anton snapped. "It'll happen soon enough." As he slid the strip free of the lock, the hatch vibrated to life, "And there it goes!"

The hatch slid into its housing and a corpse bounced against Derain.

"Yowie!" he shouted in surprise as he shoved the body away.

The crewman's carcass ricocheted off a wall and disappeared into the distance.

Anton sniggered uncontrollably, "You got spooked by a dead guy?"

"Shut up!" Derain launched himself through the hatch and down the hallway as Anton's laughter rippled along behind him.

***

Luli sat on the decking with the memory cores in her hand, murmuring to herself, "Yes, every single one of you is important to me. Even if I am the only one left to remember who you were."

She cradled them against her chest as she rose and wandered back to Doc. The robot ran a physical diagnostic on its systems as it slid back and forth on the tracks. As she watched, Doc righted one of the operating tables and slid it back into its locked position. As three of its arms shifted the other table to its proper place, the automaton chirruped at her.

Luli looked up in confusion, "What are they? They're the memory cores of the other deep spacers." She fondled one as she explained, "Each one carries all the memories of that one person; their thoughts, their desires, their fears, and their actions. An almost pure construct of the person's character and experiences."

Doc responded, "Du sae tad?"

Luli laughed, "Of course I do. Just like you do, my friend."

"Sa chu ta dae dom sa?" Doc asked after a moment of silence.

Luli stared at the cores that hung loosely from her fingers, then her gaze returned to the patient automaton on its tracks, "Wasn't one of them tampered with? Well, Jarl wasn't right in the head..." She stood silently in thought, "I hadn't thought of checking the cores for corruption..."

"Che che..." Doc chuffed.

"Thanks, Doc!" Luli's eyes glinted with excitement, "I could go through Jarl's memories and see where he went wrong!" She hurried out of the sickbay and toward the lift, "The answers to my questions have been right in front of me the whole time!" She lifted the cylinders triumphantly, "Maybe all of the secrets are here in my hands!"

seventeen

Mystery Train

Captain Ariel Kahn stared through the bow port as the Copperhead slipped closer to the end of the wormhole. Strange objects glinted out past the edge of the darkness of normal space. The freighter swept through the jump gate ring and entered the Orsova system. The only military presence was the standard two-ship complement, one cruiser, and one destroyer. But those strange objects kept catching the light and glittered with menace.

"Are those..."

Mr. Leon glanced over as Ariel's grip on the edge of the console tightened in concern, "A defensive satellite grid? I told you this was a heavily guarded system. I don't often make mistakes, Captain."

She grinned, "But you do make them..."

Jon Gray Lang

Siede huffed in the background, "I don't know why they didn't just take it the first time or the second. Sending our ident, again."

"I'd take your ident on the first try..." Hung said as he leaned into Siede's seat.

Siede's laughter was loud, "As if I'd offer it..."

Mr. Leon ignored their banter. This was the first of dangerous points in the mission. If the gate station personnel flagged their ident, Station S-3465 wouldn't allow the Copperhead into their airspace. Of course, if the gate station personnel didn't take it, the military would burn them without a second thought.

Mr. Leon's lip curled in amusement. It just so happened that the ident they were broadcasting was as real as the delivery manifest to the station. "Patience is the key here, simple patience."

"What was that, Mr. Leon?" Captain Khan asked.

Siede's voice cut through, "Ident has been accepted. Navigation, point us toward shipyard S-3465." Siede smiled with a wink, "And straight from the gate station operator, get there posthaste!"

"Excellent," grinned Mr. Leon. He turned to the Captain, "It was nothing, Ariel. Just that patience and honesty are our strongest tools."

***

The wormhole collapsed when the tail end of the luxury liner burst into the Orsova system. As the energies of the wormhole dissipated around it, every light on the hull sparked into existence and the ship glittered in the dark.

"Broadcasting ident," Thadie said in the silence.

Captain Kaur hid her nervousness as the liner slowly moved forward. They had entered the system on the edge of the asteroid belt that encircled the dwarf star. Out past the nose of the vessel floated the shipyard. In shape, it resembled a squat saucer. A series of cages built of girders radiated outward from the center. In many ways, it resembled a mechanized flower of sparkling lights in the blackness of space.

A couple of single-seat fighter craft shot out from deep inside the surrounding asteroid field. Their dampening shields dropped and they slowed to match the speed of the Peking Empress. They floated just within firing range.

"Looks like we have an escort, people," said Captain Kaur.

Far off to starboard, sublights burned briefly in the dark, then faded from view.

"There's another ship on its way to the station," said Latiff. "You think that one is with us?"

Harjeet shrugged, "Maybe? I only know our part in the plan. Our employer may have more than one hand hidden under the table."

"Knowing his rep and the bunch we've got on ice in the ballroom, you can bet he does," Ovi grimaced as he watched the two fighters for any sudden movement.

The station's beacon lights appeared and blinked through a repetitive signal. Thadie triggered a patterned signal back to the station and waited for the confirmation. Within a few minutes, the comm board registered a tight beam connection.

A relaxed smile graced the lips of Comms Officer Dimba, "They've accepted our signal, Captain. Waiting on tight beam communications for further instructions."

Harjeet nodded. She perused the initial summons they had received for anything out of the ordinary, but found nothing. As they grew closer to the station, the blackened hulls of M Series destroyers hung like shadows under the flashing security strobes.

"How many of them are in their berths, Latiff?"

"Hard to tell. Seven, maybe ten? Ones with complete hulls, anyway."

"Looks like close to twenty slots, though some of them are empty," added Officer Vadik.

"A lot of them still look like they're under construction," Ovi observed on closer inspection.

"Have we been paid enough for this?" asked Latiff.

Harjeet crossed her arms, "We'll find out soon enough."

"And there they are," said Thadie as she gestured toward the station. "Routing instructions to navigation, sir. We're to head to port nine."

Captain Kaur waved at the bow port, "Well then, head that way. And don't keep the others waiting! Tell our guests where we are!"

The pilot murmured from behind the faceplate, "Heading changed by one degree to port nine. We should arrive in a quarter-hour."

Thadie threw a sharp salute to her Captain. She pushed the ship's comm and announced, "Arrival in Orsova system completed. Prepare for docking at the station. Nonessential personnel into cold storage. Bridge out."

The next ten minutes passed in tense silence. The station grew larger as the ship crept ever closer. A heavy thud passed through the Peking Empress as it coupled to port nine on the station. The crew held their breath as the station's security scanned the ship for life signs. If all went according to plan, the scan would reveal only a skeleton crew aboard the luxury liner. No one spoke a word.

The comm chirped. Thadie quickly answered the signal, "Peking Empress is here. Awaiting further instructions."

"Please have the active crew come down," was the reply. "We will have a shuttle dispatch you to the jump gate at the earliest convenience."

"Understood. Peking Empress out." Thadie turned to Captain Kaur, "They want the active crew on deck."

Harjeet Kaur, no longer the Captain of the Peking Empress squared her shoulders. "No time like the present, people! Run docking procedures and bring her down. I'll be at the airlock waiting for you." Her eyes grew sharp, "Do not disappoint me."

Her bridge crew watched as she headed toward the lift and disappeared behind its doors. Harjeet knew her crew would be on deck once they were done. The rest was up to Mr. Leon.

**

The Copperhead's sublights burned briefly as the freighter plied its way toward their destination. A long vessel maneuvered into a port on the starboard side of the Station S-3465.

"That must be them," said Captain Kahn. "Any new instructions from the station, Siede?"

"Nothing yet, Captain."

"Keep her straight, Siew Lian. Won't be much longer."

"You sure, Cap?" asked Reynard.

Captain Kahn looked over her shoulder, "Apparently these builders need the real thing. Where did you dig up these surge beans, Mr. Leon?"

"They're from a backwater moon in the Goma system," answered Hung. "I might be able to scare some up for a pretty lady like you... if the price is right."

Reynard laughed, "The best in all the systems, I hear."

Mr. Leon smiled, "Only the best for our military, Mr. Faragoi."

Ariel suddenly squinted, "What are you doing

up here, Faragoi? Shouldn't you be at the docking tunnel?"

He smiled nervously, "Um, of course, Captain. On my way back now." He saluted before he bolted for the hatch of the bridge.

Siede Geist cupped her ear and listened intently before she turned to Ariel, "They want us to head to port seventeen. It's on the other side of the station."

"That is going to be far away from the action." Acknowledged Ariel with disappointment.

"We can make it work, Captain," answered Mr. Leon.

Ariel looked out the bow port and could see the Peking Empress docked on the other side of the station. The plan had called for both ships to be near each other so they could overwhelm the local security force. But that wasn't going to happen now.

Ariel crossed her arms over her chest as the Copperhead slowly closed with the station. A couple of single-seat fighters swung around and kept pace with them. Siew Lian kept the merchant ship steady as he brought it up against the station's port.

"That's the problem with plans, they rarely work out," She gripped, still unhappy with the sudden change.

"What was that, Captain?" asked Ms. Geist.

Ariel's lips curled into a smirk, "Just me lamenting our inability to see into the future."

Reynard Faragoi's voice came through the

ship's comm, "We have a tunnel lock with port seventeen. There is a squad of armed troops awaiting us, Ariel."

"Thank you, Reynard," replied the Captain. As the docking clamps settled onto her ship, a rumble trembled through her hull. Ariel looked over at Mr. Leon. He stood there with his hands behind his back, smiling at her disarmingly.

"Well my friends, this is the big moment," she said. "There is no turning back now."

eighteen

Death and the Lady

Deep inside the wreck of the M33, Anton's voice chattered in the comm, "Up ahead. Do you see it?"

Derain shot past him and pulled himself to a stop by grabbing onto the open hatch. As he peered down the passageway a crystallized blood droplet shattered against his faceplate, "I think we're in."

Anton floated onto the bridge and collided with a body that had seen better days, "Whoa!" He quickly disentangled himself from the corpse, "I think we found the bridge."

"You think?" asked Derain sarcastically.

"Yeah, yeah, laugh it up." Anton pointed to a large screen, "That should be the comm station. You check where they kept the Lieutenant so we can search for her. I'm going to see if I can get this junker to run a parts list. I'm pretty sure Barney is going to want to go shopping."

Derain glided over to the comm station. "Uh yeah, you do that..." he muttered noncommittally.

"These bridge systems should still have some power," Anton babbled into the comm. "A pair of localized power backups should be in place for these kinds of scenarios."

"Someday you'll have to explain to me why you would know that."

"Used to be a freedom fighter, remember? It's one of those things you just learn. Anyway, they built these things to take a beating." Anton grunted as he slid a power cable back into place, "There we go."

The console lights flickered into life and bathed the bridge in an eerie glow. Derain brought up the latest bracket of communications, both internal and external. The comm logs were filled with pretty standard ship talk until a half-hour before the M33 ruptured. Internal chatter burst into strings of commands. Most called to block access to a shuttle before incendiaries set off alarms on several decks. Then it flipped to coded combat jargon between what appeared to be three separate factions. Derain scratched his head as he sifted through the information, "What in the hell caused all these splinter groups? I got the impression our interrogator ran a tight ship." He glanced at the corpse in the Captain's chair and spotted the bloodstain on the front of his uniform, "Hmm, guess not."

"What?" asked Anton.

Derain waved him away and returned his attention to the comm list. A large file had been sent out by tight beam to the Ankara system jump gate. A single shuttle had blasted out of a firestorm taking place in the hangar bay right after it was sent. Then the FTL drive was engaged and its destination changed. "I don't recognize these coordinates."

Derain keyed back to the shuttle command. He played the recording into his helmet, "Shuttle Three requesting disembarkation. Passenger Manifest, Dr. Judith Wyeth, Yeoman Hamza Fitzpatrick, Lieutenant Galena Chadov, sedated."

Derain scrolled through the recording and his hands knotted in frustration, "No, damn it. No!" His fists pounded against the console screen until the plas-glass cracked. "No! Her blasted shuttle got away." His head bowed, "All this death on my hands and she remains unscathed. It didn't even touch her."

Anton looked over in concern. Derain didn't usually show strong emotions, or emotions in general, really. "Hey man, what's wrong?"

"That murdering psychopath and her prig got away..." he choked. "They took Galena, too."

"What psychopath?"

Derain's hands gripped the console tightly, "Dr. Judith Wyeth. So close, so damn close."

"Wait, let me get this straight. You blew up this whole ship just to kill her?"

***

With a sharp ding, the lift doors parted and Luli stumbled out. She slowly made her way down the hallway distractedly flipping through the metallic cylinders in her hands.

"Which one should I choose first? I wonder what it will feel like?"

She slapped against the hatch control and stepped into her dark cabin. Her body fell back onto her bed. With a yank, she opened the top drawer of an end table. Her fingers fished out a spare interface cord that matched the one for the coupling unit on the bridge.

Luli rolled the cores in her hand, closed her eyes, and picked one. The core had an B carved into its side. "The Major says go with Vijay's core and so I will."

Her eyes played over the cylinder until she found the central jack point located in a tiny crevice on the unit. Eagerly, she slipped the jack into the memory core's port, then slid the other end of the cable into the port behind her ear.

Her vision dimmed then went black. She gasped in elation at a banner that played across her sight; B-10 191.

***

Anton shouted as he bounded toward Derain, "It's not as if we aren't in enough shit. Shit that you dragged me into, by the way! You blew up an entire destroyer just to complete a hatchet job? With Galena still on board on this boat? Seriously, what the hell? What the fucking hell?"

"It was my last shot at Wyeth! Mr. Leon reminded me of that so that we could escape. You've heard the rumors about how he handles a failed contract, right?"

Anton balled his hand into a fist and punched Derain in the chest, "You were going to risk all of us, because he might want your head? You knew that going in." He turned away and glared at the bounty hunter, "Why did you agree to the damn thing in the first place?"

Derain sighed and tried to relax, "I had nothing. A big fat zero on leads for Luli. That little monster said he had a lead on her, but it would cost me. So, I took it."

"But a kill contract?" asked Anton. "How far down are you willing to go?"

"It wouldn't be the first one I've taken. Might be my last, though." Derain's nostrils flared in fury, "And don't get all high and mighty on me, Rabbit. It's not like I'm a pirate who gutted merchant ships and left nothing but bodies in my wake, right?" His eyes gleamed, "Not like some people in here."

Anton gulped in shock. "What?"

"And how far would I go? As far as it took," Derain retorted. "All the way, if needed... for a friend." His eyes cut into Anton, "Wouldn't you?"

"But you could've killed all of us!"

Derain moved toward him, "Are you dead? Doesn't look it. Are we free now? Yes. It was a calculated risk and I'll pay the price for it, not you. So shut your mouth."

The flat coldness coming from his eyes made Anton question everything he knew about the man. *'Danger! Danger!* screamed his sense of self-preservation.

Derain broke eye contact, "At this point, I would've done the job for free. She killed all of my kin to get at me and she got away with it!"

Anton's data pad blinked in the dim light of the bridge as it finished the download. "I think we have everything we can use for now. I'm heading to the kitchen for some supplies. You coming, Derain?"

Derain's nostrils flared as he glared at Rabbit. Anton slowly took a step back to clear a path through the open hatch of the bridge. "You coming, Derain?"

Derain's angry eyes glowed in the dim light, "Yes. It is time to go."

The bounty hunter bounded past the ex-freedom fighter and out into the hall. Rabbit breathed a sigh of relief and followed the man down the hall back to the Waratah.

***

Barney stabbed the control button and tapped his foot as the lift slowly rose to the top deck. As soon as the doors parted, he pushed his way through them. In a few quick steps, he bounced through the bridge hatch. Jacquie stood with her hands on her hips in front of the comm console.

"Jacq, I don't think I can get this steel behemoth up and running under its own propulsion. The sublight cores are shot. It would take a miracle."

When Jacquie turned to face him, the sight of salty tears tracking through the grime on her face brought him up short. Her data pad blinked incessantly as a long list scrolled over its screen. Her voice choked as she uttered, "I know."

Barney had seen her this way only once before. The dark memory of the pirate attack that killed her parents flashed across his mind. '*My fault,*' his conscience whispered.

He threw his arms around her in a strong embrace, "I must have missed something, lass. It can't be as bad as all that. We'll find a way to get her flying again. We'll figure it out."

She settled into the warmth of his hug and wrapped her arms around him in return. Neither of them made a sound as they stood this way for what felt like hours, but in truth was only minutes.

Jacquie laughed as she released the engineer, "We may have to try Anton's asinine idea of dragging the Matilda behind the Cyclops and Waratah."

"It might work. I haven't seen him since our escape. What is he up to?"

Jacquie waved her hand at the bow port, "He and Derain are out there avoiding me... as they should." She glanced around the bridge and then out into the hall, "Luli has been gone quite a while, too. Have you seen her?"

Barney looked perplexed, "I thought you knew where she was?"

Jacquie keyed the comm to the cyborg's cabin, "Hey Lu? Are you in there? Lu?"

There was no response from the comm, but in the distance an agonized, piercing shriek rippled through the ship. In startled recognition, Jacquie gasped, Luli!"

nineteen

I've Got You Under My Skin

Galena tried to open her eyes, but she couldn't fight past the med tube's tranquilizers. She was aware, but not awake. "Where am I?"

A dry laugh filled the hollow place she found herself in. "The gnat has questions? You exist in the plane between. So much time has passed since I was last here."

"What? Who are you?"

"I am what's left of you. Or what will be."

Galena wanted to back away from the thing, but there was no way to escape her dread.

The mysterious voice just laughed, "There is no form in the between; there is only consciousness. It surprises me that a worm such as you can exist here at all."

Galena kept quiet and tried to dispel the fog in her mind. Indistinct shapes crowded around her

Jon Gray Lang

in the haze. *'What are they?'*

The vague outline of a shuttle grew more distinct, hurtling through the layers of the universe. Where the ship's computer was housed, a bright blue mist pulsed brightly, then dimmed, then glowed again in its calculations. Small blips slipped to other sections of the shuttle's systems.

Two humanoid shapes hovered just beyond her reach. Bright pink limned in purple light coalesced from their brains, uniting their intellects in a thin connection of thoughts, ideas, and theories. Misunderstandings sparked in scarlet between their two minds.

With great effort, Galena whispered, "I can see their conveyed thoughts, but do they not understand one another?"

The mysterious voice responded, "They lie to each other in an effort to hide their true knowledge. Your species is rotted through with deception."

"My species?" Galena questioned. "I am not one of them. They are natural-born, I was created."

The gravelly voice chuckled behind her, "More lies. You and they are the same."

When Galena looked around, the vague outline of her body swung into view. Shifting her eyes upward, she saw what looked like synapses in the shape of her brain radiating with rosy light. In the frontal lobe, light the color of magenta burned brightest. As she stared at it, she noticed large tracts of the synapses were dim and some were barely lit at all.

Jon Gray Lang

"Is that the machine in my skull?" she asked.

"Harbinger," clicked the voice. "Unnatural creations that your species built. And now it is opened."

"Opened what?" asked Galena as she looked to her left.

What she saw now shocked her to silence. The form was larval, but resembled an isopod. Bracketed segments ran like flexible plate armor down its luminous form. Its inner body was covered in tiny legs that writhed and wiggled.

Her voice quavered, "Is this you?"

The creature ignored her and the orbs that seemed to be its eyes suddenly glowed a sickly greenish hue with a center blacker than the void, "It grows nearer! I can sense its touch."

"What grows nearer? What do you mean?" she cried.

Pale blue light from the machine within her grew brighter as tendrils sprouted and spread outward. They wrapped tightly around the entity and it struggled against their embrace. The being choked against the tightening of the mechanized strands. The greenish light that emanated from the thing grew weaker.

A blinding flash of light startled Galena and she screamed in terror. An inky viscous liquid enveloped her and everything went dark. She felt herself sinking back into oblivion and blacked out.

The shuttle's comm kicked on, "Welcome to the Malina system, Shuttle 501-S. You are free to

Jon Gray Lang

make your way to the planet Jard."

***

The Malina system hung like a jeweled necklace past the ring of the jump gate. As the shuttle passed through, the energies of the collapsing wormhole spattered against the hull. A request for identification came over the comm.

Fitzpatrick smiled over his shoulder, "Doctor, we've arrived."

"I heard the comm, Fitzpatrick. Get this shuttle to Ogun and make haste. It feels like time is running out."

Fitzpatrick brought up the local star map and the planet that hung closest to the star of the Malina system swung into view. He stared at the chart and poured over the readout. "Ogun? But it's lifeless. The planet doesn't have an atmosphere."

"Did I ask you to tell me about the stupid rock? No, I told you to get this shuttle there."

Fitzpatrick hunkered down at her berating and muttered, "Captain Kaplean at least treated me with a modicum of respect." With unneeded force, he completed the calculations on the nav system. The shuttle's engines burned bright for a minute then shut off as the small vessel escalated away from the jump gate.

"We're en route, Doctor. Our arrival will be in three days."

"Good," she replied. "Now, get me a cup of

surge and be quick about it. Then keep quiet, because I need to think."

Fitzpatrick's hands knotted into fists, "Of course, Doctor, I'll get some surge started for you."

Dr. Wyeth waved him away in disdain as she moved over to the med tube. She crouched over the unit and peered through the plas-glass at Galena. The latest medical chart generated on the built-in screen. Judith rested her chin on her open hand as she assessed the damage done to Galena's battle computer. As the genorg slept, the tiny machine had run filaments down her spine. It had grafted itself around her nerve clusters, but stretches of the filaments were unresponsive. The Doctor reached for a tumbler that hovered within her view. The heat from the surge it contained radiated through the cup and warmed her hand.

Fitzpatrick growled, "I'm taking a nap. You can have the first shift."

"Fine," the Doctor answered offhandedly as her fingers traced the dead sections on the chart.

***

Dr. Wyeth stared blankly at the data pad in her hand before her brain registered the blinking interface on the med tube. She raised the now empty cup to her lips, sucked in air, and grimaced.

"Might as well get started," she muttered as she wandered over to the kitchenette.

The kettle was still warm, so she refilled the

cup Fitzpatrick had brought her. She sipped the surge savoring its energy boost as she returned to the med tube. The interface blinked warnings for the patient sleeping inside it.

Judith growled, "Your time abroad has poisoned you in more ways than one."

Her fingers traced over the command to rouse the occupant before she pushed it. The seal broke on the lid and the pressurized gasses dissipated in a huff. She watched Galena's face closely as the genorg slowly awakened.

Judith set the cup of surge down and activated her data pad. She set it to record and spoke, "The subject, Galena Chadov, subject ID 4296-E-2631-H, shows signs of fatigue and minor malnutrition. The subject has suffered blows to the skull. Damage to the battle computer wired to her brain, probable. The subject also shows signs of infection, early stages only ."

Galena blinked in confusion as she struggled to sit up. "My friends!" she blurted. "They're going to be executed! I have to save them!"

Judith's eye's widened in surprise, "Friends? The others from that freighter?"

Galena nodded as she pulled against the restraints that held her in place, "Why am I...?"

Dr. Wyeth smiled as she took a long sip from her cup. "You are restrained for everyone's safety, including yours."

"Mine?"

"Yes. Do not forget that it was you who

sought me out and asked for help."

Galena nodded with a vague sense of remembrance. Her voice trembled when she spoke, "I have... hurt my friends and I do not wish to hurt them more."

Judith scribbled a note on her data pad, "I am sorry to say that your friends are probably dead by now. That halfwit of a Captain wormholed into the center of a star."

Struck by surprise and a sudden sense of loss, Galena turned away. Tears dribbled down her cheeks, "What is this water that comes from my eyes? Why does my chest hurt? What is happening?"

"Be calm. It is emotional pain for the loss of your... friends," answered the Doctor. "There is no hope for them, Lieutenant. But there is still hope for you. Can you tell me how you hurt them?"

Galena nodded soberly and fell into the response patterns she'd learned from birth. "There are blocks of time that are missing from my memory. At those times, I was not under my own volition. I became a danger to those around me." She looked up at the Doctor, "Am I salvageable, or have I finally reached my terminus date?"

Judith glanced at the interface reading; the warnings had cleared. "I believe that I can help you, but I require more information."

"What information do you need from me, Dr. Wyeth?"

Judith whispered the command phrase,

"Initiate 231, stroke two." She watched the genorg's eyes glaze over, "Report."

A flat voice emanated from the genorg, "Damage sustained to the main unit. Loss of three hundred thirty-six sensors in shell organism. Continued control obstructed by foreign element. Shell organism's defenses hampered by infection."

"Conclusions?" asked Dr. Wyeth.

"Prompt repairs or terminate shell organism."

"Thank you," Dr. Wyeth said as she snapped her fingers. "Close program."

The battle computer disconnected and human personality filled Galena's face again. "You slipped away there. Are you ready to answer my questions?"

Galena blinked momentarily before she replied, "I am ready."

Judith reviewed the data pad in her hand, "Let's take a few steps back. You were our primary test subject for genorg use on the war front. Which, in my opinion, was a successful test. None of the other subjects managed as well as you. It is because of this that I had you brought back to me after the Timmony Bay incident. Are you with me?"

Galena nodded, "I remember."

"Good. At the time of your return to me, we were running reconnaissance tests in the 'de trop aspect' with multiple failed results. It was surmised that your experiences made you more prepared for... unexpected change." Dr. Wyeth consulted her notes, "Modifications were made for your continued survival."

"The operations?" asked Galena.

Judith nodded, "The operations were necessary. Previous subjects had an unsettling response to the environment. It was hypothesized that the modifications from the Prime would give you extra tools to survive within the alien environment."

Galena tapped at her temple, "The machine. It has assisted me at other times."

"You're aware of it?"

"It is the cause behind my blackouts."

Judith smiled, "I can tell you that it is not the cause. Due to your repeated contact with the 'de trop aspect', your body has become infected. The machine, as you call it, has kept you in one piece, but it is crippled."

Galena visibly shivered as her fingers touched her face, "And the contamination has spread?"

Dr. Wyeth nodded, "The machine can be repaired, but I require more information on the infectious agent and where it came from. Do you understand?"

Galena nodded.

"The last time we saw each other is when you entered the sphere in the lab. Now, I need you to go back in your memories. We lost track of you within minutes of your entering. It was years later when Saric let us know he had discovered you in a prison detail on Udea."

"Dr. Saric found me and he tried to cut me."

"Saric was a loose cannon, but you took care

of him for me. What I need to know is what happened between those two moments in time? What did you see? What did you do? Where did you go? How did you get back?"

***

Galena studied the Doctor's eyes. Clearly, the woman was more interested in gaining information than giving aid. *'But why?'* she wondered. *'If the Captain were here, she might know what the Doctor was after. But she is no more.'*

She cleared her throat, "I don't remember much. But it didn't feel like years. Hours maybe? Maybe days?"

Dr. Wyeth sipped from her cup of surge, then set it down again, "Time flows differently there. What did you do, though?"

"The time in-between is fuzzy," muttered Galena. "I woke up on a dead space ship that a salvage crew was stripping for parts. One of them had been from Timmony Bay and recognized me as the one responsible. At the next port of call, they turned me in for a reward."

"Yes, yes. I know how you were found," Dr. Wyeth growled. "I need to know what you saw in there! What did you see in the 'de trop aspect'?"

Galena felt the heat coming from the Doctor. "I... I will try."

"Let me," whispered the sibilant voice in her mind.

She felt the being crawl around in her brain as it shuffled through her memories. Points in time flashed by as they floated to the surface and sunk beneath the waves of her mind. "Stop," she whispered as she tried to fight against it.

The voice slithered back, "Shh, insect."

Galena felt herself be pushed to the back of her mind. She could only listen and watch as the creature took complete control of her body. She felt her slow blinks as her eyes stared into the Doctor's.

There was an oddness to her voice as the creature spoke through her mouth, "I remember pieces... fragments. The helmet to my suit clicking into place as my sidearm was placed in my gloved hand. The swirling light from the orb reflecting against the walls of the chamber. Your instructions to turn around and enter the orb."

"We've been over this part already," answered Judith. "What came after?"

Galena's lips curled into a smile, "Even with the suit on, the scent of the place was strong as the bubble parted around me. The bubble flowed like oil across my faceplate and was lit with scintillating colors as if a rainbow had been shattered into millions of pieces. As my right foot joined my left, the feeling of resistance left. I was wholly in this 'other space'. The skies throbbed with a blood-like pulse and the surface below me moved of its own volition. Strange was the orchestra that surrounded me in a cacophony of cries, hoots, and howls."

Galena lost sight of the Doctor as her hidden

memories blocked out all of her senses and transported her to the 'other space'. In this dimension, time felt simultaneously an eternity and bare minutes.

She swung her head around and realized she was standing on the back of one of the large creatures she had seen inside the rift near Ninguiz. Hundreds of other enormous creatures drifted alongside this one through the never-ending skies. Fog swallowed her view as her eyes tracked the mist that formed in beads and trickled across her faceplate. Fear gripped her, "Will these monsters see me and gobble up what's left of my life?"

"Pay them no mind, worm," whispered the sibilant voice. "They cannot smell your blood, your sweat, your life. The metallic tang of the mechanical servant attached to your brain is all there is. And that does not smell appetizing to us."

"What about the ships?"

"Angry buzzing."

The voice departed, but she still could faintly hear herself talking to the Doctor. Suddenly, the guideline hooked to her grew taut. "I am too far away."

A small creature with many limbs landed on the line and crawled toward her. Its multi-faceted eyes gleamed in the strange light of this place. A larger organism swooped down and swallowed the many-legged beast in one gulp. The guideline snapped tight and yanked Galena from her perch. As she tumbled along the huge creature's back, the guideline tangled in its scales. The monster turned and bit down on the guideline to drag her back.

"No!" Galena screamed as she brought up her service weapon and fired.

The creature shrieked in pain, but continued to pull Galena ever closer to its maw. A loud trumpeting cry sounded behind her as something large swooshed past and left her spinning in its wake. It savagely tore the beast and the skies around Galena misted with blood. Suddenly, her guideline snapped and she floated free.

Galena cartwheeled as she screamed, "No! No, no, no!"

Fear smothered her in a stifling embrace and she shut her eyes. She disappeared into her past. It took all of her will to remember that she had survived this, though she couldn't recall how.

"How did I escape from here?" she implored aloud.

When Galena dared to open her eyes, she was dismayed to see that she still remained in the pod of behemoths. A twinkling light in the distance rekindled her hope as once again she wrestled with her memories. But she soon closed her eyes in exhaustion.

The mysterious voice hissed anew, "Your past cannot be changed, small thing. You must see this through." It chuckled, "I am enjoying this game of playing with you and your Doctor."

***

Jon Gray Lang

Judith Wyeth listened intently to the story being told by the drone and scribbled the points she thought were important onto her data pad. Her finger tapped absently at the screen as she focused on the facial patterns of the subject. There was something different about her now.

'*She is not herself,*' thought the Doctor.

'*If it is not her, then what?*' Her eyes scanned over her notes again looking for anything that seemed out of place.

***

"This is where you fell through one of the many weak spots your people have left in your travels," the mysterious voice burbled into her mind.

"I can't see anything?" Galena murmured in response.

She felt the dry laughter rasp against the back of her skull, "Your fragile brain couldn't grasp what it was going through, so it shut down." Galena could almost picture the entity as it pursed its lips, "Which is surprising considering the life you were dealt. What did that monster in there do to you?"

***

Light flooded the scene as Galena watched a past version of herself awaken in an ancient hallway. The pitted walls and the garbage that blocked the passage way looked strangely familiar.

"This is where we found Luli. How did I get here?" she asked.

"You fell through," the voice responded. "How do you know this place?"

Galena could sense the entity's heightened interest and fought against its fingers picking at her memories. In rebellion, she ignored the questions. Galena watched her image stand. She could almost feel the decayed walls her memory touched, along with the flakes of rust and paint her fingertips dislodged. Her image wandered through a part of the ship Galena couldn't remember. "I must be deep in the lower decks. The engine room must be nearby."

Galena checked the gauges, "Getting low on oxygen." She watched her image perform a scan for atmosphere, "And this thing is leaking atmo into space," Galena muttered. She held in her last thought, "Time... I have little left to me."

A cackle of laughter startled her. "You have all the time in the world!" the voice hissed.

Galena mentally shook herself as her memories continued wandering down the dark pathway. A hatch to the left bore the marking for the engine room, "Maybe there are spare oxygen tanks in there."

No longer a spectator, Galena felt herself merging with her memory image. She hurried to a door that hung open. As she walked through, her gauges read a thin atmosphere still remained in the room. She pulled the hatch closed and spun the lock shut. It moved surprisingly well. Her fingers fumbled with the controls to her suit and set it to collect. The inflow was slow, but she could see the oxygen gauge move upward.

The lighting in here was odd as it seemed to exude from the walls. But it was enough to see by. A hollow structure that resembled an engine cradle like the one Barney tinkered with stretched its bent and bony fingers into this world. Corrosion was thick throughout the engine room.

As she approached the controls, a brief memory of her time as a courier in the capital flashed in her mind. The old consoles flaked and separated like the layers of a croissant she had once stolen. Pleasure flooded through her. The buttery layers had melted in her mouth like nothing she had ever eaten before.

"A bright moment in all the darkness," chuckled the entity.

Galena shrank away from the memory in an effort to keep it safe, but she knew it was futile. She resigned herself to no longer having a private thought on her own.

"As you shouldn't."

The scanner that hung from her belt pinged her auditory equipment. She reached down to grab it as the pressure in the engine room changed. She heard voices coming from the direction of the hatch.

"But that shouldn't be possible," she

murmured.

Off to her left, Galena saw a male figure in a spacesuit approaching through the shadows. He appeared to be human, but his movements were mechanical. He was in deep conversation with an indistinct group that closely followed behind him. As they stepped into the light, Galena's eyes widened in recognition, "Jarl?"

The cyborg stopped in shock, but the larval creatures behind him wiggled and chattered in excitement when they saw her. It was their voices she could hear in her mind. She watched her past self scream in horror, fall backward into the empty engine cradle, and disappear through the floor.

All around Galena, a red sky throbbed like blood pulsing through arteries. The presence of the larvae's minds pressed on hers. Suddenly, the skies went dark and a new presence emerged within her. The pressure from its mind was too strong to bear and she blacked out.

***

"And then what?" asked Dr. Wyeth.

Galena's lips curled into a strange smile as she replied with a slight lisp, "And that's when I came to in a cell on the salvager's vessel. I have no memory of how I got on that other ship or even what it was called. All I know for sure is those salvagers were imprisoned with me on the Vogelgesang. Your Dr. Saric kept asking them questions about the derelict as he cut into their skulls looking for what I assume was in mine."

Judith lifted the cold cup of surge, took an unpleasant sip, and frowned, "Saric was always a fool. Growing old didn't help matters."

"Do you know what he was searching for?"

Judith shook her head and pursed her lips, "No idea really. After I released him from the family contract, I no longer concerned myself with his whereabouts."

Galena nodded, "It must have been before my gestation period."

"No, he was still working with my father and mother back then. You were weened in an off-planet factory and shipped to one of the learning facilities that dot Consortium space." Judith grimaced, "The factories have all been closed now and only a handful of the learning facilities are still in use. Such a shame. My grandmother's great work brought so low."

"Your grandmother started the genorg project?"

Judith noticed the emphasis on those words, but dismissed it, "I am surprised a genorg would be curious about its beginnings." She shook her head slightly as she resolutely drank the last bit of cold surge and returned to her data pad.

"Dr. Wyeth, ever since I first saw the sphere, I have often wondered... where did it come from?"

Judith answered without thinking, "It was discovered by a salvage crew on the rotting carcass of an old cruise liner. It had strange properties that intrigued my great grandfather, so he purchased it from them."

"Had he seen one before?"

Judith smiled, "His great grandmother had told him stories of something similar she had come across on one of her journeys. If I remember the story correctly, she had seen it on an old trawler from the Sol system that was dead in space. She left it behind, but always talked of going back for it." Judith's eyes gleamed, "What she had taken from it had more value at the time anyway."

"What did she take?"

Judith noticed a change in the genorg's voice and looked up. The medical interface on the med tube was flashing in warning. The restraints across the genorg's legs were undone. Galena's hands now grasped the sides of the med tube and there was an eagerness to her that was unsettling.

"I'm not talking to Galena right now, am I?"

Galena's head shook in the negative, "No, Doctor, but we know you. We know you well."

Judith stood up and the chair fell backward behind her, "You shouldn't be here. How are you here?"

"A door opens both ways, Juuudith." Galena pushed hard and came to her feet in a single sweep. "Now tell me why you opened it?"

Fear seized the Doctor, "You can't exist in our dimension!"

Galena took a step out of the med tube. Her

eyes grew inky black, "This place belonged to us before your species crawled free of the muck. It is you who treads where you should not."

Judith knocked over her empty cup in her attempt to get away and it smashed to the floor. Galena's hand clamped down on her shoulder and slammed her to the decking. The Doctor was strong, but the genorg was unnaturally stronger. In a split second, Judith found herself flipped and pinned to the floor. The genorg's face hovered above hers and she could feel its hot breath. Black liquid formed into pregnant drops that gathered in Galena's eyes, poised to fall on Judith's cheeks.

Judith struggled with all her might to get free and shouted the emergency code, "Little devil with the wooden feet! Little devil with the wooden feet!"

Galena stopped pushing. The rivulets of dark fluid retracted into the genorg's eyes. The entity fought for control, but the machine was implacable.

It cursed the Doctor, "You will live as all humans do! Cruel, short, and futile!"

The genorg's eyes cleared and she sprang to her feet in parade rest. The dull voice of the battle computer spoke, "Foreign element contained. What are your orders?"

Judith scooted away and ordered, "Get back into the med tube immediately and restrain the shell!"

Dr. Wyeth sucked in big gulping breaths as the drone entered the med tube. Reaching up, she slapped the controls to lock the unit and render its occupant unconscious. She stayed on the floor until her heart stopped hammering in her chest. "They're more intelligent than expected and they're learning. What did I miss?"

twenty

Dream a Little Dream

A loud ping woke Fitzpatrick from his slumber. He looked around blearily as he realized it was a proximity alert from the shuttle computer. It pinged again as he wiped the sleep from his eyes.

"Are you going to turn that off?" he asked.

When he didn't receive a reply, he shrugged himself up into a sitting position. There was no one at the pilot slot. Farther back in the shuttle, he spotted Dr. Wyeth on the floor addressing the rigid form of a drone standing in parade rest. He could hear the Doctor's voice, but couldn't make out the words. The genorg replied to the question with a flatness that struck him as odd even for a drone.

The alert pinged again. Fitzpatrick grumbled as he flopped into the pilot seat and pulled up the sensor screen. An attack satellite arced past the bow before its attitude jets brought it to a standstill in front of the shuttle. A weapons lock alert sounded loudly as a large vessel off to the port side set the proximity alarm into a frenetic pace. The comm rang out, "Shuttle 501-S prepare to be boarded. I repeat, prepare to be boarded."

"Doctor? Are you expecting company?"

"I'm in the middle of something, Fitzpatrick. What is it?"

The shuttle shook when a garishly designed ship swung up to the side. There was the distinct clank of a boarding tunnel against the hull. Then the sound of the shuttle's outer airlock cycling open resonated through the bridge.

"We're being boarded!" Fitzpatrick shouted as he ran to the airlock with his service pistol gripped in his hand. With a hollow boom, the inner airlock door began to cycle open.

Dr. Wyeth sauntered into the main compartment of the shuttle looking nonplussed. "I do not have time for this! What is with all the banging?"

Fitzpatrick waved her back as the airlock parted enough for an armored glove to appear through the opening. He grabbed the arm and swung his pistol underneath, "State your purpose or suffer the consequences!"

The arm tried to twist free. He clamped down on the limb and pulled his pistol back, but something smacked against the weapon. The pressure of a finger tapping against his shoulder registered at the last moment.

Jon Gray Lang

"Release it, Yeoman," commanded Dr. Wyeth. "I've been expecting them."

He looked over his shoulder and felt a sharp slap against his cheek. The shock of its sting caused him to release the interloper's arm. Then, as the airlock cycled completely open, two heavily armored guards shot into the shuttle and slammed Fitzpatrick against the bulkhead, ripping the pistol free from his grip. The Doctor grunted at this sorry sight, shaking her head in obvious disgust and dissatisfaction.

Beyond the guards who firmly pinned him, Fitzpatrick could see two young adults as they entered the shuttle. They appeared to be identical and were dressed in what evidently was the latest and most lavish fashion in this star system: seamless, floor-length iridescent coats with stiff, standing collars that were at least double the height of ordinary ones. It took Hamza a moment to realize that one was male, while the other was female, so closely did their expensive, matching outfits hide the differences. He could positively smell the mazuma wafting off them.

Presently, the male spoke, "Judith Wyeth..."

"... You have been a very bad doctor," finished the female companion.

"Even their cadence is the same," Fitzpatrick remarked, before the butt end of a pulse rifle slammed into his gut.

The Doctor glared at the twins, "He's not a danger. Release him."

The female's shimmering outfit reflected rainbows across the walls. "This big one?" She giggled, as the guards released Fitzpatrick, "He looks delicious."

"Grown from fine stock. Wouldn't you agree, sister?"

"Some of the best in the systems!" she cooed.

"He's mine, Rana," Dr. Wyeth growled, "Not yours to ogle."

"Everyone is ours to ogle, Judith. Don't forget your place."

Judith blanked her face and bowed deeply, "Of course, Lord Jai. My apologies for overstepping my bounds. This fellow is my man at arms, Yeoman Fitzpatrick."

The young woman ran her finger along Fitzpatrick's jawline and pursed her lips in amusement. "Even up close, he is a beautiful specimen of manhood. Quite delectable."

Recognition hit the Yeoman hard and fast, and he bowed hastily, "My apologies, I didn't recognize you! It is a pleasure to meet you, Lady Rana of Khanda."

Lord Jai laughed in mock astonishment, "... and mannered as well. You always had an excellent eye for subordinates, Judith."

The Doctor bowed again. "Thank you, Lord Jai, for answering my communique. I wasn't prepared for a face-to-face meeting as I did not think it necessary. What is it that you require of me?"

Jai's smile was dark, but his eyes grew bright, "We have things that require discussion, Doctor. Your diversions have not gone as smoothly as you promised and the needs of House Khanda have changed."

Rana asked distinctly, "Where is your creature, Doctor?"

Dr. Wyeth sighed angrily and pointed toward the back of the shuttle.

Rana's eyes tracked Judith's finger, "Make sure it is restrained," she ordered. "Bring it aboard the Cithara."

"She is currently sedated, Lady Rana."

"Excellent. We can't afford another Timmony Bay, now can we?" added Lord Jai. "Please join us as soon as you can, Judith. We have refreshments!"

"Of course, my lord." Dr. Wyeth glanced at Fitzpatrick, "Stay here and keep the shuttle running."

Dr. Wyeth crossed her arms as the heavily armored guards carried the med tube into the airlock. She followed behind them. Two more heavily armored guards remained at the ready on the inside of the shuttle.

Fitzpatrick bowed, "Yes, ma'am."

***

Judith was trapped between the armored duo in front of her and the pair following up. She could barely make out the matching fop cuts of the twins as they exited the airlock tunnel.

Jon Gray Lang

"Something must have happened that would pull them away from their pleasures," she murmured. "Damn the timing."

As she walked through the airlock, the sudden light of the area she entered blinded her momentarily. She felt a hand guide her forward as her eyes adjusted.

"Too bright?" asked Rana. "You've been away from Jard too long, Doctor."

"And missed much," finished Jai. Take her to our receiving room, would you, Nigel?"

"And whip up one of your special cocktails," added Rana. "Hmm, make it three. I am feeling desperately parched."

"Of course, Lady Khanda," replied the hulking fellow who held a firm grip on the Doctor's arm.

Judith's eyes finally compensated for the light and she looked around the room as she was led down a hallway. She curled her lip derisively. A deep indigo velvet covered the walls and gold piping ran the length of the hall. As she was led deeper into the ship, she saw the twins disappear through the open doors of a nearby lift.

"Time for one of their costume changes, eh?" she asked in an attempt to make conversation with Nigel.

He smiled politely as he stopped with her next to a cabin hatch. The hatch had been designed to look as if it had been carved from a single block of steel with beautiful acid-burned patterns along its surface. Knowing the twins, it would have cost millions.

"Such a waste," she murmured.

Once the hatch was opened, Nigel pushed her through. He forced her to sit down in an uncomfortable chair that she recognized as one built for executions. Straps slipped over her wrists and she felt another one encircle her throat. Nigel tightened it just enough to keep her from moving but without causing her discomfort. He bent down in front of her and pulled straps across her ankles.

"My pardon for this arrangement, but are you comfortable, Doctor?" he asked.

Judith pulled against the wrist straps, "As much as one could hope."

Nigel performed a tidy bow before he went to the bar and began mixing a cocktail. The soft clinking of glassware was the only sound Judith heard. She was also aware that the lighting in this octagonal room was dimmer, more like the lighting found in a private booth of a restaurant. Thick, luscious animal skins covered the floor except for the bare spot under the chair she occupied. As she tried to view the walls of the chamber, her breath caught in her throat. Strange sigils painted in black ran across the floor to the ceiling at sectioned intervals. The sigils disappeared underneath the animal skins.

She grimaced, "I see they haven't lost their sense of texture."

"Oh yes," answered Jai from the dark.

Rana continued, "If one doesn't experience, is one truly alive?"

The twins wore matching skintight mirrored flight suits covered in enormous offset pockets. They were ensconced in two golden thrones that slid out from the darkness and came to a stop in front of her under a spotlight. The chairs glimmered in the beams and the twins preened in the light.

"And your sense of theater is still intact, I see."

Lady Rana tittered demurely while Lord Jai slumped languidly against the back of his chair. Nigel brought two glasses over and set them between the twins.

The two cocktails differed in colors almost as much as their garnishes. Lady Rana's beverage glowed with chartreuse and edible feathers from the garden moon Skyke bird laced the edge of the tall glass. Lord Jai's drink was simple in comparison. Titian swirls hung suspended in a cream of unknown origin while a holo of avians in flight circled above the squat tumbler.

"Dear Nigel, please serve our guest," Rana said as she took a sip. "Mmm. Excellent as always."

Jai's eyebrow shot up, "You may have outdone yourself, Nigel. This is a wonder to behold!"

Judith watched this byplay as a sour taste formed in her mouth. Nigel reappeared in front of her with a syringe held between his fingers. She felt the bite as it punctured her skin and watched as the dark liquid was plunged into her veins. Nigel withdrew the needle and placed it on a table she couldn't see.

He picked up a bowl that had colorful cobalt smoke rising from it. He fanned the smoke in her face until she was forced to breathe it in. The smell wasn't unpleasant, but it did cause her air passages to tingle.

"She will be ready for you within the minute, my Lady." Nigel bowed and stepped back.

Judith swished her tongue around the inside of her mouth, "My gums are getting dry. Is this the same admixture from my last visit?"

Nigel's voice came from behind her, "It is the same with some minor adjustments. I would be pleased if you would tell me about your experiences with the new recipe."

Judith barked a short laugh, "Of course, Nigel. As one professional to another."

The skin inside of her nostrils tightened with the expanded blood flow brought on by the smoke. "Ah... the quickened blood flow should force the drug through my body much faster. Still using tanka wood smoke as the accelerant?" she asked. "It tastes different."

"I added a little kunja herb to take the edge off."

Judith smiled, "Aah yes, I recognize it now."

Jai interrupted, "Yes, yes, Nigel. We all know you worked hard on whatever it is you gave her, but I for one would like to be back on planet. The Family Senai is throwing a huge party to celebrate our merger and I want to be there! But your creations keep messing things up, Doctor!"

"It's been a minute, Nigel. Why hasn't your concoction taken effect?" asked Rana.

Judith tried to focus on what the young Lady had said, but the chamber swam with colors that hurt to look at. Dark shadows covered in pinpricks that resembled eyes moved along the walls of the chamber to gather behind the twins. Judith blinked until the colors slowed down and gave everything a blurry aura. She watched the breath of the twins escape the confines of their toothy hems and billow into wind spirits.

Judith murmured, "I would cut back on the hallucinogen. It's a bit strong."

The raw sound of a pen tip scratching across the surface of artisanal parchment crescendoed behind her. Judith gritted her teeth until it finally stopped. "I am ready for your questions, Lady Rana, though I must inform you that the drugs are unnecessary."

"It is only because you are such a wily underling," Jai giggled.

Judith cracked her eyes open and stared at the twins. Smoke of a different color encircled their heads, "Aah, teba mist. Looking for heightened responses to visual queues?"

Rana added, "... and dangerous. Tricksome too."

Jai nodded in agreement as he threw a leg over the armrest of his throne. "You have left us in a fine pickle, Doctor. Your creatures are causing trouble all throughout the outer systems..."

"The outer systems are rife with stories of armed insurrections, stolen goods, and interruptions of supply lines. All by military-trained drones. Your genorgs, Doctor," Lady Rana finished.

Judith watched in amusement as the smoke filtered into Lady Khanda's mouth as she drew in a breath to continue.

"Not my genorg, my Lady. Let's let blame lay where it should, shall we? You stole my research and sold it to a competitor. I had in my possession the only genorg trained by me until you absconded with her somewhere on your ship."

Jai's laughter was sharp and sudden.

Rana glared over Judith's shoulder, "Nigel? You'll need to tamp down how future subject's respond to the need to tell the truth. Rudeness is not required."

"Of course, my Lady."

"It's funny that you should mention your research," Jai said. "The sightings of these armed drones number more than the batch sold to our Navy by ServLabR. Either you have trained more of these things or they're training themselves."

Judith blinked, "That's... not improbable."

"Shocking isn't it?" added Rana. "These drone soldiers are causing havoc all over the Consortium! It is looking bad for us as even our military cannot keep them contained..."

"Not to mention ruining our profit margins,"

added Jai.

Rana continued, "It is unthinkable, but material shortages are cropping up in the inner systems! Production has slowed down and it's getting worse. We've had to stretch the military thin at their bases in order to crush a food shortage riot on Heilon!"

"And the name of your drone keeps getting bandied about." Jai sniffed, "As if one of those creatures had the intelligence to put such a plan in motion. One of the other Council heads must be trying to undermine us."

"She was traveling with a merchant crew when I caught her," mumbled Judith as her mouth felt thick from the gas. "There is no way she could have..."

Lady Rana interrupted her, "We will have a public execution and declare the matter over!"

"Remove the head and the body dies," added Jai.

"What?" cried Dr. Wyeth. "No! You can't do that. She's the key! I just have to figure out what makes her special. I must get her to my lab..."

Rana stared at her, "Are you even listening? We'll have to put our plans for system expansion on hold until we can get the systems we have under control again..."

"Once that is done, we can supply you with all the genorgs you could ever want to continue your research," finished Jai.

"She's the key, damn it!" Judith implored,

"She remained untouched in the 'de trop aspect'! Even trapped in there for years, they couldn't infect her. We need her and others like her to keep those things from encroaching into our space."

Rana spoke, "You're a smart woman or at least I pay you to be. You can figure it out again."

"Besides, they haven't been seen in a year or more," shrugged Jai. "Perhaps they've moved on."

Nigel interrupted, "News just arrived from the Ankara jump gate. A gateway formed in system and destroyed a patrolling cruiser. When the destroyer went to investigate, the portal was gone. There was only wreckage left behind."

Dr. Wyeth breathed in sharply, "That's where I left the M33 behind! Have the Masters figured out another way into our universe?" She looked up and noticed that the twins were staring at her. "We still need her. None of the other subjects survived the immersion."

"We need to nip this drone insurrection in the bud. An execution of their leader will do the trick," Lord Khanda stated.

Judith could feel the truth drugs slowly lose their hold on her tongue, but it didn't matter. If the twins executed Lieutenant Chadov, then all of her work was dashed against the rocks of idiocy. There had to be a way to make them see it or to at least give her more time.

"No one would believe it was her," she muttered. "It would look like a desperate gambit by those no longer in control.

Lady Rana edged forward on her seat, "What do you mean no one would believe it. We have her here on our ship."

"How would it look desperate?" asked Lord Jai.

Judith cleared her throat, "No one would believe it, because executing one drone would look much the same as executing another. I mean, they look exactly the same for a reason. Because they are."

"And we would look like fools for killing one drone and pretending it was another..." growled Rana.

"Not even the other drones would truly believe it," grimaced Jai.

"Killing her would achieve nothing in the long run. And it would put us years behind in dealing with those of the 'de trop aspect'." Judith wheedled, "Why not give her back to me and I'll keep her secured at my lab. I'll get the answers we need to keep the creatures at bay."

"We need to do something to show that we care about the people and understand their plight. Something must be done to show that we have a solution."

Judith wiggled her fingers to keep the blood flowing. She watched as Jai and Rana slumped back in their thrones. '*Like petulant children pretending to be king and queen*," came to her mind. '*Rich and powerful fools, but fools can be led if enticed properly*.'

"What you need is a scapegoat," Judith

thought out loud. "Someone who can be linked to the problem and take the fall. That could give you time to figure out a real solution."

Jai perked up, "Someone or something..."

"... like a corporation known to produce soldier drones," finished Rana.

"Oh, that's a splendid idea," Judith said agreeably. "The House of Khanda is lucky to have you to lead them into the future. And I am truly blessed to be in your employ."

Rana laughed, "I can see that the drug has begun to wear off. The Doctor is not known for sweet talk even in her better moments. Nigel, return the Doctor to her shuttle and return the drone to her as well."

"As you wish, my Lady. May I take my leave immediately, Lord Jai?"

Judith watched as Jai waved dismissively at Nigel. The straps around her ankles loosened and then her wrists. She grinned fiercely, "I am back on schedule."

***

"Hey, Lu? Are you in there?" whispered a familiar voice from somewhere. Lu?"

The voice nagged at her like a persistent itch she couldn't scratch. She tried to ignore it as she sunk deeper into the core's memories. The voice drifted into the background as her mind viewed the world through Vijay's eyes.

The afterglow of a good set washed over her like the thin sheen of sweat brought on by the hot stage lights. It felt good to be alive, a perfect moment in time. The rest of his band watched as Luli fairly danced past him into the green room.

Vijay's eyes followed her as he said, "We'll do a couple encores and call it a night. See you back on stage in a few."

"You sure you won't need more time than that?"

Vijay laughed with the rest of the band, "Don't go ruining my reputation, man!"

Her smile lit up the room as the door closed behind him.

The ends of her hair wet with perspiration sent droplets out in a fan as she twirled and crowed, "What a great crowd! I feel energized!"

He shot glances at her swaying about in the green room as she moved to the canned music. Luli collapsed onto the couch and threw a leg over the armrest. He watched her stretch.

"My, my don't you look comfortable," he murmured.

His idle lust for her sparked her senses. Not just lust though, a part of her mind registered. Intermingled with it was love and admiration that sprung from the depths of his heart. All those waves of emotion lapped at the shore of her soul from an ocean that she willingly could have drowned in. At the same time, she knew it would have buoyed her up.

'What is this?' she asked herself. *'I've never experienced this sensation before. I... I didn't know Vijay felt this way about me...'*

There was a knock at the door and she heard her voice say, "What song are we using to start the encore?"

As he rose to answer it, Vijay replied, "Well, I thought we would..."

Suddenly, the door crashed open and three large men charged in. His heart hammered in his chest as terror hit him hard. Luli knew what was coming and struggled to find a way out of the memory.

The stun stick was jammed into Vijay's chest and she felt his heart stutter from the shock. With the sudden inrush of pain, every thought escaped her. Only the horrible realization that Vijay/she had left Luli/herself in a dangerous situation.

"There is nothing I can do, there is nothing I can do!" his/her mind screamed as he struggled to breathe.

A part of his view caught her get thrown against the couch as his/her skin was sliced open along the temple. He/she began hyperventilating as the nerve endings blazed with fire.

As she tried to break the connection, Luli's mind stumbled back to the memory of her fingers being broken by Jarl's henchmen. As he/she felt the plate yanked from the back of their skull, vomit gushed past her lips. Their hair was yanked back as a bloodied haze fogged up the light from the green room. The image burned into the backs of her eyelids.

Screams echoed in her mind, but she couldn't distinguish the voices anymore. The screams intensified as the skin was pulled free from his face.

***

The flight back to the Matilda was a quiet affair. Anton huddled in the copilot chair and kept his eyes straight forward. Derain focused on piloting the troop carrier back to the dark hulk of the Matilda.

Anton gazed out the bow port as they got closer to home. With a touch of amusement, he said, "I swear we've seen the Matilda in worse condition. Remember the last bunch of pirates who tried to knock her out of the sky? Didn't stop her then. And the bunch behind us didn't either. Am I right, Derain? Am I right?"

The oppressive weight in the cabin of the Waratah lessened as Derain's laugh sounded strained, but not forced. "Too true, my friend. That old boat has survived worse." His voice grew contemplative and disappointment colored the edges, "...so many bodies left in our wake. Sometimes I wonder if anything can stop us."

"Haha, sure enough!" exclaimed Anton. "We've made crap choices before and yet here we are, alive and kicking!"

"And yet here we are," muttered Derain after

a long stretch of silence. "Those we love either stand with us or lie in the ground behind us. How much more death can we be a party to?"

Anton wasn't sure what to say. He'd never heard Derain talk like that. He tried his best to muster up some excitement, "We'll make it out of this one."

Derain continued as if he hadn't heard, "All dead except your Lieutenant. She and her many sisters still live. Should we try to find her? With the weight of karma on our backs, who else would warrant us as saviors?" Derain's throat closed as these words escaped.

Anton's shoulders tightened at the mention of Galena. He looked down at the cracked and filthy gloves that covered his morally blood-stained hands, "Who else, except maybe ourselves?"

***

Jacquie and Barney bolted out of the lift as soon as the doors opened wide enough to allow it. They ran up to Luli's cabin and Jacquie hammered at the door. She screamed, "Luli! Open the door! Open the door! Luli?" She grasped the handle, "Damn it! She locked it!"

Barney shoved Jacquie aside, "Allow me."

He grabbed the T-handle and leaned into it. The handle didn't budge at first. His muscles bulged with strength and a metallic grinding noise came from the lock. A loud pop was followed by the T-handle spinning freely.

The door swung open. Luli lay on the floor in a pool of vomit. Her eyes hung open, but were rolled into the back of her head.

Jacquie dashed in. She dropped to her knees and swept up the pilot, "Luli, can you hear me? We're here with you. Me and Barney are here! Come back to us."

Luli blinked and looked around in confusion as drool dribbled down her chin, "What? Where am I? Where is Vijay?"

"You're on the Matilda, Lu."

Barney spotted the cord running from the back of her skull. He grasped it and yanked it free. Luli shuddered as the jack popped out and fell against the side of her bed. Barney reeled the cord in and the memory core plopped into his hand.

Luli squeezed her eyes shut as she grabbed her head, "By Tom, my head hurts..."

Jacquie tried moving out of the way, but it was too late. Luli's forehead came crashing down against her knee. Luli pulled away as Jacquie slipped backward and fell to the decking.

"Oh, shit!" cried the Captain as she picked herself up. "Tell me you're alright!"

Luli cradled her head with both hands, "I... I think so. Gods..."

"What by the ancestors is this?" yelled Barney. He grabbed Luli by the shoulders and yanked her up to face him, "What are you doing with this?"

She looked away as guilt flitted across her

face.

"Barney!" cried Jacquie. "What are you doing?"

"Deep diving into a dead man's memories?" he continued. "No fear of getting lost there, huh? Leaving the rest of us with an empty husk? That your idea?"

"What are you on about?" Jacquie appealed as she pulled him away.

Barney released the cyborg as he brandished the memory core, "This can kill you as surely a bullet."

"I have to find out why..."

Jacquie glared at the engineer as she importuned, "Find out what?"

"A quick pathway to death by dreams," Barney spat. "You know this is why memory cores are no longer legally installed in humans, right? A black market for stored memories sprung up on my home world in the early days. Thought they could see a better way to the future by having a window to the past. It didn't help them none. All they did was get lost in someone else's mind until they starved to death."

Luli tried to yank the core out of his hands, "I need to know what pushed Jarl to kill us!"

"Well, you're old enough to know better!" Barney shouted. "By the Major! Go and kill yourself then!"

Barney threw the memory core against the back wall and stomped out of the cabin. His voice echoed back as he disappeared down the hall, "Why even bother trying to rescue you if you're only going to kill yourself anyway? Be damned to the ninth level then!"

Luli ignored him as she stumbled over to her bed and searched for Vijay's core. Tears blinded her eyes. She wiped at them and screamed with every ounce of rage she could muster. She screamed again and again.

Jacquie hesitantly went to comfort her friend, but her arms were batted away. Luli slid down the wall of her cabin and wailed in anguish.

***

By the second solar day of their voyage through the Malina system, Hamza Fitzpatrick began to wonder if he had chosen the right person to follow. Passage through the system had been easy, but it was feeling more like a last chance than a new beginning.

Dr. Wyeth had said almost nothing since her meeting aboard the Khanda vessel, Cithara. She had promised him a meeting with the higher-ups and she hadn't lied. But it hadn't gone the way he expected. His desire had been that it would lead to the command of his own ship. After the few words he had shared with the Khanda twins though, he didn't hold out hope. The Doctor's reticence to talk about the meeting didn't fill him with good feelings, either.

He thought back on his assignment to the

M33. His benefactors, the Family Senai, had adjusted the ship's manifest and he was added as crew. He was to be their eyes and ears on the ship. Rumors said that Captain Kaplean was securely in the Ganbat Clan's pocket. They had covertly been making gains in the Consortium and the family wanted in on the secret.

Dr. Wyeth's arrival had thrown Fitzpatrick's early efforts to the wayside. She had searched him out and quickly enticed him with promises from the House of Khanda. He had taken the bait once she had told him that she had the support of twelve of the twenty-three ruling families behind her. What looked like a quick rise up the ranks would only take the capture of the drone they now had on the shuttle. It had cost much more than that and he had yet to see any benefit. Instead, he was taking the genorg to a burnt rock near the local sun.

"I should've stuck with Kaplean until directed otherwise," Hamza grumbled as the planet Jard fell behind the shuttle. "There is nothing to be found so close to the sun."

He glanced over his shoulder at the woman who held his contract. Just as she had for the past hour, she studied a holo of the drone's body. She would run simulations with different blends of poisons injected into the body while her fingers manipulated the strands of broken filament. He heard her curse as she swiped at the holo. Every single simulation had ended with the death of her puppet.

Jon Gray Lang

He grinned in glee at her failures, then his face fell. That woman could make or break him and there was nothing he could do. Unless another offer floated his way. That offer would have to include a council majority at that.

"Let's see what's out there, eh?" he murmured.

He surreptitiously brought up the comm system and wide beamed a message back to Jard. He still had a few contacts in some of the other council families. Maybe one would lead to something that would get him out from under her without anyone losing face.

"One can hope," he muttered as he crossed his fingers.

twenty-one

Along the Road to Gundegai

Anton scrolled through the list of replacement parts from the M33's inventory as the Matilda swung into view. He brought up the scans of her sublight engine racks. They had not sustained any obvious damage with their fall back into normal space. But he couldn't make heads or tails out of the reports for the FTL drive.

His only experience with wormhole drives was the jump gates and that had only been as a passenger when passing through one. He closed the report and glanced out the bow port. They were cruising straight toward the Matilda and it was pleasant to watch it increase in size as they drew closer.

He stowed the data pad into the large breast pocket of his spacesuit and settled back in the copilot's chair.

"Contact in three minutes," Derain said as he fired the starboard attitude jets to bring them back on course.

Anton glanced over his shoulder at the back of the troop carrier. He had ransacked the kitchen stores and the Waratah was packed floor to ceiling with boxes. While he had been at this, Derain had disappeared and found the armory. There were a handful of crates stacked on the rumble seats with military stamps across the seams.

Anton unhooked the seatbelt as the hangar bay beckoned. When the Waratah passed through the doors, Derain set the ship down on the deck. The hatch opened and Anton hopped out. As his mag boots grabbed onto the decking, he pulled on the ties floating loosely in the hangar bay. The two of them tied down the troop carrier quickly. They unloaded the boxes and crates and stacked them near the airlock entrance.

"Hey Derain, help me with this, would you?" Anton asked as he clambered to the roof of the lander.

Derain bounded up next to him. They undid the cords that held the comm array in place and carefully lowered it to the hangar deck. They each picked up an end and walked it out to the landing deck that ran the length of the aft end of the Matilda.

"Thanks, Derain, I can take it from here."

"Alright. I'll get your list to Barney," Derain replied as he turned around and headed back into the hangar.

The hangar bay door clanged shut as Anton murmured, "I hope they had an easier time than we did..."

***

Barney sighed as he entered the bridge, "Lost my temper, damn it. Not the best time either. I've been losing it more frequently of late."

He cupped his forehead when the blinking icon on the nav console caught his eye. He walked over and triggered the damage report that Jacquie had generated. His lips furrowed in a frown as his heart plummeted. "Another sign that we're truly screwed."

The clomp of magnetic boots against the deck reached his ears. He glanced over his shoulder as Derain stepped through the hatch. Barney was somewhat taken aback to see anger and despair staring back at him.

"You alright, Derain?"

The bounty hunter's gaze dropped as he brandished his data pad, "Anton said you'd want this."

"Oh?" replied Barney. "Where is that thief?"

The tension broke as a half-smile flitted across Derain's face, "The thief, as you call him, is out on the hull right now. He's installing the 'lightly used' comm array so graciously donated by the Consortium."

"Donated?" Barney stared at him quizzically before he saw where Derain was pointing. "Aah." He flipped the data pad on and scanned the information there.

"Is this...?"

Derain's smile grew a little larger, "... a list of parts in storage on the wreck? Yes, it is. We offloaded a bunch of supplies. Take a look and see what we should go back for." Derain suddenly yawned, "Anyway, I'm headed to my cabin. I need some time to myself."

Barney barely noticed as the bounty hunter left the bridge, "Sure, you do that. I think we all need a moment, to be honest."

Barney's eyes went wide as he perused the report on the data pad. He began to vibrate in excitement as he scrolled further down the list, "We might be able to get this old bird out of here!" he exclaimed.

Halfway through the third page, he bounced over to the comm and flipped it to ship wide, "Jacq! We've got a shot at getting the Matilda up under her own power!"

***

Jacquie shifted on Luli's bunk. As she tried to get more comfortable, she realized a metallic object was pressing against her hip. She reached down and recognized what it was as her fingers closed around it. She rolled the memory core back and forth in her palm. Her fingertip felt along the rough edge of a gouge caused by the jaws of a spanner. The engraved lettering caught in the light held her eye's attention. They had grown dark with age. She let the core slip from her fingers and it tumbled into the sheets, "So much desire for such a small thing..."

The lights in the room grew dim as the Matilda's brain aligned the ship into what it considered late evening. Jacquie was struck with the need to yawn and did her best not to move. Luli had fallen asleep with her head resting on Jacquie's lap. She slowly stroked Luli's hair back from her face. The stitches were beginning to melt away, leaving fine scars behind.

"Not as bad as I feared it would be," Jacquie whispered as she continued to brush through Luli's hair.

Dr. Sinix had done incredible work, but the damage was deep. Luli would never again have that ageless look. Worry creases had begun to etch their way into the folds of the dermis near her eyes and around the corners of her mouth.

"We all get old, don't we?" Jacquie mused. "Even you, Luli. Even you."

The comm crackled abruptly in the room and Barney's voice crowed, "Jacq! We've got a shot at getting the Matilda up under her own power!"

Jacquie smiled, "Finally." She stroked Luli's cheek, "Good news, Lu. We can get out of here."

***

Jon Gray Lang

The shuttle 501-S continued drifting through the center of the system and the bow ports went dark to compensate against the light from the central star. Instruments read that they were coming closer to the innermost planet. Fitzpatrick tapped at the console in boredom. Ogun was now visible, but he still couldn't understand why Dr. Wyeth wanted to go there.

She had kept the conversation short every time he had asked. In fact, she had mostly ignored him the entire flight except to tell him to get the surge going or to bring her something to eat.

The nav system chimed once it got within a certain distance of the planet. Wherever she wanted the shuttle to go would have to be done under manual controls.

Fitzpatrick spoke, "We're on manual controls now, Doctor."

"Aha!" she cried in the background as her latest simulation reached completion. "Success! There may yet be a way to beat them back."

Hamza pounded the console and glared back at her, "Doctor, we are here! Now, where on this godforsaken rock are we going?"

She looked up and saw Ogun floating out through the bow port, "Why didn't you tell me we were here?" She saw the anger in his eyes and dismissed it, "Never mind. Ogun has a moon that is in a very tight orbit. Once you see it, send a wide beam comm and the tower personnel will guide you

Jon Gray Lang

in."

She stood up and rested her hand on his shoulder, "We are almost there, Fitzpatrick and the future looks bright."

***

Anton slid the last bolt into the base of the replacement comm array and felt the drill clatter once the bolt locked in. He slipped the drill into the bracket holster on his waist and surveyed his handiwork. Rewiring the housing had been a relatively simple process. The hardest part had been lugging the awkward comm array up here from the landing deck. With that accomplished, Anton had assured his friend that he could finish this without any assistance, but he knew that wasn't the real reason he had refused Derain's help. Actually, it had taken this work time alone for him to realize that the bounty hunter's recent outburst had truly scared him.

"He just needed a moment to cool off..." Anton muttered for the hundredth time since they had left the wreckage of the M33. "Then again, don't we all."

He accessed the primitive interface built into the comm array and had it run a diagnostic. He watched as the colored columns slowly built onto each other only to peter out. As the last column went dark, they all spiked suddenly. At the same time, tiny lights glittered far off into the distance.

Anton squinted at them and tried to see what was out there. The blast of static through his internal comm surprised him. He lurched back in surprise, "What the...?"

The static cut in and out for a minute or so before he distinctly heard, "Hello? Hello? Is someone out there?"

***

Barney barely noticed as the lights dimmed on the bridge. He was hovered over a schematic holo expanding part of the image, "Let's see if I can cut this flange work with this shunt. I might have to finagle this conduit to slide into the elbow, but then everything should feed through just fine."

The Matilda continued comparing the parts list Derain had provided against her damage report. Each time there wasn't a match a chime rang. Once the comparison was done, a different tone sounded. Barney looked away from the schematic and wandered over to the nav console to peruse the two lists. There were gaping holes between the two, but it wouldn't keep the ship from flying. An amused whistle spontaneously burst through his pursed lips. Then he began humming to himself.

A blinking icon on the data pad caught his eye so he tapped it. An image of Anton giving the thumbs up popped onto the screen. Behind it were the images Anton had taken of the engine racks.

"What is this?" Barney cried. "By the Gods,

Rabbit! Brilliant! Even with all the drek everyone gives you, you still come through in the end."

The comm station suddenly lit up like a light show. Then it went dark. Barney moved over to it as it lit up again.

"External comms are back up!" crowed Barney. "That's two for you, my boy!"

It went dark again before another splash of lights crossed the board and an unknown voice called out, "Hello? Hello? Is someone out there?"

Barney backpedaled away and bounced into the weapons console. The voice kept talking as Barney ran a check on the weapon's systems. They were dead.

Panic struck him as the voice kept calling in the background, "Oh shit. Oh shit, oh shit!" He cycled the internal comm to ship wide, "We have incoming! Everyone, we have incoming!"

***

Anton's mag boots detached from the upper hull of the Matilda. He cut back on the jet pack as he settled on the landing deck outside the hangar bay. Once both boots had clicked, he waited until the hangar doors opened enough to let him through. He bounded past the tied-down ships on his way to the airlock. His patience began to wear thin as he waited for the airlock to cycle through its processes.

"C'mon, damn it! Come on!" Anton grumbled. "Finally!" he shouted, as the airlock cycled open.

Within two steps he was inside and pounding the buttons for the airlock to cycle closed. As the light turned green, he twisted his helmet off and pulled the suit down. The inner airlock opened just as he was kicking the boots off. He bolted through the hatch.

He ran down the hallway and grabbed at the bridge hatchway. He threw himself in and barely avoided crashing into Barney. He tripped and stumbled against the pilot's chair.

"Someone's out there, Barney! And they're coming right at us!"

"I heard them! Do you think I'm deaf?"

"Well, what are we gonna do?" Anton implored as he slumped to the decking.

Barney glared at him, "How should I know?"

Jacquie stomped onto the bridge carrying Luli on her shoulder, and Derain entered right behind them.

Jacquie radiated confidence, "I'll tell you what we're going to do! We're going to convince them that they have what we need and they're going to give it to us!"

twenty-two

Every Stone

"Prepare for station docking. Bridge out," played over the ship-to-ship comm on the Independence. An aura of heightened anticipation radiated over the bridge crew. This was to be the biggest action they had ever participated in and failure could mean the end of everything.

Rex looked up and gave a slight nod to Captain Delta, "I'm sorry, but you will need to finish that tea now."

A somewhat dissatisfied expression flitted across her face as she gulped down the rest. She saluted him and like clockwork, all the genorgs disappeared into the med tubes that had been brought up to the bridge for this purpose.

Rosa Keri watched Rex from the pilot's seat and waited until the last of the crew had found their spots and begun the stasis process. She stood up and stretched like an alley cat before she moved closer to him.

"You think this is gonna work?" she asked.

He smiled up at her as he finished his cup of tea, "It has to or every action I've taken up to this point is for naught."

"Getting all those ship crews on the Empress and convincing them to go under stasis was some trick," she said sardonically. "You do have the Devil's tongue, it seems."

"Only when it's needed and only for those willing to listen," he replied. "Besides, those crews lost their flight licenses. Each of them dirt-sided by the system because of their support, no matter how little, for revolutionaries like yourself." He shrugged, "With the Consortium taking away their livelihood over the principle of ideals, it was easy enough to convince them.

"Still a silver tongue," she grinned at him. "Should I get you to your tube so we can wrap this step up?"

Mr. Leon smiled back, "For someone with such a darkened history, you are incurably gracious."

They both stood up and slid into their med tubes. As the doors closed over him, Rex hoped that the timer would release them at the right moment. "Oh, timing, such a cruel and uncaring mistress."

***

The Copperhead penetrated deeper into the

system. A proximity alarm rang instantly before it was cut off. Siede spoke into the ship's comm, "Peking Empress sighted off starboard of the station. Siew Lian, compensate for additional craft."

"Compensating."

Hau Hung glanced through the bow port, "Is that really the Empress?" He nudged the pilot, "When I was little, I thought I could scam my way aboard her."

Siew replied, "I used to dream of piloting her. Just seeing that grand old lady out here is damn close to a dream come true."

Mr. Leon gripped the railing, "You may get your wish yet, Mr. Hau. Did you get your package dropped off in the asteroid belt?"

Hung leaned into the back of the pilot's seat, "My connection said they dropped it off a month ago. It should still be out there."

Mr. Leon nodded, "It's good to hear that." He crossed his arms as he addressed the crew, "The station will do a complete scan of the ship and we can't set off any alarms. Get the remaining soldiers in stasis as soon as possible."

Ariel walked over to the comm station and addressed the group, "Alright everyone. We've got enough med tubes here for all of you except the bridge crew. Everyone in!" She looked at Mr. Leon, "Are you ready to get this show on the road?"

"I am almost ready, Captain," he replied. "Siede? Would you please prep the program that I handed to you earlier today?"

"Of course, Mr. Leon. Did you want me to run it now?"

"Yes please, Ms. Geist," he replied over his shoulder.

"Done," she answered.

Ariel Kahn crossed her arms as she looked the small man up and down, "What do you have up your sleeve?"

Mr. Leon walked past her and chuckled lightly as he wandered through the hatch. "Oh, nothing so grandiose as I am sure you must be imagining. Just a simple draw for our flighty followers."

"Oh?" she responded. "How wonderful."

***

Anton piloted the Cyclops back through the hangar bay doors on the Matilda. He and Derain had taken turns running out to the wreck of the M33 as Barney's list of needed replacements grew. As the Cyclops skidded to the decking, Anton flipped through his data pad one more time. The list was definitely getting shorter again as all the small bits had been gathered up and brought back. Only a couple more trips then it would be on to the really big stuff.

He popped the airlock hatch on the small yacht and strapped the craft down to the hangar decking. With a couple of deft moves, he removed the large bundle on the side of the ship and hung it off the walls of the hangar bay. He entered the airlock with a satisfied air of accomplishment and made his way to the bridge.

In response to the recent wide beam message, everyone had been working with a passion to get the Matilda ready. Although this was taking a toll on their sleep, great progress had been made. The fuel and water tanks had been patched as needed and even Doc had gotten the sickbay into working order. Just the simple task of shoveling out all that plas-glass had taken nearly a full day to complete.

Slowly but steadily, things were improving, though. The main sublight engines were still down, but the attitudinal jets were still working. The coil guns still needed to be replaced but one of the missile tubes was functional again. However, the targeting board on the bridge was completely shot.

"But that is why I dragged this mass of wires and chips all the way back," Anton commented as he stepped onto the bridge. "Hey Jacq, mission accomplished."

Jacquie pulled herself out from under the weapons console and grabbed at the item in his hand, "Great! We might have something to shoot with now." As she took the item and scurried back under the console, she asked "Any news on our friends out there? Any threat potential?"

Anton sighed as he flopped into the pilot's seat, "Nothing new I'm afraid. They're definitely getting closer, but no clue as to what they're doing way out here or if they're interested in us in particular."

Derain walked in clutching a bundle of cabling. "Hey Jacq, we got the engine room cleaned up, but it looks like the fiber from the bridge snapped somewhere. I've got some replacement here... Oh, hey Rabbit, any luck on that module?"

Anton pointed down at Jacquie's legs sticking out from under the weapons station and crossed his arms.

"We're getting down to just the big stuff then," Derain pondered. "Any news on our visitors?"

"I was just telling Jacquie, they're getting closer, but that's about it. Hopefully, once the sensor array is functioning, we can learn more."

Luli strolled in yawning and stretching. Anton gave her a quick once over. Noticing that the flesh was starting to grow back along her hairline. The scars didn't look as angry and red as they did a few weeks ago. Beyond all that, she seemed to be more comfortable with herself, back in her skin as it were. Some of her sass was returning, too. An oddly satisfied smile lit Anton's face before he looked away.

"I'm here for my shift, Jacq. Oh, hey Rabbit, you back already?" Luli blinked at him. "Any news on our friends?"

Anton grinned as he said, "Well, as I was telling Jacq here, nothing new really."

Barney wandered in and bumped into Luli. He looked up at her and his eyes fell, "Morning, Luli. Jacq, I've triple-checked the connections out to the engine housing and everything registers clear, just the engine cores are trashed. Oh, hey Anton, any news on our friends?"

Anton laughed as Jacquie pulled herself free from the weapons station, "By the Major! Will you all stop asking him the same stupid question? The only thing new is that they're getting closer!"

Barney looked affronted, "Well, excuse me. How am I supposed to know what was said before I got in here? Tom be damned! Are you done with that yet, Derain? We haven't got all day!" he shouted as he stomped off the bridge.

"Man, everyone seems so tight," Anton muttered. "Hey Barney, come back!"

Barney popped back in through the hatch, "What do you want?"

Anton pulled out his data pad, "The parts list is getting pretty short. Mostly just big things left now. I'm thinking for the engines, you should come along and supervise."

"Aye, you might be right," muttered Barney. "If'n any of you cut the wrong line, it could go boom. Then it's just a waste."

Jacquie growled, "No. You should stay here and help out, Anton. Barney and I will go work on retrieving those engine cores. What do you think Barney? It'll just be like back on Calgorlie."

"No one knows this ship better than you lass, well except for me," grinned Barney. "Derain, finish running that line and get it connected. Ms. Qing, you okay to take over for Jacq?"

The pilot nodded sleepily as she ambled

toward the toolbox, "Yeah, yeah. I am good to go!"

"Rabbit, think you can crawl on the hull and pull the old coil guns off?" asked Barney.

"Um yeah sure, Barney," shrugged Anton. "Might take more than me to push them out into space, though. But I can get it done."

"Great!" shouted Jacquie. "I've been under this damned console way too damn long. Barney, let's go."

"After you, lass."

Jacquie stepped out into the hall, followed closely by Barney.

Anton watched them go and shrugged, "You've all been planning this since after I left, haven't you."

Derain laughed and clapped him on the back while Luli giggled in the background. "Of course we have. Come on and help me run this line. We can get to those guns once that's out of the way."

***

Luli waited until they left the bridge. Slowly, she slid another memory core out of her flight suit pocket. "Only two left," she mused.

The others had been wonderful and enlightening up until the murderers appeared. And that hurt each time. Living that moment over and over through the eyes of people she loved was tough. Luli had found that replaying Vijay's memories before the... end had become a way to cope with the loss of the others. It didn't make the scenes any easier to sit through, but opening her eyes afterward was easier.

She scoffed, "Barney doesn't approve at all, of course. But isn't he younger than me by close to half a century? Anyways, it doesn't matter now that I'm down to the last two cores."

She was certain the end would be just as brutal as the others had been, but she knew what to expect. The same three faces would appear and then the shock stick to the chest. Then would come the pain of having her flesh peeled free of her skull while her overtaxed lungs struggled to breathe. Finally, it would all go black. She shivered at the thought.

Yannick's had been the worst. Those goons had made it almost ritualistic. A bloody room that had rumbled like a space station and covered in writing she didn't recognize. They never asked any questions. None of it made any sense. She still hadn't learned anything about the purpose. And the lack of having some kind of understanding for the diabolical events ate at her.

"Why did they do it? What did they want?" she asked out loud.

She glanced down at the core nestled in her hand. Palba was next. She hadn't had the strength to dive right into Jarl's, but she was running out of excuses to keep avoiding it. She turned the core marked with a P over, "Was Palba the first victim of Jarl's or the first collaborator like he said?"

"I'll know soon enough," she muttered as she strung the jack from the memory core to her port. "And I would know it now."

***

Luli closed her eyes and sensed the glitches that formed in her mind as the banner popped and hissed. Full immersion took her breath away as the core's memories skipped and dragged her along.

"I want my mommy!" wailed a little girl standing in front of an open grave. The incessant itch of a sweater as Palba crammed for a test late into the night. Awe at the strength of Palba's mechanical hand as she slammed her fist into the wall with no pain. Flying a colony ship by the seat of her pants as a meteoroid shower tumbled into her path.

"Damn it," cursed Palba. "I'm barely out of the system and nothing said anything about asteroids!"

The colony ship rumbled under her feet as she stroked the attitude jets hard to port. Small chunks of rock pinged against the hull as she edged it out of the way of the storm. Open space beckoned with safety as a small asteroid slammed into the back end of the vessel. She struggled to bring the colony ship back on course. As the meteoroid cluster disappeared behind her, the memory cut to black.

"Touch..."

"... miss..."

"... you."

A long empty corridor opened up before Luli's mind. A corridor she recognized so well.

"So alone..." murmured Palba as she looked into one of the med tubes. Her hands pressed down as her breath steamed against the glass, "So alone. Is there anything for me out there? Or do I travel on a ship loaded heavy with the souls of the sleeping forever?"

Luli's heart weighed heavy with remembrance. The long nights through the skies of eternity with no one but herself for company. She had touched the glass and asked herself the same question.

The sharp grain of static sent Luli reeling from the memories. She blinked for a moment until the ethereal whispers of a flute resonated against the plas-glass of the bow port. She felt Palba's fingers press the keys in a battle against the isolation.

"I know this tune," whispered Luli.

The memory shifted as the song stayed the same. Around Palba were the other deep spacers in a dingy bar on the edge of the universe. As the song changed to another, she felt the eyes of the concertina player on her. Heat rose to her cheeks.

He beckoned her to follow him to the bar as the band took a break. "I like the way you play. My name is Jarl, what's yours?"

She nearly choked on a mouthful of wine, "I'm Palba. Did you disembark recently?"

His laughter stole a passage into her heart and

his hand felt good on her arm. She lost track of what they were talking about, but it didn't matter. She could stay right here forever.

A high-pitched whine kicked Luli out of the recollection as the core malfunctioned. "Ow, so loud." The whine cut off and she was plunged into a dimly lit room. Palba's thoughts focused on the touch of Jarl's lips as they kissed their way along her neck and chest. Each one brought an electric warmth to her nerves. His mouth traveled further down her body and she moaned..."

Luli pulled herself out of the memory and breathed heavily for a minute. "Silly me. I should've expected that."

As Luli closed her eyes, she returned to Palba. Digital imperfections marred the nuance of the tiny wedding ceremony. Happiness colored every moment until it ended abruptly. Palba stared out the bow port as they left another planet behind.

"Monster machine!" screamed the inhabitants. "You should have died long ago! You're nothing but walking corpses! Less than human! Get out of here! We don't want your kind!" The curses hurled at her and Jarl cut her deep to the core.

"How could they say that to us?" she murmured. "Didn't we bring them here? Why did we even bother?"

She felt Jarl's hand holding hers tightly. She looked over and his smiling eyes burned the sadness away. He brought her palms to his lips and kissed them soundly. "I love you Palba, and you love me.

That's all that matters."

The memory broke apart and an empty blackness held Luli in place. Suddenly, a bottle shattered against the bow port of the Demetrius. Palba brought it in for a landing at the biggest spaceport in the Consortium. As she stepped off, a rock burst against the hull. Palba pulled her pistol free, but Jarl simply covered her hand and led her to the runner waiting on the tarmac. His smile calmed her and she slipped the pistol back into its holster.

The scene jumped to a garishly decorated room and a teenage girl in the finest clothes Palba had ever seen greeted them. "Nigel, do not keep our guests waiting!"

An older man of a great height stooped into a bow, "Of course, Lady Rana. Would you care for a refreshment?"

Palba's eyes tracked across the room. Thin lines that she originally mistook for pinstripes turned out to be lettering in a language unknown to her. A drink was placed into her hand and she took a sip. After that, she had no memory of the place.

Palba's eyes slit against the bright light, "Oh, my head. What's this?" She realized that the belt holding her in place was built into the copilot seat, "When did we get back to the ship?"

"Just now, really. You had an adverse reaction to your beverage, my dear," Jarl grinned as he programmed in coordinates on a slip of paper into the nav system of the Demetrius.

He kicked on the engines and the Demetrius

lifted away from the tarmac. His eyes sparkled strangely in the light, "No more visiting all these worlds that are the same. No more dealing with humanity in all its disappointing nature. We have an adventure ahead of us, my love."

A bright strobing light shattered the smile and dropped Luli onto the ship from her nightmares. The Polypheme stretched out in front of her in both directions. Palba stood over the ship's computer and listened while Jarl wandered the empty corridors. Snatches of conversation came through the comm, but little of it made sense.

"Her eye was stolen..."

Palba keyed the comm, "What was that, Jarl?"

"The eye has the secret. It knows the way..."

Jarl sat across from Palba at the dinner table. He had been acting strange as of late. Jumping at shadows and talking to himself. She spooned him a ball of protein and tapped at his plate. He ate absentmindedly tore at the ball and placed the pieces in his mouth. His eyes kept searching for something past the hatchway.

"What is it you're looking for?"

Surprisingly, Jarl responded. "I saw a genorg today, or was it yesterday? Did she steal it?" He shook his head vehemently, "No! It was already gone by then. Gone..."

"What was gone?"

His eyes darted to her and his head tilted to the side, "She has a piece of the map."

Palba woke at the sound of Jarl's voice.

Jon Gray Lang

He muttered, "She has a piece of the map. Must find a way."

"Who are you talking to Jarl?"

His teeth glinted in the dark, "I know of a way."

The memory stretched and Luli felt disconnected from herself. A persistent clicking sounded in her head and transformed into drumming. Her eyes/Palba's eyes throbbed to the beat.

Palba's fingers feverishly searched the database of the Polypheme for some security footage, any security footage. Her vision blurred and she sensed another presence on the bridge. She glanced around but there was no one there. "Only a shadow cast by nothing."

The computer pinged and a string of old security feeds appeared. She clicked the first one and a woman in very old-fashioned clothes filled the holo.

"The discovery of the engine has opened up new pathways in space transit we never thought possible. Is there another dimension that will ease travel for humanity? We will find out today with the first test of the 'de trop' engine."

The security footage shifted to the bridge and deep space hung out past the port windows. Off in the distance hung a blue planet that tugged at Palba's memories. "The first jump will be short, just out past the Asteroid Belt. And here we go!"

A recognizable sight to Luli's eyes flooded

Palba's mind as the huge ship slid into a tear in the universe. The pulsing skies offered none of the creatures Luli expected to see and the Polypheme fell back into normal space moments later.

Palba shifted in her seat, "What the hell was that?" She clicked the last entry marked as TEST. The same woman in clothes before either deep spacer's time appeared in the center of the holo.

"Doctor, do you have anything to tell our audience as we prepare for the final test of the 'de trop' engine?"

A well-dressed fellow walked into the image on the holo and chuckled, "Only the fastest way to travel through the universe known to man! And here we go!"

That same sight enfolded Palba/Luli as the bubble of bloody light swallowed the Polypheme. This time the skies were filled with the monsters Luli knew so well.

Their god-awful shrieks buffeted the large ship. A leviathan reached out its mighty paw and its claw carved a rent into the hull of the Polypheme. As atmosphere bled out, smaller creatures hooted in fury as they slammed their bodies against the hull looking for a way in.

By the Devil Tom, what are those?" screamed the reporter.

The man shivered in terror, "I don't know."

The screams of the others on board could be heard as the smaller things struggled through the hole in the ship to get to the passengers.

Abominations slithered and flew past the security cams as they latched onto the people still in the corridors. Blood stained the walls and carpets as more beastly things hopped and crawled past.

"Lock the hatch!" shouted the well-dressed man. "Lock the fucking hatch!"

Tears streaked down the woman's face, "It's too late..." Her shriek was cut short as a worm-like fiend attached itself to her face. Blood spurted onto the camera lens and the feed suddenly cut.

"This can't be real?" whispered Palba as she stared in horror at the blank screen. The holo flickered to life and active cameras showed the humans caught out in the open transforming into something else.

Luli's mind whispered, '*The same as it was on the Avadora.*"

Palba turned off the feed and wept. She missed hearing the hatch open as Jarl walked in. He stopped and stood in the middle of the room and raised his arms outward.

Palba wiped at the tears that ran freely down her face, "What are you doing?"

He smiled and opened his eyes, "Stretching. Thank you for being here."

Palba fell into his arms and held on tightly, "I want to leave this place. Can we please get off this ship?"

He stared into her eyes, "You are always here with me, my angel."

Luli felt the blade thrust into the hollow of

her neck and her squeal turned into a gurgle as her blood poured out of the wound.

A part of Luli was cognizant enough to pull the core free and chuck it across the room. As she shivered in fright on the bridge of the Matilda, Jarl's voice permeated her mind, "I'm setting you free."

twenty-three

Wandering Star

Anton stripped out the last bolt on the aft coil gun. He threw a quick nod to Derain and they both pushed the behemoth free of the hull of the Matilda. The two of them watched it float out into the orbiting space junk. Beams from the Cyclops and the Waratah played along the hull as they made their way back from the M33.

It was a concerted effort for the two ships to haul in the giant net filled with one of the smaller engine cores salvaged from the wreck. The yacht and the troop carrier spread out slowly. They brought the engine core down as carefully as they could. It settled onto the small landing strip that ran above the main shaft.

Their suit comms crackled and Jacquie's voice came through, "Think you two guys could stop littering up this area of space and help us get this core stowed on board?"

"As you wish, your Captainness," answered Anton.

Derain replied, "Of course, Captain."

They winked at each other, hopped off the back of the hull and angled toward the runway decking. Almost simultaneously, their mag boots clicked on the deck and their forward progress came to an abrupt halt. In a couple of minutes they managed to untangle the net from the engine and strapped the core down to the runway.

"Hey, Barney, where do you want this?" Anton commed back.

Barney's voice came through, "Right there should be fine. Just make sure it is tied down tightly. It's going to have to sit there until we're able to sling it into an open bracket."

"Got it, Mr. de Lagnel," replied Derain. "Good hunting for a matching second."

Barney's voice crackled out of the comm, "Can you believe that this is just an attitudinal jet of that monstrosity?"

"Let's go, Barney. The sooner we're back, the sooner we can get them installed," said Jacquie.

"Right-o, Captain."

Derain and Anton watched as the two ships rotated and rocketed back toward the floating wreck.

"Hey, are some of those lights a lot closer than they should be?" Derain asked pointing out into the vast distance.

Anton looked up past Derain's trajectory,

"What's that thing way out past them? Is that a comet?"

As if listening to their conversation, both suit comms chattered, "Is there someone out there? Hello?"

Anton stared hard at the small craft that approached the Matilda. The comms continued chattering the same question.

"I really think that's a comet they're chasing," said Anton.

Derain responded, "What does it matter if it's a comet? You should be more concerned with who they are."

"... is there someone out there?"

Something about the accent of the chatter struck Anton as familiar. All of a sudden, he threw his hands up in surprise, "No way! Can it be? Is it really?" He hammered Derain in the arm, "Can you believe it?"

Derain looked at his friend as if he had gone mad, "Believe what?"

"Don't you know who they are?" cried Anton as he spun around and grabbed Derain by the shoulders. "They are D'ziageno! They're following that comet!" He shook Derain, "They're on the hunt for zotti glands!"

"What are you talking about?"

Luli's voice came through the comms, "D'ziageno? Way out here? By the ghost of Tom, I never believed I would ever get to see them for real!"

***

Jacquie piloted the Waratah back over the horizon of the Matilda with the Cyclops close behind. Their bow lights played across the hull until Derain and Anton's forms were illuminated.

On the comm came the voice of their visitors, "Is anyone out there?"

She tamped the attitudinal jets and the Waratah sank closer to the runway dragging its end of the net. She felt the tension ease as Barney piloted the Cyclops behind her. The two ships worked in tandem and the second engine core was dropped onto the runway.

"Lock her down, guys!" she ordered. "Then uncouple the net."

Derain replied, "We're on it, Jacq."

The voice of the visitor played across the comm again, "Hello?"

Her breath quickened, "Could it be?" She keyed a separate comm channel for the Matilda, "Luli, please respond."

"I'm here, Captain."

Jacquie tensed up, "Do we know who our friends are?"

Barney interjected through the main comm, "Snug that engine core up with the other one. See if you can tie them together."

"There are only so many tie-downs on this boat, Barney!" Anton responded.

Jacquie held the Waratah steady as one of the

men unhitched her end of the net. "Did you hear me, Lu?"

"It looks like they're sending a contingent our way," replied Luli. "Maybe a couple of tugs and something larger. They should arrive in a few days, if their speed doesn't change."

"But, who are they?"

"You're both free to go," Derain said into the comm.

"On my way in," answered Barney.

Jacquie kept an eye on the Cyclops as it slipped past her and flew inside the hangar. She turned the troop carrier around and floated in behind the yacht.

"Anton thinks he knows who they are, but he told me not to say," answered Luli. "He wants to be the one to surprise you."

"Of course he does," Jacquie nettled in irritation.

"The net is tied down. We're heading in now."

"I'll be right with you, Derain," replied Jacquie as she set the Waratah down. She killed the engines. With everyone's help, it was short work getting her strapped to the decking. Then they all headed into the airlock.

After the chamber was pumped full of breathable air, the inner hatch swung open. The good-natured banter of her crew calmed Jacquie's nerves a little as she pulled herself free of the spacesuit. She hung it on the rack next to the others and slipped her helmet onto the shelf. The others did the same.

As they all readied for the hatch to open to the rest of the ship, she grabbed onto Anton's shoulder, "Luli said you had a thought on who our visitors are. Care to share?"

"The stars aligned perfectly, Jacq! It has got to be the D'ziageno! Can you believe it?"

Jacquie's heart skipped a beat.

***

Barney sighed when he found Luli. In a quiet corner of the cargo bay, she was sprawled almost completely flat on her back across the crates that she had set up to sit on for another one of her sessions. Her eyes were closed and a sleepy, but happy smile curved her lips.

Barney walked over to her and gave her a nudge, "It's time for your shift. Lu, wake up. Wake up, Lu."

He spied the slim wire snaking out of the back of her skull. He followed it to the memory core which was enclosed tightly in her fist. It didn't take much for the cylinder to slip free of her fingers.

"This is going to cost me..." he muttered as sadness dominated his rough face. He pulled the jack free of the port.

Luli's eyes snapped open and a brutal hardness filled her gaze once she saw Barney. She snatched at the cylinder in his hand and he let it fall freely. As it clattered to the decking below, she screamed, "Give it back!"

"Luli," he muttered. "You have to stop. Vijay is dead. Riding in his memories isn't good for you."

Luli growled at him, "I know he's dead, Barney. I was there, damn it." She sighed deeply, "They're all dead and gone. Even Palba's memories are lost forever. And I still don't know what drove Jarl to do what he did."

He stood in front of her with his head down, "I know you miss them, Luli. If I could take your pain away, I would. Even if it cost us our friendship." His eyes glistened as he held her in his gaze, "I want you to be happy and this is only leaving you stuck. You aren't moving forward."

She reached down and put the memory core back into her palm. A shudder escaped her, "I am stuck, Barney. I... I didn't know what I could have had, if I'd only looked. I didn't know how he really felt about me, but when I go in there, I do." She dropped the cylinder and it clattered against the decking, "I'm such an idiot."

Barney smiled half-heartedly as he patted her on the shoulder and dropped down beside her, "Aren't we all?"

Luli leaned into him and sighed, "Sometimes, I just want to be loved and Vijay loved me. And I didn't know." She turned toward him, "How could I have been so blind?"

Barney rested the side of his head against her cheek, "If it helps, I love you, Lu. I always have."

Luli smiled in response, "And I love you too,

Barney. But, you know what I mean."

The smile on Barney's face grew sad, "Oh, I know, lass. I know exactly what you mean."

***

Derain walked into Jacquie's cabin as she stepped out of the fresher. From across the room, he admired her while she pulled on some trousers. She caught him looking and didn't seem to mind.

"You called for me, Jacq?" he asked as she took a seat on the edge of her bed.

"We'll be meeting our visitors soon. I have some history with them, if they turn out to be who we think they are. They can help us or leave us high and dry." She tied a light blue sash around her waist, "I can't have them smelling trouble I don't know about on my boat. I have to know what goes on under my nose, the good and the bad."

Derain smiled quizzically, "Yeah, of course. I can understand that. What do you need from me?"

She stared at him with a bit of concern in her eyes, "I need to know how you conned Rabbit."

"Conned him how? What do you mean?" he asked as he leaned against the wall.

"The man does stupid things, but he's not crazy."

Derain laughed, "Are you sure about that?"

She smiled in return, then grew serious, "What do you have on him that made him jump the Matilda inside that man-o-war?"

Jon Gray Lang

"You sure you want to play this?"

At her nod, he replied, "He owed me."

Jacquie sighed as she stood up and threw her vest on, "And you gave him no choice?"

Derain's shoulders straightened and his voice turned glum, "I didn't. And before you ask, I would do it again."

"You'd drag him into this even looking back at it? Were all those lives worth it?"

Anger creased his face as his hands curled into fists, but he didn't move an inch. His voice came out hard and cold, "Those lives, as you call them, destroyed my family all to track me down. And you want to know why? All so they could catch their little genorg pet that you took on board. And I'm not saying you didn't make the right choice in regards to Galena, but my family suffered the cost of that decision. So don't begrudge me mine."

"Only some of those people did that to you, Derain. Not all of them," she rebutted.

"Like that pirate crew you spaced? Were they all responsible for the deaths of your parents?" He turned the handle to the hatch and stepped out into the hall, "You should look in the mirror before you cast that accusation, Jacq. I'm not the only one who's willing to take it too far."

She shrank back as the hatch to her room clanged shut, "What is happening to us?"

***

Jon Gray Lang

A long habitat cylinder was pulled slowly toward the Matilda by two shuttles. Luli watched from the bridge viewport until they disappeared from view. She opened up the ship's comm, "Hey Jacq, our visitors should be locking onto the airlock soon."

"Got it, Lu," replied Jacquie. "Go ahead and make your way down here. They're going to want to meet you."

"On my way down now." Luli pulled the plug from the back of her skull and settled back into the chair. Her hands twirled one memory core in particular that hung around her neck and clinked it against the others. "Come on Vijay, let's go meet the D'ziageno. They're more of a legend than we are."

***

Jacquie seemed antsy as she waited at the airlock. The cargo bay rang with clanks as the tunnel locks engaged. As the lift settled onto the decking, Luli stepped out. She made her way over to Derain. Jacquie looked back and smiled. Anton and Barney chatted together while Luli draped an arm over Derain's shoulder and leaned into him.

She felt hesitant to break the camaraderie, but it was better to be prepared. "I need everyone to line up and be fully visible, alright? Keep your hands open and empty. They can be reticent and not very trusting."

There was a heavy knock on the airlock and

Jacquie strode over to open it. The inner hatchway opened and in marched a bizarrely garbed trio. A stocky woman marched forward and planted her feet heavily against the deck. To her left was a heavily built man who easily stood taller than Derain. Slowly, a motorized chair rolled into the cargo bay in which an old man who appeared to be asleep was seated.

"Here arrives the Clan Father of Baptiste," announced the stocky woman. "Pay your obeisances!"

Jacquie stepped forward and bowed to each of the Clan Father's guardians. She made her way forward and took the old man's hands. She brought his fingers to her lips and kissed each one with reverence.

"Clan Father, these are my people," she said as she pointed out her crew. "Barnabus de Lagnel of the Titan home world. Luli Qing, who is one of the deep spacers that paved the pathways here. Anton Roane, who fought for all the peoples of the systems on the surfaces of other worlds. And Derain Tiwi, hunter of those who have done wrong. Though you may not remember, I am Jacquotte Delahaye, named after my great-great-grandmother of the clan. I captain the Matilda, though she flies no more."

Derain leaned over and whispered into Anton's ear, "Why did she list you before me?"

"Rules of a clan greeting are oldest members first, but they really mean whoever has been with the family longest."

"Ja... Jacquotte? Of the Matilda?" muttered the old man. His eyes lit up with happy recognition and glowed with intelligence. "You... I know you... though you were small the last time I saw..."

A pleased expression beamed from Jacquie's face. "You do remember me? I will never forget you, my paw-paw."

"Give me a hug, young traveler," he cried as he slowly rose from his chair. Old as he was, he was still an imposing man. Jacquie stepped toward him and he clasped her in a big bear hug. "Aah, lost daughter. It is good to have you home."

***

The Clan Father's habitat detached from the Matilda and was pulled away from the hangar when Barney gave the signal to the Waratah and the Cyclops. Two long lines were attached to each of the smaller ships from anchor points built into the hull of the Matilda. Barney closed the hangar doors and headed to the airlock chamber.

Both ships slowly increased their momentum until the cables stretched tautly. Within a few minutes, the Matilda began to lumber its way after the towed habitat.

Derain's voice came over the comm, "Any idea how far we have to go, Jacq?"

"I can't imagine it's too far," added Anton. "Dragging a habitat can't be the most efficient way to get around."

"That's how the clans mostly travel," added Jacquie as she had the Matilda extrapolate their trajectory. "They have some larger ships, but most of the people live in the 'habs'."

"They're chasing that comet, aren't they?" asked Anton.

Jacquie was silent for a moment, "The clan is on the hunt and we will all have to participate in the practice. Even though I have been recognized as family, help doesn't come for free."

twenty-four

Guns for Hands

First Officer Ghilzai headed the column that made its way down the boarding tunnel from the Peking Empress. He could see Captain Kaur waiting patiently for them at the dock of station S-3465.

"No longer the Captain now, I guess," he grinned. "More like Pirate Captain Harjeet Kaur."

Latiff Ghilzai nodded at the statuesque woman who stood front and center faced by a line of armed security personnel. He took up position to her left as Petty Officer Vadik moved to her right. The rest of the bridge crew lined up alongside them. A tenseness filled the air as each of them was checked for weapons.

The officer in command of the security force indicated a passageway to the right, "Please follow me to the waiting area. We will have a shuttle ready to take you home within thirteen hours."

Jon Gray Lang

"Any chance of a beverage while we wait?" asked Harjeet.

The officer shook his head and walked down the passageway he had indicated.

"I wasn't that thirsty anyway," she muttered.

As they followed the officer toward the right passageway, one of the security personnel ran up to him, "Sir! Sir! We are getting multiple life sign readings from the docked craft."

The Officer instantly pulled his sidearm, turned and aimed it at the heart of Harjeet, "Arrest these people immediately!"

Petty Officer Vadik grinned as she tackled the Officer and shouldered him directly into the wall behind. "By Tom, I've been itching for a fight!"

***

Captain Kaur yanked the pistol out of the hands of the man nearest her. Vadik cackled as she slammed her fist repeatedly into the man's face. Latiff charged into the line as the security forces scrambled to bring their weapons up to bear. He was quickly followed by the remainder of the Empress' crew and the fight became hand to hand.

Harjeet cycled the pistol through the round sitting in the chamber and it exploded into plastic fragments against the armor of a security person. "Damn flechette rounds!" she cursed.

Within moments, she had almost emptied the hundred round clip into the ranks of security personnel. Luckily, some of the rounds splintered in between the crevices of the armor and pierced through the skin underneath.

A handful of the guards had enough time to drop back and bring up their weapons. As they depressed the triggers, more flechette rounds spewed into the battle. Screams of pain erupted amongst her crew. As the security team prepared another volley into the crew, a crowd of heavily armed mercenaries charged down the ramp from the Peking Empress.

"Took your damn time getting down here!" Harjeet cried. As the last round slithered its way down the barrel, the pistol flew from her hand and smacked into the helmet of one of the guards. Ovi saw the opening and wrestled him to the ground.

Commander Etsiddy led the charge and laughed as he shot one of the security guards in the chest, "It is always best to arrive in the nick of time!"

Harjeet just shook her head, then grappled a security man as he tried to run past her. "Always talking bigger than your britches, aren't you, you big bastard."

"Jong! Catch that one!" The big man laughed, "Always, Harjeet, always!"

An even bigger woman tore past Commander Etsiddy and tackled the runner to the ground. The remainder of the security personnel were quickly apprehended. More mercenaries bolted out of the boarding tunnel and dispersed into the corridors.

"And that's how you subdue someone!" cried

Petty Officer Vadik as she slammed the last standing security guard to the decking. "All right, Cap, where to next?"

Harjeet studied her petty officer in amusement. "Etsiddy, get those command crews to their new ships or this whole mission is going to hell in a handbasket." She nodded as he threw her a salute, then charged after his team and deeper into the station. "As for you, Ghilzai, make sure the rest of our passengers are out of stasis. We need to get out of here as soon as we can."

"Aye, aye Captain," shouted Ghilzai.

Harjeet's hands settled on her hips as she gazed at Vadik, "As for us, we keep the Empress ready to launch!"

Petty Officer Vadik laughed as she saluted, "It'll be good to have a ship of our own again, Captain Kaur!"

"Won't it though."

***

Rex walked out of the Peking Empress hold and down the long airlock tunnel to the station. He spotted Captain Kaur standing with her hands on her hips in the open on the station decking.

"How goes the plan, Captain?" he asked.

Her lips curled at his arrival. "As well as such a harebrained scheme can go. The ship crews are headed to the vessels that you brought them to steal."

"And Etsiddy?"

Harjeet laughed abruptly and loudly, "That giant maniac and his team are leading the charge. But if I know him, he's probably sowing this station with bombs as we speak."

At his relatively pleased expression, she shot back, "You hired that madman to blow this station to kingdom come? Are you crazy?"

Rex gazed at her, "I always hire the best."

"You lunatic!" Harjeet grabbed her comm and yelled into it, "Everybody, get a move on! This job has a shorter time limit than we thought!"

***

Once Ariel and Mr. Leon met up with Mr. Faragoi at the tunnel entrance, the Copperhead's comm went off, "Captain? The two tailing fighters have peeled off and are headed toward the asteroid belt."

Mr. Leon just smiled up at the Captain as she responded, "Thank you, Ms. Geist." She looked over at Reynard, "Did you bring up the crates for the station?"

He indicated the seven crates stacked near the hatchway.

"Excellent. Well, let's get this over with," she responded, stepping into the tunnel.

Mr. Leon followed her as a handful of other crewmen grabbed the crates and entered the passageway. The tunnel ended at an open hatchway into the station. Facing them was a single officer and five guards. As Captain Kahn stepped up to the security team, her people stacked the crates in two piles in front of the soldiers.

Captain Kahn stuck out her hand to the officer and said, "Good day, sir. I am Captain Ariel Kahn of the Copperhead. And you are?"

The officer ignored her and watched as her people disappeared back inside the tunnel. He walked over to the crates and wiped a finger against the one on top. He inspected the seals for tampering and besides a light marring, they were intact. The officer straightened up and tucked his arms behind his back.

Mr. Leon stepped up to the officer and proffered the shipping manifest, "Please sign here to indicate that you've accepted the delivery." He leaned in and gave the officer a sly wink, "If you look in the crate marked in orange, you'll find that special addition that you requested.

The officer looked down at the somewhat shorter man and distaste was writ large across his face. He turned away from Mr. Leon. Ariel stifled a small laugh behind her hand as Mr. Leon angled his way back into the man's view.

Mr. Leon smiled ingratiatingly at the officer. He indicated the crate with the orange markings, "The twenty-year-old whiskey would be in this one, sir. And I must say, it did take a long while to track down a bottle of that particular distillery. It seems to have sold out in just about every system. I had to contact a collector for it and it cost me more than I had bargained for." Mr. Leon simpered up at the man, "Your gain and my loss."

The officer sneered, "I am afraid you have the wrong person."

"Oh, well my apologies," replied Mr. Leon. "If you could sign off on the manifest, we'll be on our way."

As the officer begrudgingly signed the manifest, he turned away from the crew of the Copperhead. Mr. Leon gave the man a slight bow and made his way back to the airlock tunnel. Captain Kahn followed after and almost ran over Mr. Leon's acolyte, Mr. Hau, just inside the tunnel. He seemed to be counting silently to himself with a smug grin on his face.

Mr. Leon spoke into the shimmering air that filled the tunnel, "Omega, make sure none of them escape. Once you hear the signal, cut external comms." He turned to Ariel, "Captain? Would you follow me?"

"I know this isn't a routine delivery, Mr. Leon, but what do you have up your sleeve?" she asked as she followed him back onto the Copperhead.

Suddenly, an explosion tore through the crates that Reynard and his fellows had stacked up at the entrance. Ariel looked over her shoulder and watched as a row of shimmering blurs exited the tunnel followed quickly by the rattle of gunfire. She distinctly heard Omega's voice issuing commands.

"Thank you for setting up the package, Mr.

Hau."

Hung bowed, "Glad to be of service. You know how much I like surprises."

"What have you dragged me into, Mr. Leon?"

Mr. Leon waved her back to the Copperhead, "Just a little thievery, my friend. We are going to liberate some of these FTL-capable destroyers."

Ariel Kahn stopped at the hatch to her ship in shock, "We are? Whatever for? How?"

Mr. Leon grinned up at her, "What else would I do with a hold full of soldiers, Captain?" He shook his head lightly, "Never mind the fact that my other ship has at its disposal many crews that are looking for ships to command."

"But why?"

The echo of gunfire receded into the distance, but it didn't abate whatsoever.

Mr. Leon scratched at his chin. "Why? For the cause, Captain. For our mighty cause."

twenty-five

Cowboy

Omega and her squad carefully walked down the corridor. The explosion had blackened the walls and left the security team in a state of confusion. Some of them wandered aimlessly through the wreckage calling for their friends. Before they even knew what hit them, the shimmering forms of genorgs wandered through the smoke like ghosts.

"Jamming their comms," a genorg whispered.

"We're under attack!" shouted one of the soldiers before the impact of a rifle shot sent her spinning like a top.

"Run!" screamed another.

The remainder of the security forces took off down the corridor from which they had come.

"To me!" ordered Omega as she broke into a lope. Her optical camo held as she ran through the cloud of smoke, followed quickly by the other genorg soldiers. As she kept pace with the security personnel, one of them fired blindly over her shoulder at them. It was a wasted shot.

As they went further into the shipyard station, Omega passed a shaft leading off to the left. "Xi-53, take your squad and cut the external comms!" she ordered.

"Understood!" shouted the genorg as six shimmering forms shot off to the left.

Omega and her team continued straight down the hallway. A round ripped by from behind and slammed into the back of a straggler. Suddenly, the lights glared and a siren began squalling.

"Alarms tripped!" shouted Omega. "Come on, soldiers. Time to get this done!"

***

Siede Geist flagged down Ariel, "Captain, those escort fighters are circling back this way."

Mr. Leon scowled, "The ruse is up, folks. Now we're in it for the long haul."

Captain Kahn hopped into the seat at the weapons console and secured her safety belt. "Make the announcement. Siew-Lian, pull away from the station. Siede, notify the Empress."

Siede opened the ship-wide comm, "Prep for battle people. We have two incoming."

"We just need to keep them focused on us," muttered Mr. Leon. "The mission is to get those destroyers out of here."

Jon Gray Lang

Do you have something planned for those fighters?"

Mr. Leon just glanced back at him.

"Oh," Hung laughed nervously, "Of course, you do."

***

The hangar bay doors of the Peking Empress swung open to empty space. The Independence slipped free of the hangar and headed toward the circling fighters. The ex-pirate ship spun on its axis and the thrust from its engines lit up the darkness.

On the bridge, Rosa Keri grinned like a wolf when she spotted the two fighters arcing their way back to the station. "Get those coil guns prepped, Alice! We've got fish to fry!"

Alice stared blankly and shrugged in confusion. She cycled the weapon's computer through its paces, "Coils are prepped, Commander. What do fish have to do with it?"

That grin didn't leave Rosa's face. She had studied the configuration of this boat from every angle and knew exactly what it had been re-purposed for. "That pirate Captain must've been a fool to lose her to the Matilda."

"What was that, Commander?" asked Alice.

"Nothing Alice," she answered. "You have that long-range missile lined up?"

"Yes, Commander."

"Send it on its way and bury it deep."

Jon Gray Lang

"Missile away, sir."

Rosa couldn't get over it. The engines on this boat were overpowered. Whatever lunatic had put in over-sized sublight engines had only thought about outpacing their quarry before lighting it up with the sheer number of weaponry on board.

"Launch one of the small rockets at them, Alice. We need to catch their attention."

The afterburner of a rocket arced its way toward two fighters. They split out from each other when it came in range and swung toward the aggressor near the space station.

Carla spoke from the comm station, "Getting chatter from two more fighters on the solar side of the station."

"Got it, Carla," replied Rosa. "Notify the Scorpio to cover our backs."

"On it, Commander." Carla sent a direct beam comm to the Peking Empress with a request for assistance. Minutes later, the Scorpio slipped out of the hangar bay of the Peking Empress.

The old mining ship's attitude jets sparked and the brute of a craft rose slowly up above the station. The two fighters from the far side of the station swung out to follow the moving vessel. Rosa kept an eye on their allied ship until it was directly in the path of the two fighters.

"They're on it," Carla stated.

"We've been lucky so far, sisters," Rosa called out. "Only four small fighters and communications still appear to be jammed."

A small burst of light blossomed off starboard and Carla growled, "Confounder is down. Radio comms are back up, Commander."

"Guess I spoke too soon," grunted Rosa. "Have they tried sending a comm to the jump gate personnel?"

Silence reigned supreme before Carla replied, "Comm chatter seems to only be directed at the shipyard station."

***

The Copperhead pulled away from the shipyard. Siew Lian fired the attitude jets and the freighter rotated to port as it flew over Station S-3465.

"They took out the confounder," said Siede. "External comms are live."

"What's out there?" asked the Captain.

The nav holo bubbled up from the table and the shipyard station took up a large portion of the view. The Peking Empress was still connected to the station dock while the two merchant ships exited its Ro-Ro bays. Hovering on the outer edge of the scan were four smaller craft making a beeline for the other vessels.

"We need to protect the Empress, Captain," said Mr. Leon. "She's our ticket out of here."

"You heard the man, protect the Empress." Captain Kahn settled against the weapons console, "I'll take weapons. Siew Lian, you keep us aloft."

"On it, Captain."

Mr. Leon glanced over at Hau Hung who looked pale. "You are sure the package is out there?"

"As sure as I can be," replied Hung.

Mr. Leon nodded and his gaze swung back to the bow port of the Copperhead.

Captain Kahn was surprised to see so much stress on Mr. Leon's face. She had never observed the man to be anything but cool as a hydro-vegetable.

Her mind took a detour as she struggled with the fruit, "...watermelon?"

"What was that?" the man asked with a bemused expression.

Now he looked as placid as a lake. Ariel murmured, "Just trying to remember the name of a water plant. Is all well, Mr. Leon?"

His gaze swept toward the bow port, "Just waiting on our distraction. I dislike waiting for things out of my control."

Suddenly, nonsense chatter exploded over the comms.

Mr. Leon tapped his curled fist against the bulkhead, "There it is." He smiled at Ariel, "Like clockwork. It is the waiting for the gear teeth to click that I detest."

Captain Kahn walked over to her comm officer, "Siede, can you see if you can find our contact on the station and the location of her team. We're running out of time and need to get a move on."

***

Delta stood in front of the ruins of the hatch to the command center. Rex had been right. The Consortium commander of the station had been a paranoid man. He kept all the construction crews under lock and key in the lower levels of the station. Besides a handful of security teams roaming the upper decks, the station had been nearly empty.

She stepped into the command center as Rho-11 rigged the small explosives for the ready room door.

Rho-11 stepped back and shouted, "All clear?"

Once she heard the response "All clear" from everyone, she shouted, "Fire in the hole!"

With a loud burst, the door shattered into splinters. Three genorg troops rushed through the fragments to surround the commander they sought. Delta strolled over to the cowering man as he hid behind what little was left of his desk.

"Well, well, well," she grinned. "Exactly the person I needed to find. I am in need of the access codes for... what did he call them? Oh yes, that string of black pearls out there."

The man just pointed to a lockbox built into the wall of the room. He went back to cowering under the bristle of weapons pointed in his direction. A tsk escaped Delta as she waved Rho-11 over to the safe.

"You've got this?" she asked.

The genorg nodded and clapped a digital breaker against the surface. Within a minute, there was an audible click and the door swung open.

The panicked commander looked up at the click and shouted, "No, wait!"

Rho-11 waved a scanner over the opening, but made no move toward it. A warning beep echoed in the ready room before it changed to a high-pitched whine.

Sparks and smoke poured out of the safe as Rho-11 just glared at the man, "This isn't our first bullfight, mister."

Delta smirked at her sister, "Where'd you learn that one?"

Rho-11 laughed as she pulled out a stack of data cards from the opening, "From the dancer on the Matilda. She always had a funny way with words."

Delta's comm chirped. She stepped out into the main room of the command center and looked on appraisingly. Her people cut off all access from the lower and upper decks to the wings of the station for the completed ships. In fact, Zed-321 was already on the comm channels with the crews of the soon-to-be liberated ships.

She clicked the comm, "Delta here."

Siede's voice echoed tinnily from the speaker, "Position and timing?"

"COC and we will be running the data cards

soon. Delta out." She grinned at nothing in particular, "Liberated, yes I like this word. It feels free."

***

Rosa glanced back as nonsense chatter exploded from the comms. "That the signal, Rex?"

At his nod, she threw him a quick salute and kicked the thrusters on. The two fighters wobbled in response to the noise, but strayed back into the path of the Independence. Rosa barked, "Alice, rockets away!"

The deck rumbled as the starboard missile left its tube and arced out toward the two ships. Moments later the port tube launched its payload and its afterburner blazed after its twin. Rosa kicked the port side attitude jets and the Independence pushed hard to clear its path. The two fighters swung out in separate arcs to avoid the two missiles then swerved back in, headed toward the Independence. Two fiery explosions lit up the asteroid belt.

"Damn it! Must've hit a gas pocket or something!" yelled Rosa. "The jump gate must have seen that burst. We're going to have company!"

***

A small fighter flew past the nose of the Scorpio and it arced its way into a wide angle. The

Scorpio kept lumbering forward on its course into space.

Tau-SA43 commented, "Gamma, Copperhead says to expect heavier ships en route."

Nu-M12 cycled the weapons to live and nodded in agreement. Gamma pushed on the ship's controls; the old mining craft dropped its nose and rolled to port. She looked up and calculated their position based on what she could see.

"The Scorpio's a weird boat," Gamma muttered. She hadn't had much training on other vessels and this one wasn't like the others. It was older than the Independence and simpler than the Matilda. The nav station was tied directly into the pilot's console. The only other stations were weapons and comms.

The ship was slow and its armaments were only meant for close range. Its main compensation was that the entire bridge was made out of industrial-grade, armored plas-glass. It sat on the front end of the ship like a dimple. All of the short-range cannons bristled outward around it. The only weapons not on the nose of the craft were the manual belly guns.

Gamma looked up and tracked the fighter. "We need them to come in closer. A lot closer."

Nu-M12 was quiet as she poured through their options, "She's built on a defensive platform."

"We have to wait for them, then," groused Gamma.

The ship continued on its slow course until it

swung out broadsided in front of the Empress. One of the fighters swooped in and launched a series of rockets at the Scorpio. The rockets burst harmlessly against the heavy plating.

"This thing is built to handle asteroid fields," laughed Nu-M12. "Your little toys aren't going to penetrate its skin."

"She's still got weaknesses. Drop the dampers to protect the engines," commanded Gamma. "Tell the belly gunners to be on the lookout."

"On it," replied Tau-SA43. She opened the ship-wide comm, "Prep those coil guns, sisters. Don't waste ammo, if you can."

***

Inside the hold of the Scorpio, Moraldi had his back pressed against the bulwark. The rumble of small impacts on the skin of the ship reverberated all the way down to where he stood.

"Those crazy genorgs took my tub into a fight?"

He pasted his ear against the bulkhead and felt more than heard the pitter-patter of small rockets detonating against the hull.

His mouth curled into a dark grin, "Where are you on that lock, Mbuni? Those damn drones have got to be distracted right now. This is our chance."

The dull thunk of the lock plummeting to the floor resounded in the hold.

"All done, sir."

"By the Major, we're taking my ship back!"

***

One fighter pulled in tight and rattled the hull of the Independence with incendiary rounds and launched a guided missile at the flight deck. The automatic defensive gun's chain fired heavy-metal tipped rounds at the missile and it burst apart right in front of the viewport. Little flecks of metal showered the window.

The fighter flew too close to the ship and the defensive guns spun to engage. The little fighter couldn't pull away fast enough; it was riddled with holes and plummeted toward the station.

"One down, Rosa!" cried Alice. "Coil guns locked on secondary target."

Carla looked up from the comm console, "We're being hailed by the local cruiser. They're asking for ident."

"Ignore it for now," commanded Rosa. "Are they moving toward us?"

Carla was quiet for a long time.

"Well?" asked Rosa.

"Both of the capital ships have shifted their flight toward the station," Carla replied.

"Inform the Empress. It's time to tuck tail and run."

***

Moraldi and his crew snuck quietly out of the hold. The ship rang with a cacophony of impact pings and the shouts of orders. The heavy-throated boom of the belly guns echoed down the corridors. Moraldi waved them forward. As they came to a corner, Mbuni ran ahead and threw a sleeper lock on the single genorg guard. She went down quickly and their immediate vicinity was clear.

The ship bucked from a heavy explosion. Moraldi just chuckled. He patted the nearest bulkhead, "My Scorpio can take a pounding. It's what she was built for. Am I right, boys?"

"Right you are, sir," answered Suarez.

Mbuni scouted ahead, but quickly returned, "Couple of groups of them women on the hull guns and then it's clear." He looked at Captain Moraldi, "What's the plan?"

Moraldi bent down and took up the guard's rifle. He threw it to Mbuni and looked him dead in the eye, "We take back my ship, damn it. We take the bridge and then the rest of her.

Suarez's teeth glinted in the low light, "What about the drones?"

"Any that survive, we sell as quick as the mazuma can be flipped," answered Moraldi. "Got enough troubles in my life, don't need to be dealing with this nonsense."

***

Jon Gray Lang

"Independence says they got their two. They also report that the local heavies are making their way here," said Tau-SA43.

"We'll need to pick up the pace then," muttered Gamma.

"The fighter on the port side looks like he's gunning for the bridge!" Tau-SA43 shouted.

"Light it up, Nu," replied Gamma. "I'll keep her running straight."

There was a hush as the fighter changed its trajectory and swung into a flight path heading toward the bubble of the bridge. Gamma kept the Scorpio straight and the fighter made its way closer. A couple of missiles fired off its fuselage, but the little craft kept flying straight at them.

"Almost in range," murmured Nu-M12. "Firing... now!"

A wall of irradiated rounds blasted from the cannon cluster that covered the nose of the Scorpio. The fighter didn't have a chance. It tried to pull up and away, but only shrapnel sliced through its underbelly. The ship disintegrated into fragments and the Scorpio plowed straight through the wreckage.

"Looks like the other fighter is pulling away," Tau-SA43 said. "Head back to the Empress."

"On it," replied Gamma.

Suddenly, the hatch opened and a rifle fired a volley through it, into the bridge. Gamma was hit in the shoulder and she rocked forward in the pilot's chair. Tau-SA43 turned around, but was too slow to avoid a spanner that cracked on her skull. Nu-M12 was yanked from her chair by Iago, who grabbed her gun and pointed it at her.

"Take my ship, will you?" asked Moraldi. "Not my damn ship! Curse you all! Tie them up, Mbuni."

twenty-six

Son of a Preacher Man

It took over three solar days for the Matilda to make the trip to the clan's home. The Cluster, as it was called, was made up of a collection of old ships, habitats, and other canisters rigged together that allowed the group to travel through space while maintaining an atmosphere. Each piece was daisy-chained to the others to form a complex knot that carried with it a standing within the clan and the power related to it.

The Clan Father's habitat was pulled into the center of the Cluster and quickly reconnected to where it normally lay. The Matilda, on the other hand, was moved to the outer edge. Older canisters, some that dated back to the earliest days of colonization, drifted beside the outer edge along with the husks of long-dead vessels with solid hulls.

The Waratah floated closely to one of the

nearest hulks. Derain hopped out of the rear of his troop carrier and unclipped the line to the Matilda from his craft. With a deft move, he turned himself around and ignited his jetpack. The small jets flared briefly as he arced his way out toward the pitted and ancient bracket that hung from the decaying hulk. He pulled on the loose cable and clipped it onto the hardware. "Cable attached. Heading back now."

"Got it," answered Anton.

The Cyclops made its way toward another canister and edged just past it. Anton popped out and detached the cable from the yacht. He floated over and snapped the cable into place. "Matilda is linked."

"Good to hear," answered Jacquie. "Come back in. We've been summoned to the core. Suit up to look fancy, but not too fancy. Oh, and Derain, no weapons."

"What? I'm not always armed..." grumbled Derain.

Luli glanced sidewise at the bounty hunter, "Try not to blow them up, would you? It's hard to make friends with the dead."

***

The core of the Cluster was more space station than ship. The long fuselage was dotted with modules placed in what seemed incongruent places. Expanded tunnels had been left attached between some of the larger sections and shielding had been built up to protect many of them.

"Strange way to get around," muttered Derain as the Waratah slowly flew past it.

"The Cluster has been traveling for hundreds of years. As the family grows, it grows, too," explained Jacquie.

The hangar bay doors lay open on the central ship of the Cluster. The Waratah flew in and landed in the expansive bay. Shuttles and other small craft flew in after them. A large number of them already covered the decking.

The hangar doors stayed open as the hatch on the Waratah opened up. A guideline had been run out for safety since the gravity was light. Jacquie clicked a small line from the belt of her spacesuit to the guideline and waited while the rest of her crew did the same.

They walked into the open airlock and unhooked from the end of the cable. The airlock hatch closed behind them with a whump. Breathable atmosphere slowly filled the compartment in a steady stream. Once the light panel turned from red to green, Jacquie's crew undressed in the open area. They hung their suits on the remaining hooks. Jacquie ran her fingers through her hair and gave Anton the eye.

"You be on your best behavior. Got it?"

Anton zipped a finger across his lips, "I will keep my mouth shut, Captain. I promise."

"Good. Same goes for the rest of you." Jacquie gave each of them the evil eye then knocked on the inner hatch.

The hatch swung open and Jacquie and the crew stepped out. A long dim hallway lay ahead. Every few meters there stood an armed individual on either side. They were a mix of genders, but every one of them was of an imposing stature or build. An older woman stood near the airlock control panel. She stepped forward and bowed slightly. Jacquie bowed deeply to her. The woman draped a long and decorative stole around the Captain's neck.

"The Clan Mothers await you inside," atoned the woman as she stepped back.

As Jacquie moved forward, Barney took Luli's arm and they followed her. Anton reached out his hand and grasped Derain's. Derain shook him off and glared at him. Anton hid his amusement behind his hand.

The five of them proceeded down the hallway and past the armed guards. They passed through large ornate doors at the end into an elaborately ornamented ballroom.

Ancient glory still shown throughout the chamber. Old chandeliers winked in the light from the vaulted ceilings. Beautifully decorated tile covered the floor and intricately carved wood paneling covered the walls. Massive pillars reached up from the floor and held onto an upper deck that encircled the entire room.

At the far end lay a raised dais surrounded by long scarlet curtains. As Jacquie made her way toward the stage, faces stared down from the upper deck and marked her progress. Members of the D'ziageno slowly filled in the room on all sides. Each of them studied the crew of the Matilda as they walked by.

***

Derain looked around at the crowd, but no one made eye contact. He leaned over to Anton, "Do they seem judgy to you?"

"Still feeling that sting from Luli?" Anton grinned. "Well, they are a very private people. They rarely let non-family inside as most deals are made on the ships and stations of others. This is a once-in-a-lifetime experience."

Derain nodded in understanding, but wished he had the comforting weight of a pistol at his side. Not to mention his boot knife. He listened in as Barney and Luli pointed out various things in the ballroom that they either recognized or had heard of. He also kept an eye out for an exit strategy.

When Jacquie reached the dais, two guards blocked her way. Their armor looked ceremonial, yet functional. Unlike the guards in the hall, each of these wore a decorative crimson sash at the waist.

"Ooh, Guardians of the Mother's Table," murmured Anton. At the bounty hunter's questioning look, Rabbit whispered, "You know the D'ziageno are made up of clans. Well, each branch is headed up by a matriarch. The family matriarchs vote one of their number into the position called the All-Mother. They act as the de facto head of the table and can overrule all. There can be a lot of infighting amongst the family heads. You know, based on salvage rights, hunting quota, food, and water rationing, and such."

Derain nodded in understanding as he noticed each of the guards bore a well-used assortment of weapons.

Anton continued, "So the clans needed an impartial group to enforce the peace, as it were. And that's the Mother's Table Guardians. I'm sure you noticed the guards near the airlock each wore different colored sashes to represent their clans. As you can see, the Guardians are the only ones allowed to wear the red."

Derain stared at the two people in front of Jacquie and noticed others in strategic locations wearing the red sash. "Red, huh?"

Anton nudged him in the side, "It means, to keep the blood. You know, inside of the body."

"How do you know all this? Why do you know all this?" Derain asked perplexed.

"My dad used to tell me stories about them when I was little," he answered. "I think he ran with some exiles before I came along and they must've made quite an impression. When I found out that Jacq was part of a clan, I badgered the hell out of her for more information on them."

Anton looked up into Derain's eyes, "Listen," he said in a hushed tone, "They don't meet a lot of people way out here. I should warn you that they'll probably want some of our DNA to keep their genetic stock diverse."

Shock made Derain stare at Rabbit, "What?"

Anton continued, "They might go about it the old-fashioned way or the scientific method. Now shush, the ceremony is about to start."

The curtains opened and revealed a large round table. Seated around the table were women adorned in decorative colored fabrics, heavy jewelry, and odd bits of tech. The women ranged from middle-aged to grandmotherly. One of the red-sashed guards stood behind each chair. Two of the guards stood behind the center chair and the woman in that chair was easily the oldest at the table. But her eyes burned bright with intelligence.

"There are only eighteen clans in total?" asked Derain.

Anton replied, "In this Cluster, yes. There are other ship clusters out there, though. And each of those clan heads represents huge families. You can kind of get a feel for it, if you look around. Each of the families incorporates their clan color into their garb."

Derain studied one of the women on the dais then looked through the crowds at those wearing yellow. The sheer number took his breath away. He glanced at the stage and noticed a woman wearing a familiar hue of blue. His eyes traveled back to the Captain and he saw the same color on her, "So, that's why Jacquie wears that shade of blue all the time. I thought it was just because she liked it."

"Crazy, right?" answered Anton before he felt the sharp jab of an elbow.

"Shut it, you two," Barney whispered.

The woman at the head of the table rapped her cane against the tabletop and the chit-chat throughout the ballroom died down.

"Let's bring this to order. I'm not getting any bloody younger," ordered the table head. She gestured with her cane at Jacquie, "You, young lady. Step forward and explain yourself."

Jacquie looked up in concern and took a step forward, " I am Jacquotte Delahaye, lost daughter of the Clan Baptiste..."

"Yes, yes I can see that," grimaced the old woman. "But why are you here?"

"Umm," Jacquie stumbled. "My ship is dead and we..."

The old woman rolled her eyes and rapped her cane against the table three times. "Tell us something we don't already know, if you please.

Jacquie's eyes grew wide at the woman's shortness, "My apologies, your..."

"Just answer me this and make it quick," bellowed the All-Mother of the Clan Mothers. "What do you want from us?"

In a rush, Jacquie blathered out, "Can you help us get our ship running or drop us off somewhere that can?"

"Yes to dropping you off," muttered the woman at the head table. "See your own Clan

Mother for other assistance. Meeting adjourned!" she cried as she banged her cane rapidly against the tabletop.

The scarlet curtains quickly closed and the populace began to head back out to their ships. Two of the red sashed guards approached Jacquie and her crew and a couple of guards wearing the pale blue sash arrived behind them.

One of the crimson-sashed guards beckoned to Luli, "The All-Mother of Clan Mothers wants to speak with you. She is not a patient woman. Please make your way forward."

Luli looked back and Jacquie pushed her toward them, "Go! It's a once-in-a-lifetime experience! See if you can warm things over for us."

"What about you guys?" she replied.

Anton threw a thumbs-up, "We've got our own thing to attend to."

"If you would come this way, please," stated the larger of the two blue sashed guards.

Jacquie nodded and followed after them with Anton and the rest in tow. Derain looked back, though and watched Luli disappear into the crowd.

***

"Let's go meet the All-Mother," Luli said as she walked behind the red-sashed woman. She picked up her pace to match the woman's stride and tapped her on the shoulder, "I'm Luli Qing. Could I ask who you are?"

"You may call me Daniela and he is Antony," the woman replied. "We must hurry as it is bad for us to leave her waiting."

Antony nodded as they all hurried past the dais and into the hall behind it. The three of them moved quickly down the hallway. When people saw the red sashes, they stepped aside to clear a path. In a short distance, Antony slowed down and knocked on the door of an unmarked room.

Luli patted her hair to smooth it, but was careful not to stress any of her fingers in the process. There was a second knocking pattern on the door to which Antony tapped out a staccato rhythm in reply. The door opened and a young girl, maybe twelve or thirteen, stood there. She gazed frankly at the cyborg with a small frown on her lips.

"You're a deep spacer?" she asked.

Luli blinked a moment before she replied, "Yes. Yes, I am."

"I thought you'd look a lot older," the young girl replied as she moved out of the way. "Come through, please, and take the first left. Grandmother will be in the second room."

Luli nodded and walked in. Behind her, the girl confronted the two guards and dismissed them, "Grandmother says she doesn't need you. Go stand guard in the hallway or something."

"But what about her safety?" asked Antony.

The girl put her hands on her hips, "Not your concern. Now shoo! Shoo."

Luli found the first left and took the turn.

The walls displayed an old world glory. A plaster-like substance ran the entire length and was separated by wood trim. Paintings of old earth decorated the walls every few meters. Carpet that had once been plush, but now had a valley carved into it by footsteps, covered the floor. She stopped next to the open door of the second room.

An old woman's voice called out, "Come in and shut the door behind you. My great-granddaughter is a nosy one."

"I heard that, grandmother," said the young girl as she waved the cyborg through the doorway.

Luli laughed, walked into the room and slid the door shut behind her. She found herself in a room half as large as the lounge on the Matilda. Ensconced in a high-backed chair sat the All-Mother of the Cluster, who moved two long needles back and forth in a mesmerizing pattern. It took Luli a moment to realize what it was she was doing.

"You're knitting."

The old woman smiled, "I am at that, though it is an activity I have little skill for." She set the project to the side, "It helps me to relax. Now, Ms. Luli Qing, I have long looked forward to talking with a deep spacer, but I never thought I'd have the chance. And then you arrive! But from the way you hold yourself, it looks like you need to talk to someone else as well."

"What do you mean, All-Mother?"

The old woman sighed, "Please sit, please sit. And you can call me Lucia. Pomp and titles are for the males."

Lucia waited until Luli slid into a soft wingback chair. "You wear your troubles on your brow like a crown and leave them there to shine. What is troubling you?"

"I don't think anything is troubling me..."

"Tut, tut woman. Why do your people treat you as if you're made of glass? Except for the little one. That one seems to be cross with you."

Luli stared blankly at the portable heat source rigged into the center of the room. "How would you know... How can you tell?" She shook herself, "It's a very private matter and I don't know if I want to share."

"Who better to share it with than a complete stranger? Especially one who doesn't have many circulations left to her?" chuckled Lucia. "Come on, out with it, girl."

Luli's hands curled into fists and pain pulsed up her arms. As she relaxed her fingers, she released the breath she didn't realize she had been holding in. "Can I have your promise that anything I say won't leave this room?"

"Nothing said leaves this room. By the devil Tom, I barely leave this room. Ha!" Lucia cackled for a moment before she peered at the necklace of memory cores that adorned Luli's neck. "What are those little tubes around your throat?"

Luli's scarred hands reached up and stroked one of the cores, "These? These are... these are all that I have left of my fellow deep spacers. My oldest friends."

Lucia sighed, "So the rumors are true, then. None live but you. Yes, yes, news travels even to out here." She looked up into Luli's eyes, "What are they to you, though?"

Luli cleared her throat and straightened her back. Her voice took on a matter-of-fact tone, "I'm not sure how much you know about us deep spacers. Each of us was augmented, rebuilt in a way, into a being that could handle the long journeys out from the home system of Sol. Part of that rebuild created a digital backup of our thoughts, our dreams... our memories. Each of these cores contains the memories of a deep spacer." Her hand fell back into her lap as she closed her eyes, "Sometimes, I connect to them and live in their minds as they go about their last days."

"I can understand wanting to see old friends, I truly do," murmured the old woman. "But is it not dangerous?"

"It's more a matter of needing to know why they were killed than wanting to see them again," rebuked Luli. "At least it was at first. I... I've learned things that I hadn't seen when they lived, and realizing what I lost because of that, it torments me."

Lucia smiled and reached out to pat Luli on the leg, "Aah, heartbreaking is the unknown love that was lost. Young lady, the past is a strange place to live. There is always more to learn there, but at the same time, it keeps you from the joys of your life in the present and the possibilities of your future."

"My life," Luli growled as she caressed one of the cores. "What could you possibly know about that?"

"I have had many old friends whisper secrets in my ear before they left this life. More than I care to remember." She smiled sadly, "One that stands out was from an old woman. I had secretly loved her as a young girl, but had been afraid to ever tell her about it. Many years past those early days, she returned from a hunt. She was horribly injured and wanted to speak with me. In her last breath, she told me how she had always loved me and never dared to say a word. As she died in my arms, my heart couldn't let go of the what-ifs? For months afterward, I would play out our possible futures and find myself weeping. I ignored my duties and everyone around me. As patient and understanding as my people were, it still hurt those who depended on me, that still lived and loved me."

"But how did you handle what you had missed out on all because you hadn't seen it?"

"It took time, but in the end, I came to terms with it. I had made my choices, both good and bad, and lived my life. And I still do, though Tom only knows why." She mused, "Maybe in the next life, I will make different choices and live a wholly different story. I did learn from that experience, though. Now, I rarely hold back from letting my feelings be known." Lucia sighed as she rubbed her hands together for warmth, "Did you at least learn why your friends were killed?"

"I know who ordered them dead, but I haven't gone through these memories yet," Luli replied as she held up one certain core. "The others were so beautifully flawed and their lives ended in such pain. I... I am scared to look into his mind. He imprisoned me and stripped me of what's left of my humanity. What if I see something I can't handle?"

"You are as human as you have always been! And will be until the last breath you take! Nothing can take that from you! Never believe otherwise," admonished Lucia.

Luli's eyes widened in surprise and her hands gripped the armrest at the flash of anger from the old woman.

"Fear may keep you safe in the short term, but it doesn't help over the long ride to the end." Lucia's eyes held Luli still, "Face those fears and learn from them. No matter how much it hurts. And you need not face them alone."

***

Anton hummed to himself as he followed Jacquie out of the ballroom. They took the second right into a hallway that was bereft of people. Anton glanced over his shoulder and noticed two more blue-sashed guards coming up from behind.

"Captain, we good?" asked Derain.

Jacquie nodded, but didn't say a word. Barney grunted as he rolled his sleeves up. They kept quiet as they were led deeper into one of the wings of the huge vessel.

Anton wondered aloud, "Where did they find this old liner? She's in great shape considering the age."

A man's voice answered from behind, "She was set to be turned into scrap when our people were being pushed off the core worlds. She was granted to us as a way to leave."

"Given to you? Huh. I always thought the exodus was just an old story," Derain exclaimed.

"The exodus is no story," answered the woman to the right. "Our nomadic lifestyle was found to be incongruous to the values held by the core world governments. They rounded us up, locked us on board, and told us to leave the system. This is the truth for every Clan. The only difference is the starting world."

"Still one hell of a ship to be given to you," Anton said as he admired the beautiful woodwork.

The man to the right behind him chuckled. "The center of our home is a beautiful craft, even though her FTL core and other vital systems were stripped clear of her. The first years of our people were spent keeping the atmosphere in and the sublight engines running."

"Sounds familiar," quipped Barney.

"Never mind that her food stores were light for the sheer number of us," continued the woman to the right.

Jacquie chimed in, "The clan's exodus

continued as they were turned away from each world they traveled to. Some would grant our people supplies, repair materials, or smaller ships. The clans took the hint and kept to their nomadic ways. The outer worlds didn't mind them as traders. Supplies are more important than who brought them."

"Now that sounds familiar..." muttered Anton.

Jacquie continued, "The clans made a subsistent living until they heard the call."

"What call?" asked Barney.

The two guards at the front stopped and nodded at the two guards flanking a door. The door swung open and revealed a dimly lit hallway further in.

"Treat the Clan Mother with all due respect," stated the female guard to the right. "Your honor rides on this, lost daughter."

***

"I have so many questions for you, Ms. Qing," said Lucia. "What was life like in the Sol System in the before? Has humanity changed so much from those days? I know things have changed in the time of my short life compared to yours, but at the same time, it all seems familiar."

Luli reflected for a moment, "My life in the Sol System was much simpler than it is now. Each day was filled with transporting ore from the mines to the refinery and enjoying my time with friends and family. But you're right, it isn't that different these days. I still transport cargo from one place to another. The people in my family have changed, but my days are still spent with them in everyday activities."

Lucia grinned, "The normalcy of it keeps the insanity of the dark moments in check. I feel the same."

"It does," Luli contemplated. "Maybe I have been ignoring them and didn't realize it."

Lucia gazed at the cyborg as she gave deeper thought to her conclusion. Some of the worry lines that had etched her deceptively young-looking face disappeared.

Slowly, Luli looked up and took one of the All-Mother's hands, "Thank you, Lucia. It feels like a weight has been lifted from me. I didn't know I needed to talk to someone about this. I can't thank you enough."

"Then I would ask a boon of you, Ms. Qing."

The smile on Luli's face broadened, "Anything. I feel that I owe you."

Lucia settled back into her chair, "We will be making port in a few weeks and we must increase our stock of Dsup medical supplies before we arrive. We are preparing for one last hunt."

Luli's brow wrinkled, "What can I do?"

Lucia rolled her eyes, "The males and their pomp. The Clan Fathers and the hunters will be leaving soon in their small ships and they always want a big party when they come back."

Luli's eyes dimmed.

"We have heard wondrous things about the deep spacers and the music they remember of our forebears."

Luli muttered, "I can no longer play..."

Lucia continued as if she hadn't been interrupted, "Songs rich in the history of the peoples from the Sol System."

"I hate to disappoint, but I will have to turn you down, All-Mother," replied Luli.

"You will do anything but that?"

"I cannot play anymore." Luli held up her hands and put the bruised scars on full display. "My hands are no longer what they were."

"But that is all I will accept from you, deep spacer," growled the old woman. "Is your voice broken?"

"Well no..."

"It's settled then!" cried Lucia. "Many of us can play instruments to accompany you. We need to hear you sing. Please, do not deny my people a story for them to talk of for generations."

Guilt and fear wracked Luli. She thought about being on the stage under the lights for all to see. They would see the damage done to her. They would see that she was not entirely human. Her breath caught in her chest, "Why am I afraid?"

"Do not let anxiety hold you back. I beg you."

Luli gulped at the air and hardened her resolve, "I will sing for you, Lucia though I may quaver at first."

"I could expect no more. Now, shall we confront the curse you bear around your neck together?"

***

Jacquie entered the backroom first and was led to a long couch. The rest of her crew shuffled in and slid over to sit next to her. Facing them was one of the women from the dais. She looked younger than she had initially appeared. The Clan Father they had met earlier sat to her right. The couch was flanked by a young man who flipped a knife in his left hand. On the other end was a girl who must have been his twin. She sat there with a deck of cards splayed on the table and a well-used pistol strapped across her belly under her ample bosom.

"Cousin," announced the Clan Mother. "It has been too long since we last met."

Jacquie peered into the woman's face, "Salome? Is that really you?"

"It is!" she laughed. "I never thought we would see each other again. But once I saw those eyes, I knew it was you."

"Nor I," laughed Jacquie. "You have grown so much since last we met as little girls. And now Clan Mother!"

Clan Father sighed, "She is new to the position with the passing of my wife. Though my

Jon Gray Lang

niece has learned quickly."

"All because of your teaching, grand uncle," she replied. "Otherwise, I wouldn't have lasted a day amongst those sharks."

Jacquie looked from one to the other, "Is there trouble between the clans?"

"No more so than usual," replied Salome. "But those with more experience will take everything they can from those without it."

"A hard deal, then."

Salome smirked, "Yes, a hard deal. But rare is the deal that is easy."

"Rare indeed," smiled Jacquie. "Shall we get to it then?"

"Pleasantries afterward," nodded Salome. "Under clan rules, we give you and yours shelter until such time when you can make your leave. How will you compensate the clan in your time of need?"

Jacquie swallowed and clasped her hands together, "Clan Father says there is a hunt coming up soon."

Clan Father nodded and Jacquie continued, "We can take three seats at no cost to the clan. But I need at least two of mine to remain behind to continue repairs for my vessel. Would this blood price suffice?"

Salome's eyes never broke from Jacquie's face, "Three is many for you. Can you afford their loss if the hunt ends poorly?"

Derain whispered to Anton, "What hunt are they talking about?"

"They're hunting for adult zottis on the comet they chase," answered Anton.

"Zottis?" Derain frowned in confusion.

Anton muttered, "Thermozodi? Umm, Water Bears?"

Derain frowned again.

"You know, Tardigrades. They live and feed off the water of the comet."

"Ah. But aren't they microscopic?" asked Derain.

Anton shrugged, "Something about them traveling in low gravity increased their size. They can get up to a meter or a meter and a half in size. They're hunted for their Dsup protein. It's an ingredient in radiation protection."

"The clans haven't been adjusted to handle solar radiation?" Derain uttered.

"Oh, they have," answered Anton. "But there are many in the core worlds who refuse the DNA additions. They considered it unethical and impure."

"And there are others on my home world where the alteration didn't take, so they need the medication to survive in space," Barney added.

Jacquie slowly turned and faced her crew until they sheepishly stopped talking and looked away.

Salome's laughter changed the mood in the room. "Let my daughter read the cards and we will decide on the number of your people then."

Jacquie stuck out her hand and they shook on it, "We will do as the seer says."

The teenage girl closed her eyes and waved

her hand over the deck. The first card pulled was Temperance while the second card was the Six of Swords. The third card was The Magician and completed the line. She placed the fourth card, the Two of Cups above The Magician. The fifth and final card was placed underneath The Magician. It was the Queen of Coins.

The tarot reader looked over the cards and stated, "The journey will be dangerous, but if successful, bounteous. Only two should go, mother."

"Thank you daughter," replied Salome. "Who do you choose, cousin?"

"Count me in," Anton shouted.

Clan Father smiled at Rabbit's exuberance. "Would you join us on the hunt, lost daughter? It would mean much to me and the family."

Jacquie smiled and shook his hand, "I would be honored. She glanced over at her crew, "Barney, will you and Luli work on the Matilda as much as you are able? Derain, can you help them out?"

"Of course."

Jacquie turned back to Salome, "How far out are we from the nearest port?"

"Scrapheap is almost a month out," answered Clan Father.

Salome clapped her hands together, "The deal is made. It is time to celebrate the return of our lost daughter, though she stays for only a short time. Bring forth refreshments!"

A line of heavily laden trays were brought in

and placed around the room. As these bearers stepped back, music began in the distance and drew closer. Dancers followed shortly behind. The front door to the suite opened and more members of the Baptiste clan piled in."

"Come cousin, dance with me!" shouted Salome.

Jacquie leapt up from the couch and grabbed the hand of the Clan Mother. The two of them joined in a dance and were quickly surrounded by other members of their clan.

Derain's brow wrinkled in confusion, "I don't understand. Why didn't Jacquie try to find her clan after her parents were murdered?"

Barney watched as Salome and Jacquie whispered and laughed, "She can't rejoin the clan. She will always be a lost daughter."

"Why is that?" asked Anton.

Barney sighed, "The Matilda met up with her Clan Father when her parents were alive and Jacquie was taken to the Cluster. They offered her a chance to rejoin the clan. But she said no as she would have had to leave her parents behind."

"Why would she need to leave her family behind?" asked Derain.

"Because her mother had refused to rejoin for the same reason years before," answered Barney. "Once the offer is made, your decision holds until your dying day. If Jacquie has children, they would be given the same choice at some point. If they say yes, they would leave with the clan representative on that day and rejoin the clan. If they say no, then they can never rejoin."

At the perturbed expressions, Barney shrugged, "It is their way."

twenty-seven

Bottom of the Deep Blue Sea

Lucia, the All-Mother, turned the lights down low and the room grew dim. She hummed softly to herself while Luli made herself comfortable on the long couch with the age faded upholstery. After the cyborg woman closed her eyes, Lucia shooed her great-granddaughter out of the room.

"My friend, we are alone now. It is now just you and I," whispered Lucia.

Luli's voice quavered, "I still have reservations about doing this."

"What do you fear, deep spacer?" Lucia asked. "You have seen more of the worlds of humanity than any other living being. You have seen the accomplishments and the failures of our species more than any other soul. So, tell me, what do you fear?"

Luli haltingly answered, "I fear seeing myself

in his eyes, in his memories. I don't want to know what he thought of me in those dark moments."

"You speak of your friend turned tormentor Jarl?"

Luli nodded and her fists clenched tight. The skin along the scarring whitened.

"Then why do you do this?" Lucia walked over and held Luli's hands until they relaxed, "What do you hope to learn?"

Luli's gritted her teeth, "I have to understand why. Why did he do what he did?"

"Then look only for those answers and nothing else," Lucia replied. "But there is more. What is it that you truly fear?"

Luli continued to hesitate. The answer came shakily to her lips, "That I'll find out..."

"Yes, what is it you fear to see?"

"That I'm not human. That I never was," Luli whispered. "That I'm only machine."

Lucia squeezed her hand hard enough to make it ache. "Is that all? I can help you with that! Do you fear? Do you love? Do you believe that you are human?"

"I do, yes."

"Ha!" barked Lucia. "Then your fear is allayed. Let's get on with this. I am an old woman and the number of my remaining days left grows short."

***

Jon Gray Lang

Luli closed her eyes and slipped the cylinder into her right palm. She clicked a thin cable into the core and draped it over her shoulder. Then came the feel of static as she clicked the other end of the cable into her own port.

As the interface completed the connection, she saw herself through Jarl's eyes. Beaten and bloodied, but not broken. He read the anger in her face and understood it as acceptance of his fate. The knife plunged into his throat. The remembered pain swallowed her in an intense wave and she did her best to weather it. With a quick twist, the knife's edge severed his spinal cord and everything went black.

"It's not real... it's not real... it's not real..." Luli whispered as she focused through the jagged noise of the cut nerve endings. She cycled back into Jarl's memories to when she was first brought to that husk of a vessel.

The name came to her unbidden from his thoughts, '... *the Polypheme.*'

"Her eye was stolen," echoed the words from his memory. The image of an empty cradle for a huge sphere flickered across her mind.

"A jump engine," she mouthed.

His memories segued back to her tied to the chair. Her form glowed within a halo of golden light. His disappointment and anguish bubbled to the surface, "Am I not the one? Is she the one to bear the message?"

Jon Gray Lang

***

Lucia watched as Luli shook in anger. She held tightly to the cyborg's hands and attempted to calm her, but made no other actions. Eventually, Luli's grip loosened and her breathing grew relaxed.

Lucia's comm lit up and her Doctor's voice came through, "She spiked there for a moment, but she has leveled out."

***

Luli cycled further back through Jarl's memories. She searched for the times when he captured the others, but there were none. Each time his memories only showed his henchmen delivering him the memory cores. She scrolled further back still.

Suddenly, Palba was laughing. They were holding hands and the presence of intense love affected Luli. She looked through Jarl's eyes and recognized the cockpit of the Demetrius. The whorling sides of a wormhole tunnel flashed by the bow viewport. The tunnel twisted and shattered against the fuselage as the Demetrius flowed out into normal space.

"It's exactly where Lady Khanda said it would be!" asserted Palba. "I'm getting a reading from a large object off the starboard side."

Jarl laughed, "She wasn't lying? It's really out there?" His hand slipped inside Palba's, "Let's go

Jon Gray Lang

exploring."

The Demetrius rolled to its starboard side. Far off into the darkness, they could just make out the faint glow of another vessel. As the Demetrius closed the distance, the mystery ship grew more distinct. A sickly green mist that faded in and out hovered around the craft. Palba coasted as close to the ancient tunnel point as she could. The attitude jets fired and the Demetrius slowly settled in space. Jarl unstrapped from the nav console and floated over to the airlock. He keyed in the code and the Demetrius's tunnel expanded outward.

He could barely contain his excitement as he shrugged into his spacesuit, "Something new for us to see. A new experience."

"I'm almost ready," Palba said. "Don't you go ahead without me!"

"Better hurry then!"

The Demetrius shook as the tunnel banged against the hull of the old ship. Tiny robotic legs walked the tunnel over to the clips on the derelict vessel and forced a connection. The tunnel's width shrank about three decimeters before the green light for a solid connection flashed success.

Jarl cycled the hatch open and pushed off the decking. He rocketed down to the other end and his boots clicked to the tunnel floor. There was an old keypad on the right side. As his gloved fingers brushed the metal flakes away, Palba landed beside him.

"I said wait for me," Palba groused as she

slapped him on the back.

"You haven't missed anything," Jarl replied. "Looks like the keypad is too corroded to use."

"I bet there isn't any power, either." Palba pulled out a driver and worked at a panel on the left side of the hatch. Once the panel tumbled free, she reached in and pulled a lever. A small panel ground its way down and revealed a crank. "Did you bring the bar?"

"I left it on the ship," Jarl replied.

"Typical," grumbled Palba. She turned around and launched herself down the tunnel back to the Demetrius.

Jarl slid a driver out of his belt pouch and wedged it against the face of the keypad. The cover popped off and dust particulates floated free. The fibers inside the hollow were exposed at the end.

He muttered, "Looks like these have been spliced plenty of times."

The outer surface of the fibers was pitted, but not broken. He slid his data pad into the open slot until he felt the click of a solid connection. With a swipe, he had it run a diagnostic.

Palba landed next to him and slid the bar into the crank. The gearing protested and rust frittered off in ribbons, but eventually, the teeth clicked into their slots. She turned the crank and the outer lock slowly parted open. She kept at it and the gap grew wider.

Jarl pulled his data pad out and pushed the keypad cover back on. "You were right. No power, but the fibers are good."

"I'm always right." Palba grunted as she pushed the lever down, "Why don't you take over on this?"

Jarl laughed, "You're almost done. I'll do the inner one."

Palba muttered under her breath, "Typical."

The outer hatch opened and they stepped inside. They played their flashes over the inner hatch and saw that the plate over the crank was already exposed.

Palba slipped the bar in and stepped out into the tunnel. "I'm going to grab the portable power unit. See if we can get her primary system up and running. Be right back."

Jarl nodded as he set to work with the bar. The inner one cranked open easier and didn't require as much elbow grease. There was no atmosphere bleed when the hatch cracked open. "Either it's been bled out or left open to space." After he had the hatch completely open, he stowed the bar on the back of his suit.

Darkness was all that he could see past the hatch. He played his flash over the interior. Dust hung in the vacuum and only moved once he disturbed it. The walls were blank of any color, just a dull gray, and also showed signs of corrosion. His flash shown off into the distance revealing piles of refuse that hung suspended where they had been left.

Palba's flash shown in before she popped

inside the vessel, "See anything?"

"Not yet," replied Jarl. "But I waited for you. Good idea on the porta-batt. You're always thinking ahead, aren't you?"

"You know it. Let's get this show on the road."

"After you," Jarl said as he floated behind her.

The only thing they found was more detritus. The first side hall had been barricaded with tables, chairs, and even an old door. Through bent girders, space showed out past the barricade. They made their way back to the main hall and headed further in. As Jarl passed a room where its door hung open, a ghostly shadow moved.

"You see that?" asked Jarl.

"No. Where?"

"Over there," he said as he moved through the doorway. His flash played across the room, but the only thing inside was the remnant of a bed. "Nothing. Must be my eyes playing tricks on me."

They proceeded on their way. Another hallway had been blocked off with just about everything not nailed down, but beyond the barricade the passageway looked intact. When they turned back to the main hall, a faint shape loomed up into the hallway behind them. Completely unaware of the presence, Jarl and Palba calmly continued their tour.

Eventually, they made it to the bridge of the ship. Electronics were pulled free of their housing from what should be the navigation system. The pilot's section was gone, only stripped bolt holes left in the floor marked where it had once existed. A ragged hole showed through the plas-glass of the bow viewport.

"Looks like a violent end," whispered Palba.

"Or salvagers," replied Jarl. "That looks like the main power coupling. Let's see what still works."

Palba placed the power unit next to the coupler and plugged it in. The main computer warmed up and blinked into life. An error message flashed across the interface followed by the ship's schematic that highlighted where the damage was.

"Doesn't look too far away. Just further down the main hallway," Palba stated.

"I'll go take a look," answered Jarl. "Turning on my tracker and suit map is now engaged. You tell me when I'm close."

Palba nodded, "Suit map engaged and paired. And there you are. Waiting on you to get your ass moving."

"Yes, sir!" saluted Jarl as he laughed.

He went back down to the main hallway and took the indicated left. Everything here looked the same as in the rest of the ship, except for some crisscrossed burn marks spattered on the walls. He slowed down and played his flash around, but didn't see anything out of the ordinary.

"You're almost there," stated Palba through the comm. "Should be on your left."

Jarl relaxed and pushed off the wall, "What am I freaking out about? All this damage happened a long time ago. Besides, this thing is open to space. Nothing can live here."

The scorch marks became more prevalent the farther along he went. His flash played across the rug that showed a large section of it was blackened with soot. His light traveled up again from the rug to the scorched walls that bubbled out and looked as if it had been liquefied.

Something caught the light of his flash and glinted. He floated toward it. It was a human arm bone that stuck out of the blasted wall next to a melted hole. Other pieces of bone were bonded to the wall as well and inside the hole lay a burned human skull next to a ruptured power cable.

"You're right on top of it..." said Palba.

At the same time, Jarl said, "I think I found it..."

***

Jarl turned the burner off and inspected his handiwork. He felt pretty confident that the fiber was reconnected. He slipped a shield sleeve over the exposed cable and flipped the shrink on. The shield billowed out at first, then it sucked into itself and grew skintight on the repair.

He spoke into the comm, "Told you it wouldn't take too long. Try it now."

Palba's voice came back, "Switching it on... now."

Jarl looked around and everything remained

dark. "Nothing seems to be happening. What's the read-out say?"

"Looks clear. The bridge is lit up. You're not seeing anything?"

Lights began flickering far down the hallway near the turn-off for the bridge. Some of the lights popped and fizzled out, but the lighting continued to kick on in spurts. As the lights flickered to life around Jarl, he thought he saw a large, spindly thing standing erect just at the edge of the shadows. But when the lights flickered on above that area, there was nothing there.

"I'm going to need to get the processing for my eyes checked," he grimaced. "Damn things are ghosting for some reason."

Jarl spoke into his comm, "Looks like we're good down here. How about up there?"

"The main computer is coming up, but it speaks a weird language I'm not familiar with. Archaic maybe. This ship is much older than it looks."

"It looks pretty damn old," he replied. "I'm going down to the engine room to see what's left."

"Go ahead. I'll see if there is anything worth salvaging from the computer."

Jarl clicked his comm off and settled the burner back into its holster. He pulled up the suit map and overlaid what the Demetrius had seen of the hull. The suit computer ran a quick comparison and built a rough guide from what information was available. Three sites blinked on the pseudo overlay as locations for an engine room.

"Well, I'll check the closest one and see what I see."

***

The first location turned out to be a large medical bay. What was left of the operating tables was crusted with what he could only imagine was old blood. A huge dent defaced the surface of one table; another had been slammed into the cabinetry and crushed. Jarl gave the medical bay a cursory glance with the assumption that the area had been picked clean of any supplies and equipment. He placed a red 'X' on the pseudo map and moved on to the next possibility.

Palba's voice came through his comm, "I found her name. She's called the Polypheme."

"The plot thickens..."

"I pulled the vessel layout and the ship is pretty large. Sending it to you now."

Jarl laughed, "You're kind of taking the fun out of exploring, Palba."

"Think of it as a treasure map, then. And no one knows where the treasure is hidden."

"Ooh, fun. I'll do that."

As the download completed, he discovered that the room he was heading toward was listed as the water filtration chamber for the ship. "Ha! That's not what I'm looking for. On to the final secret room, then."

From the layout Palba had supplied, the ship listed four decks. The airlock had been on the third deck while the fourth deck was just the bridge. The empty shaft of a lift materialized on the right and he dropped down with a little push. As he floated past the second deck, the roof of the lift appeared below him. The access panel on top disconnected easily and he dropped in.

The lift doors were bent in, as if something very large had tried to get inside. There was enough space for Jarl to wiggle his way through. He shook his head then took a quick right toward the aft of the Polypheme.

On the map, the indicator pointed to the room on the right, three doors up. Humming to himself, he pushed off the wall and floated toward the marked entrance. His magnetic boots clicked onto the ceiling and he spun to face the large circular hatchway. It had been left open.

"This is the place. Hey Palba, I'm heading into the engine room now." He didn't wait for a reply and walked in.

The engine room was a complete disaster. The monitoring equipment had all been yanked out. Bare wires and fibrous cables floated loosely in the equipment bays. Random chunks of circuitry hung from its housing. But it was the strange thing in the center of the room that made him stop and stare.

An immense cradle stood empty and its prongs reached out like fingers from an enormous hand. From its design, it should hold a sphere roughly five meters high.

"What is that for?" he wondered out loud.

A strange sibilant voice whispered in his mind, "It holds the gateway..."

"Who said that?" he asked as he looked around. But he found himself alone. There was nothing to see.

Luli's eyes popped open and she stared at Lucia. "What, by Tom, was that?"

***

Luli saw the concern in Lucia's eyes. "I'm fine. I just had to get out for a moment."

"Should you take a break?"

Luli shook her head in the negative. She closed her eyes and reengaged the connection to Jarl's memory core. She was dropped back into the engine room.

She felt his hand reach out to the cradle. A bone-chilling iciness seeped through his gloves from the metal.

"How strange," he gasped. "It's so cold!"

Again, he heard that sibilant voice speak, "It harbors its loss of purpose as the body does not forget."

As Jarl felt an icy hand grip his shoulder, he turned to face what was there. An odd being that was more larval than anything else stood behind him and he could see right through it. Its seven other appendages grasped at nothing while the appendage on his shoulder moved to his chest.

"What are you?" asked Jarl. "Who are you?"

A sound just on the edge of his hearing emanated from the apparition as it faded in front of him. Suddenly, the appendage on his chest moved to his faceplate and a bright flash scrambled his brain. Random memories of the Sol System cycled through his thoughts. A sense of need overlaid each one until he could think of nothing else. Slowly, his world slipped away and he blacked out.

When he came to, there was no one else with him in the engine room. He knew something was amiss, but he couldn't remember what it was. His gloved hands cradled his helmet as a single thought burned in his mind. He whispered into the open comm, "... home."

"What was that, Jarl?" Palba asked.

His lips twisted as he replied, "Find the way home. We need to find the way home. Find the way... the way... way home... home..."

***

Luli pulled herself free of Jarl's memories and felt Lucia's hand grasping hers. "What's wrong?" she asked.

"You started repeating things," said Lucia. "Over and over you said, 'Find the way home, and then your breathing became labored. Are you alright?"

Luli looked up at her, "I, I think so.

Something happened to him out there but I don't know if it's real."

"Real? Why not?" asked Lucia.

Luli thought on that question, "Well, the memory core remembers what the personality remembers and just like human memory, it can be faulty. It can change over time, so it's not always the truth."

Lucia asked, "What do you want to do?"

"I'm going back in," Luli stated. "I need to see what he did to Palba."

"Alright, If you think that's wise."

***

Luli let Jarl's memories enfold her mind. After so many dives into the others, she felt she had some modicum of control. She quickly sifted through the individual points in time until she found one that called out to her. As she fell into it, the darkness of the in-between parted.

"She has a piece of the map," whispered the alien voice in the back of his mind.

Jarl stared at Palba sleeping peacefully beside him. "I know," he growled. "But there's no way to take it without killing her."

The voice hissed, "But you must find the way."

"I know," Jarl whispered to Palba as he stroked her hair.

He closed his eyes, reviewing a mental

inventory of their needs and accomplishments. Repairs on the Polypheme had taken months to complete. On the command deck, the bridge viewport had been patched with plasteel and re-pressurized. The first and second decks had been undamaged. Fuel had been siphoned from the Demetrius and the power was now functioning throughout much of the ship. There wasn't an engine to work with anymore. The only concern that remained was the gigantic rent in the starboard side on the third deck.

They had made their home in one of the suites on the second deck as they worked on the vessel. Palba had chosen it because it had a kitchenette. He smiled as he stirred their meal in the single pot she had let him take off the Demetrius.

"I think we should stay here and see what else there is to find," Jarl mentioned offhandedly.

Palba looked up at him, "Do you think there is anything worth finding that wasn't already taken? There can't be many places left to look for anything of worth. The ship was stripped by salvagers."

"Yes, but the computer still works and most of the Polypheme is undamaged," replied Jarl. "I mean, isn't this what we were looking for? Something new? Something different? Not another barely inhabited rock struggling to get by? Just a place of our own."

He glanced over his shoulder at her, "Besides, I have the feeling that there is undiscovered treasure hidden on her. Something important with immense value."

Palba sighed in resignation, "If it's that important to you, we can stay for a while longer. I'll pull some plating off of the Demetrius and repair the hole. At least get her spaceworthy."

A different time floated to the surface and he stood staring at the empty cradle in the engine room. By now, the outside hull was patched and the entire ship had atmosphere. With only the two of them on board, it was kept to the bare minimum needed.

They had searched every room on the ship and nothing of value had been found, only corpses. Long dead corpses had barricaded the rooms and suites on the third deck. It had been grisly work, but the last of the bodies had been cleared away and sent out to space. He fell into the moment.

He released his end of a body and watched it float away through the tear in the hull, "That is the last one."

He glanced at Palba and noticed that she looked quite ill. She turned away from him and rested her forehead against the wall.

He reached out his gloved hand to touch her and flecks of decaying matter puffed free. "Are you alright, Palba? You don't look well."

Her voice shook, "I'm not alright. We just threw fifty-three bodies into the void. All of them died trying to escape something."

"But we're the only living things," he replied. "Just you and I."

She avoided his contact and nodded, "I'm

sure we are. But something ripped a hole in the Polypheme. I would feel safer if we left the barriers up."

"The garbage?" he frowned.

She nodded as she turned away, "I need to be alone for a little while, Jarl."

He watched her walk away and a feeling that he was missing something niggled at his brain. His sightings of the shadowy form were becoming more frequent of late. The strange voice whispered to him even when he was sleeping now. But he never mentioned it to Palba.

He closed his eyes in thought and when he reopened them, he stood alone in another part of the ship. "She wouldn't understand," he reasoned aloud. "I barely do myself."

"What was that?" asked Palba as she entered the engine room.

Jarl smiled, "Oh, nothing."

Palba wrapped her arm around his back and squeezed him, "Okay. What do you do down here, anyway? You come here a lot."

"I'm searching for something," he said as he pulled her into an embrace. His cheek rested against the side of her head. His eyes traveled down the back of her skull and the premonition hit him, "The secret is there."

"Yes," Palba said, but her voice sounded alien.

A glow emanated from around her and the strange voice spoke while her lips moved, "The way home is trapped within my crude shell. I am a guardian as you are the messenger. Ethereal beings meant to guide the way..."

"You know what I've been searching for?" he cried as he squeezed her hard.

"I'm not sure?"

It felt like another time jump had occurred as Jarl struggled with how his memories of a moment ago led to a much later moment in time. A single thought danced through his mind, *'The secrets lie within. A single cut placed here and simply move the flesh.'*

He found himself in the dead center of the bridge. His arms were outstretched and his eyes closed when he heard the hatch open.

"What are you doing?" asked Palba.

He smiled and opened his eyes, "Stretching. Thank you for being here."

Palba returned his smile as she moved into his arms, "I hope you didn't miss me."

He stared into her eyes, "You are always here with me, my angel."

He thrust the blade of the small knife into the hollow of her neck and twisted the handle. Her connection to the rest of her body was cut and she slumped to the floor. He rolled her to her side and cut the skin away along her scalp.

"What are you doing to me? Why can't I move?" she whimpered. "What is happening!"

"I'm setting you free."

Jarl came back to himself and stared down at what was left of his dear Palba. Her once beautiful face was now horribly marred by his shoddy cutting.

Jon Gray Lang

"I... I already did it, didn't I?" he asked into the silence.

Palba's lips moved and the serpentine voice spoke, "You set my ethereal being free from its physical prison. Feel no guilt messenger, for what was done was right."

"This feels wrong..." Jarl held back tears as he brushed a strand of hair from his wife's face.

Palba's lips moved and the otherworldly glow brightened, "My love for you is real, Jarl, But there is more work to be done. I have called friends to help you complete your task. Be quick about it and come back to me. The Fates are harsh mistresses and they do not suffer fools long."

Jarl felt the arms of his dead wife close around his waist and pull him into an embrace. He closed his eyes and cried into her shoulder.

***

Luli choked on her tears and wanted to flee, but another memory tugged at her. She felt drawn to it, and as hard as she tried, she couldn't escape its pull. Its maw opened up and swallowed her whole.

The call was loud to his/her ears and it could not be denied. Jarl's eyes bulged in their sockets and his arms opened wide.

"Can you see them? They are all around us!" He threw his head back, "They bless us with their presence!"

The Polypheme twisted in space as it had

been doing more frequently of late. Darkened shades slithered out of the walls and the rot of old vegetation burnt in the air.

He looked down and Luli Qing, the last of the metal guardians, cried out, "Gods! Are we jumping?"

The crash of a gong reverberated loudly throughout the ship. He could see the sound waves moving slowly out in concentric rings. As each ring passed, the beings that lived here with him grew more visible and solid.

"Nine stand in a circle with me at the center! Each one part of a whole that differs from the last!"

One creature stood up on its abdomen waving its five legs that grasped at the empty air. Another slithered inside the carapace of the large insect it wore like armor as the shell molted. The third's body undulated wildly as its unending length vanished into the distance. The air beat in waves from the entity with hundreds of wings, all while the other watched with its thousand scabrous eyes.

Their voices leaked out as they stared into his eyes, into his soul, "We see the thing inside and the thing inside sees us. You must find the way home."

Luli screamed in horror as she realized they were talking to her through Jarl's memories. She felt more than heard Jarl's mad laughter. The room spun as he danced a jig in the center of the chamber and the creatures clapped along. She felt his air being choked off and struggled to breathe as his systems shut down.

Jon Gray Lang

She sensed the connection to Jarl's memory core being yanked free and her breathing stabilized. She opened her eyes and stared into Lucia's.

"I thought I was losing you," Lucia said as she inspected Luli's face. "Did I do wrong?"

"No," whispered Luli. "You saved my life." She pulled the old woman down and hugged her fiercely. "I can never repay you for this." Her tears burst free in a torrent.

She sensed Lucia stroking her hair and felt comforted. But a remaining thought burned in her mind, '*Must find the way home.*'

twenty-eight

Red Skies

Onboard the Peking Empress, Thadie Dumba monitored the comm channels from their allied ships in space as well as the comms from their teams on the Shipyard S-3465.

"The Independence says they've taken out their attackers."

"Go ahead and send out the call to bring them home, Thadie," replied Captain Kaur.

"Message sent, sir. Scorpio says they are on their way back."

"Where are we on the thievery?" asked Hau Hung.

Thadie held the headphone close to her ear, "Hold on that. Please repeat. Relaying message. Make haste, Captain."

Thadie turned around, "News from the Copperhead. Consortium fleet from the jump gate is incoming. Only a matter of time before they get here and disrupt your party."

Mr. Leon nodded in understanding. "Contact the teams inside. We need to hurry this up." I'll send a direct request to Delta's team.

"Contacting now, Mr. Leon," replied Thadie.

Captain Kaur gripped the railing. "Warm up the sublights and have the crew at the tunnel ready to cut it free."

***

Mr. Leon's voice came through Delta's comm, "What's our progress?"

Delta handed off the last security stick from the ship's vault before she answered, "Runners are on their way. Only nine of the thirteen pearls are fully functional. Two are only shells and one is missing its FTL drive."

"Probably the one prepped for the Empress' FTL drive. Get those key cards to the crews. We have big ships incoming and we lack the firepower to take them on."

"Understood," replied Delta. She cut the comm and looked over at a man cowering behind his desk. "You have any genorgs on the station?"

As he shook his head in the negative, Delta looked over at Rho-11, "We need to get this natural-born to the worker bay before we head back home. On your feet, mister. You get to live another day."

***

Etsiddy handed off the last key card to the crew, "Head to docking ring twenty-three and double time!"

His comm rang and he answered, "Etsiddy here."

"Pack up your team, Etsiddy. We've got incoming and it's time to leave," said Thadie.

"The last crew is boarding now. We'll be heading out soon enough. Etsiddy out."

Once the airlock to docking ring twenty-three closed, he addressed his team, "Time to get out of here. Head back to the Empress!"

Most of the mercs headed out as commanded, but only Jong hung back.

"Come on Jong, get a move on!" cried Etsiddy.

Eventually, Jong sauntered past with a grin plastered across her face. She winked as she walked on by.

"What have you got planned?"

She replied with a twinkle in her eye, "Nothing much, sir. Just got one of these destroyers synced to my data pad. I'm gonna fly it out of here."

"Ha! You ain't no pilot," he laughed. "You'll just crash it into something."

She just winked again.

***

Jon Gray Lang

Deep in the center of the saucer-shaped station was the main lift to the living quarters. The workers were sequestered here per the orders of the man Delta and Rho-11 dragged along behind them.

"Pick up your pace, Commander," growled Rho-11 as she shoved him forward.

Out of nowhere, a shot pinged by his head and he dropped to all fours. A small contingent of the station's security team bolted around the corner. Delta dropped to a knee and raised her rifle. Rho--11 slammed her back against the passageway wall.

"Get down, idiot," she cried at the Commander. Another shot splintered against the plas-tile on the wall. In wide-eyed panic, the man scurried away and disappeared around a corner.

Delta's rifle barked three times before she scooted back to where Rho-11 stood. Rho-11 sighted down her rifle and squeezed the trigger. A cry of pain indicated her shot had found its mark as a body at the end of the hall toppled to the ground.

Rho-11 cursed as splinters of plas-tile shot past her, "They've got us locked down."

Multiple shots rang out as Omega's team came bounding up from behind the security squad. They whittled away at them until the team broke for cover.

"Ho, Omega! We lost the station Commander," Delta shouted upon her sisters arrival.

"Leave him," cried Omega. "You heard the

Jon Gray Lang

call, Delta. Time to go!"

"Right behind you, sister!" she cried.

The two of them formed up with Omega's team and ran for all they were worth to the Peking Empress. They didn't encounter any opposition along the way. They rushed past Mr. Vadik who stood at the airlock.

When they passed him, he commed up to the bridge, "That's the last of them. Go ahead and break free, Captain Kaur."

***

The Consortium cruiser Puno coasted toward Shipyard S-3465. Small bursts of light popped in the space around the station. The only legible radio chatter came from one of the patrolling fighters. The rest was garbled nonsense.

"Still nothing coming from the station?" asked Captain Takahashi.

Comm officer Engels just shook his head. "Besides the single fighter, the only other channel in use is scrambled. We're working on breaking the code as we speak."

"Go ahead and open the comm from the fighter for now," ordered Captain Takahashi. "Let's see what's going on."

"The channel is up. Radio delay is forty-three seconds," answered the Comm Officer.

The bridge hissed with static before a woman's voice came through, "... lost my wingmate

and it looks like Team Two is down as well.
Awaiting orders. Is there anyone out there?"

"This is Captain Takahashi of the Puno. Who
is this and what do you see?" She drummed her
fingers against the armrest as she waited for the
reply. "Anything pulling up on the scanners yet?"

"Only five heat sources are showing, sir," the
Sensor Technician answered. "That includes the
station and the fighter."

The static suddenly dropped in volume,
"Finally. This is Lieutenant Deahl. The station is
under attack by a band of pirates! I count four ships
total! Please tell me you're on your way here."

"The Puno and the Luyang are on the way to
you," replied the Captain. "Our arrival is..."

Officer Engels interrupted, "... twenty-three
minutes, sir."

"Twenty-three minutes," continued the
Captain smoothly. "Four ships you say.
Armaments?"

"Captain!" blurted the Sensor Technician.
"Multiple heat sources have appeared around the
station."

"How many, Mr. Lewis?"

Technician Lewis was quiet as he tracked the
new sources, "Four, no five. I mean six." He
glanced over his shoulder, "Not including the
previous five. And there is another."

Lieutenant Deahl spoke, "Merchant class
vessels with an assortment of armaments. General
pirate trash, but they know what they're doing. They

took out three fighters without setting off any in-system alarms."

"What were the latest jump gate entries?" asked the Captain.

"Only one entry, sir," replied the Comm Officer. "Supply delivery for the station. There is a manifest for a luxury liner to be decommissioned for their FTL drive as well. Hmm, ident was received from the Peking Empress after wormhole entry."

"Seven minutes out, Captain. We should have visual now," stated Technician Lewis.

"Making my way to you, Puno. Lieutenant Deahl out."

The bridge crew watched as nine of their destroyers left the space dock. They were closely followed by the luxury liner. Bringing up the rear of the fleet was an old ore hauler.

***

Captain Moraldi yanked Gamma out of the pilot's chair and dumped her unceremoniously on the deck. "Now, what star system is this?"

Mbuni tied Gamma's wrists together and let them fall into her lap. He dragged her across the floor and propped her next to Tau-SA43 and Nu-M12. Moraldi tossed him the rifle. A wicked smile lit up Mbuni's face as he leaned back and pointed in in the genorg's direction.

"I don't know where the hell we are," muttered Suarez. "This system isn't on our charts."

"Mbuni, make her answer my damn question," Moraldi ordered.

Mbuni slammed the rifle butt into Gamma's shoulder, "You heard the man. Where'd you take us?"

Gamma brought her knees up to her chest, "We're in Orsova."

"Where in the cursed heavens is that?" grunted Suarez.

***

"Can you see anything about the pirate ships, Mr. Lewis?" asked Captain Takahashi.

The technician replied, "No weapons showing on the liner. The other pirate ship is heading directly to her. First one in range is the ore hauler."

"Inform the Luyang to immediately fire on that ore hauler," ordered the Captain.

"Message sent, Captain," answered the comm officer.

"Three minutes out," stated Technician Lewis.

The Luyang's engines burned hot and it blasted past the Puno. The port-side missile tube on the destroyer flashed as a long-range missile launched toward the hauler.

***

"You're going to want to dock in that liner, and you need to do it now," murmured Gamma.

Jon Gray Lang

Moraldi growled, "I'm not going anywhere you want me to.

"By the devil Tom, we've got incoming!" screamed Iago Suarez.

The Scorpio rocked hard to starboard as a large missile impacted the side plating. Superheated metal bubbled up and spilled out into space. Alarms blared loudly as the ship listed to one side.

Mbuni lost his footing and fell hard to the deck. Gamma rolled over and slammed her knee into his face. With her hands still tied, she grasped the grip of the rifle, aimed it at Suarez, and fired a burst. The rifle fired again with a cluster of rounds that smacked into the comm station and drilled into Iago. He slumped in his seat as a small fire started at the base of his console.

"Get us in the Tom-be-damned hold of the Empress, if you want to live," barked Gamma.

The hull chimed like a gong as three coil gun rounds smacked against the Scorpio's side.

***

Rosa fired the bow attitude jets to slow the forward momentum of the Independence. As the Peking Empress grew closer, she floored the starboard jets to push the vessel in the right direction.

"Carla? Send the code now!" commanded Rex.

"Tight beam code sent," she answered.

"Awaiting reply."

The hangar beckoned welcomely. The Independence rocked as the port jets fired to slow down its swing. The Empress's docking claws reached out for the ex-pirate ship and the hull boomed with the connection. Rosa killed the engines and let the Empress deal with the inertia.

"And we're in," Rosa shouted. "Begin the shutdown process."

"Hold on that for a moment," ordered Rex. "Did you get a reply yet, Carla?"

The genorg shook her head in the negative.

"Leave the comms active, Carla," ordered Commander Keri. "Go ahead and shut down the rest." She glanced over at Rex, "Escape is our only option. There's nothing else we can do."

Rex looked grim, but he nodded, "We did what we came here to do. One can always hope for the little extra."

Carla shouted excitedly, "I received a tight beam response. The order has been received."

Rex laughed with gusto, "Sometimes I forget to have patience."

***

Deep in the asteroid field, the artificial intelligence of a planet-killer missile suddenly activated. A transmission had been received by laser and it required a response. The artificial intelligence housed within the fuselage was only a simple machine. It was designed for a specific purpose and couldn't process commands outside of its original function.

The intelligence surveyed the instruction code for any anomalies. No errors were highlighted and the command code was accepted. The machine verified the security protocol and it registered as acceptable. A response was tight beamed back to the originating source, but the source had moved. The missile scanned the surrounding area until it found the source. The reply was sent out again.

The orders contained in the tight beam code were simple. The missile brought its engines online and began to warm them up. Its targeting computer locked onto the requested power source on the edge of the system.

"Targeting acquired... Warhead armed..."

The engine flared brightly and the missile nudged its way free of the asteroid field. Once it was clear, the engine burned hot until its fuel was exhausted. With no gravity wells near enough to disturb it, the missile continued to pick up speed.

***

Captain Kaur shouted over the din of her crew relaying information, "Do we have the other ships on board?"

Latiff pulled his headphones clear, "The other two are locked down. We're just waiting for the Scorpio."

There was a commotion at the bridge hatch as a squad of genorgs entered, dressed as Consortium jackboots. Armed to the teeth and streaked with soot, their weird green eyes glowed under the bridge lighting. Harjeet wouldn't want to run into them in a dark alley, never mind having them on her bridge.

'*They're part of Mr. Leon's package,*' she thought. That's when it struck her, '*He carries the same kind of intensity that they do. Are they mimicking him or is there something deeper?*'

Harjeet looked out the viewport and saw Consortium vessels as they swiftly came into view. One of them made a beeline for the shipyard and released a barrage on the Scorpio.

"We'll give them three minutes. In the meantime, wind up the FTL!" she ordered. "This is going to be rough and tight!"

"On it, Cap!" shouted Ovi. "She's wound and sound!"

***

Moraldi stared down the barrel of Gamma's rifle. The nav screen was filled with the movement of other ships and debris. Warning lights blinked rapidly and bathed the bridge in a staccato of darkness. In the flickering lights, Moraldi glimpsed Mbuni's crushed skull. He also spotted Suarez's body draped over a chair and saw blood splashing against the decking in slow motion.

Gamma growled, "We need to get into the

hold of that liner before we die out here. Do you understand me?"

Moraldi could feel a bead of sweat rolling down his cheek. The ship rocked as another missile slammed into the fuselage. Seconds later, a single fighter swooped past the bow and pelted the hull of the ore hauler with depleted uranium rounds as it flew away from his ship.

A very young genorg, not much older than twelve, stumbled onto the bridge. Blood seeped from her scalp and a bruise was forming on the side of her face. "Captain Gamma! I'm sorry, but the prisoners have escaped! Oh!"

As Gamma turned to the bridge hatch, Moraldi reached for the pistol that lay in his lap. In a swift move that appeared as slow motion in the blinking lights, he released the flight controls and brought the gun up to bear on the genorg.

"This is my ship!" he screamed as he pulled the trigger. The round slammed into the genorg's chest and knocked the rifle from her hands. He aimed his pistol at the other genorg and fired a second shot.

As Tau-SA43 shifted out of the way, he saw the little genorg at the hatch yank a huge pistol free from a belt that encircled her coveralls.

"No!" screamed the little girl as she sent a bullet slamming into his chest. She flew back into the corridor from the recoil and disappeared from view.

Moraldi looked down in confusion as blood

Jon Gray Lang

pumped freely from his body, trying to understand what shouldn't be possible. "How could a drone shoot me?" he stammered.

Suddenly, Gamma filled up his entire view as she ripped the pistol free from his numb hands, "To be honest, it's very easy."

The sound of his own gun firing point-blank in his face was the last thing he heard.

"Tau? Are you alright?" Gamma asked.

"Well enough, Gamma."

"Go check on Phi-IK97, will you?" Gamma asked as she dragged Moraldi's body out of the pilot seat and settled into it. "Without her, this would have gone very poorly for us."

Phi-IK97 shuffled back onto the bridge, "I'm alright, Captain." The young girl looked down at the gun that trembled in her hands, "My first time shooting a natural-born." She bent at the waist and threw up everything she had eaten.

Tau-SA43 grimaced, "It won't be the last." She flashed a comm to the Empress, "Scorpio is en route Empress. I repeat, Scorpio is en route."

Gamma guided the ore hauler to the Empress's hangar as Phi-IK97 continued to heave behind her.

***

"Luyang reports direct hits, sir," stated the Comm Officer of the Puno.

On the nav holo, the crew watched as the ore

hauler continued to trundle its way toward the luxury liner.

"Those old asteroid belt haulers have some heavy plating," remarked Technician Lewis.

The Captain raised an eyebrow at him.

Lewis continued, "I used to serve on one before I got my commission. Sir."

Captain Takahashi crossed her arms as she ordered, "Gunnery, target that liner."

"Still out of range, Captain. We might hit the station in error."

In a matter of moments, a mass of wormholes sprang up. The stolen M class destroyers vanished inside the wormholes as they collapsed behind them.

"They're getting away," griped the Captain. "Are we in range yet?"

Due to its increased speed, the Luyang overshot the shipyard and began a wide curve outward to swing back. All of a sudden, bursts of light burned brightly all around the shipyard. The station exploded and fragments spun off in all directions. Surprised by the explosion, the crew of the Puno barely noticed the Scorpio as she slipped into the Peking Empress to moor at the dock inside.

"Firing now," stated the Gunnery. "Spray Pattern Alpha."

The cruiser rumbled as five missiles were launched one after the other. The missiles arced their way to the luxury liner. But it was too late. A wormhole opened up in front of the Peking

Empress and the ship disappeared from view.

***

The planet-killer missile gained in speed as it streaked through the night sky. At its current velocity, there was very little that could stop it from reaching its target. The artificial intelligence settled into a feeling of contentment its makers would have found uncomfortable.

"The mission has a success rate of 93.7 percent."

***

The Puno's Comm Officer received an incoming tight beam message from the jump gate personnel, "Captain Takahashi, the jump gate's perimeter defense system has discovered a small object on a collision course with it."

"Mr. Lewis, can you confirm?"

Technician Lewis frantically checked the onboard sensor suite and it registered a match to the jump gate's findings. "The object is set to collide with the ring. Backtracking its trajectory, sir. It came from the asteroid belt."

Captain Takahashi gripped the railing and bowed her head, "Expected collision time?"

The Sensor Technician ran the calculations. "Collision will occur in ten minutes."

"Even with a full burn, we're a good forty

minutes out," growled the Captain.

"What about the destroyer?" asked his gunner.

"The Luyang is even further away. Swing us around and get us headed back." The Captain cursed under her breath. "Inform the Luyang to sweep the shipyard for survivors."

The heavy cruiser burned its attitude jets hard and the ship lumbered along its axis. Once it was facing back toward the jump gate, the main engines burned fiercely enough to arrest their momentum deeper into the system. The cruiser took valuable time away as it struggled to break its momentum, but the pilot finally succeeded. The ship slowly picked up speed.

The comm officer spoke up, "The object has been identified as a planet-killer missile, sir. It is still two minutes out."

"Where did a band of pirates get that kind of hardware?" Captain Takahashi pondered aloud.

"The defensive satellites can't get a fix on it. It is moving too fast."

"Tell them to initiate station abandonment!"

"I lost them, sir. The laser comm isn't responding."

Abruptly, a new sun sprung briefly into existence where the jump gate had been. The light was so bright that the bow viewport darkened to compensate. When it finally cleared, the jump gate was gone.

twenty-nine

Chain of Fools

"Hurry it up, outsider," called out the son of the Clan Mother of Baptiste. He grinned and popped through the hatch on the shuttle Burton.

Anton grimaced as he yanked the last strap free of the ship, "Almost done, Leopold." He quickly rolled up the strap and secured it to the hangar decking.

With practiced ease, Anton bounded off the floor and hooked his hand on the hatch frame. With a quick twist, he corkscrewed in past the hatchway and shut the airlock. His feet landed on the transport shuttle deck and he grabbed a seat back to bring himself to a stop.

Leopold smiled, "Nice moves outsider. You are to sit there."

Rabbit plopped into the proffered seat and clicked the belts closed. He was just in time as the

Burton shot out of the hangar and threw him hard into the foam padding. Other ships left the hangar bay at a more relaxed pace. The space around the Cluster was cluttered with small ships.

"Thanks for giving me a moment, Leopold," groused Anton.

The young man laughed and patted the pilot on the shoulder, "Tone it down, cousin Ama. Seems our guests are a bit rattled from your exit."

Jacquie kept an eye on Leopold as Ama killed the afterburners. The brash pilot threw a wink at Anton before she brought the Burton in line with the other shuttles.

"You marking, Ama?" asked Jacquie.

A lascivious grin crossed the young woman's face, "Just checking the mush. Why? You got a contract?"

Jacquie smiled back, "No, no contract. Isn't no gorja, savvy." She glanced over at Anton and smiled.

Ama laughed long and hard, "Sight on that aye."

Anton looked back and forth between the two of them, "What's going on, Jacq?"

Leopold's lips curled into a half-smile as he clicked the comm over to the shuttle fleet, "Burton's a go."

Other voices played over the comm until each ship had given a reply. Finally, the command came down the line, "Cluster still within range of the gravity well of the comet. Five hours out at hard burn, setting for seven hours. Watch your fuel. Fortune says the hunt will be good. Hunt leader out."

"Clan Father, should we prep the hold in the meantime?" asked Jacquie.

"Just call me Nani," he replied. "Leo, take the outsider with you and get the hold prepped. We'll be right behind you, so no trouble, eh?"

"You can call me Anton, alright?"

"Come on then, outsider. Prep should only take a couple of hours. Then maybe a game of chance?" asked Leopold.

Anton nodded a bit hesitantly before he followed Leopold into the hold.

Nani gazed into Jacquie's eyes, "Are your people up to giving the tocher or token? The clan needs the diversity, daughter."

"Putting my mark on that one," Ama cried out. "Even if he say no."

"Just fly the ship, Ama," Nani chided.

Jacquie grimaced, "I'll talk to them."

"We're including you too," Nani added. "You have enough differences we can give in trade to the other clans."

"Understood," Jacquie said as she closed her eyes. "Should we help the boys before they get in a fight?"

"Ha! That Leo always lookin' to swing fists," crowed Ama.

"Ama!" Nani chided.

***

Back on board the Matilda, there was a chirp and the airlock at the cargo bay cycled open. Luli stepped on board then waved back at the ship that had brought her home. She looked around and saw Barney standing near the sickbay with a sweeper in hand.

"Gone for a long time, weren't you?" he asked. "Your meeting with the All-Mother go well?"

Luli smiled a bit, "Well enough, anyway. She had a lot of questions and I did my best to answer them."

The lift opened and Derain walked out holding a wiring harness. "Hey Barney, this harness looks fried. We have any thin gauge fiber laying around?" He looked up, "Oh hey, Luli. We were beginning to wonder if you were coming back."

Luli laughed, "Of course, I'd come back. The Matilda is my home."

Stiffness left Barney as he said, "Glad to hear that, lass." He glanced over at the bounty hunter, "There should be some spindles in the machine room. You'll find the splicing kit in there, too."

Derain nodded and hopped back in the lift. "I'll get this harness repaired and we should be able to get the port side attitude jets working..."

The doors closed and muffled the last words he said. Luli walked over to Barney and stopped beside him. He looked up at her and she seemed more relaxed, less cagey.

His eyes traveled down to her wrists, "How are your hands?"

"My hands?" she replied. She held them up and wiggled the fingers. "They hurt less and I'm getting some range of motion back. They still feel mushy with a tough skin, though. Like potatoes." She saw the concern in his eyes. "Which reminds me, the All-Mother asked me to perform for the Cluster. They'll have a big celebration once the hunters return."

"What did you say?"

"She convinced me to say yes, though I am still hesitant."

Barney asked, "Would you play?"

"She got me to agree to sing, because I said I can no longer play." She waved her hands around and the scarring down the back of each finger stood up like harsh ridges. "But I think she wanted me to try. How are repairs going?"

Barney sighed for a moment, "The hull is in better shape than we first thought. Most of the hardware is where it's supposed to be. You know, comm array, coil guns, and all the parts we could salvage from the wreck. But a lot of the internal wiring is shot. Weaponry circuits are fried, dead fibers run to the sublights and some of Matilda's data bundles are charred."

"Which ones?"

Barney laughed, "Only some of the important ones like targeting and navigation."

Luli thought back a moment, "I can replace

most of the missing navigation. Actually, I can add even more to it." She jingled the memory cores.

Fear flickered across Barney's face before he was able to hide it, "Um, that would be great, Lu. Having the Matilda operate in the literal dark of space is not where I want us to be."

"No problem. I'll get started on that," she replied. "What else can I do to help get her shipshape?"

Barney rubbed his chin and furrowed his brow. "See if you can get Matilda to route out every bad wire, fiber, and bundle. The sooner we know how big of a mess we're dealing with the better. In the meantime, Derain and I will keep replacing what we've found so far."

"I'll get started on it now," Luli said as she moved toward the lift.

She could hear the Titan muttering to himself, "... already running out of materials. Don't know how I'm going to get her space-born..."

***

By the time Jacquie and Nani made it to the hold, Leo and Rabbit had the hold partially prepared. Pens had been set up to keep the water bears contained. The two joined up with the rest and assembled the remaining pens. Each pen was given a portion of the waters needed to fuel the ship as well as to keep the zottis alive.

Leopold wandered over and checked the stasis

generator. Once it was turned on, the zottis should go into their hardened catatonic state for the return trip. "She's ready, Nani."

"Are you going to pull some fuel water while we're out there?" asked Jacquie.

"That's the plan, cousin," answered Leopold. "You ever pull ice while deep in the solar winds? Makes harvesting the zottis a moonwalk in comparison."

Anton grimaced, "Should make for an exciting ride, then."

***

Luli slid into the pilot seat of the Matilda and pulled her knees to her chest. She pulled the loose end of the jack from underneath her interface unit and plugged it into the back of her skull.

"Matilda, I need you to run a diagnostic on every system. Pinpoint where the connections break using your best summation. Update me after each check."

Luli waited for the guttural reply from the ship, or at least that is how it always seemed to her. Although no sounds emanated from the Matilda on the bridge, a series of lights scrolled through patterns on the pilot's screens. The lights all flowed to a single point of light that blinked rhythmically.

Luli nodded and said, "Start with navigation for now. Next, check life-support systems." Luli paused while the computer queried her. "Yes, I understand that most of your star charts were wiped. I will see about getting them replaced. For now, just verify that the linkages are working correctly."

The nav console lit up, then went through a series of light patterns. Luli leaned her head back into the headrest and her fingers strayed to the cores around her neck.

"We can replace the missing maps, can't we?" she asked. Her fingers undid the clasp on the back and the cores piled up in the palm of her hand.

The fingers of her right hand slipped into the pocket of her flight suit and pulled out the small device that one of Lucia's people had given her. Inwardly, she smiled down at the multi-connector. It took only a few moments for her to unclip each core and to slide jacks from the device into the end of each one. Her hands draped the cord around her neck and closed the clasp on it.

Her left hand held onto the single jack from the device and her fingers rubbed against the dual opening. Her right hand reached back and clamped onto the jack in the back of her skull. All of the lights on the nav console blinked solid and then went out. A report on the nav system scrolled directly into Luli's mind and she studied it.

"Hmm, disconnect between port side to bow tracked to five meters from sensors; total three. Schematics generated." Luli shunted the information to a holding file for her data pad. "Prepare for chart download. Breaking contact now."

Luli slipped a cable jack into the port behind her ear, then attached the other end of the cord to the multi-connector. She closed her eyes as the link engaged. "Let's see, search for star charts only and remove duplicates."

Her eyelids fluttered at the huge amount of data that flooded her brain. She waited for her processor to wipe the duplicates from the search. She gazed at the wealth of information that remained. Many of the charts found were ones she didn't have.

"Well Derain, looks like you're going to get your wish," she muttered as she sent the information to the Matilda. Warnings blinked as eight files pulled up as being incomplete. "Eight files..."

She opened the eight files and had her processor connect them. Her body became still as a stone as words tumbled past her lips, "...home. Must find the way home..."

***

In the darkness of space, a wormhole opened and the Peking Empress flowed through. The lights along the fuselage sparked into brightness as other wormholes opened up nearby.

Captain Kaur wiped at her brow, "That was the third jump, Mr. Leon. I don't know about you, but the Empress and I need some time to recuperate."

Mr. Leon smiled, "I do, as well. How many of ours made it, do you think?"

Harjeet glanced at the monitor as more ships popped through around them. "Any unsolicited followers, Mr. Latiff?"

"None so far, Captain."

"Keep the FTL spun in case we need to leave in a hurry."

"Of course, Captain."

Mr. Leon chuckled, "Harjeet is no longer a Captain. You should refer to her as Admiral."

"Ha!" laughed Harjeet. "Me, an admiral? Never thought I'd see the day." She grinned at Mr. Leon, "Well then, War Master, what's our next objective?"

Hau Hung entered the bridge bearing a tray of steaming cups of tea. He moved around the room and handed each of the bridge crew a cup. He gave the last cups to Mr. Leon and the newly minted Admiral Kaur. "A successful raid deserves a reward."

"Is that my special tea?" asked Mr. Leon as he savored its aroma. "You've outdone yourself, Mr. Hau!"

Mr. Leon took a sip and smiled with joy. "So, Harjeet, here's our next agenda. We cut the Consortium off from the outer systems. We break their control of the jump gates and then we take the war to the inner systems."

Captain Kaur blinked, "Just us?"

The smile on Mr. Leon's face changed into

something more wistful, "Oh no.   Not alone, Admiral. We are far from alone in this. You'll see."

thirty

Sometimes I Feel Like a Motherless Child

The line of shuttles and ships streaked toward the comet that dominated everyone's view. The comet was a young one as the local star system hadn't shredded it down to smaller fragments. The main body of ice and rock measured out close to eighty-nine kilometers and luckily had an end-over-end slow tumble to it.

Eight of the twelve ships from the cluster spread out to overtake the comet. They slowly formed into a cone shape in front of it and hovered as close to the surface as their pilots could handle. The other four hung back from the comet and deployed nets.

The nets were to catch ice chunks for water

retrieval. They were also there to catch anyone who might fall off of the comet, including the zottis. There were stories when the nets didn't catch a hunter and they had sailed off into space never to be seen again.

Ama flipped the Burton over so that the top of the ship was closest to the surface of the celestial body. Leopold opened the hold doors and Anton spotted the lumps of the water bears that dotted the comet's surface.

"This comet is too far out for the zottis to be feeding," said Nani. "Take point, Leo."

Leo's laugh echoed in the comm. "You ready for some fun, outsider?"

With a long cable attached to his back, the young Baptiste jumped free of the shuttle and triggered his jet pack. With the attitude jets angled upward, he dropped to the surface of the comet like a stone. Ice puffed up from his landing as his boot claws dug into the frozen surface.

Anton gave his line some play and leapt out of the hold. He tapped the jet pack button and the engine nozzle burned hot for a second. He plummeted toward the comet below and landed heavily. His left boot claws stabbed into the ice as his right foot bounced off the surface. He pulled his body down to his knee and regained his footing. The right boot claws clamped into the ice.

Leopold laughed and turned away, "Not bad, outsider. The hard part is over. Now we catch some bears." He unhooked the line and sank the tip into the ice.

"You can call me Anton or even Rabbit," he grumbled as he did the same with his line.

Leopold shrugged, "You are an outsider. It is good for you to remember that."

The young man uncoiled a line at his belt and threw one end to Anton. After Anton clipped it to his harness, Leo did the same. The two moved away from the shuttle and disappeared over a craggy hump on the surface.

***

Jacquie watched as the two of them disappeared from view. She keyed the comm, "You come back, Anton. You promise me?"

Static broke up his reply, but she still heard, "I'll... back..."

Ama's voice came over the comm, "Comm channels go crazy around this comet. Nani thinks it has metallic deposits running through it."

"I can speak for myself, Ama." Nani addressed Jacquie, "I've been running hunts since before I was Leo's age. We always had comm issues on this one. Something funny in the ice."

"Or just metals," Ama interjected.

Nani groused, "Or just metals. Now we wait until they bring back a zotti and we reel it up. Shouldn't be more than a half-hour for the first one.

***

Anton watched as Leopold stopped to inspect a large bulbous rock that was partially submerged in the ice. He walked over to inspect the rock and noticed it was oddly familiar looking. Segmented plates ran the length of the tube-shaped stone.

Leopold reached for the cutter at his belt. "It's a big one. We'll have to cut this one loose."

Anton glanced over at Leopold as his cutter arced brighter than the suit flashes. "This is a water bear? I was expecting something more alive-looking."

"The comet is too far out from its star," Leopold answered. "They go hard and hibernate until it's warm enough."

"Huh," grunted Anton. He pulled the cutter handle free of his belt and bent down to the side of the zotti. His cutter arced and he warmed the ice near the bear until he could wedge a gloved hand underneath. He followed Leopold's lead and warmed the ice that ran the length of the creature's flank.

"Should be good now," Leo declared as he turned off his cutter. "On a count of three, we both lift and it should pop free."

"Got it," Anton replied as he stowed his cutter. He could feel the ice boiling around his fingers and crystallizing. So he wiggled them.

"One. Two. Three and lift."

Both men lifted the hardened body of the water bear free of the ice. Tiny ice crystals blew free and swirled around.

"We need to move slowly and safely. Keep each raised foot close to the surface," Leopold instructed. "One slip and we could all slide off into space."

"Hence the nets?"

"Exactly. Small shuffling steps until we get to the lines. We get this bear into the hold and head back for another one."

"They're a lot larger than I expected. How many are we looking to harvest?" Anton keenly inquired.

"Only a little over eleven hours left on a full rotation," answered Leopold. "As many as we can get."

***

"I can see them coming back over the ridge," said Jacquie as she peered through the bow port.

"Get ready to haul up the first one," replied Nani as he activated the winch.

Jacquie floated back to the hold and hooked to a guideline. Nani nodded at her and pointed down. Two space-suited figures carried a large tubular rock over to the secured lines. They placed the zotti into the net that hung from the two cables. The net glinted in the light from their flashes as it was securely fastened around the water bear. Nani cycled the winch and brought it up into the shuttle.

Both he and Jacquie grabbed the net and

pulled the zotti free. They carried it over to one of the open pens, gently placed it inside and closed the lid over the top. Then Nani revved up the winch again to return the empty net to its starting point.

He glanced at Jacquie, "Now we keep doing this for the next twelve hours."

Ama's voice came through the comm again, "I'm going to need someone to take over for me in the next hour. The cosmic winds are tossing the Burton around like a leaf in a gale."

Jacquie keyed her comm, "On my way to you after the next ice bear comes up."

***

Anton trudged behind Leopold over the jagged ice field. Ice crystals pelted both of them and rattled off their spacesuits. Loose particles crunched under their feet as their boot claws dug in to grip the surface of the comet.

This was their fifth journey across the ice and they had to go farther out on each excursion. The buffeting solar winds, their slow steps and the exertion of lugging the cumbersome zottis were taking their toll. Anton had already slipped once when his claws missed biting into some of the holes they had left on one of their previous trips.

Leopold's hand shot up and waved to Anton. Anton lumbered his way over as Leopold bent low to examine something. The carcass of a tardigrade lay exposed. It had sunk into itself and its scales lay scattered about.

Leopold pointed to a puckered hole in one of the tardigrade's plates, "This one got old. If you look there, you can see where another zotti drained it of its fluids." Somberly, he turned toward Rabbit, "They can be dangerous when they're active. This is why we only collect them twice in a cycle. Once before they wake up and once right after they hibernate. They're more docile before they wake, but require more feeding. They require less feeding right after they hibernate, but they're harder to deal with then."

"We have anything like that to worry about now?" asked Anton.

"We'll avoid the more lively ones." Leopold stood up and stepped away from the carcass, "Let's get back to the job at hand, eh?"

***

Jacquie wrestled with the shuttle controls as the comet moved underneath the ship. This was her sixth time in the pilot's seat and her stamina was waning. She and Ama had traded pilot duties to keep the exhaustion at bay. In another hour or so, they would switch again and Jacquie would assist Nani once more with lugging their quarry into the hold and into the pens.

"Only a few more hours to go and we can finally head back to the Cluster," Jacquie murmured.

"What was that?" Ama asked.

Jacquie just smiled, "Just getting tired and looking forward to our return trip."

Ama slipped into the co-pilot's seat. She buckled the safety straps and settled her hand on the steering mechanism, "Ya, these hunts get ya beat. Don't worry though, Nani will take us back once we break free."

Jacquie glanced over at the young woman, "Gods, won't that be nice."

Suddenly, a glimpse of something outside their craft abruptly averted her attention. "What is that?" Jacquie blurted.

"Pull up!" cried Ama.

Jacquie yanked on the steering and their shuttle slowly climbed. She stared out the port window and spied the huge chunk of ice that spun toward the ship. Smaller particles of ice spattered against the windshield, but the chunk passed harmlessly below.

Ama cried out, "Watch out! A big piece like that usually means something bad happened."

Jacquie frowned, "Wish we could contact the boys below and tell them to be on the look-see."

***

Anton grunted under the bulkiness of his end of the zotti. He shifted his grip a little so they could fit the beast through the narrow, high-walled valley that lay between them and the shuttle. He and Leopold flipped it to its taller edge and held it up high.

"This is going to be hard, outsider," cursed Leo.

Anton cursed under his breath and said, "That figures. These things aren't really built for carrying."

The sucker-like mouth of the tardigrade was perfectly in line with Anton's helmet. When he slipped to one side, the water bear shifted and pursed its mouth against his faceplate.

"Aah!" he screamed. "It's ugly and it's moving!"

"We have to hurry then," cried Leo. "Otherwise we'll lose this one!"

They both readjusted their hold on the zotti, determined to resume their journey at a quicker pace. After only a dozen steps, though, Leopold stopped abruptly and stared straight ahead. Anton looked up in confusion that cleared up instantly when he saw the reflection of fire flickering across the young man's faceplate.

"Oh, no," Leo whispered.

***

There was a brief flash of light far ahead on the comet's surface. That was immediately and completely obscured by the cloud of dust and ice that billowed up around it.

Radio chatter exploded from the ship's comm, "Shuttle down... Impacted... Alert!" Static drowned out the rest.

"Damned   dinlows!"   cursed   Ama.
"Unseasoned pilots with more bravado than brains!
It's gonna get ugly, cousin. Go let Nani know we've
got trouble!"

Jacquie released the controls and felt Ama
take over. She popped the seat harness and leapt out
of the seat.

"On it," Jacq barked, as she shot out of the
cockpit.

***

Particles of dust and ice pelted Leo and
Anton as they struggled to get the zotti through the
narrow pass.   But the thing's six legs started
wiggling. Anton gave another push and the creature
slid most of the way through the chasm.

"Push again, damn it!" shouted Leopold. "We
got wreckage coming up fast!"

Anton dug in with his boot claws and pushed
harder. The zotti popped out into a wider clearing
and knocked Leo to his ass.

"Duck!" Leo screamed.

Without a second thought, Anton dropped to
his knees and none too soon. A section of a shuttle
wing spiraled into the tight valley and slammed hard
against the ice behind him. A ragged strip of metal
caught on his back and ripped through the material
of his suit. It carved into the flesh of his shoulder
and arm before it spun away.

Anton cried out in pain and grabbed at his shoulder. Small bits of metal, plastic, and ice buffeted his suit. One piece of debris the size of a large platter shattered against his back and laid him out flat. His boot claws lost contact with the ice and he skittered forward.

He could barely hear Leopold's voice coming through the comm as his spacesuit alarms went off. He scrabbled for a handhold, but his fingers couldn't find a purchase on the ice. Leo reached out his hand and their fingers touched, but Anton slid past too quickly.

Anton rebounded off a boulder and floated away from the surface. He blinked and tried to think as his suit cut off the atmospheric flow from his neck down. In desperation, he searched for the tiny grappling hook launcher that he wore at his waist. His fingers latched onto the device and yanked it from his belt.

Through bleary eyes, he sighted down to the icy surface of the comet and fired the hook. He felt the lifeline go taut before he blacked out from the pain.

***

Jacquie reached the hold and clipped in her guideline. She flew over to Nani and grabbed his clip. "You forgot to click in, old man!" she shouted. "We've got at least one shuttle down on the comet. So, expect some crazy maneuvers."

Jon Gray Lang

"Damned dinlows," Nani cursed. "Their pride won't let them give up on a hunt. But, when they get all tired, they put us all at risk."

The shuttle dropped and the surface of the comet rapidly drew closer as the craft descended. The whole ship yanked sideways until it was perpendicular to the comet. Nani lost his grip and slid toward the open hold. Jacquie leapt toward him and grabbed his arm. He looked up and smiled, but the smile faded into an expression of extreme pain.

Jacquie cried out, "No! No, no, no!"

A slender piece of metal protruded from his belly and out past the hold. Jacquie could see crumbled bits of plas-glass that dotted its edge as it twisted violently and ripped open Nani's belly. Blood spurted from the wound and froze into tiny red particulates.

She felt his hand grow slack in hers. A wail of grief escaped her as she pulled him into her lap and held him close. The shuttle righted itself and more chunks of the wrecked ship flew in through the open hold. She hugged Nani close to her chest and tried to staunch the blood. But she knew it was too late.

***

The ride back to the cluster was a somber one. Three ships had been lost due to the initial crash. Two of the retrieval teams on the surface hadn't escaped the debris and were lost. The flight

Jon Gray Lang

crews for all three ships were gone. The rest of the hunting parties had been retrieved, but many were injured.

"Like Anton," whispered Jacquie.

He was still comatose. Ama had sprayed plasflesh into the slit of the spacesuit and Leopold had done a quick repair on the suit to keep it from losing any more atmosphere. Jacquie had kept the shuttle on course for the Cluster. Nani's body was back in the hold with the captured zottis.

"A dangerous flight indeed," Jacquie grimaced as tears threatened to fill her eyes.

Leopold whispered in her ear, "But bounteous. Our hold is full and we only suffered the loss of one. Though our loss will weigh heavily on us, other clans have suffered far worse."

Ama added, "So soon after the last Clan Mother, too. But Salome is strong. She will keep us together. I am not so sure about the Jati clan. They are a small family and their Clan Mother is old. The strain may be too much for them."

A ping sounded on the nav system. All three sets of eyes strained to peer into the darkness. Faint pinpricks of light rewarded their efforts and a collective sigh of relief rose up among them.

"Soon, we are home," murmured Ama.

thirty-one

My Name is Human

"Shuttle 501-S, you are cleared to land. Head to Pad 3-B and make it quick. A solar storm is expected to hit within the quarter-hour."

Fitzpatrick spotted the blinking circle for Pad 3-B through the dust and clouds that permeated the small moon's atmosphere. "Tower, Shuttle 501-S is making our final approach to Pad 3-B."

Yeoman Fitzpatrick landed the shuttle he had been trapped in for a week on the requested pad. Once the landing skids settled, the landing surface slowly sank into the ground. When it had fallen below the sixty-meter mark, an iris above cycled shut. He sat back and released the pilot controls. The shaft grew dark and it felt as if the shuttle was being taken deep inside of the base on the tiny moon.

Lighting flashed once the landing pad had

Jon Gray Lang

sunk past the base of the shaft into the hangar bay
proper. After the pad completely settled into the
floor, there was a knock at the airlock. Fitzpatrick
cycled it open and two armed guards stood at the
ready just out of physical range. He spoke over his
shoulder, "We've landed and we have visitors."

"Of course we have visitors," Judith sharply
replied.

She jockeyed the med tube past him and slid
it through the open hatch on its one functioning
anti-grav unit. He decided not to assist her as the
med tube swung off to the left out of her control.
Dr. Wyeth waved two of her orderlies over and
pointed at the errant anti-grav bed as it floated to a
stop next to one of the guards.

"Get the subject prepped for surgery as soon
as possible. Understood?"

"Of course, Doctor," replied one of the
assistants while the other went to collect the med
tube.

As they walked out of the hangar, Fitzpatrick
moved up to join her, "Do you need any further
assistance from me?"

"No," she replied. "Major Diego will find you
a space to crash." She turned and held him in place
with her eyes, "Do not get complacent. I may have
need of you at a moment's notice."

"Of course, Doctor. Where would I find the
Major?"

She ignored him as she spun on her heel and
followed the scientists with the genorg subject.

Fitzpatrick sighed as he rubbed the stubble that had grown in on his jawline. He glanced at the two guards. One had followed the Doctor. The other one, a stocky but powerful fellow remained in place, listening intently to his comm. As the Yeoman approached, the guard shut off his comm and pumped Fitzgerald's hand.

"I am Corporal Cook, sir, but everyone calls me Jerr. Per the Commandant, You'll be bunking with me..."

Fitzpatrick muttered, "It's been a while since I had a bunkmate and I can't say I'm looking forward to having one now."

Cook stared at Fitzpatrick's knuckles and noticed the damage that still had not fully healed, "Give it a chance, sir. I think we'll be great bunkmates. Come this way; I'll see that you get settled in."

Fitzpatrick shook his head and followed the Corporal into Dr. Wyeth's moon base.

***

Dr. Wyeth arrived at the medical bay in her surgical gown. She elbowed her way into the operating room and let the door swing closed behind her. Her assistants had removed the patient from the med tube and were carefully monitoring the genorg's sedation. The Doctor studied her subject, one Galena Chadov, case ID # 4296-E-2631-H, who laid before her on the operating table. Galena's head and neck were held in place by a clamp built into the table. Her hairline had been shorn down to the scalp and shaved smooth. Dotted ink lines encircled her skull.

Dr. Wyeth's medical assistant and a surgical nurse silently stood on either side of the table, awaiting their instructions. Judith surveyed the scene and noticed a bottle in a temperature sleeve that sat next to the operating table.

"Is this the synthesized biochemical solution?"

"Yes, Doctor."

"Prepare a syringe of it now. This is all going to come down to timing."

The nurse slipped a needle into the solution and filled the vial to the two-millimeter mark.

Dr. Wyeth slipped her data pad from her apron, "Cut the skull open to allow access to the chip. I will be perusing my old notes."

The medical assistant selected a scalpel and sliced into the genorg's flesh. As the skull was exposed, the old incision from her last surgery appeared. It had left a bony ridge that was still visible.

The grinding sound of a bone saw filled the operating room as Judith flipped through her notes and flashed a sardonic smile, '*So long ago. An epiphany in the middle of the night. All to combat the things in the darkness.*' She glanced up when the bone saw went quiet. '*She still lives. It worked, but not how I expected.*'

Judith slipped the data pad back into her

apron and moved toward Galena's open skull. The crown of bone was set aside on a metal table just off to the left. The drone's brain was now exposed to view. It looked like a sea sponge cradled in the shell of her skull.

An odd thought struck her, '*Similar to the way the hell portal sits in its housing. Now let's see what they did to you. What weakened you enough for the Masters to gain a foothold?*'

With gloved fingers the Doctor grasped the lobes of the brain and widened the folds. Interwoven through the tissue of Galena's brain lay tiny glass-like filaments that ran down toward the base of her skull. The visible ends of the filaments connected to a small oblong device that had a crack running the length of it. She reached in and plucked the tech unit free of the subject's brain. Inside the casing was a tiny board with an array of ancient chips, but the board was cracked in a spider web pattern of fine lines that could shatter at any moment. Parts of the chipset showed evidence of previous self-repair attempts. The unit looked very fragile.

"Isn't the use of augments illegal in the Consortium?" asked the concerned nurse.

Dr. Wyeth glared, "Such things are only illegal if one declares intent and asks for permission. And I do not have time for that."

Where the oblong device had been nestled into Galena's brain, the Doctor also discovered tiny fragments from the case. And something else lay in wait there. Judith reached in to move the fragments around. But as she lifted the largest piece up, a black viscous fluid dribbled out from underneath.

"Inject the solution directly into this alien substance," she commanded the nurse. "We have to eliminate its control of the subject before it's too late."

Alarms from the monitoring equipment started blaring as Galena's heart began to palpitate erratically.

"She's flatlining," announced the assistant.

Dr. Wyeth shouted, "Be quick about it! Faster!"

The nurse slipped the needle into the center of the dark fluid. She pressed the injector and the solution bubbled up from inside the aqueous material. Where the two liquids touched, a flat grayish fluid was left. The black liquid veered away from the solution and more of it bubbled up from between other folds of the genorg's brain. The nurse drove the needle deeper into the brain tissue.

"Capture that liquid!" ordered Dr. Wyeth. "We cannot let it escape! All of it must be neutralized. Every last drop; do you hear me?"

The medical assistant grabbed a kidney tray and held it under the subject's head. Fluid dribbled into the tray. He ran a retractor along the folds and tried to force more of the alien material into the pan. The liquid slithered away and pooled higher up in the open cavity.

"Not like that," Dr. Wyeth growled as she

grabbed the suction vacuum and placed the nozzle directly into the main puddle of the material. The vacuum sucked greedily at the fluid. The viscous stuff tried to flee, but it couldn't escape the vacuum's strong suction. As the last of the fluid gurgled down the suction tube, Dr. Wyeth shoved the vacuum into the assistant's hands. The monitoring system's alarm stopped and was replaced with the sound of a normal heartbeat.

"Make sure you remove every last drop from the subject and from the vacuum. All of it. Now get out of my way."

Judith turned her attention to the damaged chipset connected to Galena's brain. Her headlamp played over the component and a burned fragment caught the light. She slipped in her tweezers and pulled lightly on the piece until it snapped. Brittle filaments attached to the piece crumbled as it was removed.

"I seem to have found the problem," Judith grinned as she dropped the piece into a tray. "Nurse, bring me a spool of filament and the nano-splicer. It better be in catalog drawer F-13. Be quick about it!"

The nurse rummaged through the wheeled cabinet. Dr. Wyeth lit the fuser and melted the board's fragments back into one cohesive piece. She took the nano-splicer out of the nurse's hand and set it on the board. When the spool of filament was dropped into her hand, she set the nano-splicer to rewire the board. Her nurse took the fuser from her other hand and retreated to the far end of the operating table. The autonomic device pulled filaments free from the spool and reconnected the board's circuitry. It ran querying tests until it completed the repair process. The nano-splicer shut off when a sharp ding signaled completion of the task.

Dr. Wyeth studied the repair diagrams provided by the nano-splicer as she set the chipset loosely back in place. She teased out the bits of unconnected filament and pulled them free of the genorg's brain. "These have definitely found their home haven't they?" She said, amused at the length of some of the strands. "It exceeded what I had thought it capable of. Will the wonders of old tech never cease. Fascinating."

She dumped the thin strings into the tray and completed a final inspection before she nestled the oblong device back into its place. There was a wet-sounding squoosh as it reseated itself into its wedge.

Dr. Wyeth stepped back. Galena's dog tags glinted briefly in the overhead lighting. Judith gripped them and broke the cord that held them around the genorg's neck. She dropped them into her right pocket and pulled off her gloves. "You can close the skull now. The subject's brain will be as good as new once it regrows its connections." Dr. Wyeth grinned eerily as she left the operating room. "We can drive those creatures to extinction," she mused.

Following the data from the nano-splicer's

report, the Doctor generated a digital copy of the device on her data pad. She grabbed her comm, "Rossi! I'm sending you the schematics for the device. Begin manufacturing and set up a schedule to get them installed in some of the spare drones. Finally, some progress!"

Judith left the medical bay and headed off to her office.

***

Galena woke and found herself in strange surroundings. Medical tile covered the walls of the small room and the lighting was incessantly bright. She covered her eyes with her hands and discovered that she was no longer restrained. She pushed herself up into a seated position and studied the space she occupied.

"Strange and yet familiar," she whispered. "I have been here before. But when?"

She hopped off the bed and landed on her feet. The jarring sensation sent rivulets of pain into the base of her skull. Her left hand cupped her forehead and touched the bandages that encircled it. She stumbled over to the large mirror on the wall to examine herself.

The bandage hung loosely around her head. She slowly unwound the wrap and tugged at it where it became sticky. She crumpled the bandage in her hand and dropped the blood-crusted cloth onto the floor. Her eyes followed it as it came to rest near her feet.

Slowly she looked back toward her reflection. The white hair along her scar had grown long in the time since she had last seen herself. The black mane around it had grown shaggy as well, but not as long as the streak of snow-white hairs. Her fingers felt along her scalp and found the closed incision from the Doctor's surgery.

"Is this new?" she asked quietly in the empty room. A cynical smile she had seen the Captain use graced her lips, "My head feels like patchwork, so who knows how new it is."

Her hands fell to her chest. With practiced ease, she slid the zipper open down the front of her coveralls. As the clothing fell away, she inspected the rest of her body. Her fingertips traced the scars that the mirror displayed unapologetically. Some part of her wanted to catalog them.

"This one is old, from the cave-in on the moon that killed many of my sisters." Her fingers followed a scar that encircled her right bicep, "I remember this one. The owners had let the stamping machines at the factory go past their safety parameters and I almost lost my arm. My sister next to me had her legs crushed in the accident. She was retired." Galena also found the almost invisible scar right underneath her left eye, "The ring an inner system senator wore that cut into my face. I never understood what I had done wrong."

Her fingers touched the puckered scar from a bullet wound, the jagged edge of an old knife injury, and the spot where her left shoulder hadn't reset correctly. Newer bruises decorated her frame and blended with the older ones.

Her hands slid to where her dog tags would normally lay, but the ornament was gone. Shock hit her and she checked the pockets of her coveralls. "Where did I lose them? When did I lose them? Too many opportunities to have lost them forever. The Captain would say I'm a right mess," she laughed, but her mirth rang hollow.

She felt the being's sense of amusement enfold her, "A right mess you are. But never alone..."

thirty-two

This Night

The ships from the hunt arrived at the Cluster. Each one slowly discharged their contents of Thermozodi into the pen habitats. When they were done, they circled back out and returned to their clan collectives.

The Burton swung out to the rear of the cluster. Ama hit the attitude jets as the craft approached the Matilda. As the shuttle slowed, Leopold extended the tunnel. Once the connection light turned green, Ama killed the engines and hopped out of the pilot's seat.

Leopold and Jacquie picked up Anton; Ama joined them at the airlock.

"Has the debt been paid?" Jacquie asked as she cycled the airlock.

"The debt to Clan Baptiste is no more," Ama intoned.

The two women shook on it before they headed into the Matilda. It took all three of them to carry Anton through the tunnel and hoist him into one of the med tubes.

Anton woke as he was placed inside, "Did we make it back?"

Jacquie smiled down at him, "We're back home and our debt is covered."

Anton grunted as the bandage on his back pulled on the edges of the cut. "Did we pay in blood?"

"Blood and lives, but that is the way of the hunt," answered Leopold as he flashed a smile. "Fast thinking with your pocket barb, outsider. You have earned my respect."

"And you have mine, Leo," replied Anton with a smile. "Where is the old man?"

Jacquie bent down and squeezed his hand, "He didn't make it back."

"That's why we're doubly glad you did," Ama said as she ran her fingers through his hair. "You and I have a prior accord. I expect to see you up and mobile for the celebration."

"The celebration?" asked Anton. "Wait, we have an agreement?"

"Ta ta, pretty man," she said as she gave him a wink. "Come on Leo, let's head back home."

The two left the cargo bay and disappeared through the airlock.

Jacquie laughed at his confusion, "Get some rest and we'll take a look at your back later."

Jon Gray Lang

"What did she mean by agreement?" he mumbled as the med tube closed over him.

***

Twenty-four hours later, the summons was sent. Everyone aboard the Cyclops tingled with excitement as it flew into the hangar of the main Cluster ship. Paper roses and lanterns festooned the upper rafters of the bay. A ceremonial guard made up of all the Clan Mother's guards lined the hallway past the airlock.

Barney turned away from the port window and glanced at all of the people around him; his family. "Well, might as get this show on the road."

Jacquie stood at the airlock hatch on the small ship, "That's right. Helmets on folks. That includes you, Rabbit."

"I'll need help with my helmet clips. I'm still having trouble with my left shoulder."

"I got you," replied Luli.

Derain looked over the heads of the crew and winked at Jacquie, "It feels good to have us all back together."

"It does," replied Anton. "I only wish Galena was with us to make it complete."

Luli clipped his helmet closed then picked up her own. "We'll find her."

"Even if it takes years, we'll find her." With a grim expression, Jacquie clamped her helmet to her suit, then cycled the airlock, "We don't leave anyone behind."

As soon as they passed through the airlock and entered the Cluster, they popped their helmet clips. Immediately, the throbbing pulse of festive music filled their ears. They quickly removed their spacesuits and hung them on the available racks.

"Sounds like your kind of party, Jacq," quipped Anton.

A woman wearing the red sash of the All-Mother stepped into the chamber. "If you'll follow me, Ms. Qing."

Luli looked up as she slipped her foot out of her suit and slid a boot over it. "Sure, just give me a sec."

"You got this, Lu?" asked Barney.

She hung her suit up, closed her eyes, and exhaled slowly. "Yes, I can do this."

Jacquie wrapped her arms around Luli, "We got your back, if you need us."

They all embraced their pilot without hesitation.

"We love you," murmured Derain.

Barney smiled up at her, "Knock 'em dead, hon."

Anton pulled her ukulele out of its hard case. "I think you'll need this," he said as he handed it to her.

"Hello there, old friend." Luli flipped it over and studied the repairs that ran the length of the little wooden instrument, "Now, you and I both bear scars." She shook herself and smiled, "Well, let's give this a try." She followed the messenger out of the room.

Jacquie put her hands on her hips and announced, "We're to process with Clan Baptiste tonight, but if any of you want to step out, that's fine."

"We're all behind you," said Derain. "Lead the way, Captain."

As a team, they stepped out into the hallway and walked past the ceremonial guards for the Clans. They passed through the tall doors of the auditorium and stopped just inside. The ballroom was packed and the music was loud.

Jacquie searched the crowd and eventually found Salome. "Come on, this way."

As they approached her, Jacquie bowed slightly from the waist and said, "Good evening, Clan Mother."

"Just call me Salome tonight, cousin. I happen to agree with the All-Mother that titles get tiresome. All of you, please, feel free to mingle. Tonight is going to be glorious."

Anton suddenly felt a hand slip through his arm and clasp his hand.

"You're mine tonight, pirate!" Ama laughed as she dragged him to the open dance floor.

He could feel the plasflesh on his back stretch, but luckily, the wound only itched now. He gave the woman an appraising glance, "Do I have a choice in this matter?"

Ama pulled him close and guided his hand to

her backside, "None whatsoever."

Derain shook his head and laughed. Suddenly, another arm reached around his waist and pulled him toward the dance floor as well, "Whoa!" He lost sight of Jacquie as he melded into the crowd.

Barney felt a hand on his shoulder and turned to see a middle-aged man. "Excuse me, sir. Would you care to dance? I or my clan mate would love to partner with you."

Barney took notice of the lovely woman standing beside the fellow and replied, "Why not both of you?"

The older gentleman's face broke into a wide grin as he took one of Barney's hands and his partner took the other. They disappeared into the crowd.

Jacquie slipped a rack of vials in coolant sleeves from her inner vest pocket. She handed them to Salome, "Tocher is paid."

"And tocher is accepted," Salome answered as she slipped the vials up one of her voluminous sleeves. "We will be making port at the Scrapheap to trade in our catch. As much as I hate to see you go, we will have to leave you there."

"I have only heard tales of that station, but none of them were good," replied Jacquie. "Is there no other place?"

Salome sighed and held Jacquie's hand, "It is the only port we will see for over a year. As much as I want you to stay, we cannot afford to house your people."

"And I made my choice to stay outside the clan long ago," Jacquie said. "You have treated me and mine far better than I had the right to expect."

Salome nodded and squeezed Jacquie's hand, "Shall we head out onto the dance floor?"

Jacquie bowed, "After you, cousin."

***

The red-sashed woman directed Luli through a door that led to a stage, then bid her adieu. The area behind the curtain was a flurry of activity as different acts awaited their times to perform. The dissonance of various instruments and human voices should have put Luli on edge, but she found it calming.

"It's been a long while since I last heard this cacophony and I miss it." She mused, "Too much silence as of late."

As a dance troupe concluded its number, cheers erupted from the audience. In a few short moments, the dancers passed by Luli as they left. Some of them glanced at her with wonder in their eyes but Luli kept her eyes shut and focused solely on her breathing.

"This is nerve-wracking," she groaned. "Why am I getting so worked up? I've done this hundreds of times. I've got to focus on the good things; on what I still have."

The next act rushed onto the stage, but she

barely noticed. All of her thoughts were focused internally as she recalled past events.

Her lips curled into a tiny smile as Luli thought of her Poppy singing to her when she was just a little girl. She remembered one of the many jams, when she and the other deep spacers had played together and all the times she had sung to a teenage Jacquie when the nightmares woke her. The time she and Anton sang together on the way to one of her shows evoked a spontaneous giggle. And last came the memories of being the only one awake on the colony ships. She had sung just to keep her mind occupied and her fears at bay.

From the stage came the announcement, "And up next is Luli Qing! She is the last living pilot of the ancient colony ships. She only has one night to play for us! And that night is tonight!"

Luli's eyes opened slowly and a sense of wellbeing filled her heart, "I've always had myself to believe in..." She looked down at the scratched and dented ukulele in her hand, "and, of course, you too, my friend." She curled her hand into a fist. The spiderweb tracery of scars from the surgery caught the light and glinted in the stage lights, "And that hasn't changed."

***

Derain was engaged in conversation, but glanced away when Luli's name was announced. From the corner of his eye, he saw Anton look toward the stage as well. He glanced around until he spied both Jacquie and Barney staring intently at the M.C. as he concluded his introduction. The curtains parted and Luli walked... no... she strutted onto the stage.

The spotlights swung down to highlight her as her boot heels click-clacked loudly across the wood floor. Each member of the Matilda's crew could feel her eyes as she scanned the crowd for them. The audience had hushed in awe and anticipation.

A mournful smile clouded her face, "As we all travel through the infinite darkness, is there a harsher mistress than time? She knocks us down when we don't see her coming and leaves us lost."

The crowd couldn't take their eyes away from her as she moved across the stage.

"She shows us that life in all its magnificence is still a fragile thing. It can end in an instant. And for those of us left behind, every loss we experience is a painful lesson. No matter how many times we experience it, we live through it. But the pain runs deep. Deeper than we ever think possible. Yet it is those very moments that remind us how wonderful and rare the highs of life are."

She dropped to her knees at the edge of the stage and her gaze swept over the crowd, "Have we all not suffered grief? Yet we continue to live?" Her voice choked as her eyes glistened under the hot lights of the stage.

Luli jumped to her feet and her voice carried into each corner of the ballroom, "We must continue living. We live for those we've lost to time. And tonight we say farewell from the depths of our heart."

Applause filled the room as her sweet voice lilted over the crowd. Her voice was strong as she sang, acapella, ballad lyrics that ached with bitter sadness. Some of the older listeners sang haltingly to half-remembered tunes from a time when their great-grandparents had sung to them so long ago.

Luli moved to the center of the stage, gingerly plucking the strings of her father's tiny instrument. As her confidence grew, so did the tone of her ukulele. Then something strange began to happen. As the stage lights followed her, a glittering halo radiated from her form.

The inner light that seemed to grow within her was a transformative sight to see. The entire crowd was enraptured as Luli continued to sing a song from long before even her time,

"You have soiled it,
You have soiled it in exile,
In the empty foreign lands.
Oh Yiannis, my Yiannis
In the empty foreign lands..."

***

Barney slipped the door open and stepped out into the hall. He looked back into the room and smiled as he watched the woman roll over and drape her arm across her clan mate. He sighed, pulled the door closed, and ambled down the empty hallway. Heaps of detritus scattered along the route confirmed his impression that last night had been one helluva party.

As he walked toward the lift, he discovered that the main Cluster ship had been opened up to all the clan members to recuperate from the festivities of the previous evening. People were sleeping on the floor and in the random seating areas of the ship. Each room he passed was loaded with people still in the throes of passion or long collapsed from it.

Barney smirked, "The modesty of the streets of my home world wouldn't last a day on a ship like this."

He strolled past the ballroom where he saw a security man lay a blanket over a reveler who was splayed out on a table. Barney shook his head in wonder. From the ballroom, it was only a short walk to the hangar. As he rounded the corner, he came across Derain and Jacquie holding hands in the waiting area. Both of them were suited up except for their helmets.

"Morning, Captain. Morning, Derain," said Barney as he got closer.

"Morning, Barney," Jacquie replied as she pulled her hand free from Derain's.

Derain's hand closed reflexively, but his expression never wavered. "Morning, Barney. Was the evening to your liking?"

"After Luli's performance, it could only go

downhill," grinned Barney.

"Hey, I heard my name," Luli yawned as she came around the corner. "It better be only good things." She winked and initiated a full body stretch with her arms raised high above her head.

Jacquie whistled, "Well, someone looks like they're feeling better!"

Luli blushed and curtsied, "I definitely needed last night more than I thought. It was good to say goodbye and then 'Oh, hello there!' That hello was worth it."

"Your performance was amazing, Lu. Otherworldly, even," Barney gushed. "I've never seen one like it."

"Only the best for my friends and family," she laughed. She yawned again and looked around quizzically, "Where's Anton? He's not down yet?"

Jacquie looked smug, "Um, no. He's had a rough week and could use some time to recuperate. Besides, someone has special plans for him for the next few days."

Barney asked, "How are his wounds from the hunt?"

"Last he told me was that they were closed up solid, but they itched like the Devil," replied Derain with a knowing smirk.

"He's in good hands, though," Jacquie assured them all. She settled her hands to her hips, "So, is everyone ready to head back?"

Her people responded by slipping into their spacesuits and grabbing their helmets. She nodded and picked up her helmet, too, "The Cluster is set to make contact with our next destination in a couple of solar days. We'll be stuck there until we can get the Matilda working."

"All the heavy lifting is done," said Barney. "Aside from getting the sublights reseated, we're down to running new fiber and cabling through her. Then we'll find out how many node points and modules are completely blown."

He sighed, "Frankly, the rewiring is going to be slow and painful, but I don't know what we're going to do to fix those modules. Those things are old, pre-Consortium old, at a guess. I might be able to rig up some replacements, but we're going to need access to parts."

"Well, we're in luck then," replied Jacquie. "The place the clans will drop us should have the biggest selection of old parts in the whole damn galaxy."

Luli's brow furrowed, "Where's that?"

"We're going to the Scrapheap," Jacquie answered. "Then we're going to find Galena."

Derain chimed in, "No matter where she may be."

thirty-three

The Songs for Chapter Titles

As in the previous books, so the tradition continues. The chapter names are song titles and each one is part of Ms. Luli Qing's performance roster. This list of songs helped set my mood for the various chapters. Only certain versions were used. If you'd like to hear them, here they are:

☐ Crazy Horses - The Osmonds
☐ Gun Fever (Blam Blam Fever) - The Valentines
☐ Always on the Run - Bosnian Rainbows
☐ Sad But True - Metallica
☐ The Trooper - Iron Maiden
☐ Cruel Melody - Black Light Burns
☐ Laisse Tomber Les Filles - Frances Gall
☐ Captain of a Shipwreck - Neil Diamond
☐ Heavy the Beat of the Weary Waves - Closed

Jon Gray Lang

Circuits
- [ ] The Passenger - Iggy Pop
- [ ] Anonymous Club - Courtney Barnett
- [ ] SAIL - AWOL Nation
- [ ] Rabbit Rabbit - My Jerusalem
- [ ] I Drove All Night - Cyndi Lauper
- [ ] Space Junk - DEVO
- [ ] Under the Milky Way Tonight - The Church
- [ ] Mystery Train - Elvis Presley
- [ ] Death and the Lady - Clifton Hicks
- [ ] I've Got You Under My Skin - Frank Sinatra
- [ ] Dream a Little Dream - Ella Fitzgerald & Louis Armstrong
- [ ] Along the Road to Gundegai - Slim Dusty
- [ ] Every Stone - Jonny Houlihan
- [ ] Wandering Star - Portishead
- [ ] Guns for Hands - Twenty One Pilots
- [ ] Cowboy - Jonneine Zapata
- [ ] Son of a Preacher Man - Dusty Springfield
- [ ] Bottom of the Deep Blue Sea - Missio
- [ ] Red Skies - The Fixx
- [ ] Chain of Fools - Aretha Franklin
- [ ] Sometimes I Feel Like a Motherless Child - Odetta
- [ ] My Name is Human - Highly Suspect
- [ ] This Night - Black Lab

The title of the book is also a song:
- [ ] Secret Matilda ---------------- Husky Loops

Jon Gray Lang

Now the team readies to find Galena and to face the future. Read the thrilling conclusion of the series in Waltzing Matilda!

Jon Gray Lang

***

About the Author

Jon Gray Lang was born in Australia before being hastily relocated to the United States where he wrote a handful of screenplays, shot a few films, and even threw his hat into the acting ring. But with a life-long love of science fiction, it was only a matter of time before he bit the novel writing bullet and wrote the award-winning five book science fiction series, Saga of a Space Freighter. When he's not typing away at the keyboard, he's busy fighting with rapiers, skiing the Rockies, or banging out tunes on a ukulele... just not all at once... No matter how hard he tries.

Please follow him on:

JonGrayLang.com
facebook.com/JonGrayLang
twitter.com/Jon_Gray_Lang
instagram.com/jongraylang

<<<<>>>>

Jon Gray Lang

www.ingramcontent.com/pod-product-compliance
Lightning Source LLC
Chambersburg PA
CBHW020503020726
47493CB00001B/161